CW00855543

Titles by Collette Scott

Forever Sunshine
Hannah's Blessing
If We Dare to Dream (The Evans Family, Book One)
Through Winter Skies (The Evans Family, Book Two)
Eyes on Tango (The Evans Family, Book Three)
Kat's Last Chance (The Evans Family, Book Four)
Terri's Gift (The Evans Family, Book Five)
Cooper's Choice (The Evans Family, Book Six)
Sunshine Rising (The Evans Family, Book Seven)
Hope is Calling (The Evans Domination, Book One)
A Blessing in Disguise (The Evans Domination, Book Two)

Hannah's Blessing

By
Collette Scott

This is a work of fiction. Names, characters and incidents are the products of the author's imagination or are used fictitiously. Any resemblance to actual events, locales, or persons, living or dead, is purely coincidental.

Copyright © 2011 by Collette Scott

All rights reserved.
For information address Marimay Publishing, P.O. Box 11821, Tempe, AZ 85284

ISBN-13: 978-1463539962
ISBN-10: 1463539967

Acknowledgements

This one goes to Caitlin, Shannon and Brynn. You three are my world. Without your love and support, I would have been lost.

To my Massachusetts family – thank you all for your support.

To my Arizona family – words just can't express my gratitude to you all.

Special thanks to Jenny and Betsy for your input.

Chapter 1

With a sudden squeal of the tires, the midnight black Mustang stopped in front of a long-legged blonde dressed in skin-tight black jeans and a black tank top. Over the rumbling engine, an unseen neighborhood dog could be heard barking while the driver revved the car impatiently. He reached across the seat to open the door. The woman at the end of the driveway hastily tossed her pink overnight bag in the back and climbed in. No sooner had she shut the door than the Mustang was pulling away with another swift chirp of the tires.

"You're late," the blonde whined.

She pressed the power button and rolled down her window. Cool night air entered the car and filtered out the aroma of her perfume.

"I've had a bad night," he replied.

She was instantly contrite. Her full lower lip pouted and she reached over to place a well-manicured hand on his thigh. Peter Somerset glanced down at the smooth hand and compared it to his wife's.

Diana's hands were dry, and her fingernails were brittle from cleaning and cooking. Unlike Camille, she never took the time to paint them anymore. In fact, she did not care about her appearance at all. What had happened to the popular catch he thought he had snared? Had their child stolen all of her sex appeal away? He stomped harder on the gas in frustration and maneuvered onto the highway, heading west to the hills. If it was the last thing he did, he was going to enjoy his weekend outside of the city.

As long as he was far away from Diana and Hannah, he'd be fine. Just fine. It did not bother him that Diana knew he was going to a cabin for the weekend with another woman. He did not care that she had cried when she said their marriage was over. Though her money had been good, he was having a hard time finding anything interesting about her now that it was gone. And he knew that Diana understood that as well.

"What happened, babe? Did you and Diana have another fight?"

"Yep," he snapped, steering onto the open road. "I told her we're through."

A smile curved Camille's painted lips for several minutes. She turned to look out the window and remained silent. It was another thing he liked about her. She did not fight with him, and she had a fat wallet. Two very good qualities; the ones he liked best in a woman.

After a while, she reached over, and her hand began to caress his thigh. "Good."

"No, it's not good. Why did you come to the house? Hannah told her you were there."

"So what?"

"So? She could use that during the divorce."

Peter's foot pressed harder on the gas pedal, and the sleek car sped up smoothly. He was tense all over, but Camille's hand was distracting him all the same. The lights of the city had turned to the blackness of the mountains ahead. He could already feel the chill in the evening air through Camille's open window. He deftly maneuvered the car into the hills, enjoying the curves and dips on the road. The vehicle hugged the pavement, compelling him to speed up even more. At this time of night, there were very few people out, so he felt confident about putting his car through the paces. He knew Camille loved the way he drove, and he strove to please her as he had never pleased his wife. Right now, he had to ensure he stayed on her good side, for he would be dependent on her soon.

"What's wrong with starting a new life? Without Diana and Hannah. Let them do their own thing. After all, it's like the two of them are peas in a pod." Camille's hand crept further up his thigh, getting tantalizingly close. "I can give you everything you need, baby."

Peter's sharp inhale came through clenched teeth. How could he think about his nagging wife and child when this beautiful woman was teasing him to distraction?

His fingers gripped the steering wheel harder when he heard the sound of the zipper on his black slacks being released. They were almost there. The cabin was just up the mountain. Ten more minutes. He gasped. Her cool fingers surrounded him.

When her mouth came down upon his erection, he nearly lost control. Though he was still upset and angry, there was no denying the soft pull of her mouth and teasing intensity of her tongue. One hand left the steering wheel to roughly grasp her head and hold her in place as he sped up even more. Diana and Hannah were forgotten as Peter allowed his lover to distract him.

Then the deer appeared in front of him.

With a shout, Peter's foot quickly shifted from the gas pedal to the brake, but he knew it was too late. He struggled to free his hand from Camille's stiff hair, but he succeeded only in tearing free strands of her mane. She responded by biting down on him in a wail of alarm and pain. His hips bucked, sending her head into the steering wheel with a dull thud.

Then they were off the road; the headlights shining on nothing.

Peter closed his eyes tightly before the first impact came. The front end of the Mustang buckled as it landed on the soft shoulder of the cliff. A loud bang sounded before he was slammed in the face with the air bag, driving Camille's head into his abdomen with so much force that he could not breathe. Then she was gone, her feet flying out of the open window. However, he remained with the car, toppling head over heels. The pain was excruciating, and he was unable to catch his breath.

Suddenly he was rolling, his body tumbling free of the driver's seat to go with the car to the bottom of the ravine.

"Hannah?" Peter gasped, his last thoughts of his beautiful child. "God forgive me."

Relief flooded through Peter as the pain began to ebb away. He was vaguely aware of the car coming to a halt and everything going quiet. It no longer mattered. Peter knew it was time.

~

Diana Somerset came awake from her dream with a gasp, her eyes fluttering open to the gray light of dawn. It streamed through the window via the cracks in the blinds, offering enough light for her to see the untouched side of the bed where her husband of six years used to sleep.

Today was his funeral.

The car accident that had taken his life kept replaying itself in her mind, a mind now filled with guilt, as though she was somehow responsible for his irresponsible actions. Pieced together from what she had learned from the police, she had envisioned the events of that night over and over again until they now invaded her dreams.

She replayed their final words countless times.

"You're leaving again?" Diana had asked.

"I am."

4

"Will you be coming back?"

"No."

Through tears that she had bravely held in, she stared at the man she had promised to love and cherish above all others. "May I ask…" she began. Then her voice broke. "Peter, do you not care about our marriage anymore, or that I want out?"

Slowly, so very contemptuously, his gaze had traveled from her head to toe. His lips twisted just before he answered. That single word that had dashed all of her hopes and dreams. They had sealed the deal.

"No."

She had known that he was leaving that night, had even slammed the door behind him when he stormed out after those final painful two letters. Locking the door behind him, she had picked up all the evidence of their altercation and locked herself in the bedroom to nurse her wounds. When she had gone to bed that night, she had known that the time had come to make a change. She just had not realized that change was being forced upon her by the hands of fate. After eighteen months of watching her marriage crumble around her without doing anything to stop it, she now understood that Mother Nature had taken the reins from her hands and had settled the matter for her. She no longer had a say in her future; it was out of her hands.

In the privacy of her bedroom, she allowed the tears to spill. Tears of regret, tears of relief, and tears for the man she used to love with all of her heart trickled down her cheeks. This was her time to grieve, away from onlooker's eyes. All too soon, she would have to face his friends. She would have to hold her head high as they whispered behind their hands about how Peter had died, about Camille's presence in the car, and the bruise high on Diana's left cheekbone that remarkably showed signs of being obtained around the same time as the accident. Yes, their final altercation had not gone well, cumulating into physical violence borne from frustration by both parties. They would never have a chance to discuss it, though Diana doubted he would have wanted to try.

Soon she would have to face her future bravely. However, at this moment, she was free to be weak. To grieve. To wonder what she had done wrong.

Wiping away her tears, Diana tossed back the covers on her bed and made her way to the bathroom. A long hot shower eased some of the tension in the muscles of her neck and shoulders and washed away the last traces of her sorrow, but it did nothing to ease the ache in her heart. Like a song stuck on replay, she heard the guilt in her mind reminding her that she had not been careful in what she wished for. What she had wanted was her freedom. She had gotten that for sure, but she received that gift at a great cost to herself and others.

Hannah would grow up never knowing her father. Although, with the way things had been going, Diana wondered if that was a good thing.

More guilt immediately settled onto her tense shoulders.

She stood before the mirror on her dresser as she dressed, critically taking in her appearance through blurred vision. These past few months had been the most difficult. Late nights of worrying about Peter's philandering and partying had seen her once-rounded figure grow thinner from exhaustion and loss of appetite, and dark circles dulled her normally bright blue eyes. Her wavy blond hair was now dry and limp from the pressure and the stress. Once considered a knockout, she no longer had the time to make herself as beautiful as Peter had wanted her to be. That was a point he had made repeatedly. In recent months, she had not even had the urge to try.

Smoothing her black dress over her hips one last time, she sighed and turned away from the mirror. Hannah still needed to get ready, and they had to leave soon. She had more important things to worry about. No more time for self-pity.

Though she had arranged a quiet graveside funeral, she was amazed to see so many people congregate around his casket. She only knew a small portion of the group, and they avoided her intent stare with the shifting eyes and shuffling feet of those who knew too much for their comfort. Several times she caught some of the men in the group protectively covering their privates with a pained groan. So, it was no secret what the police had determined as the cause of the accident, she realized with a touch of humiliation. When they caught her furious stare, they turned away in embarrassment. Not too long ago, those men had flirted shamelessly with her. Now they glanced at her out of the corner of their eyes in pity. She and Hannah stood alone by the minister, dressed in their best and remaining dry-eyed and solemn while all his friends in their flashy, high-fashion clothes and lithe, well-toned bodies cried and mourned around her.

The day was cool and sunny, perfect for a funeral, and the high altitude air was fresh and clean. Diana held onto Hannah's hand tightly as she took several deep breaths. Hannah was not yet five-years-old, and she had not taken the news very well. With her youthful lack of wisdom, she could not understand that her daddy would never come home again. She wanted to know why and sent a barrage of questions Diana's way. They were questions she did not have the strength to answer yet.

Why?

Diana could not say why. It was not her decision.

The morning after the accident, Hannah had awakened to find their elderly neighbor dozing on the sofa while Diana had gone with the police. She had been worried when her mother returned pale and numb with shock. After Diana had told her there was a bad accident, Hannah had cried. However, the tears were more from confusion than comprehension.

Diana wept too. She wept bitter tears of anger at her husband. How could he be so foolish and remove himself from

7

his daughter's life so permanently? She remembered the look on his face again. Apparently, he had not been considering either her or Hannah at the time, and he had made it plain that he regretted their marriage. That look of pure contempt he had given her before he stormed out the door would stay with her for the rest of her life. She had certainly learned her lesson, and she would be damned if she ever fell that hard for a man again.

"May he forever rest in peace..."

The minister's final words rung in Diana's ears as she slowly lifted her chin. The silence only lasted a moment before more wailing captured Hannah's attention. She turned her head out of curiosity, and Diana gave her a quick tug on the hand to keep her focused. At the same time, they heard a car door open from somewhere behind the long line of cars parked along the side of the dirt road leading up to the freshly dug grave. How rude to interrupt, Diana thought, although she was not surprised. The tightknit crowd that Peter had grown friendly with was not necessarily a respectful group of individuals. Disturbing the somber silence of the last rites fell right in line with their standards. In fact, she half-expected that once the grave was filled, most of them would return to celebrate with him one last time. The idea filled her with disgust.

Again, Hannah's head swiveled toward the distraction. Now was not the time to lose the child's attention. With as much grace as she could muster, Diana gave Hannah another tug, this time pulling her forward so they could drop the rose her daughter clung to her chest into the gaping hole. She could feel the stares upon her, watching her every move and waiting to see her break down. But no, she would not give them the satisfaction. Her child squeezed her tightly when she saw the pastel floral casket cover that Hannah had chosen after Diana had flat-out refused the red rose arrangement designed to show everlasting love. No, they certainly had not shared that. The one that Hannah had picked out

8

sported colorful blooms of pink, white, orange, lavender and green roses, lilies and mums - more suitable for an Easter celebration but acceptable for a daughter's final gift to her father.

"Mommy, is that Daddy in there?"

Diana nodded solemnly. There was someone behind her, watching her. The hairs on the back of her neck stood up in warning. Yet she remained cool, refusing to give in to the unspoken pressure.

"But why?"

"We can talk all about it later, honey. Now give Daddy your flower."

Hannah cautiously approached the casket and threw down the single pink rose Diana had given to her. She stared at it intently, her small face a mask of concern. Then she grasped her mother's hand again. Diana did not bring a flower for him. As it was, she had a hard enough time gracing his casket with such an expensive waste of beautiful flowers. His final and most public humiliation had left no doubt with his friends that their relationship was long over. Why bother faking it after his death?

They stepped back to watch the casket slowly descend into the grave, and Hannah's voice took on a new urgency. "Mommy, why are they putting Daddy in that hole?"

Feeling that heavy stare was irritating Diana. She longed to turn around to see who was watching her every move, but her daughter's growing panic required all of her strength now. She leaned slightly to whisper in her small ear.

"It's okay. Daddy's in Heaven now looking down on us. We're just putting his body to bed."

"But why, Mommy? Why can't he go to bed at home with us?"

Diana smiled gently. "I'm sorry. It's not his home anymore. He's up in Heaven now. That's where he's going to live. And in Heaven he doesn't need his body. So it's just you and me at home.

9

But don't worry - Daddy will always keep an eye on you. He'll smile down at you and send you kisses. Now hush up and listen to the minister. He's almost done."

Hannah frowned, obviously wanting to ask more questions. However, she held her tongue and made her mother proud.

The minister glanced at Hannah and smiled gently. Then he blessed the casket one last time. "Now go in peace, and peace be with you."

The congregation murmured their response and slowly began to melt away. No one approached Diana, nor did she want them to. She could not guess how many of these women her husband had enjoyed a relationship with.

They eyed her speculatively as if to say "now I know why he strayed from home," and it hurt her more than she cared to admit. Though not a vain woman, she knew that she too had once been fresh and beautiful like them. However, her husband's constant verbal abuse and lack of interest had chipped away at her self-esteem until she had little left. She had been at the point where she no longer cared enough about recapturing her former beauty.

Things would change now, she thought with a firm resolve. For whatever reason, she had been given a chance to start over again with Hannah, and she intended to do just that. Though her last five years had not been joyous, she still had Peter to thank for the gift of Hannah. She had her daughter, and that was all that mattered now.

Taking a deep breath, Diana approached the minister to thank him. He shook her hand and reached down to stroke Hannah's cheek.

"Will you be all right, Diana?" He asked softly.

She managed a small smile. "We'll be fine."

"How about financially? I know it took all of your savings to pay for this. Will you be okay?"

"I have a job. I've already looked into going full-time. Once I find a good daycare for Hannah, I'll take the extra hours. Thank you for your concern."

He nodded. "My parish will do whatever they can to help. You need only ask."

She reached forward and squeezed his hand. "Thanks so much. I appreciate everything you've done so far, but I'm sure we'll be fine."

As Diana watched the minister move away, she again felt the gaze on her back. Glancing around her quickly, Diana noticed that almost everyone was returning to their waiting cars. With heads bent together in quiet words of soothing, Peter's friends silently made their way away from her. They were leaving her and Hannah all alone.

Alone. She was alone again.

Well, not completely. She still had Hannah, and Hannah was all she needed. She might be alone, but she would never be lonely while she had her precious child.

With everyone moving on, Diana gave her husband's casket one last long glance. The colorful flower arrangement seemed so out of place residing on the final resting place of a man whose heart was as black as coal. Tilting her chin, she took a deep, shaky breath and let it out slowly. Why, Peter, she wondered. Why did you have to do this to our marriage, to our child, to us? Even as her agonized heart asked the question, she knew the answer. It was clear almost from the beginning. He had never loved her as much as he loved himself. She had foolishly lived a lie, hoping that he would see the good in her and overcome his selfishness. However that would never be, and she had learned a valuable lesson. Never would she succumb like that again.

Confident that most everyone had gained enough distance from her for her and Hannah to depart, she began to head back to her car. The prickly feeling on the back of her neck had not eased, but she felt fairly certain it was paranoia. Then she noticed the long, black stretch limousine. Standing beside it was a tall, lean man as dark as the vehicle. His black hair was professionally trimmed and stirred only slightly in the mid-summer breeze, and even from the distance, she could tell his black tailored suit was top dollar. Hanging open and flapping lightly against his slacks was an elegant lightweight overcoat. A large, hulking blond man stood beside him. Although not as expensively dressed, he stood proud and tall and frighteningly impassive. Diana shivered. He appeared to be some sort of strong arm or perhaps a bodyguard. Had Peter gotten involved with thugs, too?

From the distance, she could feel his penetrating stare and shivered. A feeling of fear filled her at his intensity. Oh no, she thought with a touch of panic, what kind of mess had Peter gotten into? And more importantly, what did they want with her?

~

Devlan Doyle crossed his arms over his chest and frowned as he scrutinized his sister-in-law. During the end of the service, his eyes had remained on her hastily pinned golden hair and trim back, not moving away even when she bent to speak to his niece. All he remembered of his sister-in-law was how beautiful and vibrant she had been and how proud his stepbrother was to have captured her. Looking at her now reminded him how destructive his stepbrother had been. Not content with even the best, he always felt as though he deserved better.

It was sad that he left such a trail of devastation behind him.

He saw the bitterness in her profile when she turned to speak with the minister. It made her appear harsh, and his astute gaze carefully took note that she had not shed one tear. Even from a distance, he could grasp her disengaged countenance. She acted like a woman who no longer felt with her heart. While the other attendees held handkerchiefs and dabbed occasionally at their eyes, Diana remained stoic and grim. And once the minister said his final words and the guests began to mingle, not one person approached her or looked her way. She remained rigid as they meandered off, with her child by her side impatiently scuffing the green grass with the tip of her shoe.

The child.

It was the child that brought him here, he reminded himself, not her.

With Peter's death, Devlan was faced with a problem. Unfortunately, he did not like problems. They were a nuisance. While there definitely had been no love lost between him and his closest remaining family member, his lawyers had advised him that the death of his younger stepbrother had changed everything. A serious problem, he was told. His entire estate would now be left to a four-year-old child, and though he had no plans of dying in the near future, Peter's accident reminded him that no one could ever be sure. Now this child, a child that he had never set eyes on before this very day, was his heiress and would remain so unless he married and had children of his own.

Hannah Somerset stood in line to inherit one of the largest software companies in the world. Now Devlan's first priority was to ensure that the girl was in good hands. Peter's influence could not have been all that good, and he was feeling the first stirrings of doubt about Diana now that he was seeing her again. Not only had she stayed with the squanderer, but looking at her now made him even more concerned. Though he had been prepared for the possibility that her good looks hid the truth like Peter's once did, all he saw was an angry and bitter woman. He knew he had to pay his last respects and see for himself the child that was all he had left of family, but he viewed the whole debacle with distaste and irritation.

Such a shame.

His attention was brought back to the present when Diana

moved away from the minister and glanced around. Her cool gaze took in the mourners as they wandered away, but still her face expressed no emotion. Then her roving gaze met his. At that point, everything about her changed. As soon as she noticed him standing by the car, her whole posture stiffened, and the hand that gripped Hannah's noticeably tightened. She spun on her heel and rushed back to the road, hastily pulling her child along beside her and away from him.

With some surprise, he noticed Diana had taken her own vehicle to her husband's funeral. She came to a sudden stop beside an older-style compact car while she fumbled with her keys, refusing to look in their direction. Pushing away from the side of his limo, Devlan turned to his companion with an almost imperceptible nod.

"Okay Mike, let's get this over with."

"Right, Mr. Doyle."

The two men approached Diana and Hannah, stopping her as she buckled the little golden child in her car seat.

"Excuse me, Mrs. Somerset."

Diana startled visibly and backed slowly out of the car. As she straightened to greet him with her dark blue eyes wide and wary, Devlan's breath caught. Despite her rundown appearance, she was still a stunningly beautiful woman. Her classic features belonged on the cover of a magazine, not in a graveyard with dark circles under eyes that were wide with what appeared to be fear.

Even though there was no make-up adorning her smooth skin, she was by far the loveliest woman he had seen in attendance. The black dress that covered her trim form had seen better days and hid what he remembered as a perfect figure, but still Devlan could feel his heartbeat quicken when he stared at her.

Just like it had six years ago.

Taking a deep breath, he forced his thoughts to return to the present.

"Yes?" she replied.

When she answered, he noticed the slight quiver in her voice and wondered about her nervousness, but before he could continue, a perceptible change came over her. Almost as though someone had flipped a switch, some of her tension eased. As she stared up at him, her head cocked slightly to one side, and her lips turned down in a slight frown. He could tell by her squinted eyes that she was struggling to place him.

"Devlan Doyle, Diana. Peter's stepbrother. We met briefly at your wedding."

That easing tension suddenly returned in full force. Ignoring his outstretched hand, she inclined her chin defiantly in refusal. As he studied her, he watched a flash of distaste in her gaze before she carefully schooled her features to reveal no hint of her feelings.

With the grace of a debutante, she nodded coolly. "It was nice of you to come all the way out here. What can I do for you, Mr. Doyle?"

Devlan smiled thinly. It seemed she held him in as high esteem as he held her. He glanced down at the child, and his smile grew. Hannah was beautiful, the spitting image of her mother, and to his untrained eye she looked exactly like a four-year-old girl ought to. To all appearances, she looked healthy and well-cared for, and, at the moment, her bright-blue gaze, so similar to her mother's, was glued to him and his big friend curiously.

"Hi Hannah, I'm your Uncle Devlan."

She smiled shyly and glanced at her mother for approval, but Diana stood with arms crossed under her deceptively round breasts. Never one to refuse an invitation, his gaze shifted to the firm mounds she had hidden behind her dark clothing, even though his actions made Diana's scowl deepen.

"Mr. Doyle, why are you here?"

Devlan knew this was the moment Diana would change her

attitude toward him. Mention money to a woman, and they were putty in your hands. With a cool smile, he reached into his pocket and handed her a business card. "I'm here to ensure that Hannah will be okay."

"'Okay'?"

"Yes. With Peter gone, she'll need someone to watch over her."

"Watch over her?"

He nodded impatiently, growing irritated that she kept repeating his words. "Yes. She is, after all, the only family I have left. I want to make sure that she's well cared for."

With a curt nod of her head, Diana pressed her lips together with finality. "Thank you for your concern, Mr. Doyle, but Peter's 'departure' has not changed a thing. I can assure you that Hannah was fine before and will continue to be fine now that he's 'gone.'"

She had just dismissed him, of that he had no doubt. Devlan realized his mistake just before the icy words escaped her stiff lips when her gaze turned as cold as the mountain peaks around them. He had misjudged this woman, forgetting the class with which she had conducted herself when they had first met. Apparently, his brother had not stolen that from her along with everything else.

With reluctant admiration, he studied her closely. The light breeze stirred several loose strands of her hair across her face. The thick, sun-streaked mane was a texture and color that women would pay for in the hairdressers' shops. Her slender fingers, with unpainted and closely cropped nails, reached up to carelessly curl the wayward strands behind her ear as her eyes narrowed under his close scrutiny.

Frustration hardened Devlan's jaw as he hurried to make up for his blunder before she turned and left him standing in her dust. Never before had he had trouble speaking to a beautiful woman, and he refused to allow this one to be the first.

He cleared his throat meaningfully before he answered. "I

meant financially, Diana."

"Financially?"

Still with arms crossed, she raised her gaze to study him steadily. It was then that he noticed a fading, yellowish discoloration around her left eye. Though wisps of hair had been strategically placed to try to cover the mark, apparently she had forgotten when she tucked those strands behind her ear. He wondered where the mark had come from as his voice grew hard that someone had dared to mark her beautiful face. "Yes, financially."

"And what do you want from me in return?"

Her sarcasm was not missed, but the truth was that he had never given it a thought. His concern had been solely focused on Hannah, and he had never considered Diana. However, he was a man, and her cold words planted sudden ideas and images in his head. His eyebrows rose as he scanned her from head-to-toe.

"I can take care of you and Hannah. That's why I'm here. What you give me in return can be worked out."

Diana glanced down at the business card with distaste. Then she met his gaze coolly and handed the card back. There was a strange look on her face as her full lips turned down. "Hannah's fine, Mr. Doyle. I have a job and can take care of her. She is, after all, *my* daughter. If you were so concerned about her safety, you should've come a long time ago. Your help may have made a difference then, but it's too late now. Hannah and I just want to move on with our lives and forget all this." She indicated with one hand toward the casket before turning back to her car. As if in afterthought, she sent him one last icy glare over her shoulder. "Thank you for coming to pay your respects."

Devlan watched in stunned surprise as she hastily opened the car door. With a flash of her shapely leg, she was in the car and fastening her seatbelt. Then the engine roared to life, and she put it into gear roughly before pulling away and showering them with dust, just as he had expected.

Mike jumped back, whistling under his breath. "Well, how do you like that?"

When there was no returning answer, Mike glanced at him. Ignoring his questioning look, Devlan continued to watch her drive away, frowning thoughtfully before he responded. "Find out everything you can about her. Debts, job information, what she's been doing. Also check out Hannah. I want her medical records and any hospital visits she might have."

"Why, what's up?" Mike asked.

"She had a black eye, Mike."

"So? Maybe the two of them played it rough – with each other or with others."

"No, not her… I want them watched."

Devlan was surprised at how angry he felt. It was a damn crime to be marring such a beautiful woman. She was the type that a man showed off proudly by displaying her on his arm, not one that was knocked around until bruises marred her smooth skin.

Diana's cryptic words echoed in his ears. He needed to know what had happened. Most of all, he wanted to know what Diana meant when she said his offer to help was too late.

"Yes, sir."

Devlan nodded slowly, his mind whirling like the leaves in the breeze. His problem had suddenly grown more complicated, for now he was intrigued by his sister-in-law. There was something different about her, beginning with her disdainful reaction to him. She had taken him completely by surprise, and he had momentarily lost his composure. That was a victory on her part. After all, there was one thing he had learned in his time, and that was that women loved his money. At least in his previous relationships, the women he had dated proved to appreciate his status and wealth more than he did – an apparent misconception that had kept him single and skeptical for so long. She had been different, and her reaction to him both excited and challenged him. Not interested in his money? In fact, it seemed only to increase her dislike.

However, despite his surprise, he was not completely blinded. Diana Somerset had let some emotion slip, and his astute business sense had detected her faux pas. There had been fear in her eyes when she looked at him, and he had noticed loneliness behind her self-righteous anger. He suspected that the loneliness he saw was not for the death of her husband but perhaps for being alone. He wanted to know why.

Well, he would find out. His people would find out everything there was to know about her. It was only a matter of time. Though he was not yet sure why, the urge to help that woman made him burn with an urgency that he had never before experienced. He wanted to help her more than anything else in his life.

Chapter 2

Diana glanced one last time in the rearview mirror of her car. She saw the bodyguard jump back, but Devlan remained where he stood, allowing the dust to spatter his expensive suit. His face bore a thoughtful expression as he watched her leave, and with a shudder she realized that would not be the last of Devlan Doyle.

She took a deep, shaking breath and brushed the hair away from her face once again. How dare he insinuate that she should take up with him? *He could take care of her.* Like it was some sort of honor. No, she could take care of herself and Hannah just fine. All she needed was time to get reorganized and take stock of her life.

No, another man was not what she wanted or needed right now, especially her husband's womanizing stepbrother. She shuddered at the thought. Oh yes, Peter had told her all about him when they were first married. How Devlan went from one woman to another, keeping track of his conquests by carving notches in the hardwood of an Irish walking stick his father had given him. How ridiculous and childish, she thought as she glanced back one more time. A total commitment-phobe refusing to ever commit to anyone, he played the field casually, and if one woman grew too attached, he immediately ended the relationship. It must have run in the family, she thought furiously. What a creep.

Still seething, Diana maneuvered her small car into traffic, trying to focus on Hannah's soft singing in the backseat. But no matter how hard she tried, all she could hear was Devlan's deep, seductive voice telling her that they could work out her repayment. How could that man have such a nerve? At her husband's funeral? The gall of it made her feel ill. No, she had already made a promise to herself. After Peter, she would never fall blindly for a man again. And that included Devlan Doyle, for all his sexy charisma and confidence. She certainly would not fall for those dark blue eyes and sensual good looks. So he had a fit figure and was gorgeous, but he also had a track record that would out-do Peter's. No, she told herself yet another time, another cheating man was not what she needed. Not now; not ever again. She would not be one of his conquests.

She and Hannah would do fine. Once she took stock of their assets and cashed in Peter's life insurance, she would finance a sum for Hannah's education and maybe use the rest to pay off their mortgage. Then she could find work more leisurely and perhaps stash up enough to open her own shop. This was her time to start a new life. She was free to do whatever she and Hannah wanted to do.

Her only regret was that she had not done this a long time ago.

~

The office she sat in had a row of windows against the wall, but it did little to ease the dreariness of the dark wood desk and black, upholstered plastic and aluminum chairs, one of which she now sat on. A half-dead plant was also housed in black plastic, and the pot sported the white and brown wounds of overwatering and leakage. Diana studied the fine veins on a single leaf, struggling to remember all the parts of a plant that she had learned long ago. Blade, vein, margin and petiole... Then the man looked up and blinked at her.

"I'm sorry, Mrs. Somerset, but we've given him as many

extensions as we could. The mortgage hasn't been paid in a year."

Diana sensed the blood draining from her face and closed her eyes briefly. She could not be hearing what she thought she was. Hoping it was all a bad dream, she slowly re-opened her eyes. Unfortunately, she was still in the same dreary office sitting across from the same somber man.

"I had no idea we were in arrears, Mr. Simms, but certainly if I can pay what we owe, they'll let me and Hannah stay in our house?"

"Well, we'd have to have everything you owe in back payments. Can you come up with that kind of cash?"

"How much are we behind?"

The bank manager stared down at the papers on his desk. "Uh," he stuttered, his face flushing to his light brown roots. "Mrs. Somerset, you'd need to pay twenty-thousand dollars."

Diana gasped. "You can't be serious. Surely there's something you can do."

The manager looked over his glasses at her. "Foreclosure proceedings have been in process already. Letters have been sent. Unless you can pay it all, I'm afraid there's nothing I can do."

"Wait a minute," she said. "Peter's life insurance policy is with this bank. When I get the cash from that, would it be enough to pay off the mortgage?"

Mr. Simms looked at his computer screen with a frown. When he turned back to Diana his face was grim. "I'm sorry… the insurance policy was cashed in six months ago. The only accounts I have listed for you are your savings and the joint checking. There's a savings account for Hannah, but that has a zero balance."

Diana felt her world come crashing down. Gripping the edge of his desk to prevent herself from pulling out her hair, she peered at the squirming manager in desperation. "He emptied Hannah's account too?"

The manager looked at his hands. She knew he felt as awkward as she did, and she knew that it was her fault. She should never have trusted Peter.

"If I sold my car, would that be enough to postpone the foreclosure?"

"What I would suggest, Mrs. Somerset, is that you sell what you can before they seize your house. Or try to sell your house quick. Pay off what debts you can under bankruptcy and start anew. If you'd like, I can give you the name of a lawyer..."

Diana could feel tears burn her eyes and blinked rapidly. One by one, the salty drops escaped, running unchecked down her pale cheeks. Avoiding her gaze, Simms found an invisible speck of dust on the framed photo of his two beautiful children and busied himself with wiping it away.

Hopelessness devoured all of her good intentions. There was nothing she could do. Dreams shattered, she understood clearly that she could not pay off the mortgage and purchase a shop. He had blown through it all, every last penny. It was one more ambush Peter had won.

All because she had let him.

Nodding slowly, Diana reached for the number. She stared at the card through blurred vision, and a solitary tear dropped onto it before she tucked it into her pocket.

Coming to her feet, she managed a tremulous smile at Mr. Simms. "I'm sorry to take up so much of your time."

Fumbling in a nearly empty desk drawer, he handed her a box of tissues. She pulled two out and crumpled them in her fist with a short laugh of embarrassment. "Thank you."

"It was no trouble, Mrs. Somerset. Let me just say how very sorry I am. If you need any help that I can give you, please don't hesitate to call me."

She snorted. "How about a loan?"

Simms laughed awkwardly and led her to the door. Holding it

open, he allowed her to pass. She knew he was as eager as she to escape the awkward situation. As she turned to say goodbye, he smiled again.

"Please believe that I've done what I could."

"I know you did."

She nodded one last time and walked away.

~

"Diana Marie Halliday. Born December 7; age 29. Parents died in small plane crash when she was eighteen and in college. She majored in finance with a minor in business management. Graduated with honors at age 21. Smart chick. One steady boyfriend. Took parent's money and invested it. Started work straight out of college as a manager at a bookstore. Met your brother. According to my sources, he wined and dined her. Swept her off her feet. They married and had a baby within a year. They bought the house for the baby, using part of her trust fund as a down payment. Peter had odd jobs here and there; Diana kept working part-time at the bookstore. Hannah was born in September, four-years ago. No exact date for when Peter started cheating, but he has a list of women trailing after him."

"You were right, by the way."

Devlan glanced up at Mike, his brows raised. "How so?"

"She didn't sleep around from all appearances. She's kept pretty much to the straight road... despite the cheating husband."

"Mmm." He waved his hand, indicating to Mike to continue.

"Okay. Peter drove the Mustang involved in the crash. Bought new."

Devlan nodded.

"Diana kept the Corolla we saw her in. She also managed to have a private savings account that she stashed money into. According to the minister, that was how she paid for his funeral.

He told me Peter stole and squandered everything else away."

"Does she have any money now?"

"Nothing. Not a dime. In fact, there's so much debt over her head now, she's completely broke."

A finance major? Devlan shook his head in disbelief. "How did she not know?"

Mike glanced down at his papers. "He controlled everything. I don't think she had much of a choice… Let me leave it at this: He didn't allow her to find out. He was an overbearing bully that liked to shout as loud as he could. Her paycheck was direct deposited into their joint checking account. How she managed to store away what little money she had was a stroke of pure luck or genius on her part."

Devlan's lips thinned. "Well, I guess she's better off without him. Did you happen to find out why she stayed?"

Mike shrugged. "Beats me. Although, since she lost both her parents, it appears as though she might've stuck around for Hannah's sake. An old friend at her last job mentioned that she was known to say that she thought it important that Hannah have both parents."

"But if the parent isn't good for the child?"

"That's just it. He may have worn down Diana, but everyone we spoke to all agreed that he never hurt his daughter. Her medical records are impeccable. No accidents, no bumps or bruises. Healthy as can be. Besides, from what I've learned about her – if he touched his daughter, Diana would've torn him to pieces."

Shaking his head, Devlan wondered if he would ever understand women. "But she allowed him to hurt her? That makes no sense."

"I'm not so sure it was a regular thing," Mike offered. He glanced down at his papers again. "I could only find one episode for her at an emergency room, and that was recent. Three cracked ribs. Bound and sent home with no questions asked. Reported she fell down the stairs while home alone."

Devlan's brow rose. "Okay? That's possible."

"They live in a ranch house, no basement."

Devlan nodded curtly in understanding, and his jaw tightened in anger. Women. They were all trouble, every last one of them, and this particular woman was bothering him more than she should, which annoyed him even more. He should not give two hoots that this woman appeared to be pure, honest and simple. It should not bother him that life had dealt her an unfair blow by his selfish stepbrother.

Yet that sad look in her eye still haunted him. She was completely alone now, with a small child to care and provide for, and financial ruin hanging over her head. Despite all that, she still had flat-out refused to accept the help of the last member of her extended family.

"I gave my connection at the bank your card. He was told that your lawyer's handling Peter's estate, and you're power of attorney. That way he can release information. He's sure to call you."

"Excellent. Good work Mike, and thanks."

Mike nodded and backed out of the room. Before he shut the door behind him, Devlan glanced up. "Mike, do me another favor. Keep that watch on her."

Mike's eyes widened in surprise, but Devlan did not notice. "Sir?"

"Desperation can force people to act in reckless ways. I need to make sure she doesn't do anything too drastic. Hannah's my priority."

Though he knew that he was not fooling Mike any more than he was fooling himself, Devlan continued to study the papers in front of him as the door closed behind his closest friend and most-trusted employee. He knew Mike would remain discreet and do as he asked. In fact, he thought with a small shake of his head, Mike was more like a brother to him than Peter had ever been.

Forming a steeple with his fingers, he rested his chin upon them as he continued to go over the information Mike had given him. Behind him, the sun continued to rise above the hustle and bustle of downtown Los Angeles, but he barely noticed. In the quiet of his office, with only the sound of his employee's muffled voices to distract him, he wondered what it was that had forced Diana to make such sacrifices and fall so hard. If it was love, he hoped he never fell in love.

The intercom buzzed. "Mr. Doyle?"

Devlan pressed down the button to answer his secretary. "Yes, what is it, Kathy?"

"A Mr. Simms, from the bank, sir. He says it's important."

Devlan frowned. Then he saw the name on his desk. Ah, yes. Simms was Diana's banker. That did not take very long.

"Put him through," he said grimly. He reached for the handset as soon as the light blinked. "Doyle."

"Mr. Doyle? John Simms."

"Yes, Mr. Simms, what can I do for you?"

"Mr. O'Hare told me that you are the power of attorney to Peter Somerset's estate, and that I should contact you with any updates."

"Yes, I'm aware of that."

"I spoke with Mrs. Somerset today and have had a chance to review the accounts. I know you're in charge of his remaining estate, and I'm hopeful that things can be settled quickly on your end."

"There are a lot of debts?"

"Well, yes, sir. Quite a bit of defaults."

"I see. Is Diana financially stable?"

Simms cleared his throat. "I can't really say, sir. I'm sorry. I know he was your brother, but she's still alive and most of the accounts are in both names. I'm borderline breaking confidentiality now."

"I understand, Simms, but I'll personally handle his debts with the fund in my control. Pull a bureau on my brother and have it ready. My secretary will wire the funds for you to settle the debts. In fact, I'll buy the mortgage and sell the house outright."

"Yes, sir, Mr. Doyle." The relief in the banker's voice was so apparent that Devlan almost smiled.

"Oh, and Simms? Your secret is safe with me as long as mine is safe with you."

"Of course, thank you sir."

Devlan smiled. "Thank you. Rest assured that all my brother's debts will be handled."

"I'm on it now."

Devlan hung up the phone and sat back in his chair, spinning it around until he faced the window. Outside, the city of Los Angeles came alive in the steamy summer sunlight. How fast-paced and different life here was compared to the relaxed atmosphere he had witnessed in the quiet suburb of Denver. The cost of living for one year in his house in Brentwood would probably cover all of Peter's debts in Denver, but inside his office on the top floor, Devlan shook his head in self-reproach. He was taking on a huge responsibility; one he was now absolutely certain Diana would not want him involved in.

However, he reminded himself yet again, it was really for the child. While the gossip columns might accuse him of not having a heart, never in a million years could he allow the last remnant of his family to suffer needlessly. Not while he had the means to fix things. He was not that selfish and cold.

Diana was just an added distraction.

What did it matter that his heart fluttered in his chest when he thought about all the pain she had been through? It had nothing to do with her. Not even because she looked so vulnerable behind her tough-as-nails exterior.

His gaze scanned the horizon, staring out at hazy Los Angeles around him. The heat here was stifling, but he had enjoyed the brief reprieve at Peter's funeral. Back in Colorado, the snow had almost completely melted from the high peaks in preparation for the new snow coming soon. As he pondered the differing climates, he wondered what Diana was doing at that moment. She had just left the bank. Chances were that she was heading home to pack. Where would she be when the weather turned?

Closing his eyes against the strong California sun, Devlan envisioned Diana as he had always remembered her. The stunning bride dressed in an ivory silk sheath gown that had clung to her curves like a fitted glove. He still remembered that day as if it were yesterday. She had been so happy, her young face glowing with hope and happiness in the candlelight. Peter, too, had appeared happy until he arrived. Without as much as an invitation to stay and dine with them, Peter had demanded that he leave.

How jealous his brother had been, jealous and selfish from the first moment he had arrived on the scene. Despite the eight year age difference, Peter had constantly tried to best him. It was a feat not accomplished until he had found Diana. Peter glowed with pride over having landed her, and for the first time Devlan had to admit he was envious, especially when she smiled at him. It had reached her bright eyes, the skin around them crinkling endearingly, and her laugh was clear, contagious, and so full of joy.

A knock on the door broke his reverie, and he turned away from the window reluctantly. "Yeah."

Mike came strolling back in. "Simms called already?"

"Word travels fast," Devlan said with a grimace.

"I was in the office." Mike took the seat in front of Devlan's desk and leaned forward. "What's going on here? What's making you do this?"

Devlan shrugged. "I need to make sure that Hannah's well cared for. If not, she'll be in the custody battle of a lifetime."

Mike shook his head. "No, this goes beyond that. What did your brother do that makes you feel so guilty?"

Devlan laughed shortly and came to his feet. "Believe me, Mike, it's not Peter. I have absolutely no loyalty to him at all."

Peter had been the sole black smear upon his father's good name. His elderly father had found Peter's mother somewhere in Las Vegas and brought the pretty woman home with him. She had died three-years later from a sedative overdose, leaving her thirteen-year-old son behind. However, Peter had not missed his mother. Even at a young age, he was spoiled and wanted so much more than he deserved. His mother had been merely the key to his stepfather's money. Unfortunately, when his stepfather died six months later from a heart attack, the only money he had left Peter was stashed away in a college fund. He depleted that by the end of his sophomore year, and that was when he found Diana. She had money left to her by her deceased parents, and apparently the lovely face and charming personality that went with it was an added bonus that he took advantage of.

Devlan's hands curled into tight fists. It sickened him that it did not take Peter long to squander her money as well as her love. Now he and Diana were left picking up the pieces.

Everything Peter had touched he destroyed, but it was not out of guilt that Devlan was trying to clean up after him. No, there was something else that tugged at his heart like a child on someone's coattails.

However, even he was unsure exactly what that was.

~

Hot tears burned Diana's eyes. She struggled to keep them in, but it was too hard. No matter how quickly she blinked, the persistent moistness welled and overflowed. Sighing sadly, Diana resigned herself to allowing the tears to fall while she drove home from the bank. There was no holding back anymore; she no longer had to hide her true feelings. While Peter used to ridicule her whenever she felt down, he was gone now. It was time to let it all out. Now, before Hannah saw her.

She pulled into the driveway and stared at the small ranch-style house she had called home for the last five years. It rested in a quiet, family-oriented cul-de-sac, where SUVs were parked next to bicycles, and community parks were overflowing with block parties. While the sad memories had begun to outweigh the good ones in recent months, it was the house she carried her newborn baby home to. It was the only home Hannah had ever known.

She was glad Hannah was not there when she had received the news. She could not imagine trying to answer the questions the child was sure to ask. She needed time. Unfortunately, that was a luxury she no longer had.

With shaking fingers, she unlocked the door and went in, taking note of how quiet the house was. There would be no more arguments. She had thought she was finally free now that Peter was gone, but he took with him everything she owned. How could she have been so ignorant, so foolish to believe in him, or so blind to the reality of her life?

Sitting down hard on the couch, Diana sighed as she placed her face in her hands. She deserved a good cry. It was a long time coming. Once she was done crying, she would move on and make new plans. There was much to do and she needed to get started. She could survive this; she was tougher than she thought. At least, that was what she kept telling herself.

So why did she feel so alone?

~

"That's the last one." Diana sat back with a sigh and glanced around her at the empty house.

Her neighbor, Mindy, with her chocolate hair drawn back in a ponytail that bunched in the hood of her black, green and gold CSU sweatshirt, entered the living room carrying Hannah's favorite stuffed bear. "Wait a minute. I have one more."

"I don't have any room. We'll have to let Hannah carry it."

Mindy nodded and enthusiastically viewed the room. "Then that's it. Let's go."

"Yes. I have a lot of unloading to do when we get there."

With a strength that belied her petite frame, Mindy picked up the last box and carried it to the small rental truck parked in the driveway. Her husband, Allan, called for Hannah and their son, AJ, who came running with squeals of delight. They were quickly loaded into the truck with Allan.

Diana lagged behind. With a heavy heart, she walked through her house for the last time. Dust motes danced in the sunlight streaming through the windows, and echoing footsteps replaced the sound of Hannah's laughter down the narrow hallway leading to the bedrooms. No beds remained in those rooms anymore. In fact, there was nothing left. Everything was swept clean. Only emptiness remained, and it left her with a hollow feeling.

After committing everything to the back corners of her memory, Diana returned outside to the brisk morning chill and joined the others. The "For Sale" sign in her front yard told it all. It was over. This part of her life was now one experience from which she had learned. From here on out, she had the rest of her life ahead of her.

In a stroke of pure luck, Diana had received a call later in the afternoon after her visit to the bank. Fortunately, Mr. Simms had located the account that Peter had put the money from their savings in. While it was not enough to bail out her mortgage completely, she was able to pay off some of their smaller debts without having to sell her car. He had guided her through signing all the necessary papers, and then he told her that she could move on. After selling and donating her extra furniture and most of Peter's belongings, Diana packed up what little remained from block yard sales and prepared to move to her new apartment.

The apartment she took was a small three-room place in a newer complex close to Hannah's preschool in Westminster. Small but clean, the single bedroom was all she could afford for the time being. While not the lifestyle Hannah was used to, Diana was sure that she was young enough to adjust. Once she had explained why they had to leave, Hannah had accepted it reluctantly, but Diana had felt the first stirrings of hope for their new future together.

"Are we ready?" Diana asked. Though the words were hard and stuck in her throat like spoonful of peanut butter, she thought she matched Mindy's enthusiasm.

The kids in the truck shouted their eagerness, and Diana smiled in return. Allan, on the other hand, rolled his eyes, but his voice was teasing. "I knew I'd be the one stuck with the kids. I just knew it."

Diana gave him a grateful smile. "I can't thank you enough, Allan. You and Mindy have been a great help."

"It's no problem, Diana. I wish you had come to us a long time ago. Perhaps we could've helped you more than this."

Diana could feel a blush rise to her cheeks. Allan was not a small man, and the fierce frown on his face spoke volumes. How she hated that her neighbors had learned what had happened.

"I'm okay, and Hannah's great. We'll manage just fine," she said lightly.

"It's the hidden scars we're afraid of, Di," he said pointedly.

Diana could feel herself squirming under his scrutiny. This line of discussion was not the direction she wanted to head into. Not today. "You know, these past two months have done wonders for Hannah. She's started her new school, and I've found this new apartment. Losing the house right after Peter has been hard, but we'll manage. We just need a fresh start."

"Well, I know a few guys who would love to help you, Diana. Just give me the okay, and you'll have your pick."

Diana laughed, a genuine giggle that came from deep within and made her eyes sparkle. She liked that she was able to laugh again. "I'm not ready for that yet, Allan, but thanks. I'll definitely keep your offer in mind as winter sets in."

He grinned and revved the engine. Diana waved back and crossed her neatly manicured grass one last time to reach her car, starting it up, and leading the way to her new place. As she pulled out of her neighborhood one last time, she glanced in the mirror and saw the truck following behind. It reminded her that not everyone was selfish and cruel. There were good people out there that were willing to help. Like Mr. Simms at the bank and Allan and Mindy. Thank goodness she had been able to keep her car, and thank goodness she had finally found some friends.

Chapter 3

Their new home was small but safe, despite its location on a main thoroughfare. As she and Hannah settled in, there was a lot to keep them busy and the adjustment went well. The new routine suited them both. As fall approached, Hannah began Kindergarten, and Mindy kept her after school until Diana was done with work. At the same time, Diana started full-time at her job, and the extra money was well worth it. They were starting over on their terms.

Although this new lifestyle was busy, Diana and Hannah still managed to keep some quality time together. Though she never thought it possible, she and Hannah had grown even closer. Without Peter's constant harassment, Diana was able to become her old self again, and her evenings with Hannah were shared with plenty of giggles, hugs and kisses.

It was just the two of them, and they were a team. After Diana picked her up from Mindy's house, she would prepare dinner, and Hannah helped her clean up. Then they would spend the evenings together, completing Hannah's homework, reading, doing household chores, and preparing for bed before another busy day arrived. Hannah chose the outfits; Diana tucked her in. So full of each other, Diana rarely had use of the electronic sitter. The television set resting on the used entertainment center was reserved for weekends and special occasions.

However, it was through the television that Diana again saw

Devlan Doyle.

Three months had passed since he had confronted her at the funeral. Though at one time certain he would be harassing her more regularly, she had not heard from him since. It later dawned on her that his professed concern had been just a courtesy, and neither she nor Hannah had made his cut. Surprisingly, she was comfortable knowing that they probably would not ever see or hear from him again. He was from a part of her life that she would just as soon put behind her. Nevertheless, when Diana heard his name on the evening entertainment show, she could not resist her curiosity.

She was up to her elbows in Hannah's bath bubbles when she heard the announcement, and her ears instantly keyed in to what was being said. Cursing her interest, she tossed down the towel and came to her feet. Though she knew she was being silly, she hurried into the living room and stared at the set. Tall, dark, and oh so debonair in his black tux, he beamed at the cameras with the stunningly beautiful woman on his arm.

Nah, she confirmed in her mind, he had not spared them a thought since the moment he left Denver.

"And high-fashion model Roxanne Lemieux showed up at the premier with none other than Devlan Doyle, business tycoon and rumored producer. There has been talk of Doyle teaming up with Hugh Davis, a close friend of Roxanne's, for a new project, though neither party will comment on it. While Doyle claims merely to enjoy the beautiful model's company, the pair has been seen together at several functions, although neither will admit to a serious relationship. As you know, Roxanne is the former wife of Director Wayne Moore, and Doyle has been linked to several beautiful actresses including superstar Catalina Jasper..."

With an exasperated sigh, Diana turned away. Those brothers may not have been bound by blood, but they certainly shared the same fear of commitment. She and Hannah were so much better off without them in their lives, and it had been foolish of her to watch because the sight only served to ruin her mood. Seeing Devlan flashing his white teeth in a friendly smile for the cameras with a stunning model on his arm made her jaw clench, even as it reminded her of the lack of companionship in her own secluded life. What one took for granted, another could only dream of.

She went back to the bathroom and sat on the lowered toilet seat thoughtfully. Hannah was still happily playing with her dolls in the bath and did not look up when she returned, so Diana watched her idly as her mind drifted back in time to the first time she had seen Peter's handsome brother. It seemed so long ago, though really only six years had passed. Her forehead puckered in remembrance. He had changed a bit since that night so long ago. There were more lines around his large blue eyes, and his face had thinned slightly over the years. Perhaps that was why she had not immediately recognized him.

Devlan Doyle. A man as dark as his step-brother was fair. When he had arrived at her wedding reception in his form fitting black suit that almost perfectly matched his hair, he had immediately drawn attention. Whether it was because he arrived during the toast to the bride and groom or because he was just a mesmerizing man, his presence had taken the attention away from his brother. And Diana clearly remembered that Peter had not been happy about it.

Though Peter had told her Devlan never lacked for female company, he had come alone to their wedding. Her curiosity, along with everyone else's, drew many interested stares his way. However, his focus remained on the head table – on her and Peter. Much to Peter's dismay, Diana's eyes were drawn to Devlan's instantly, and she felt her new husband stiffen beside her when her gaze locked with the enigmatic man's in the doorway. While she told herself it was just the interruption that made her return his steady stare, in truth it was because he was so darkly handsome and had such bright eyes. They were mesmerizing. His intense blue orbs had focused solely on her, and he studied her intently. The way he had stared made her shiver, but she had been helpless to look away. There was no denying it; the man was not only handsome as sin, but sexy as well.

As though in a trance, she had broken away from her guests as soon as possible and approached him, smiling cheerfully and stating her welcome. He had grasped her hand in his and held it longer than necessary, leaning forward to offer a kiss to the bride.

At the time she had been blinded by hope, so Diana had not seen the warning sign in Peter's jealous reaction. After watching his brother's appreciative appraisal, he had risen and approached Devlan before he had completely lowered his lips to her cheek. There was a heated discussion, with Peter doing most of the gesturing, and Devlan left quietly without another word. His parting gaze had left her feeling somehow unsatisfied, but her idealism quickly brushed aside the compelling attraction.

It was much later in their honeymoon that Diana had mentioned the incident. Peter had shrugged it off and told her about Devlan, how his stepbrother had stolen his inheritance and used it to buy into a huge corporation that was struggling. He took it over and slowly expanded it before using every trick in the book to cheat Peter out of his share. After hiring smooth talking lawyers to scour every document, Devlan ruthlessly swindled Peter out of his wealth.

At the time, Diana had sympathized with Peter. He had painted the perfect picture of a family embezzlement, of a selfish and ambitious man who had forcefully gone after what he wanted without considering those he hurt. She had put Devlan Doyle out of her mind, burying her curiosity behind her righteous anger and indignation.

Diana grimaced. What a naïve fool she was. She should have known then that she had married into the wrong family. If they would cheat each other so horribly, why would she be treated any different? Back then, her love was blind, and she had been captivated by her new husband and the promise of a happily ever after. Today, she just felt foolish.

She was still resentful as she drove Hannah into school the next morning. Both men had the ability to wreak havoc and cause trouble in her life, and she no longer needed that stress. She and Hannah were much better off without them. Hannah could remember Peter the way she wanted to, and Diana could move on.

Pulling the car to a stop across from the school, she reached to the backseat and gave her daughter's leg a tickle. Hannah giggled and pulled her leg away. "Mommy, stop that!"

She smiled at her daughter, feeling a surge of love for the child. "Okay… I go into work late today, so I'll see you tonight after dinner. I love you."

"I love you too, Mommy."

Hannah was smiling happily, and it made Diana's heart want to sing. Yep, she thought, much better off as just the two of them. Hopping from the car, Diana went to the back door to collect Hannah, who waited impatiently as Diana unbuckled her car seat and helped her out.

"Come on, Mommy."

Diana raised her eyebrows and took her daughter's hand. "Don't fret, silly. We're early."

"I know, but you take so long. Why do you take so long?"

"Because I'm old," she muttered.

Hannah giggled. "You're silly, Mommy."

"Yeah, yeah. Come on, let's go."

They crossed the street together, with Hannah dragging her feet through the fallen leaves. Fall was coming fast, Diana thought, and that meant more winter clothes for Hannah. After that, Christmas would be upon them. What would she do then? Could she come up with enough money to make her daughter's dreams come true?

The kids were all lining up outside on this blustery morning, and after bending down to give her daughter one last kiss, Diana sent her on her way with the rest of the group. She watched as Hannah was enveloped into the smiling group until she was out of sight before hurrying back to her car.

She was just opening the car door when she heard Hannah call for her. Turning back, Diana watched in confusion as her daughter ran toward her, not minding the road or the oncoming traffic. In her hand, she held a paper, waving it excitedly, while behind her, the teacher was calling out to her to stop. When Hannah did not respond, the teacher broke away from the group of children to give chase. Soon all eyes were upon her, but still Hannah paid no mind.

With a frightened scream, Diana held out her hands, but she was too late. Eyes wide, Diana viewed the oncoming disaster with horror. Hannah had finally stopped, but she halted in the middle of the road. Her eyes were round with fear as she stared at an oncoming car. Too fast. It was moving way too fast. Without considering her own safety, Diana forced herself to move. She was running, screaming, waving her hands as though she could stop the accident by her own force of will.

It did not work.

There was a horrible squealing of the tires and a sickening thud, and Hannah was suddenly sailing through the air and landing with a dull thump several yards away.

"Hannah!" Diana screamed, her hands going to her mouth in horror.

Still running and screaming at the same time, she fell to her knees beside her daughter. She barely noticed the pain when they struck the hard pavement.

"Don't move her!" Suddenly there were people everywhere, and the sound of running feet echoed in her agonized mind.

"Hold her head still."

There was blood seeping from a wound on her head, but Hannah was still breathing and her eyelids fluttered. Diana grasped her head and held on, taking the handkerchief someone handed her and pressing it to the gash on her forehead.

"She's breathing!"

"There's so much blood. Somebody please call for help," she cried.

"They're on their way, ma'am. Just stay calm."

Diana wanted to scream that it was not their child lying broken in the middle of the street, but there were so many voices that she knew no one would hear. She bit her lip until it bled in an effort to keep her panic at bay.

One of the mothers bent down next to her and wrapped her arms around Diana's shoulders. "It's okay, Diana. Everything will be okay."

Diana's eyes filled with tears as she fought back the anguish. Right now, she was not sure that Hannah would be okay.

After what seemed an eternity, she heard the sirens. They sounded loud in the sudden hush of the children and parents gathered around her. She could hear the increasing urgency in their voices and felt the cold hand of terror take a hold of her heart.

Please, oh please, don't take my baby too.

~

"There's been trouble."

Mike's unceremonious entry into his office brought a warning frown to Devlan's face. Already in an irritable mood, he raised his weary gaze to his closest associate. He had spent the evening in the spotlight with Roxanne again, something he dreaded doing. It had been a long evening listening to her endless chatter, and an even longer night trying to be rid of her. Now he was back at work with hardly any sleep and sporting a headache to worsen his mood.

"I hope this is good, Mike."

"I just got a call from my guy in Denver. It's Hannah Somerset. She's in the hospital."

For the briefest of moments, he struggled to place the name. Then it hit him. He sat up straighter. "What happened?"

"Hit by a car this morning by an uninsured motorist. She's got serious injuries."

He dragged his hand slowly down his face. Of all the luck. Though he wanted to just shout out a curse, he knew that it would not help matters. Right now, he needed to keep calm and take immediate action.

"Okay. Get the jet ready. I want to be there within the hour. Is she in a trauma center?"

"They sent her to Denver. Just arrived."

Ignoring Mike's curious glance, Devlan pressed the button on his desk to page his assistant.

"Kathy, cancel all my appointments. I'll be out of town for an indeterminable amount of time. And call in any contacts we have in Denver. I need to find the best pediatric orthopedic surgeons, neurologists and whatever else may be needed for a child struck by a car. I'll send you details as soon as I get them."

"Yes, sir," came the crisp response.

Devlan collected what papers he needed and placed them in his briefcase. His headache and his frustration with Roxanne would have to wait. In fact, everything would have to wait. Diana and Hannah needed him now and he had a plane to catch.

~

Diana stood by the nurse's station, ears attuned to the activity

42

in the trauma room while she struggled to keep from barging in. One nurse had told her in an overly patient and calm voice that there was a tube to Hannah's lungs, and they were giving her oxygen to keep the swelling in her brain down. They would soon be getting x-rays, and then they would be sending her for a CT scan. While they were doing all this, they would continue to stabilize her. If she would just take a seat…

No, Diana would not just take a seat. Though the words were meant to reassure her, it did little to help. Tears continued to roll down her face, and she paced and worried while her heart screamed out for her child. Why could it not be her on that table? She should have done something to stop it from happening. Something more. While she waited in a hallway with bated breath, her daughter could be dying without her.

She was still hovering as close as she could get when the emergency room doctor approached her. "Mrs. Somerset?"

She nodded.

"Is there anyone else with you?"

"Uh, no. I'm alone," she whispered. Yes, she was very alone. Hannah was all she had.

His face was solemn as he led her to the family waiting room. The room was empty now, but he shut the door behind them for even more privacy.

"I'm Doctor James Haverill. I'm the Emergency Room physician on duty this morning. I have some good news and some bad news."

She nodded her head weakly.

"We've got some swelling in her brain. We also found some bleeding into her pelvic cavity. There's a question as to the stability of her pelvis, but right now it appears intact. One of her femurs, the thighbone, is fractured and the other leg shows some bending, which is not unusual in a child since their bones are so flexible. Fortunately, the break is not within the epiphysis, or growth plate. It's the head injury we're concerned about. It can be fatal or at least permanently damaging…"

He stopped and gave her a moment to ingest everything before continuing. "I have a neurosurgeon on the way. He's very good; the best in the area. We need to operate immediately to get the bleeding controlled and the swelling down."

"Do whatever you must, just please let her be okay."

He shook his head solemnly. "I can't tell you for sure if she'll be okay. It's far too early. We have grave injuries here that we must treat carefully."

Diana blinked away fresh tears. "Do what you have to."

He nodded and gave her hand a squeeze. His hand was warm and strong. "I'll do my very best. We all will. Betty over there will have papers for you to sign."

A tremulous smile crossed Diana's lips, and she watched the doctor hurry back down the hall. She sank to the sofa and ran her hands through her hair as a moment of panic filled her chest. What if something went wrong and she did not have a chance to see Hannah and tell her how much she loved her? Unable to stop the frantic pounding of her heart, Diana bit back the despair that threatened to overcome her. First Peter, and now Hannah. How much more could she take?

Struggling against the tightness in her chest, Diana mentally shook herself. Hannah needed her to be strong and in control right now, and she owed it to her daughter to be so. Inhaling another deep breath, she let it out slowly in an effort to ease the growing pain in her breast. She had to get moving - now.

It was through blurred vision that she saw the tall, broad shouldered man in a dark suit race past the door in the direction of the nurse's station, but he stopped in his tracks and turned back when he saw her.

"Diana?"

Diana stiffened at the sound of that deep, seductive voice.

She knew that voice. She had just heard it on the television. Why was she hearing it here?

She wiped at her eyes quickly, trying to clear the tears before he noticed her show of weakness. Then she met his concerned stare. Astonished, she realized that it really was him. From the television the evening before to standing in the middle of the family waiting room, Devlan Doyle appeared to be everywhere.

"What on earth are you doing here?"

He came to tower above her, looking fresh and clean and smelling of expensive cologne. Though intimidating in his power suit, his face was grave, and worry glittered in his eyes. "I came as soon as I heard. Where's Hannah? Is she going to be all right?"

"They don't know yet," she whispered brokenly.

"I'm so sorry."

She nodded and looked away, unwilling to share her pain with him, but Devlan was not having it. He reached down, captured her hands, and pulled her to her feet. Too stunned to resist, she stiffened when he suddenly enveloped her in his arms and pulled her close, his hand smoothing her hair down her back. She remained rigid until his husky whisper reached her ears.

"You're not alone, Diana. I'm here to help in any way that I can."

Alone. She had not felt this alone until the idea of losing her child became a sudden reality. Now everything seemed so tenuous, so many unknowns, and his small gesture of kindness was all it took to break down her resolve to resist. Her tears overflowed and ran in a silent stream down her cheeks. How had he known how alone she felt?

"I'm so afraid that she'll never know how much I love her."

"Doubtful," he said forcefully.

Devlan's hands tightened encouragingly. He did not seem to mind that she was crying on his fancy suit, which probably cost as much as her monthly salary. In fact, by the racing of his own heart, he appeared to be as frightened as she was. Surprised by his sudden vulnerability, she began to weaken. His touch was gentle and soothing, and it was so welcome during this time of uncertainty. Surely he could make matters all right. He said she was not alone.

How easy it would be to fall back into that trap.

Quickly changing the subject from her traitorous thoughts, Diana took a deep breath. "The doctor said that she has swelling in her brain, and both her legs are injured. She might also be bleeding into her pelvis. What will happen now?"

She could feel Devlan nod as his chin came to rest upon the top of her head. "I've already called in favors from some friends of mine, Diana. They'll work on Hannah to the best of their abilities. She'll pull through. You have the best in the area to help her."

As his words sank in, Diana suddenly realized just how bizarre his presence in the hospital was. It was almost surrealistic. She stiffened and pulled away from him, leaving the comfort of his arms with the suspicion that things were not what they seemed. Reaching for another tissue, she took a moment to regain her composure. She could feel his intense gaze upon her as she moved away to a safe spot within the small room.

"How is it that you're here, Mr. Doyle?" She managed a shaky laugh. "I mean, how did you hear about the accident and get here so quickly?"

There was a slight hesitation before Devlan answered, and his gaze did not quite meet hers as he spoke, which only increased her suspicion. She watched him warily as he focused on his clean, short fingernails. "I was already here, Diana. I was upstairs in a meeting with upper management. I'm doing some work with the hospital. There was a lot of talk about the accident, and when I heard Hannah's name I came down."

Diana was not sure she believed him, but judging by his

sharp appearance she suspected he was doing some sort of work. Whether or not it was upstairs was another story altogether. However, he did have the means to help her, and at that moment Hannah needed all the help she could get. The police had told her that the driver could not show proof of insurance, and that did not bode well for her at all.

She nodded slowly and sat back down on the couch, keeping a safe distance between them. Her guard was up again, and she intended to keep it that way. No, she *needed* to keep it that way.

Seeing her continued hesitation, Devlan took a step toward her and spoke quickly. "Let me help you help your daughter, Diana. I can do it. I can ensure that she has the best medical care available, with specialists in every field."

"I am capable of taking care of Hannah, Mr. Doyle."

He nodded impatiently while his hand waved away her words dismissively. "I know that, but I'm offering you financial help. You have no insurance. How will you pay for her care?"

The warning bells that had rung when she first saw him were an all-out cacophony of noise now. Her eyes narrowed until they were almost slits. "How did you know that?"

"Common sense, Diana." When she continued to stare at him suspiciously, he shrugged. "You just started full-time, did you not? Does your job offer you benefits immediately?"

She grimaced. He was right. "We're covered as of the first of the month."

"You see? You can't get her the care I can. Trust me, Diana. I'll do my best for her."

"But why? I can offer you nothing in return. You know I can't repay you; I have no money."

"I don't want your money."

Their gazes locked, but Diana held her tongue and waited for him to elaborate. Tense moments passed until his gaze slipped away from hers to travel her length. Unlike Peter's scathing and contemptuous look, Devlan's was warm and appreciative, and Diana felt the power of it all the way to her toes. He cleared his throat, but his voice grew deeper when he finally answered her unspoken question. "There are things other than money that you can offer."

She could imagine what that meant.

Though her mind screamed that she was being foolish and reckless, her heart told her that nothing mattered more than her daughter. She would do anything for Hannah. Taking a deep breath, she met Devlan's gaze steadily. "What would I have to do?"

"I'd expect that you return with Hannah to L.A. I can take care of you both there. Hannah will have the best medical care that money can buy. We can discuss repayment options at a later date."

"I'm still not sure I understand," she said with a quick shake of her head. "Why would you do this for us? We're nothing to you."

He recoiled in surprise, and a fierce frown appeared on his face. "Nothing?"

As his blue eyes darkened in frustration, Diana realized that he was not a man used to being questioned. Judging by his glare, he apparently did not like that she did just that. When he finally spoke, his voice was clipped and cold and she shivered at his tone.

"I'm offering you the best of care for your daughter. Take it or leave it. But I'd advise you to reconsider your stubbornness and think of how far you will go for Hannah… I'll be out in the hall."

Chapter 4

Diana watched Devlan back from the room and shut the door behind him with a gentle click. The smell of his cologne remained behind, a tangy male scent that tickled her nose. She could tell that it was costly. Of course, everything about him spelled out quality. She knew he was wealthy beyond belief, and that meant he had the means to help Hannah.

His words still rang in her ears. How far would she go for her child?

She was not that stubborn. She would do anything for her baby.

If the steamy look he had given her was any indication, he did not want her money. No, he wanted something else from her, and she could think of only one thing that might be. Was she prepared to get involved with a man who would surely break her heart? Was she willing to put aside her firm decisions to get her life and confidence back before allowing another man into her life, especially a man that would surely bring havoc?

Entering a relationship with Devlan Doyle would cause trouble. But Hannah needed his help, and unfortunately, she had no way of giving her everything she needed without taking Doyle up on his offer.

Diana came to her feet. Nothing mattered as much as her daughter. She would do whatever it took to get the best for Hannah. Closing her eyes briefly, Diana stiffened her resolve and took a deep breath to give her strength. She reached for the door handle and grasped it tightly, knowing that once she opened that door she would seal her fate. She would find a way to steel her heart against Devlan Doyle; she would not allow it to betray her again.

"I'll take it."

Devlan stood by the nurse's station with his companion, the same man he was with at the funeral, speaking in hushed tones. At the sound of her voice his head swiveled slowly in her direction, and his triumphant gaze penetrated her very soul. With an almost imperceptible nod, he straightened and joined her again. "They're taking Hannah upstairs now. I'll bring you up."

"I'll go anywhere. I'll do anything. Just help her."

Devlan responded with a quick nod. "I'll take care of it."

"I'm counting on that."

His hand came down on her shoulder and gave it a squeeze. "Don't doubt me. I always keep my word."

When she immediately stiffened, his hand dropped to her arm. Without another word, he guided her to the nearest elevator and up to the surgical floor. There he stood aside so she could exit the elevator but did not follow. "Mike will stay with you. I have to get some work done, but I'll be back when they're done. If you need to reach me, Mike will take care of it."

Diana glanced at the burly blond man with a little trepidation. She had never met a bodyguard before. As if in answer to her unspoken question, he smiled cheerfully down at her. "Hello, Mrs. Somerset."

She managed a small smile. "Please call me Diana."

Mike glanced at Devlan, who nodded shortly before the elevator doors closed again. Stuck alone with Mike, she began walking down the hall.

"Can I get you anything?"

Diana shook her head. All she wanted now was reassurance

that Hannah would be okay. Unfortunately, that meant another waiting room. This one was sporting four white walls, a sofa and several chairs. Magazines rested on the battered wooden coffee table, most current but well read. Everything was clean and well-kept, but missing her laughing daughter.

Sinking into the chair closest to the door, Diana stared at her feet. As she glanced down at her worn jeans, she noticed for the first time Hannah's blood staining her knees and thighs. Fresh tears pricked her eyes as an image of the accident scene flashed behind her eyes. There had been so much blood and so much noise. For as long as she lived, she would never forget the sound of that sickening thud.

Please let Hannah get well.

~

Devlan exited the elevator and strode toward the exit. The bright late-morning sunlight greeted him, and the cool fall air went right through him. Squinting against the glare, he shivered and pulled his jacket closed as he approached the waiting limo.

"Chilly out today, sir?" The driver asked.

"I left in too much of a hurry to grab a winter coat," he muttered.

"I have the heat running in the car."

The driver opened his door and stood aside while Devlan climbed in. Once in the privacy of the dark interior, he leaned his head against the seat and closed his eyes. Though he was used to sudden events and immediate reaction times, this morning had caught him completely by surprise. Little Hannah Somerset was in serious condition, and now he had to prepare for the worst case scenario.

First Peter and now Hannah, he thought in frustration. Was he destined to donate everything to charity? No sooner did the thought escape than he chided himself. After all, to him Hannah's situation was an annoyance; to her mother, it was devastation.

His irritability must be due to the lack of sleep. He was just too old for these late nights, he concluded. If Roxanne had not forced him to escort her to another premier and the parties afterwards, he would have been more alert this morning instead of frazzled and cranky. His days of enjoying the night life were over; now they left him exhausted.

"Where to, sir?"

Devlan sat forward and pressed the intercom button. "To my suite."

"Very well."

The silent limo eased away from the curb, and Devlan settled back once more. Hannah was in trouble; her injuries serious. Now he needed to make sure that he could live up to his promise to the child's mother. He did not like promises or the commitment they required, but this time he was determined. Not only did his estate require it, but he had given Diana his word.

The elation of victory was somewhat hollow but still there. Diana and Hannah were finally under his protection. Though not exactly in the way he intended, he had accomplished what he had set out to do. Diana had relented, and he had control. The question now was whether or not he could pull it off. Not in the clear yet, he needed to demonstrate to them both that he was capable of taking care of them, and taking care of them well. He had to earn Diana's trust and prove that she had made the right choice. The only choice.

He reached for his phone and dialed Kathy. "Open the Malibu house. I need it cleaned and ready for use."

"Sir? But you've never used the Malibu house before."

"Just do it. And find a good rehabilitation center for the child. Once she's cleared to leave the hospital, I want to settle her mother there and personally oversee Hannah's rehab."

"How is she now?"

"In surgery. Too soon to tell. It's serious, though."

"Oh no, that's terrible. The poor thing. Her mother must be frantic… I'll get right on it. I've cancelled all your appointments here, but I had a problem rescheduling your golf game with Mr. Littleton. He's booked until after Christmas."

Devlan grimaced. "I'm not too concerned with a golf game. At least that was a break."

"Yes, sir. Will you be coming back today?"

"No, I've decided to spend the night here. I'm on my way to the suite now. I want to be close by when Hannah's done with surgery and has her first night."

"But you have the plane."

"Yeah, but I wouldn't want to put all my trust in an airport. Who knows what can happen?"

He heard Kathy sigh on the other line and frowned. "Is there a problem?"

"No, but Roxanne called and was expecting you for supper. She made dinner plans at your Brentwood house. She's going to be disappointed that you won't be there."

That woman was getting far too presumptuous, he thought. Inwardly he groaned in frustration, and his voice was curt when he answered. "My presence here is more important than her dinner plans."

He thought he heard Kathy giggle in the background, but she was serious when she answered. "I'll call her straight away."

"Do me a favor, Kath? Don't tell her where I am, okay? Diana doesn't need her here. As a matter of fact, don't tell anyone I'm here. I'd rather have some privacy right now."

"Of course, sir."

He signed off and glanced out the window. Clouds were slowly rolling in from the west. The sun was no longer glittering brightly through the tinted windows. Fall was certainly making its presence known here. Multi-colored leaves littered the street around him, and houses were happily showing off their Halloween decorations. Summer had ended early in this climate, and the entire area seemed different.

The three months that had passed since the funeral seemed so long ago. A lot had changed while he had observed from a safe distance, but seeing those changes firsthand had been more unsettling than he had imagined they would be. Even emotional and disheveled, Diana had regained her natural beauty. The dark circles and strain that had marred her face when he saw her last were replaced by fresh, glowing skin and laughter lines. Not only did she appear physically healthier, but she seemed stronger emotionally. Even frightened and worried about her daughter, she glowed more than Roxanne on her best day. It was a concerning reality that he found her so damned attractive, and although he kept telling himself that Hannah's health was his priority, he suspected that proving himself to Diana was playing a large part too.

That was a problem. One he did not have time to consider at the moment.

Work was his life, his livelihood. However, with the wealth came the hard work and long hours. Even a family emergency could not draw him away from the day-to-day problems, and he knew that he had plenty to do before he could rest. Perhaps that was why he had no one until now. Suddenly, things had changed. In the blink of an eye, he had a ready-made family, which surprisingly filled him with hope and pleasure rather than fear. With his money, he fully intended on drawing the Somerset ladies into his life and keeping them there until he could sort out his feelings.

The afternoon was spent in the quiet of his spacious suite working, and it was past dinner when he finally got Mike's text that Hannah was out of recovery. The surgery was successful, and

Hannah was being moved into a room in the pediatric intensive care unit. Much to his surprise, all thoughts of work fled, and his priority switched to the hospital to see with his own eyes that Hannah was pulling through. Even though he had only met her once, he looked forward to seeing the adorable golden-haired child awake and smiling.

As he entered the lobby of the hospital, he overheard a man at the information desk. "I'm looking for information about Hannah Somerset. She was brought in this morning. Little girl, hit by a car."

The woman punched in some information into her computer and then looked up apologetically. "I'm sorry, sir, but she's in the intensive care unit. Only immediate family members allowed. Are you a family member?"

The man looked frustrated. "Just about."

The woman shrugged in response. "I'm sorry, sir. Only the mother, father, or primary caregiver."

"Well, can I leave her a message? Can I at least let Diana know I was here?"

"I'll call up to her room and see if she'd like to see you. Would that be okay?"

Devlan frowned at the tall man as he walked by. He was good looking in a rough way, dressed in khaki slacks and a dark sweater. His brown hair was slicked back like he had just gotten out of the shower, and he carried a handful of balloons and a huge teddy bear the size of Hannah. Was Diana dating already? And if so, how had he not been notified?

"I'm sorry sir, but what was your name?"

"Allan."

"I told her you were here, but she doesn't want to leave the room." The woman placed down the phone and smiled apologetically again. "If you want to leave your gift, I'll make sure she gets them as soon as we can."

Allan handed everything to the lady behind the desk and thanked her politely as Devlan paused to inspect the bundle, but he looked away quickly when the other man noticed his stare. Continuing toward the elevator, he flashed his pass at the security guard. "Where can I use my phone?"

"Public areas only."

Devlan thanked him and pressed the button to the elevator. He should have thought of it himself, he thought grimly. Boy, did he have a lot to learn. Children were beyond his reasoning… Way out of his league.

As soon as the elevator doors opened, Devlan dialed his secretary once again. "Kathy, I need your help."

Scowling, he glanced around him to see if anyone was listening. Standing in the middle of the hushed hallway prepared to let everyone listening know how ignorant he had been was not something he liked.

"What is it?"

"You have children, right?"

"Yes," she said slowly.

"How old?"

"Two and five, sir."

"So you know what a little girl would like, right?"

Kathy laughed on the other line, and Devlan felt his grip on the phone tighten. Again his eyes scanned the hallway for eavesdroppers. The reminder that he was not as knowledgeable as he thought certainly stung his pride, and Kathy's gloating made it all the worse.

"Mr. Doyle, shame on you. Did you not even think to bring the child anything?"

He growled. "You're joking, right?"

"Yes, I'm joking. I'll take care of everything. Does price matter?"

"Of course not."

"I should've known."

"I'll ask you what you mean by that when I get back. Just handle this for me, and get it here as soon as possible."

Kathy giggled again, and Devlan hung up the phone with an exasperated sigh. How would he have known? He was a forty-year-old businessman, not a father.

Reminded of his earlier concern, Devlan paused and frowned slightly. He was not trying to be this little girl's father, was he? Of course not, he thought. While he would admit that he was enjoying the idea of bringing them to California with him, his reasons were simple. He needed to keep an eye on his little heiress. Besides, he knew next to nothing about this child and her mother except from what his research had told him. Sending a gift was the polite thing to do, and he had long ago learned his manners well. So why was his heart telling him that it was slightly more than just politeness that caused him to care so much for the wellbeing of these two females? If that was true, perhaps he was lonelier than he had originally thought. Once again, he concluded that he required more time to sort these strange new feelings out.

Mike was standing outside the room, and he met Devlan several doors down. His normally impassive face showed traces of worry.

"How is she?" Devlan asked in greeting.

"The doctor said something about watching the swelling in her brain. The next twenty-four hours will say a lot. They set her legs and stopped the bleeding in her pelvis. Nothing major internally, from what I overheard."

"Her mother?"

Mike shrugged. "She's with Hannah now. Hasn't moved since they let her in. She hasn't spoken much since you left."

Nodding, Devlan patted his friend's back. "Thank you for staying with her. Have you eaten?"

"Not yet. I didn't want to leave her alone."

"Go and get something. I'll meet you back here in an hour."

"Right."

Mike sauntered away, leaving Devlan alone in the hallway. All was quiet on the floor. The nurses on duty murmured in soft tones, their gazes studying him with interest. He did not notice them, nor did he return their flirtatious smiles as he normally would.

Pausing just outside the door, Devlan came up short and took a moment to absorb the somberness of the scene. Diana was as close to Hannah's side as she could get without being in the bed with her. Though her back was to him, he could see the defeat and terror in her posture. She held the child's pale hand gently and was stroking her soft skin while her face rested on the pillow next to Hannah's ear. He could hear Diana's soft sniffling between murmured words of encouragement and felt his heart give a tug.

The reality of the seriousness of Hannah's condition was disappointing. There would be no smiles this evening. Hannah looked so small in the large hospital bed with all the equipment attached to her. Her blond hair was hidden behind a pristine white bandage and there were wires surrounding her from head to toe. The beeping of her cardiac monitor struggled with the ventilator for supremacy in the otherwise quiet room.

Devlan approached silently, reaching out to place a hand on Diana's shoulder. Though she startled slightly before turning her bloodshot gaze to him, she did not grow tense as she had before. Pleased, he could not prevent the faint smile he sent her way. "Things are good so far?"

Her eyebrows rose as if to ask him how he could even ask that, but then she nodded slowly. "The doctor said that there's still activity in her brain, and the swelling isn't as bad as they first thought. We just have to wait and see."

"Excellent."

Easing away, Devlan went around the bed and took a seat

across from Diana. The suspicious wall she had erected earlier returned as she watched his every move warily. Devlan refused to let that daunt him and smiled as he stretched out his legs in front of him. Telling himself that he had broken the cycle of mistrust in men far tougher than her over the years, he was confident that Diana could be handled with time. The silence that fell between them was broken only by the sounds of the activity in the hall and the machinery in the room. They were absorbed in their own thoughts for some time before Devlan finally shifted in the hard plastic seat and captured her attention once more.

"I spoke to my secretary, and she's opening my house in Malibu for you. Once Hannah's able to leave the hospital, I'll fly her to L.A. She'll have the best pediatric rehabilitation services available there."

Diana glanced down at Hannah before meeting his gaze. Her voice was low and subdued. "Very well." He was about to comment on the resignation in her tone when her soft voice once again broke the silence. "Are you staying in town?"

"What?"

"In town. Are you staying here?"

"Yes. I'm at the Four Seasons a couple miles away. I'll stick around until Hannah's out of the woods. That way, if you need me..."

Diana remained silent as she studied him. He smiled faintly in an attempt to reassure her, but her weary gaze continued to search his face as if questioning his motives once again. Not accustomed to being regarded with such wariness and not enjoying it at all, Devlan looked away and reached into his suit pocket for one of his business cards. "Last time I gave you one of these, you gave it right back. Considering our agreement, it seems appropriate for you to hold onto one now. My home phone is at the bottom, as is my mobile."

Reaching over her sleeping daughter's legs, Diana took the

card he held out. Their fingers brushed briefly before she snatched her hand away and sat back down. "Thank you," she murmured.

"You're welcome."

"I don't use a cell phone," she offered in explanation for not giving him her number.

"That's okay. I can reach you through the hospital switchboard when I need to. They can take a message."

She returned her attention to Hannah's inert form, and Devlan stared at her head, wishing he could say something to put her at ease but knowing it was useless at that moment. He shifted uncomfortably again. "Have you eaten?"

"I'm not hungry."

"Would you like me to get you something for later?"

"No, the nurses ordered a meal for me." She glanced up and cocked her head to the side. "But thank you."

With nowhere else to go in that conversation, Devlan fell silent. Diana did not seem to mind. After another few awkward minutes, he came to his feet and stretched. There was not a whole lot he could do for her now, and she was far too preoccupied for him to press his own agenda. All he could do is remain close by in case something came up during the night. "I'll leave you two alone for now. Do you want me to arrange a ride home for you?"

Diana shook her head. "No. I can't leave her."

Devlan nodded, accepting his bad choice. Once again, he had displayed uncustomary ignorance, and he looked forward to kicking himself later. There was just something about this woman that made him nervous. He wanted her to like him. "I understand. Can I get you anything from home? A change of clothes?"

"No, Allan will take care of it. He has a key to my apartment."

Devlan was immediately reminded of the burly man in the lobby. In spite of his best intentions, he frowned. "Allan? I didn't realize you were involved."

Her head came up. "Involved? What do you mean?"

"Allan? I saw him downstairs."

A bitter smile curved her pink lips. "Do you really think me so stupid to jump into the first bed I found?"

Devlan remained cool as he answered, for how could he say that most of the women he knew would do exactly that? "I don't know, Diana. I really don't know you at all."

"You're right; you don't know me. So don't come to such hasty conclusions. Allan Collins is my friend. His son and Hannah are friends. Allan and Mindy have helped me a lot through the past few months."

Chastised, Devlan fought his surprising possessiveness. "I see. I apologize if I've offended you. I didn't mean to."

She refused to meet his eyes when she spoke next. "Yeah, well, I don't jump from bed to bed."

Feeling the tension and hostility rising, Devlan backed away. Once more, he had offended her with his clumsiness. This was not how he had expected things to happen, but it was too late now. All he could do was retreat and try again later. "Call me if you need anything, or if anything changes. Mike's coming with me now, but I wrote down the number of my suite on the back of the card."

Diana flipped the card over and stared at his bold handwriting silently while Devlan gave one final glance at Hannah and slipped from the room. Now he would track down the doctors and see what they had to say. The next twenty-four hours would be the test, and it was a test he prayed the child would pass.

Chapter 5

There was a ringing in his head, a persistent high-pitched ring. Devlan opened his eyes a crack and glanced at the clock beside the bed. It was three in the morning. Who in the hell would be calling him at this time of night?

Sitting bolt upright, Devlan grabbed his phone with a shaking hand. "Diana."

There was a slight hesitation before she responded. "How did you know it was me?"

He sank back against his pillows in relief. There was no grief in her voice. "Call it intuition."

"I thought that was something I would say."

"What happened?"

"Hannah's awake. She opened her eyes."

Devlan's smile turned into a grin. "Oh, that's great news. Did she recognize you?"

Diana was speaking quickly, and her tone was lighter than he had ever heard before. "I really couldn't tell. She's on so many medications that I couldn't be sure. But her eyes are open… She's going to be okay, I just know it."

"I'll be there within an hour."

Although he expected some reluctance from her, she surprised him by not objecting. Warning himself not to get his hopes up as he hastily threw back the covers, he realized that more than likely she was just so relieved that Hannah was finally awake that even his company was acceptable. Although maybe, just maybe, his persistent presence over the past few days might have begun to have an effect on her stubborn defiance. After all, it was well known that he was exceptionally charming, and he had been using every trick in his book to break down her self-protective walls.

Devlan rang Mike's room and told him where he was going before heading to the parking garage to retrieve the rental he had picked up for his frequent trips back and forth from the hospital. Much to his surprise, another inch of snow had fallen during the night, and it reminded him that winter would soon be upon the city in full force. He wanted to be back in L.A. long before then.

It was four o'clock by the time he reached Hannah's hospital bed. No one in the deserted hospital questioned him, and he assumed by now they all believed he was Hannah's father. Passing the nurse's desk with a cheerful smile to the night shift, he hurried along to see his family.

Diana met him outside the room, her face radiant with a bright smile. He had not seen her smile since her wedding, and the sight of her pearly white teeth felt similar to an electric shock, sending tingly waves throughout his body. It was as if years had been erased from her face with just that simple gesture, and the brief flicker of joy was like a ray of sunshine peeking through the storm clouds of those stressful recent days. Taking a deep, steadying breath, Devlan stopped in front of her, and a smile of his own creased his face, one as genuine as hers.

"She's awake. She's finally awake!"

"Now?" Devlan asked.

"No. She went right back out, but they're going to run more tests and begin weaning her from all the medications."

"That's great, Diana. I'm very pleased."

Diana blessed him with another brilliant smile before hugging her hands to her waist. "Right now, I want to go home and take a real shower, put on some clean clothes, and get a real meal."

Devlan chuckled. "Is that all?"

Her gaze met his, and a blush stole up her cheeks. As she bit her lip, he laughed out loud. Like everything else about her, her reaction to his teasing was invigorating and genuine.

Hoping to ease her embarrassment, he shrugged. "It's really no surprise. You've been living here for days. When was the last time you were home?"

"I don't even remember," she said with a chuckle.

"Well, I'm here. Why don't I give you a ride to your apartment? Then you can take your time and come back when you want."

"Would you mind?"

"Of course not," he answered quickly. "May I peek in at Hannah first?"

Devlan was aware of Diana's curious gaze upon his back as he glanced in at the child who remained quietly sleeping. Her color was better, and her eyelashes fluttered as she dreamed. It was a sight that filled his heart with joy. She was returning to the land of the living – finally. Giving Hannah's hand a gentle squeeze, Devlan smiled. Now that she was mending, he knew he had time to fulfill his promise. The worst was over. From here on out, it could only get better, and he was finally confident that he would win them both over. It just went to show that patience truly was a virtue. He could wait her out. After all, he had the means and skills to outlast one stubborn woman.

~

Diana stared at the shiny rented Mercedes and felt the first twinges of regret. Mike was nowhere in sight, and the car was much too small for just the two of them. She never should have agreed to let Devlan bring her home. Not only was she reluctant to show him her tiny apartment, but she was not ready to be alone with him either. Especially now that she was riding high with relief that Hannah was going to be all right.

"Where's Mike? Isn't he coming too?" Diana asked, glancing around.

Devlan grimaced as he shot her a wry look. "I don't bring him with me everywhere I go."

Her lips twisted into a sarcastic half smile. "I thought you did."

"No, he's asleep, like the rest of the city."

Devlan reached past her to open her door. Diana nodded her thanks and slipped into the soft, plush leather seat. While Devlan shut the door behind her and went around to his side, she glanced at the fine leather and wood interior. This was so beyond her modest means. Everything about Devlan was so beyond her.

"I'll need directions, Diana. I don't know where you live," he reminded her as he secured his tall length into the driver's seat.

Swallowing hard, Diana glanced over at him nervously. "Would it be easier for me to call a cab? You don't need to take me all the way home. You should be back at your room getting some sleep, not traversing all over with me."

"Don't be silly," he said. "What kind of gentleman would I be if I put you in a cab while I went back to sleep? Buckle up."

Diana sank back in the seat reluctantly. Her palms felt moist from her nervousness, and she wiped them against her jeans as casually as she could while she told herself to not care so much about his opinion. It was her pride that made it difficult. There had been a time, long before Peter had stolen everything from her, when she would have felt completely comfortable in the Mercedes with a man who had more money than Midas. However, so much had changed since then, and she was still picking up the pieces.

Devlan seemed not to notice her discomfort as he pulled the beautiful car out into the dark streets. He maneuvered it with ease, his hand firm on the gear shift and strong legs maneuvering through the gears smoothly. He was a piece of work, she realized grimly. There was a grace about him and a compassion she feared could easily win her over if she allowed her guard to slip. For all of his blinding success, there was absolutely no glimmer of selfishness in his demeanor. He had proven to be a hard man to resist with his sexy charm and winning smile.

"Which way?"

In a voice that quivered slightly, she guided Devlan back to her apartment complex. Luckily, he did not seem to notice and continued driving with an occasional glance around him. Aside from her directions, they passed the fifteen-minute ride in a companionable silence, but that ended when they pulled into her complex. Tucked behind a commercial area on a busy main road, the cars in the lot announced the income level of the occupants. A grim frown turned down the corners of his mouth, but before she could jump to her own defense, he scowled at her. "You live here?"

Though she had been hesitant about bringing him there, she did not fully comprehend how humiliating it would be until she witnessed his reaction. It bothered her so much more than she thought it would. After all, her monthly rent was probably what he earned in an hour, if that.

"I just recently started full-time work. I don't have a whole lot left over once the bills are paid."

"I thought your bills were paid," he snapped.

"My bills are not your concern," she replied through clenched teeth.

Devlan instantly closed his mouth and gave her an apologetic smile. His hand reached out as if to touch her flushed cheek, but she recoiled away. "I'm sorry, Diana… I wasn't expecting to find you and Hannah living like this."

"It's safer than it looks, and that's all that matters to me.

Thanks for the ride."

Devlan pulled into an unmarked spot in front of her building and shut down the car. To her growing irritation, he opened the door and rounded the trunk to gallantly open her door. When she climbed out, his warm fingers encircled her arm and remained there while she fished out her keys.

"You don't need to escort me in, I can manage from here," she said quickly.

The smile he sent her told her that she was crazy if she thought he would give up that easily. "It's quite all right. You mentioned breakfast, so I'll take you out after you shower. Besides, I'm curious to see where you live."

"But why?" Diana snapped, still stung by his earlier reaction. If he thought the parking lot was bad, he definitely would not approve of the inside. "Why are you so interested in my life?"

With a patient sigh, Devlan met her gaze straight on. "I told you before. Hannah's my last surviving relative. I'm concerned about how and where she's raised."

"And I've told you, she's fine."

One brow rose skeptically as he plucked the keys from her fingers. Frustrated, Diana knew this was one battle she was not going to win out in the parking lot. Spinning on her heel, she stiffly led him to her door, and she stood to the side while he opened it before brushing past him angrily. The dark chill caught them first, for Allan apparently had turned down the heat in her absence, and the faint scent of eucalyptus and vanilla candles did their best to overpower the stale smell of an empty apartment. While Devlan closed the door behind them, Diana reached for the lamp.

Safe inside where no one else could overhear them, she turned back to face him. "Now you listen to me," she said sharply. "I was raised with strong morals and know how to care for my daughter. I don't need you to butt your nose into my business."

When she paused, he merely nodded. Though surprised at his calm acceptance of her anger, she took the opportunity to continue her rant and express her frustration with his arrogance. "She's my daughter - not yours – and I do doubt your motives. You'd never even set eyes on her before the funeral… So where were you during the tough times? Where were you those last months of hell?"

At that point, her voice broke, and she turned away with a muffled curse of embarrassment. Pressing her fingers to the bridge of her nose, she blinked back the sudden sting of tears, determined not to let him see her pain. No, she was not ready yet to get into the tragic end of her marriage to Peter.

"Diana…"

She raised her hand to stop him and shook her head. There was no way she was going to get into this with him. Not in her living room on the day her daughter finally opened her eyes. This was a good day, and she was determined to enjoy it to the fullest. She sighed heavily. "There's instant coffee in the cabinet over the sink. Help yourself. I'm going to take a shower."

The apartment was small, consisting only of three rooms and a bathroom. There was no wall between the kitchen and living room, and Diana left Devlan standing awkwardly between them as she went to Hannah's bedroom in the back. At that moment she did not care if he felt uncomfortable. He needed to know that his arrogance was out of line, and she would not stand for it.

After closing the bedroom door securely behind her, she made her way to the closet she shared with Hannah to pick out some clean clothes. There, alongside her work clothes and worn jeans, she beheld her daughter's small two-piece outfits lined up neatly. A tender smile erased her frown as she fingered Hannah's favorite dress, and she pulled it off the hanger and placed it on the child-sized bed. When Hannah came home, she would wear her favorite clothes and be surrounded by her favorite things. No matter what it took, Diana planned to make sure that happened. Even if it meant that she played nice with Devlan Doyle. She would have to watch her temper a little better.

Jutting her chin forward stubbornly, Diana found the rest of her necessities and locked herself in the bathroom. Through the thin walls, she could hear Devlan rummaging in her kitchen and cringed. His dismay had reminded her again of how much she had lost in recent years.

When she had met Peter, she had thought he was the sweetest, most wonderful man in the world, and the way he had courted her like an old-fashioned lover had swept her easily off her feet. His promise of the family she had lost and wanted so desperately to have made her commit too quickly. He had claimed that he loved her, and she had trusted him. Though all of that was in the past, she was now at risk of falling prey to his outwardly generous and kind stepbrother. She could only hope that since Devlan had seen how poor they were, he would realize that she and Hannah had no place in his high-society life. Unfortunately, she suspected it would not be that easy.

Sighing again, Diana finished undressing and climbed into the slowly warming shower. Not long after, she heard the customary loud bang of the pipes and Devlan's muffled curse. Pressing her hand against her lips, she giggled as she imagined him jump out of his skin the way she had the first time she heard the bang. It sounded as though a bomb was going off in one of the lower floors when the hot water finally reached her apartment.

Just as quickly, she erased the smile from her face. It was not fair to laugh at another's surprise, no matter how irritated he made her that morning. For the truth was that Devlan had been nothing but kind and courteous so far, and even she had to admit that he was trying his hardest to be friendly, starting the day after the accident. He had arrived at the hospital with arms loaded with gifts for Hannah. There was a doll, a stuffed animal, the latest

DVDs, and early-reader books – anything Hannah could have possibly wanted was in his hands, and he turned it all over to her with an awkward smile.

She had been about to demand he send it all back when he had glanced at her sheepishly. "Will she like any of this?"

Despite the stress, worry and tension she had dealt with, the look on his face paired with his crazy question had caused her to giggle behind her hand. Though his cheeks had darkened, he had returned her smile and admitted that his assistant had assembled it all since he had no clue what to buy a child. In that brief shared moment, she had seen the ice wall erected around her start to melt ever so slightly. His honesty had taken her completely by surprise, and she grudgingly respected him for it.

"I can't lose my heart again," she whispered into the hot water.

She could be strong. After all, she had survived a devastating marriage, so she knew she could deny Devlan. This was for Hannah, and she would do anything for her little girl. With firm resolve, Diana finished her shower and hurriedly dressed into a warm sweater and faded jeans.

When she exited the bathroom, she was dressed casually and devoid of makeup. She carried her brush in one hand, tugging on the knotted ends of her hair as she went in search of her mysterious benefactor. He was in her small kitchen, standing by the stove and frying up some eggs, and she stood in the entryway to watch as he deftly flipped them then turned to butter the toast he had made.

"You cook?"

Devlan turned and smiled lopsidedly, and the rest of her earlier anger dissipated completely. She became aware of a melting sensation deep inside her belly and steeled her face not to respond. He was so handsome with his well-trimmed dark hair and freshly shaven cheeks, and she was disappointed to realize that he looked just as good in jeans and a pullover as he did in a tailored suit.

The man was just plain gorgeous.

"I do have a housekeeper, Mrs. Maclean, but she's a horrible cook." Turning his attention away from the stove, he cocked his head to the side thoughtfully and pointed the spatula at her as he spoke. "Have you ever noticed that some of the chubbiest people are the worst cooks? How do they do it? I mean, Mrs. Maclean reminds me of a cream puff."

Diana laughed out loud. "A cream puff? That doesn't make sense."

Unable to hide his returning smile, Devlan shook his head. "How does that not make sense? The woman is round."

"I would've expected you to be surrounded by perfect beauties all the time."

The playful smile faded, and Devlan's face grew serious as if remembering her earlier attack. Narrowing his eyes, he studied her intently. "Is that why you dislike me so much?"

Diana inhaled sharply. "Dislike you? I never -"

"Yes, you do. Don't deny it."

"I'm not," she began.

"I just want to know why," he interrupted solemnly.

"Well, I guess you're guilty by association," she conceded reluctantly.

He sighed. Obviously, he remembered how his stepbrother really was. "But you don't know me any more than I know you."

"I know," she admitted reluctantly.

"Then how can you despise me when you don't know me?"

Feeling as though she had no other choice but to come clean, she decided on honesty. It did not help that his voice had the tone of a man wounded. It made her feel guilty and ashamed at the same time. "I've heard things," she murmured, looking down at her hands.

"What could you possibly have heard about me that would make such a smart lady like you hate so much?"

"Well…"

He shook his head. "Seriously, don't actions speak louder than words? Haven't I proven that I have only your best interests at heart?"

"That's what scares me. Like I said, I don't understand why you're so interested in me."

"Hannah's your daughter."

"I know, but –"

"But what? You're family, Diana. It's my responsibility to help you and Hannah."

Family. There was that word again. She sighed. "Peter said a lot about you when we were first married. And of course, I've seen you on the television. It seems as though there's a new woman every month. I know it's not my business, but I don't trust men like that… That doesn't mean that I hate you."

"Peter said things?" His sarcastic laughter expressed his incredulity. "Oh, that's rich. Please, tell me what he said. This could be interesting."

Devlan leaned against the counter, his arms crossed as he waited for Diana to enlighten him. Fortunately the burning of the toast in her toaster saved her from having to speak. With a muffled curse, he dropped the spatula and turned around, frantically trying to get the toast free.

"Let me do it. It gets stuck sometimes," she said, coming to his aid.

Devlan stood back to allow her to free the burning toast, but suddenly her nervous fingers refused to jiggle the familiar latch correctly. Despite the charred odor permeating the kitchen, Diana could still smell his familiar cologne, and the heady scent grew stronger as he bent closer to her, as if she needed the reminder that he was so near.

"Do you need help?"

Devlan's hands came up to cover hers as she toyed with the defective lever. The large size of him briefly overwhelmed her, and for a moment, she was overcome with panic. Yet, his long fingers were gentle and warm, his touch almost feather-like, and surprisingly his palms had the rough feel of a man familiar with hard work. All too soon, she realized that it felt good, which frightened her even more.

She pulled away hastily and turned to face him, instantly regretting her sudden move. He was so close that she had to tilt her head back to look up at his face. Though the sudden jerk of her hand made the toast pop back up, and the charred remains smoldered in the fluorescent lights, Diana did not notice or care. She was consumed by Devlan's warmth and the impenetrable gaze he pinned her with. Suddenly, the kitchen was way too small for the two of them.

"It's all set," she whispered.

With a mixture of anticipation and dread, she noticed that Devlan did not back away. Instead, he reached past her to pull the hot crumbs from the toaster and toss them on the nearby plate. His voice was slightly husky as he spoke, but his words were very serious. "I don't intend on taking over your life any more than I plan to take over Hannah's. You're her mother, and as long as you're a fit mother, she should remain with you. However, if you ever become unfit, I will take her away."

When she felt herself stiffen in indignation, Devlan shook his head slowly. His lips were compressed in disappointment, but his eyes still glowed with some unfathomable emotion that she longed to explore. "I only want to help you, Diana. I realize you're fresh from a terrible situation, but you can start trusting again... You can trust me, Diana. There's no malice in my offer, and I have absolutely no intentions of hurting you or Hannah," his voice lowered. "That's the last thing I would do."

Diana's mouth felt dry, and the pounding in her chest was so forceful she feared he could see it. This was not good. He was gaining the upper hand, and she could feel her resolve slipping. He was too close for her to think straight, and then there was that strange gleam in his eye that made breathing difficult. Taking a deep steadying breath, she stared up at him with wide eyes. Time to be strong, she thought. "You may not want to hurt us, but it will happen. We'll get used to seeing you, to having you around, and then you'll go back to your life, and we'll never see you again."

Devlan's face lowered slightly. "And that would bother you?"

"Hannah wouldn't take the rejection lightly. She's just lost her father."

He bent still more, his hands coming to rest on either side of her on the counter, and his gaze fell to her lips as he spoke. "And you've lost a husband."

She let out a shaky laugh and waved her hand dismissively. "Our marriage was over a long time ago."

"Now you're afraid. Afraid because you actually do care."

Diana opened her mouth to deny his words, but it was too late. His arms swiftly enveloped her, and his lips descended onto hers in the kiss she had so feared and anticipated. No, no, no, she thought just before her eyes flickered closed. Push him away, she warned herself. However, she could feel the rapid pounding of his heartbeat against her chest when her arms reached up to grasp his shoulders, and though she meant to push him away, she ended up pulling him closer instead.

Fool!

She was a fool. Even though he felt so large, she instinctively knew he would pull back if she tried to fend him off, but she did not want to. She felt captivated by his adept lips, and when his tongue slipped forward to taste her lips, her mouth opened to allow him entrance. It angered her that she had given in so quickly, but gosh, it had been so long since she had felt even

74

slightly desirable, and he was skillful in his attempt to break her resolve. The man definitely knew how to kiss a woman senseless.

Taking advantage of her submission, Devlan's hands tightened around her waist, and his long fingers stroked her back gently. It felt wonderful, he felt wonderful, and she shivered and squirmed against the growing need pressing against her belly in response. It was a slight satisfaction to note that she had as much an effect on him as he did on her, but it also served as the final glass of cold water in the face of her conscience. No matter how good he felt pressed against her, she knew she needed to resist the growing passion between them, to keep control of her emotions, or she would be pulling off his clothes in the middle of her kitchen.

Devlan sensed her withdrawal and released his hold on her lips reluctantly. He still held her close as he raised his head, almost as if he did not want to release her at all. His eyes were warm and glazed, and he reached up to stroke her cheek. "I can't tell you how long I've wanted to do that," he murmured, his lips curving into a wistful smile.

He did? Unable to tear her gaze from his, Diana licked her moist lips and let her hands slide down his arms. Oh, did they feel good. Strong and capable for sure, but they were also adept at extreme gentleness. Her voice shook as she spoke softly. "I'm sorry, but I'm just not ready for this."

Devlan nodded and stood back, smiling as he loosened his grip on her. She turned her attention to the eggs he had made in an effort to cool the passion that had unexpectedly flared between them. "I hope we haven't ruined breakfast," she said with an awkward laugh.

"I doubt it. Let me make more toast." He handed her a plate. "Take this; I'll eat the other ones."

Diana glanced down and sniffed the food. "Whatever possessed you to cook anyway?"

"You hadn't been home in days. I figured you'd want to use up all the food. Besides, you're coming home with me, remember? We'll need to get rid of it anyway."

She glanced down at the coffee he had made. His attempt to win her over was working, and she had just learned how susceptible to his charms she was. It both frightened and intimidated her "Do we really need to go all the way to California? There must be a good rehab institution here."

"Diana," he sighed.

When he came to sit down, he was frowning, and Diana struggled to get her words out before he interrupted her. "Let's be realistic. You really don't want us hanging around. We'll just cramp your style."

Devlan spoke calmly, but his meaning was clear. He was done with the conversation and would not tolerate any more excuses. "You will not cramp my style, Diana, and you will go to Los Angeles with me. We had an agreement, remember?"

Feeling chastised, she nodded her head. "I do remember. I remember that very well."

Though the frown he sent in her direction told her that he was not entirely sure what she meant by that, she did not respond. The truth of the matter was that she was not sure what she meant either. This could be the greatest bargain she had ever struck, or the biggest mistake she had made in her life. One thing was certain, only time would tell.

Chapter 6

The brain scan and EEG came back normal, and Diana was thrilled to see her daughter begin the road to recovery. It took more time for Hannah to lose the grogginess of the medications, so her first few days were in a haze of uncertainty and loss of memory. Diana continued her vigil with silent prayers of thanks.

"The road will be bumpy," Mindy told her on the telephone. "You told me yourself that her doctor said she'd probably have no memory of the accident, but she's making great headway. You should be so proud of her."

"I know," Diana murmured. "I am. I feel as though I've been given a second chance."

It was all thanks to Devlan and his swift response. Because of him, Hannah was progressing quickly, and Diana wished he could see how far she had come already. He had returned to Los Angeles the week before, just the day after their steamy kiss in the kitchen, and without his persistent presence and eagerness to please, Diana realized that she actually missed him. He had been so reassuring and had taken over all of her worries so effectively that she actually had grown dependent on him. It happened so subtly, and she was dismayed that she felt the loss of his support. Not a great sign for her.

"Diana? Oh, it must be the stud."

Diana jumped. She had completely lost track of her discussion with her friend. "What?"

"Mr. Doyle? You know, the man who's constantly on your mind?"

"Hannah's constantly on my mind, Mindy."

"Oh, I know that," she said with a chuckle. "He's on the lower half, though."

Diana blushed. "That's not true."

"It's okay, we understand. You should've seen the look tall, dark, and devastatingly handsome gave to Allan when he went to visit you that first day. Talk about possessive."

"He did mention seeing Allan, but he didn't seem to mind."

"Allan said he was glaring at him."

"Well, I don't think it was that. Perhaps it just looked like it," Diana said hastily. "Besides, he's not even here anymore. He's in L.A."

"Oh, but he'll be back for you. Better watch out, sweetheart, that man wants you."

"Wants me? You make me sound like a dessert."

Though Mindy laughed, Diana did not join her. Her friend meant well, but she did not know the truth of Diana's association with Devlan. When the time came for her to attempt another relationship, she wanted it to be real, not some sort of agreement. Devlan had reminded her of their arrangement after their kiss, and the truth was that it made her feel cheap and used. After all, Devlan had given her his word, she had given him hers, and that was that.

She feared that her heart would pay the biggest price.

~

After the initial relief of Hannah's recovery, Diana began to dread the hospital rehabilitation almost as much as her daughter did. The pain Hannah went through those first few days was horrible to watch. Diana hovered nearby as she was slowly moved, first to a sitting position, and then to a chair in her hospital room. Tears of agony careened down Hannah's creamy cheeks with every painful movement, and though she tried to hide it, Diana cried alongside her.

However, Hannah was proving to be incredibly courageous. Her daily rehab treatments were slow but well worth it, and she continued her speedy recovery. In the middle of her second week, she was discharged from the hospital. The arrangements were made for her to attend the rehabilitation center in Los Angeles, and Diana accepted that Devlan would soon be returning.

Return he did, within hours of hearing the news. When he strode off the elevator dressed in his customary black suit and a long wool coat, all the heads on the floor turned to watch him. Devlan seemed not to notice or not to care, Diana could not tell which, for he marched straight toward her with a happy smile on his face and Mike close on his heels.

Diana turned away with a feeling of self-loathing. Of course, she was no better than the gawking nurses who watched him as though he some sort of god. She returned to Hannah's side, wishing that the child would awaken from her nap and save her from Devlan's impending arrival.

Unfortunately, she did not.

"So how's our little patient?"

Diana turned around and found Devlan standing directly behind her. He was still smiling broadly, and she noticed for the first time the small laughter lines around his eyes and mouth. It was quite appealing, almost boyish, and she looked away quickly. Holding a finger to her lips, she pointed to the sleeping child in the hopes he would move away. Unfortunately, he did not.

"That's great – privacy." He grasped her by the waist and pulled her close.

Diana's startled gasp was muffled when his mouth covered hers in an enthusiastic kiss. Her hands landed on his shoulders, and she pushed as hard as she could, but Devlan only hugged her tighter this time. His lips were soft and seeking, not hard and probing like the last time he had held her close.

"I missed you," he murmured, lifting his head slightly. "You look great."

Diana opened her eyes slowly and was immediately trapped by his smoldering blue gaze. Just like a schoolgirl, she thought, feeling a blush stain her cheeks. "Flattery will get you nowhere with me, Mr. Doyle," she replied in a shaky voice.

He grinned in answer. "Ah, but I can still try."

Despite her best intentions his enthusiasm was contagious, and she could not resist returning his smile. With a reluctant sigh, he released her, and she stepped away in the hopes of putting additional space between them to calm the fluttering of her heart.

"So how have you been?"

"Managing."

"Did you miss me?"

"No," she lied. "As a matter of fact, I've barely given you a thought."

"Liar," he said, smiling. His voice was warm and husky, and Diana felt her palms grow moist. "Trust me, I know. You've spent every waking minute thinking about me, unable to concentrate on anything all week."

Diana felt her blush deepen and turned away to hide it under the guise of collecting Hannah's things. "You're wrong."

"Ah, but you're blushing. Humor me, Diana. Tell me part of it was true?"

Diana gave him a sidelong glance. Devlan did appear hopeful, almost pathetically so, and his wistful look caused her to laugh in response.

His face softened as he took in her humor. One hand reached forward and ever so lightly touched her cheek. "You're so beautiful when you laugh, Diana. It's good to see you happy again."

Wow, she thought.

A knock on the door captured their attention, and the medical team hired to transport Hannah strode in before she could answer. She accepted the interruption thankfully and allowed Devlan to pull her from the room and down the hall to the elevator.

"I have a jet here that we'll take. Hannah will then go directly to the unit. I'll bring you there from Malibu."

"Wait a minute," Diana said. She stopped short and crossed her arms over her chest. "I can't just get up and leave now."

"Why not? Everything's taken care of."

"I haven't packed anything. I just got the news a few hours ago." Her arms went akimbo. "You're moving way too fast."

"Nonsense," he returned. "We can pack up your little place in a matter of minutes. I'll even help. Let's go, we don't want to keep Hannah waiting too long."

"You'll help?" She smirked. "So you do manual labor?"

He chuckled. "You've tasted my cooking. Doesn't that answer your question?"

"It wasn't cooking I was talking about," she said wryly.

He leaned down and whispered near her ear, so close that her hair tickled her cheek. "If you let me pack up your underwear drawer, I'll show you exactly what kind of manual labor I can do."

The memory of his fresh kiss warmed her and prompted her to use more caution. Oh, she had no doubt that he would, and even less doubt that she would be able to fight her desire for him. However, he was still far more experienced, and she was undoubtedly playing with a fire that could only burn her.

"I'll keep that in mind," she murmured.

The elevator doors opened and she ducked in quickly, waiting in the back for Devlan and Mike to fit their bulk in with the other passengers. None of them spoke while they made their way out of the hospital into the bright sunlight of the windy November afternoon.

"Car's this way," Mike said, leading the way.

Ahead idled a long stretch limo parked against the curb. As Diana climbed in, she wondered what her neighbors would think, but when Devlan slipped into the seat across from hers all thoughts fled. Diana glanced around quickly. "Where's Mike?"

"Why are you always wondering where Mike is? Is there something I should know about?"

"I was just wondering," she stammered.

"He rides up front. That's what I pay him to do," Devlan answered coolly. A laptop suddenly appeared on Devlan's lap and he began to type furiously. She was dismissed.

"Oh," she answered. Up front was more her league, too.

Devlan lifted his head a few times during the ride to fill her in on what he had accomplished while he was gone. In preparation for her temporary move to L.A., he had seen to it that she was released from her lease and a moving company scheduled to transfer her furniture into short-term storage. He had also spoken to her company and collected the paperwork for a leave of absence with a job guarantee.

All that was left was to pack up her remaining belongings. Luckily, she did not have much for Allan and Mindy to store for her, and Devlan granted her the time she needed to pack every piece of luggage that she owned to take to L.A. Toys, stuffed animals, and clothes caused zippers to bulge precariously, so she did not complain when Devlan carried everything down to the car for her with a satisfied grin on his face. Still stunned, she followed behind him in a dreamlike trance, completely unaware that Devlan had no intention of ever letting her go back.

~

Los Angeles International Airport was crowded when they arrived after a short flight in his luxurious private jet. Despite knowing that their arrangement was temporary, Diana could not help but be enthralled with the wonder of it all. Hannah would be in therapy for only a few months, and then they would be back on their own. However, it was impossible not to get caught up in the newness of her adventure, especially when Devlan made sure that she was treated with the utmost respect.

She was steered out of the airport into another long limo, this one a Bentley polished to a high gleam. She took note that Devlan stopped and greeted the driver, a young man about twenty or so who sported a deep tan and dark brown hair. Once their brief chatter ceased, he glanced at Diana and gave her a friendly smile, his hand pumping hers enthusiastically. "Welcome to California, Mrs. Somerset. I'm glad to finally meet you."

Diana smiled back, instantly liking the young man.

"This is William," Devlan announced, placing a possessive arm around her waist. As always, he ignored her when she stiffened and attempted to pull away.

"Everyone calls me Wills," he put in.

"Wills," she repeated.

"So are we ready?" Devlan asked impatiently.

Secured alone in the back with Devlan again, Diana busied herself by gazing out the window and taking in the crowded scenery while Devlan held his mobile to his ear. She wondered what kind of rate plan he was on, considering every moment that he could he was communicating with someone. To her, it appeared exhausting.

"We're on our way in now. We're taking the 405 to I10. Traffic's thick. Did you pick up that item for Mrs. Somerset and confirm the reservations?"

Diana glanced over with a frown, but Devlan only winked at her.

"Yes, and send some flowers to Hannah's room. We can't have her feeling left out."

"I don't think she'd notice," Diana said softly.

Shrugging, Devlan turned his attention back to the other speaker. "I don't care if he's complaining. Tell him I'll be in first thing Monday. We can discuss it then. You didn't book any meetings for the rest of the week, did you?" After a slight pause, Devlan ran his hand down his face. "I'll work on it tonight. You can reach me anytime in Malibu. We'll be settling in there. Just don't send me anywhere until next week. This is more important."

Diana's brow rose in surprise. Devlan was canceling everything for her daughter? Not many men she had known would do the same, but then again he was once again proving to be unlike the men she was used to.

Careful, the voice in her mind warned again.

"She's with me now. We're on our way to the house. It's all set, right?" He nodded to Diana. "That's great. Good work, Kath. What would I do without you?"

His warm tone unsettled Diana. She barely knew this man and was already envious of his secretary. As he signed off, Diana turned her attention back to the road. The highways were congested, bumper-to-bumper with pushy drivers, and the haze was thick, almost obliterating the hills to the northeast and the mountains off in the distance. Los Angeles was everything she had heard it would be. What surprised her most was that she was visiting for the first time in a way she had never expected. This was no family trip to the theme parks and beaches. Instead, she was riding in a Bentley to oversee the care of her injured daughter.

"We have a bit of a ride to Malibu, depending on traffic. Would you like a drink or something?"

"What I'd really like is to see Hannah. I'm afraid if she wakes up someplace different without me she might panic." She frowned. "I knew I should've ridden with her."

84

Devlan's lips compressed as he considered her words. "You know, I didn't even think of that. I'm not used to this child thing yet." He pressed the intercom button and heard blaring music. "Damn kid," he muttered. "Turn it down, Wills. We've had a change of plans. Head up to the rehab now, please."

"You don't have to change all your plans, Mr. Doyle. You can just drop me off if it's a problem."

Devlan laughed. "I've kissed you twice now, Diana. Don't you think it's time that you start calling me by my given name?" When she did not immediately respond, he pursed his lips playfully. "All right, let me put it to you this way... If you don't start calling me Devlan, I'm going to kiss you in public."

She blushed in answer, which caused him to laugh harder.

"Besides, this makes perfect sense. It beats running back and forth from Malibu to the city. We have reservations tonight for eight o'clock. I don't want to rush you all over, not on your first night in Los Angeles."

"Reservations?"

Diana hesitated, her stomach muscles clenching. Perhaps now that she was in California, he was anxious to begin their relationship. In truth, Diana was surprised he had not pushed her that morning in the kitchen. While he had not even mentioned their agreement since that breakfast, she had noticed that he told his secretary he was staying in Malibu with her. If she knew men at all, it was only a matter of time, and apparently the time must be coming. She was not sure how to respond.

"I made dinner reservations at a great place I found some time back. Thought you might enjoy relaxing a little and seeing the L.A. of the movies. Now that Hannah's getting the best care, you can finally relax a little."

"She had good care in the hospital," she protested.

"Yes, but these are specialists. Hannah will have twenty-four hour care and more therapists than the hospital could offer. She'll be with children like her, and there might be some near her age. Will you trust me?"

She ducked her face away from his, too afraid to say what she really felt. No, it would do her no good to place all her trust in one individual. She would trust no one but herself.

"You don't understand," she declared. "She's my daughter. I need to be with her."

"I'll call now and see if we can bump up our appointment with the admission liaison and the attending physician. They'll tell us what's planned for Hannah, who will be taking care of her, and those things. You'll be in charge of everything; just tell me what you need."

"If it matters at all," Diana said softly. "I thank you from the bottom of my heart for everything you've done so far."

Devlan beamed with pride and a warm smile appeared. "I think it matters a lot. Especially since I know how hard it must've been for you to say it."

He reached forward and placed a warm hand on her knee, and she watched as his fingers gently stroked the area around her kneecap. Despite the warning signals in her brain, she was unable to move away from the soft touch. It was foreplay, she reasoned. He was trying to break down her defenses.

Seeing her discomfort, Devlan sat back and again reached for his phone. It took some time, but he was methodical and efficient in adjusting their schedules. She half-listened to his authoritative voice as he let his expectations be known while she watched the cars meander alongside them. Her thoughts drifted as well.

Hannah would be in an inpatient facility for some time before she could go to the Malibu house with her. There, she would have several hours of therapy and educational tutoring every day until she was ready to return to Colorado. The cost, Diana feared, would be astronomical, and there was only one form of payment Devlan seemed to want from her.

Sex.

"We're all set," he announced.

Diana startled when she heard his voice, but he did not notice. His attention was focused on the traffic out the window, and the frown on his face was filled with frustration. She stared at his handsome profile, admiring his straight nose and square jaw while he was distracted.

"This is the worst way to see the city. Tomorrow, after we go to the facility, I'll be your guide."

"Oh no, that's not necessary. I'm sure you have more important things to do," she said hastily.

"You are important, Diana. You and Hannah are my priority right now. You're the only family I have, and you're visiting from out of town. Don't you think it would be pretty rude to ignore you and not take some time to show you around?"

"Well, this is a little different. We're a little different," she answered.

"Nonsense. I told you before, I need the time off. Work has consumed most of my time, and I'm due for a vacation."

She could not help the jab. "Apparently not so much time that you couldn't hit the parties."

When Devlan smiled, his bright blue eyes smiled as well. "So you noticed," he teased.

"Yes," she muttered.

"I love when you admit to it," he said, chuckling. "Ah, looks like we're finally here."

Sure enough, they had arrived, and the whitewashed modern facility caught Diana's attention. The well-manicured lawns sported paved walking paths flanked with an assortment of wood picnic tables, benches and lawn chairs to occupy the patrons. Established trees offered shade from their trim and neat canopies, and beds of perennials brightened the yard with a splash of rainbow colors.

"Very nice," she admitted.

Devlan assisted her out of the Bentley and once more wrapped his arm around her waist as he led her up the steps. Just inside the door stood a pretty young blond woman dressed in scrubs and a white coat. Beside her was a woman with fiery red hair, dressed in a plain blue business suit and low heels. They approached with wide, friendly smiles.

"Welcome Mrs. Somerset, Mr. Doyle, we've been waiting for you. Hannah's just arrived and is being transferred to her bed. We'll take you straight up to her room to see her, and then we'll sit down and chat."

Diana appreciated their enthusiasm and happily fell in step between them, peppering them with questions and concerns while they listened patiently and responded reassuringly. Devlan was left to lag behind but did not complain from his position close behind her.

Hannah was still groggy when they arrived, so after saying hello and making some introductions, Diana and Devlan were led back to a spacious office to discuss Hannah's care path. While Devlan appeared to take it all in stride, Diana found her head spinning with all of the information thrown at her. Whereas she could answer the questions they posed, it was Devlan who asked the ones about the facility. Apparently, he had done some homework about rehabilitation, and that pleased her even more than his carrying her luggage down to the car.

After performing so well with the administrators, Devlan finally allowed his more impatient side to appear when Diana fussed over Hannah for the remainder of the afternoon. With increasing glances at his watch, by the third hour he finally spoke up. "Diana, we still have a long drive."

Diana leaned over Hannah and gave her a kiss on the nose. Her eyelashes fluttered briefly but remained closed, and the nurse who had joined them smiled at Devlan conspiratorially. "She'll probably be out all night. You chose a good night to take your wife to dinner."

"If I could get her out the door, I'd consider it a good night," he responded.

Diana glanced at him over her shoulder. It was not his childish whining that caught her attention. It was that he made no attempt to correct the nurse for her mistaken belief that they were married. Interesting. Stroking Hannah's hand one last time, she finally pulled away when the nurse placed her hand on her shoulder.

"She'll sleep through the night and won't even know that you're gone," she whispered. "From what I hear, you haven't left her side yet. Let your handsome hubby take you out for a night and spoil you. Even Hannah wouldn't mind. It'll be good for you both when you come back feeling more relaxed."

Diana shook her head, fully intending to set the nurse straight. "He's not –"

"She's right, Diana," Devlan interrupted smoothly. "I bet Hannah will heal even faster when you're happier."

"That's absolutely true."

Diana scowled in Devlan's direction, but he only winked back at her. Coming to his feet smoothly, he came up behind her and wrapped his arms around her waist. Playing the husband role effortlessly, he pressed a warm and lingering kiss on her neck and smiled at the nurse. "Now you're fairly sure she'll sleep through the night?"

"I can't say with absolute certainty, but given that she's had a long day and her medication..." Her voice trailed off encouragingly.

"All right," Diana muttered. She bent and kissed Hannah's soft cheek one last time.

"It's only for one night," the nurse said. "We have your contact information if something comes up."

Hating that she seemed like an overprotective mother, Diana nodded her thanks and sent one last glare in Devlan's direction. His eyes danced with mischief and what appeared to be excitement.

Before she could find another excuse to stay, he reached for her arm and led her out of the room back toward the waiting car. Knowing it was pointless to fight any longer, she allowed him to have his way this time. After all, Hannah would be better soon. She was safely ensconced in a state-of-the-art facility with beautiful grounds and a friendly staff. They could not have asked for anything more. The best care money could buy was the gift she had received for her daughter.

For that, she had Devlan Doyle to thank.

Chapter 7

Malibu was a beautiful seaside community north of Los Angeles where the affluent lived and the tourists gaped, and it was also the place that Devlan Doyle was allowing her to stay. Yet again, she was faced with the now familiar fairytale feeling as they entered the small community, and it grew when she saw the property for the first time. His house was among the finest, hidden off the road by a gated drive. Feeling more like a movie star and less like a penniless single mother, Diana stared in awe at the well-manicured grounds tucked behind the privacy walls.

Wills spoke into the speaker, and the gates swung open on well-greased hinges to admit them. While Diana continued to gape, Devlan looked around with satisfaction. She had thought that most of the houses on the beach in Malibu were condos or narrow salt-box homes. Well, she was wrong.

The long drive circled around the front of the Mediterranean-style house. Though narrow, the yard was a plush, deep green and littered with marble statues and fountains leading all the way up to the house. Fresh flowers in full bloom lined the drive and added a splash of color to offset the dark green of the beautifully landscaped yard. Diana quickly noticed that, in addition to the garages, there was a tennis court and a large, spacious guesthouse on the property. It had the same whitewash and red-tile roof, almost a miniature of the large house. She wondered if that was where she was going to live.

The Bentley came to a gentle stop in front of the three-story house. The late afternoon sunlight glimmered on the stucco finish, enhancing its pristine exterior. As Wills held open her door, Devlan assisted her out and led her up the wide outer stairs into the expansive foyer.

The large door stood open, revealing a huge chandelier with hundreds of small lights hanging from the high ceiling. Just beneath it stood a heavy crystal table with a clear glass tableau. Her breath caught at the sheer size of it.

"That light probably cost as much as my yearly salary," she murmured aloud.

He snorted. "You're probably right. I didn't buy it. I only walked through real quick when I bought this place. I haven't had time to come here since."

Diana shot him a withering glance.

"Well, it's nice." He grinned down at her, his eyes sparkling, and his arm once more snaked around her waist and pulled her against his side. "This house is your house while you're my guest. I'll show you around, and then you can settle in before dinner."

"Wait," she said nervously. "Aren't I staying in the guest house?"

"No," he said, frowning. "I put you in the second master, with Hannah's room next door. The guesthouse is isolated. Mrs. Maclean will stay there when she arrives. She'll be out in a few days to help while you're visiting."

"Oh, I don't know about this."

Ignoring her comment, he moved further into the house, veering to the right into a spacious white-carpeted room. The room was as bright and cheerful as the foyer, too white for a five-year-old girl, she thought nervously. Every room as far as she could see was lined with large windows, granting a serene ocean view and natural lighting. She could understand why he liked the place. It had an optimistic and welcoming feel, more beautiful than any house she has ever stayed in before.

"This is the main living room."

Diana fell in step behind him, following him throughout the house. It was multi-leveled and asymmetric, and she knew in an instant that it would take her some time to find her way around. There were eight bedrooms in the main house, three masters, all with private baths and huge walk-in closets as well as balconies that overlooked the heated pool and the long sandy stretch of beach a short walk away. His prideful enthusiasm began to rub off on her as they continued the tour, and soon her intimidation was replaced by excited planning of trips down to the beach with Hannah when she was better.

Diana's room was spacious and cheery, like the rest of the house, with a huge king-sized bed, full entertainment center and whirlpool bath. Like the other rooms she had seen, her bedroom had a full wall of floor-to-ceiling windows with a view of the ocean. She glanced around in awe. "All this for me?"

Though she felt guilty that she desired to stay at the house, she could not help her girlish excitement of being treated to such luxury. She feared that she and Hannah would be spoiled forever and never want to leave.

He smiled. "Naturally... Do you like it?"

"Yes, it's very beautiful... and big."

"Yes, this room alone is bigger than your whole apartment," he pointed out.

"Thanks for reminding me, I almost forgot."

He chuckled and crossed the room, having one more surprise that he proudly showed her. Hannah's room connected with hers through a hidden door disguised as a bookshelf. "You can either use this door or have Hannah come through from the hallway."

Hannah's room was already littered with more toys than any child could dream of having. There were walls of toys and books, and Diana turned to Devlan in dismay. "You can't keep doing this.

She's going to leave here so spoiled, I'll never be able to keep her under control."

Devlan gave her a curious glance before clearing his throat. "I'll be back to pick you up at seven."

"But, Devlan," she said. "I don't have anything to wear to dinner."

"Look in your closet," he announced over his shoulder. "We picked up some things for your stay here."

As the door closed behind him, she continued to stare at the spot she had last seen him. It concerned her that he was growing more presumptuous with every passing day, and it was difficult to accept his generosity. Letting out a nervous sigh, Diana marched straight to the closet, only to gasp when she opened the doors. There was almost an entire wardrobe in there, all in her size.

"How in the..."

She began pulling the clothes off the rack and held them up to her. There was even a bathing suit.

"Who?"

She kept looking, pulling out a silky nightgown with a fine, soft matching robe. There was a fashionable pantsuit and even a couple of casual outfits. Everything she would need for semi-formal and casual dress.

"I guess he doesn't like my jeans."

Though she knew he had the best of intentions, tears of shame filled her eyes. He was trying to make her fit in the only way he knew how. She could never afford a wardrobe as costly as this, so he took care of it in his subtle and firm way. Part of her felt like Cinderella meeting her prince, but the realistic part of her was deeply humiliated.

If Devlan wanted her to look good while she was here, she would do her best to live up to his standards. She had been raised well and could socialize with the best. She could show Devlan a thing or two. Yet, her pride demanded she not keep a thing. She would leave every gift he purchased when they left.

As she was turning back to exit the huge closet, her eyes fell on the sapphire blue cocktail dress. Obviously it was for her to wear to dinner, and the gown itself was magnificent. Softly lined in silk and beaded with pearls and sequins, it glittered in the afternoon sunlight. It had been so long since she had spent an evening on the town, she could not resist the longing she felt when she studied it. It was the kind of dress that clung to her curves, requiring little or no undergarments, and she wondered if Devlan had planned it that way.

Suddenly unable to breathe, she quickly hung the dress back up and went to stand outside. Her balcony overlooked the large pool, partially hidden from the tropical trees that wound up the side of the house. It too glimmered in the late-afternoon sunlight, crystal clear and stirring only slightly in the breeze. Beyond the pool, the waves pounded rhythmically into the sand. It was a pleasing and relaxing sound that she knew would help her sleep at night.

As she leaned against the railing, she closed her eyes and took a deep breath. The soothing sounds were comforting to her ears. She realized that she had been working on nervous energy since early that morning and could use a long nap. Looking over her shoulder, the large bed beckoned, and she dropped down on her soft mattress with a thankful sigh. It had been a long day, one full of surprises. Vaguely, she wondered what would be next.

~

Devlan stood in the living room by the wet bar, idly watching the clock on the mantle. He was on his second whisky already, and yet he had only been downstairs for fifteen minutes.

"Wills brought the car around," Mike said, shutting the front door behind him. "He's ready when you are."

Devlan turned at the sound of his voice and took the opportunity to glance up the stairs again. "Great. What time is it?"

"Ten till."

"Okay," he said, sighing. "How do I look?"

Mike glanced at him up and down, taking in the sharp black evening suit with a critical eye. His eyes glittered with amusement when he answered. "I'm sure she'll find you pleasing enough, sir."

Devlan nodded again. "Right."

A slight noise caught his attention, and both men turned their gaze to the curving staircase. Diana stood at the top like an angel dressed in the sapphire-blue gown he had chosen, and his mouth went dry as he stared up at her. She was perfect, every inch of her. The dress clung to her soft curves like a glove, one he wished at that moment he was wearing.

She smiled shyly and self-consciously patted her hair when she saw him staring. The blond mane was tastefully done in a French twist with a few wayward strands escaping down to curl around her face. Her neck was exposed, all the way to the 'V' in her gown. A sudden urge to taste the exposed skin caused him to grip his glass a little tighter. When his body reacted immediately to his wayward thoughts, Devlan forced himself to look away from the gaping gown. However, it did not help when he scanned lower. The slit up the side showed a bit of her smooth thigh as she descended the winding stairs. With a sharp glance at Mike, Devlan noticed that he too was intently watching the show.

"Mike, tell Wills we'll be right out."

With as much reluctance as he had felt, Mike tore his gaze away and absently muttered a few words of acknowledgment. Devlan's eyes returned to Diana as she continued her descent.

"You look ravishing," he said warmly.

She blushed under his stare, her hands running down her sleek frame. "Thank you. And thanks for supplying me with a dress. It's a perfect fit. Just no more, ok? We've taken enough from you already."

Though he wanted to tell her that he planned on showering both her and Hannah with everything he could give, he held his tongue when her clear eyes met his. "I won't ask how you managed to find out my clothing size."

He cleared his throat cautiously. "I took the liberty of peeking in your closet that day we had breakfast. Kathy and I went shopping several days ago."

"Oh," she breathed. "You looked in my closet?"

Feeling humor would be his best defense, he winked at her. "At least it wasn't your underwear drawer. I couldn't find that... I hope you don't mind?"

"Mind? Of course I mind. You shouldn't have. I can dress myself." She shook her head. "I can't believe you bought clothes for me."

"I did." He nodded his head, still not feeling a trace of guilt. Her eyes darkened, though from anger or embarrassment he could not tell. "They're a gift from me, Diana. Would you please accept them?"

"Do I have a choice now?"

In the time that Devlan had spent with Diana, he had learned a thing or two about her temper. Her pride was obstinate, and he had obviously offended her. Now was not the time to share his plans with her. Instead, he sent his best smile her way.

"Let's go. It's almost seven. I want to take a short detour through Beverly Hills before dinner. Show you some of the sights. Are you hungry?"

"Starved."

"Good."

She paused at the bottom of the stairs, her heels clicking against the marble tiles, and Devlan still could not tear his gaze away from her. Everything about her was fresh and pure, so different from the competitive beauties in this land of the stars.

He loved that she wore very little makeup to cover her clear, healthy skin. Only her lips glistened with the tantalizing moistness of her gloss, and his chest swelled with pride as he admired her. Tonight, he had the honor of escorting her out.

Taking hold of her arm, Devlan felt her shiver. Satisfied that she was not as immune to him as she would have him believe, he led her outside to the waiting car and smiled proudly as Wills and Mike gaped. In his opinion, tonight he was escorting the most precious beauty ever.

Diana sat silently in the Bentley on their way to the restaurant while he explained some of the sights. Though she piped in to ask an occasional question, he could sense her apprehension. It almost matched his. If things went his way this evening, he had a lot to gain. His goal of having her finally accept him as a part of her life, perhaps even place her trust in him was finally within reach, but he would have to tread carefully during this critical stage. Nervous energy caused his fingers to drum against his thighs in a rapid tattoo, and he reminded himself over and over again to move slowly and remember his patience.

However, his patience was in short supply when they pulled up in front of the highly rated restaurant, and he spotted the small group of photographers standing by. As he suspected, Diana went rigid.

"Are they here for you?"

He chuckled. "You give me far too much credit, Diana. Photographers usually hang around the more popular restaurants hoping that they'll catch a shot of someone. More than likely some of Hollywood's finest are out for the evening."

"But won't they recognize you?"

"Maybe. Does that bother you?"

Diana reached up to pat at her hair self-consciously and then glanced down at her dress. "Yes, a little. I'm nothing like the women I've seen you with."

He reached forward to cup her chin. Her skin was soft, warm and very much alive. "You're beautiful, and for once I'm looking forward to spending an evening out. I'm proud to be your escort tonight, Diana. Besides, they'll probably leave us well enough alone."

When his thumb began to stroke her jaw, she pulled away and glanced out the window. "I don't know."

"I'll be right here beside you."

"That's what worries me."

Wills came to open Devlan's door, and he smoothly stepped out, turning sharply and holding out his hand for Diana. Her long, cool fingers slipped into his palm, and he gripped her hand reassuringly. They strode toward the restaurant side by side, barely drawing notice at first. However, the opportunity was too good to pass for some. Several cameras flashed in the night, and a few voices called Devlan by name.

"Good evening, gentlemen," he said to the men loitering with cameras in hand. He only paused for a moment before leading her into the dim safety of the restaurant.

"See? That wasn't so bad... and you looked great," he murmured, leaning into her soft hair. It smelled fresh and clean, a floral scent that came straight from the shower. The urge to remove the pins and set it free was strong, but he maintained his control as the young, tuxedo-wearing host approached with a wide smile to escort them to their table.

Candles were everywhere, casting a soft glow on the room ahead and lending a more secluded and romantic setting. It was just what he had planned, and he scrutinized the dim corner table they were being led to until he was satisfied with the solitude. Let the seduction begin, he thought triumphantly.

"Doyle, man, how are you?"

Devlan stopped short, his private world shattered yet again. Standing before him was an older man, about sixty, with a woman the same age. Distracted by his private thoughts, it took him a moment to place him. Then he remembered. He knew him from his golf club.

"Thomas, how are you?"

He held out his hand, and Thomas took it in a firm handshake. Diana stood beside him, smiling politely. He glanced down at her in preparation to make introductions, but she surprised him again by taking the initiative.

"Thomas, Esther, how are you?"

Devlan's eyes widened in surprise. She knew them?

"Diana? My God, Thomas, look! It's Diana!"

The older woman stepped forward and held out her arms, embracing Diana in a hearty hug. The other diners around them glared at them from their tables, irritated by the loud display, but Devlan was too stunned to intervene.

Ignoring their stares, Thomas took her hands in his and kissed her soundly. "Diana? What are you doing in California?"

"My daughter is here recovering from an accident. She was hit by a car."

"That's horrible. Will she be okay?"

Diana nodded. "We're over the worst of it."

Thomas turned his attention back to Devlan and narrowed his eyes. "So how did you meet up with Diana, Doyle?"

"She's my sister-in-law. She's staying with me during Hannah's rehab."

Thomas eyed the two suspiciously. "And where's your husband, Diana? Are you two still together? Haven't seen him since you were married. As a matter of fact, we lost complete track of you after the wedding."

"I'm a widow now," she said softly. "Auto accident this past summer."

Esther's eyes seemed to fill with tears of pity. "Two car accidents? Just months apart? Oh, that's terrible. I'm so sorry we weren't there for you. First your parents, and now your husband. Just tragic. Is there anything we can do for you?"

Diana took Esther's hands in her own. "You're so kind."

"She's fine. She's in my care now, and I'm taking good care of her." Devlan securely wrapped his arm around Diana's waist, aware by her rigid posture that she was not pleased.

Thomas raised his brows suggestively, and Devlan realized that it was fast becoming no secret how much he wanted this woman. However, the older man took it in stride and smoothly changed the subject.

"I hear you put Littleton back in his place a few weeks ago. Good man."

Devlan had to chuckle. It was true that Littleton was not a happy man, but it was not him who had set him back. "That was Kathy just doing her job."

"Ah, Kathy. And how is that beautiful assistant of yours now? God knows, man, you should just marry her and be done with it."

Devlan was aware of the strange look Diana gave him and quickly sought to diffuse the situation. "Kathy's happily married with two children, Thomas. Alas, another beautiful woman lost."

"Diana's widowed now, Devlan, perhaps she'd be the perfect Mrs. Doyle?"

Devlan's hand tightened around her waist, and he pulled her closer.

The open display proved too much for her, and she pulled back with a slight frown. "I'm not so sure Devlan's ready to settle down quite yet. Have you seen his track record lately?"

A collective gasp echoed between Devlan and their uninvited guests followed by polite chuckles. Diana's eyes twinkled mischievously when she stared up at him, and this time it was he who was not amused. His hand tightened around her waist again.

"Perhaps I'm still looking for the right woman," he muttered.

COLLETTE SCOTT

Esther smiled and pinched his cheek while Thomas leaned forward and whispered in the general direction of his ear. "Well, look no further, lad. I've known Diana since she was a precocious little girl. Never met a smarter child. You'd be wise to grab her while you can."

Devlan threw back his head and laughed. If only he knew. "I'm trying, Thomas, you've no idea."

"Well, good luck to you, then. I'll see you on the course soon?"

"Of course."

Thomas returned his attention to Diana, who was frowning at their whispers. "We must run, dear. Take a card and call me. Devlan will let you out of his sight long enough to visit with some old friends, right Dev?"

Devlan nodded reluctantly. As much as he would love to keep her all to himself, he knew that she would very openly rebel. "Of course."

"I've just arrived today, so I'm sure he'll be tired of me soon," Diana answered smoothly. He bristled again, but Esther did not seem to notice her veiled insult.

"Take care, dear, and please call soon."

"I will, Esther, thank you. Thomas, it was good to see you."

"Likewise, darling girl, now run along. Too many people staring."

Devlan grunted in agreement. So much for a quiet, pleasant evening to get to know one another. First photographers, and now some old friends. What would be next?

Despite the interruption, he soon realized there had been a benefit after all. Seeing Thomas and Esther Holmes had lightened Diana's mood considerably. She became animated, less frightened and much more talkative. With only a little prodding, he was able to learn more about her childhood in Connecticut, and the crash that made her an orphan. Over a dinner of roasted lamb and

102

pickled salmon, Devlan learned that her father and Thomas had been good friends as well as Esther and her mother. It was obvious that Diana had a happy childhood and treasured her parents very much. Once they were gone, she met and quickly married Peter in the hopes of having a family again.

In the short space of one meal, he had learned more about her than in all the time they had spent together combined. As the minutes passed, he watched her visibly relax and felt better than he had in days. Finally, he was making progress. They shared laughter as well as conversation, and her quick wit amused him tremendously. He was further surprised to see Diana's normally cool manner melt when dessert was brought out. Like a child, her face gleamed in the candlelight when she leaned forward excitedly.

"I have a horrible sweet tooth," she admitted with a wry grin.

"I'll keep that in mind."

Reaching forward, Devlan poured himself another glass of wine. It was a great Chardonnay, not too heavy, and one he discovered and committed to memory that Diana liked. He sat back and sipped it as he watched her help herself to the dessert platter. Pleased with his progress, he smiled contentedly and decided to push a little further.

"So I've heard about your wonderful childhood. Now tell me about Peter," he said.

Diana placed down her spoon and shot him a cold look. "I'd rather not ruin a pleasant evening."

In no mood to spoil the mood, Devlan nodded in agreement and flashed a smile. "Then at least tell me why I'm such a jerk."

"What makes you say that?"

"When I first met you at the funeral, you looked at me with disgust. Besides, you told me he had said things, and then there was your comment to Esther and Thomas... I'd like to know what kind of monster I'm supposed to be."

Diana glanced down at her plate and took another sip of

wine. Her discomfort was plain, but the wine she had consumed that evening loosened her tongue. "Peter said you were a horrible womanizer. He said you would never commit to anyone, left a trail of broken hearts, and used women only for sex. Afterwards, you used to mark your conquests on an Irish walking stick."

"That's actually true," Devlan admitted with a laugh. "In college I did that. But it wasn't because *I* went from woman to woman. Unfortunately, I was the one being dumped."

Diana laughed as well, her eyes revealing her disbelief. "You're a handsome man. I find it hard to believe that women dumped you."

"Well, they did. I think it was because I was too nice. Girls always look for the bad boys." When she snorted in answer, a wide grin crossed his face. "Okay, so that's a partial falsehood. What else did he say?"

"He was very explicit in detailing how you stole his share of the inheritance from your father and used it to buy into a company that took off. He was left with nothing and said that you made millions off his small share and refused to pay any of it back."

"What a bastard I was."

Diana shrugged. "Maybe he deserved it."

"Do you still believe him?"

She met and held his gaze. "I don't know what to believe anymore. One minute you're a businessman with more money than I could ever imagine, and the next you're an ordinary guy. You've bought me thousands of dollars' worth of clothes; you've taken care of my daughter's medical bills... you've done so much for Hannah and me in the past month.

"Part of me says that it's just guilt over what you did to Peter." She stopped and sighed, her eyes softening to a sky blue. Her voice was low and husky, and the sound of it warmed his bones. "Then part of me says you are a decent man who would never stoop to such heinous lows, and what you've done for me you've done because you really care what happens to us."

Unable to look away from her, his voice dropped an octave when he answered. "Is it so hard to admit that Peter was not telling the truth?"

She shook her head quickly, smiling sadly. "Knowing what I do now, no."

Devlan pressed his advantage. "None of that is true. Peter's inheritance was smaller than mine because my mother brought in the money. Peter was my stepbrother; he never even knew my mother."

She nodded.

"Before he died, my father set aside a college fund for him. That was his inheritance. He spent it all before he finished his second year of school."

"That's when I met him," she admitted softly.

"Yes, I know. He came home several times and asked me to give him a loan. The economy had just started turning, and I had put every dime I had into a failing software company. I had nothing to give him. He never forgot it, especially when I came out with our mobile software, and my company took off the following year. I expanded from there and grew by leaps and bounds. By that time, he had you and was planning to get married. He no longer needed me.

"But, I'll tell you Diana, I've never met a man who could hold a grudge like he did. He could be completely wrong and still make you feel like you were in error."

"Believe me, I know," she agreed softly.

"If you knew him and how he was, why were you so quick to think the worst?"

She was opening to him. He could see it in her eyes. All of his patience was slowly wearing her down. He could almost taste his victory.

"I don't know." She shrugged. "You're Peter's brother? After what he did to me… I guess it was easier to think the worst. That way I could dislike you and not care what you did… but you've made that so hard to do."

"Yeah, well you've made it very hard for me, too."

"I don't want to be hurt again."

For the first time, she allowed him to see the vulnerability in her eyes. She was still a woman inside underneath all that pain. With some tenderness from him, it was possible for her to heal. He knew it.

As he continued to watch her icy walls melt before his eyes, their waiter returned to slip him the check. Without even glancing at the bill, he placed his card in it and returned the slip. Then he reached across the table and took her hand within his own. Her fingers slipped around his in a firm grip, almost clinging. He had finally done it, and he was eager to show her that there was so much he could do if she would let him.

"I'm not a monster, Diana," he replied. "Nor am I anything like Peter. I want you to give me the chance to show you that."

"It's hard for me to trust," she said softly.

"I understand that, and I'm a patient man. I can wait."

"But you won't be around forever. You have a different life. A full life. Hannah and I will be an inconvenience."

"That's not true. You only see the money. You don't see that I'm a man who has only a small family left, and the means to make sure they're safe. That's my motivation, Diana. To share what I have with you."

She paused, biting her lip in indecision. Seeing her growing weakness, he jumped at the opportunity. "Let me show you how to be happy again, Diana. Let me be your sanctuary until you're confident again."

A slight, almost imperceptible, nod tilted her blond head. Suddenly, he felt a little hot around the collar, and it seemed as though everyone knew it. He sat back and glanced around, but the other diners were focused on their own business and not paying them any attention. Still, the urge to be alone with Diana, to show her exactly what he promised, was overwhelming. He had waited long enough. It was time to seal the deal.

Chapter 8

This time, Diana allowed him to slip his arm around her waist as he led her out to the waiting car, and they passed through the restaurant without any interruptions. He ushered her out the door and into the cool evening air, barely nodding his thanks to the staff as he went. His mind was whirling with plans about playing out the fantasies that he had only previously dreamed. However, first, he needed to get her alone.

Luckily, Wills appeared almost immediately with the car, and no sooner had the door shut behind them than Devlan was pulling Diana across the plush seat to his side. She gasped in surprise, but for the first time since she had melted against him in her kitchen, she came willingly into the circle of his arms. The silky material of her cocktail dress felt perfect under his heated fingers, and he enjoyed the sensation as his hands slid slowly up her back to her shoulders.

"What if they see?" Diana whispered.

"They can't, but I don't care if they could," he muttered. "You're so damn beautiful."

Devlan felt consumed with a fire of hunger. Her skin was like soft molten lava, silky smooth and burning hot to the touch, and he had never felt anything so good. She stared at him with wide eyes but did not resist when his hands tightened and pulled her forward to meet his kiss. Her willingness enflamed him all the more, and it took all of his strength to move slowly, patiently.

Though he wanted nothing less than to press her back upon the seat and make furious love to her, he restrained himself with the knowledge that his triumph was near at hand, and she deserved his full respect. Her lips were moist and pliant beneath his, and she eagerly met his kisses with a passion of her own. Much to his delight, she reached up and cupped his face, her palms firmly holding his face near. He groaned in answer and pulled her onto his lap, and when she landed so perfectly, he nearly shouted with joy. She felt so right; she fit so well against him.

"You have no idea how much I want you, do you?" He whispered before he kissed her again.

His mouth left her lips and ran alongside the underside of her jaw. She sighed in answer, her head lolling against his arm while her hands lowered to his shoulders. She tasted sweet, her own heady flavor mixed with her shower gel, and he appreciated it more with every nibble.

"Please," she gasped.

"Oh, I will, Diana. Trust me, I will."

Fast losing control, his eager hands sought out the full mounds of her breasts. Her back arched immediately in response, offering them to him freely, and he took. Yes, he took.

"Oh, yes," she breathed.

Gone was the cautious woman whose company he had so recently enjoyed. In her place was a woman with as much passion as he, and she could not stifle her soft moan of pleasure any more than he could deny the teasing movement of his hands. Smiling in satisfaction, he watched her lips part in wonder. How many times had he imagined being with her like this? He wanted more, and he fully intended on getting it.

Lowering his head, he allowed his mouth to follow his hands. With a low purr, she pressed her hands to his head to hold him in place. Though he was almost to the edge, he could not resist pulling her closer. He needed her now, and he feared he would lose his mind if it did not happen soon. Raising his head, he beheld Diana in all her longing.

"I've wondered all night what was under this dress. I want to see you, Diana. All of you." He looked out the window in frustration. "Damn it all, where the hell are we?"

~

As the car came to a gentle stop in front of the Malibu house, Devlan reluctantly released her and smoothed back her hair. Diana felt detached, like she was another person in another time when he arranged her back in her own seat. Devlan was so strong and solid as he restrained himself, but his hands were tender when he straightened her dress. Whatever happened in the morning would be soon enough to deal with repercussions, but right now this beautiful and sexy man was all hers.

"I'm afraid I can't help you more… if I keep touching you, I won't be able to stop," he said roughly.

Still dazed, Diana managed to finish straightening her dress on her own. It bore the telltale wrinkles of being bunched, and there was a moist spot over her left breast where his mouth had teased her. Oh, that mouth! She was still thinking of his mouth, and the pleasure he had given her, when the door opened and the cool sea breeze filtered into the car. Suddenly, she felt cold and alone again and could not resist reaching for Devlan and his warmth. He was there for her, his fingers tightening over hers as he assisted her out of the car.

Though he stood tall and lithe in his dark suit, his hair blowing gently in the wind, his eyes smoldered as he stared down at her. Even though he appeared to be in complete control, she alone noticed the glazed look in his eyes and the tightness around his full lips. Oh yes, beneath that collected exterior was a man burning with as much hunger as she was. It was a new and exhilarating feeling to be desired with such intensity, and she felt her power when she heard the tension in his voice.

"That'll be all for tonight, Wills. Mike. Thank you. I'll see you in the morning."

"Thank you, sir, have a pleasant evening," came the knowing reply.

Mike's fair head nodded in her direction, and Diana gave him a shy smile before following Devlan into the dark house. He reached against the wall and flicked on the hallway light before turning abruptly and sweeping her up into his arms. Ignoring her surprised cry, he lifted her against his chest, and Diana wrapped her hands around his neck as he marched up the stairs with concentrated determination.

No sooner had he reached the landing than he was kissing her again. She had no time to voice any regrets or protests, nor did she want to. All rational thought escaped her mind the moment his lips touched hers. It had been a long time since a man had touched her with such longing, and her body reacted to his tenderness with an urgency that took her breath away. This man wanted her. He wanted her with a passionate hunger she had never before experienced.

Instead of taking her to her own suite, Devlan took a right at the top of the stairs and went down the hallway to his. The room was dark and cool, with the relaxing sound of the ocean filtering in through the open balcony doors. Raising his head, Devlan gently lowered her to the bed and ran his hands down her length, eliciting a shiver from her before he paused at her feet. Though she could only see his outline in the moonlight, his soft touch spoke volumes. It was almost reverential.

His fingers were at her ankles, releasing the clasp of her sandals and allowing them to hit the carpeted floor with a dull thud. Then he was at her side again, placing feather-light kisses along her jaw. Sitting up, she pushed his jacket from his shoulders and down his arms. It landed with a soft rustle as she reached for the buttons of his shirt. However, his hands stopped her progress when he reached for the neckline of her dress. As the loosened material landed around her waist her first impulse was to cover up, but Devlan captured her hands and held them away from her.

"Don't hide from me," he ordered.

It was all new to her, she realized, to have such a handsome man stare at her with such yearning. That feeling of power rose again, and slowly her shyness melted away. He dropped to his knees before her and buried his face between her breasts.

"I've waited too long to see you like this. You're even more beautiful now than on your wedding day," he said forcefully.

"Oh," she breathed, her heart racing out of control.

Raising his head, he pushed her back on his bed, following close behind. With a soft sigh of surrender, she wrapped her arms around his shoulders and melted into him. He lifted himself on his elbows and seized her lips in another soul searing, open mouthed kiss that left her breathless.

Then the phone rang.

Please, don't stop, she thought wildly. A sudden blast of cool air against her skin announced his reluctant hesitation. By the third ring, Devlan grudgingly let her go, his breathing coming somewhat raggedly.

When he picked up the phone, his voice was harsh. "What?"

Diana heard the raging female voice on the other end of the receiver and froze.

"How in the hell did you get this number?"

She heard more raging and felt her ardor cool. Apparently, there was a woman in Devlan's life who was not happy about something.

"Yes, Roxanne, I was out tonight. Yes, it was with a blonde... She's my sister-in-law."

Diana's hands sought out the shoulders of her mistreated

dress, and she quickly covered her partial nudity. Roxanne was the woman he had been out with, and apparently they were still involved. This was news to her. Judging by the anger she could hear coming from the handset, Roxanne had already heard about Diana and was not pleased. Word certainly traveled fast in California.

Despite the longing coiled tightly in her loins, Diana felt certain the evening had definitely come to a close. Having had an unfaithful spouse, she had no interest in being the other woman this time around. She may not have known Roxanne, but she certainly did not want to steal her lover.

Devlan sounded cold and angry as he spoke, and Diana was vaguely aware that he was adamantly refusing her something. He continued to say "no" over and over, and then hung up the phone with a slam. When he turned to Diana, his face was red with anger.

"She's coming over," he said shortly.

Diana nodded wordlessly and scooted off the bed, but Devlan came around to stand before her as she was picking up her shoes.

"It's not what you think, Diana."

Her fierce frown spoke volumes, and Devlan took a step back. Taking a deep breath to calm herself, she leveled him with a cold stare. However, as cool as she tried to sound, her voice still shook when she spoke. "I had no idea you were seeing another woman. As long as you are, I can't get involved with you. I'm sorry, Devlan, but we'll have to work out another agreement, perhaps a payment plan or something."

"Pardon me?" Devlan recoiled as though she had physically struck him.

"We'll have to work out some other way for me to earn Hannah's care expenses."

"You mean you're only here to pay me back for Hannah's

care?"

As she stared at him, the flush of color in his cheeks faded to a deathly white. Unable to view the shock and dismay in his eyes, her gaze dropped to the ragged rise and fall of his partially revealed chest. "I thought… I mean, I got the feeling when you said that we could make arrangements that you wanted –"

"That I wanted you to repay me by having sex with me?"

He sounded so incredulous that Diana began to doubt herself. Cocking her head to the side, she slowly raised her gaze to meet his and instantly regretted doing so. Anger, frustration and disbelief met her wary stare. Sitting down hard on his bed, Devlan ran his hand down his face. He appeared stunned and perhaps even hurt as he lowered his gaze to the floor. His dark brows were drawn over his eyes in a confused frown, and those soft lips that had brought her such pleasure were now pressed tightly together.

"This *is not* happening," he muttered.

"Well, didn't you?" Diana asked softly.

His head swiveled in her direction, and the gaze he pinned her with was as cold as his voice. "Surely you're not serious?"

"You said we could work out an arrangement."

"You really think that I was helping you and Hannah for sex…? Lady, you rate yourself pretty high. Do you know how much her hospital bill was?"

Diana's gaze dropped to her feet as humiliation and grief filled her. Of all the times Peter had told her she was stupid, she had never truly believed him until that moment. Oh yes, she had just proven him right. What an arrogant fool she had just shown herself to be. No, her body was not worth the price of her daughter's medical bill, and he had just said as much.

"I'm sorry that you thought that, Diana. That's a pretty high insult to both you and me." He shook his head again, but this time it was with regret. "I never pay for my women. They usually come quite willingly."

"I've noticed," she snapped.

He continued to stare at the floor. Too preoccupied to see her anguish, he waved her away absentmindedly. "You'd better leave before I do or say something irreparable."

"Fine."

Diana slipped from the room before he saw the tears that filled her eyes. Retreating to her room to heal her wounds, she blinked them back furiously. No sooner had the door closed behind her than she was roughly pulling off the sapphire blue dress and throwing it in the corner in frustration. It was a shame to treat such an expensive piece of clothing that way, but she was beyond caring. She should have known better than to think her fairytale would have a happy ending. She felt like such a fool.

Taking a cool shower helped to clear her mind enough to realize that she needed to put some space between her and Devlan. Immediately. Emotions were high, and coupled with their mutual attraction she feared what their next encounter would bring. Perhaps by increasing the distance between them, they both could cool their ardor. Mind made up, she tossed some clothes in her own small suitcase and hurried down the back stairs to Mike's room.

The tall bodyguard opened his door dressed only in a towel, fresh from a shower. When he saw her, his eyes widened. "Well, you're the last person I expected to see."

"And why's that?" Diana snapped.

Though he tried to hide his shock, he still appeared uncomfortable. "What can I get you, Mrs. Somerset?"

"I was hoping you would tell me where I could borrow or rent a car, so I can get to the facility."

"You want to go tonight?"

She nodded.

"Now?"

She nodded again.

"Does Mr. Doyle know?"

"No, but he's expecting company."

Mike let out a long breath through pursed lips before nodding. "I'll call Wills and have him drive you over. I'll see about getting you a car tomorrow. Is that okay?"

Diana nodded her thanks and turned away. Behind her, Mike shook his head in disbelief. "I'll call your room when he's brought the car around."

Diana retreated back to her room. Her room. If she and Devlan had been in there, he never would have answered Roxanne's phone call. Wait, she reminded herself. If she and Devlan had ended up in there, it would have been too late. Yes, too late to stop her wayward, foolish heart. At least she had gotten a hold of herself before she had fallen completely over the edge.

She shut the door and went to stand in the cool breeze by her balcony. The sheer curtains billowed in the wind, beckoning her outside. She stepped out onto the balcony and sucked in a sharp breath. Devlan was there, standing by the light of the pool. He had donned swimming trunks and was about to dive in.

Even more beautiful than she imagined, Devlan was firm and toned, and the sight reminded her of how good he felt in her arms. Though she wanted to turn away, instead she drank in the sight of his broad shoulders as they tapered down to a narrow waist and led to long, sinewy legs that had so recently been entwined with hers. So tall and lean, he posed such a handsome sight that the ache in her belly intensified once more with unfulfilled longing.

He dove into the water and began making forceful, angry strides from one end of the pool to the other. His muscles rippled in the glittering light of the pool as his long arms cut through the water. Unwilling and unable to tear her gaze away, Diana stood in the shadows and watched while he did lap after lap without rest.

She admired his stamina even though she felt a twinge of

pity. She knew how horrible he must have felt, for she felt it, too. It was frustrating to be left feeling so unfulfilled and unsatisfied. But alas, it was not to be. Fate had again stepped in and taken matters out of her hands.

So why did she ache so much?

Diana felt fresh tears sting her eyes as she watched Devlan continue to work out his frustration. Blinking furiously, she refused to allow them to fall. She was supposed to be a strong woman now. Had she not learned her lesson when Peter died? Apparently not, for she suddenly realized that Devlan had somehow changed from a beast into a man who could easily capture her heart, and she had no idea what to do.

Run away, quick.

Hearing the phone ring, Diana stepped back inside. Wills had pulled the car around, and she knew this was her chance to escape and gain some distance. She was going to where she should have been all along. They would allow her to stay with her baby, they just had to. She needed to be safe with Hannah.

~

Devlan heard the heels clicking on the patio even from the depths of the clear blue water. He surfaced to find a long pair of shapely legs covered only by a mini skirt of black leather.

"I see you were out this evening as well," he said mildly.

"I'd like to talk to you."

"I assumed that already."

He effortlessly pulled himself from the pool and reached for the carelessly tossed towel. As he wiped his face and neck, Roxanne glared at him, her hands on her hips.

After seeing Diana's natural beauty on a daily basis, he had a hard time seeing what had attracted him to Roxanne. The exotic model he had once found tall and breathtaking was, in fact, angular and sharp. Her face was gaunt, and she was far too thin from the pressures of modeling. Her breasts were artificial, as was the makeup that adorned her sharply angled face. Diana was so much more pure and lovely, and that made his anger increase tenfold. He should be with her right now, kissing every inch of her body, not swimming off his frustration in the pool.

"Where were you tonight? Don't you realize how humiliated I am?"

"Since when do you dictate who I can and cannot be seen with?" Devlan ground out through clenched teeth.

Roxanne hesitated at his sudden anger, and she arranged her face in a pout like a sad puppy. Still, Devlan was in no mood for games. He had played enough for one night, and Roxanne's sudden possessiveness just fanned the flames.

"But Devlan, they said you were seen with a new blonde. All of Beverly Hills is talking about her." she replied, waving her hands dramatically. "Do you know what they're saying about me? 'Poor Roxanne, dumped for a blonde.'"

"They wouldn't be saying those things if you hadn't told people we were together."

"But we are together, aren't we?"

Devlan continued to dry off, his face a cold mask. No, he thought with finality, they were not, never had been and never would be. Now that he had tasted American innocence, he realized what his life was missing. He no longer cared about functions and galas. He wanted a family.

"I thought we were friends... but right now, I don't even consider you that." He frowned down at her. "I came here for privacy, and I expect to have some."

"Privacy for her?" Roxanne sneered. "Is she here now?"

"Excuse me?" Devlan asked. His voice was deceptively calm, and his brows rose over furious eyes in an unspoken dare for her to push him just a little too far.

"You're sleeping with this blonde aren't you? After all the time I've known you, you've never touched me, and now this woman – this broad – shows up and already you're in the sack with her? Who is she? What does she have that I don't?"

"Careful," he warned.

"I haven't even begun to push my limits, Devlan," she shot back.

He scowled. "She's from out of town, and I'd like to preserve her privacy."

"Ha," she jeered. "You're too late for that. Look in the tabloids tomorrow, honey, she's sure to be all over them."

"Let yourself out," he snapped. "Now."

Fully exasperated with all females, Devlan stalked away with Roxanne's bitter laughter ringing in his ears. If she was right, there would be a lot of explaining to do in the morning to Diana. He let out a weary sigh and headed straight for her suite, knocking on the door softly. This whole evening had gone from bad to worse in just a matter of minutes, and he knew he would get no sleep until he worked things out with Diana.

"She's not there, sir," Mike said, coming up the stairs behind him.

Devlan turned around quickly, his frown fierce. "Where is she?"

"Gone, sir. With Wills."

"Where did he take her?" Devlan frowned at the sound of panic in his voice. What was it about this woman that made him so crazy?

"To the facility. She packed a bag and asked to borrow a car. I told her Wills would take her, just in case."

Not knowing what else to say at that moment, he smiled grimly. "Good thinking, Mike. Thank you."

"Wills should be back soon. They left a while ago."

Devlan nodded and stepped away from the door. He was

about to turn around and take a cold shower when Mike called out softly to him.

"Sir?"

"Yeah, Mike."

"You really botched things, if you don't mind my saying so."

Devlan rolled his eyes. "Tell me something I don't know."

"She's falling in love with you."

Damn, how hearing those words made his heart race with excitement, and it would have made all the difference in the world if she had not taken off on him again. Once more, she had left him in the dust. Shaking his head, he smiled wryly at his friend. "Not after tonight, Mike. Good night."

Chapter 9

For three busy weeks, Diana managed to avoid Devlan. Once Mike delivered a rental car, she commuted between the facility and the Malibu house without encountering him alone. Luckily, the staff there welcomed her with open arms and encouraged her participation in helping Hannah get well, and despite her distress over Devlan's harsh words, Diana had never felt happier. Hannah was recovering quickly.

By the end of the third week, the brave little patient was walking with the aid of a walker and only a minimal amount of pain. Thrilled, Diana stood by and watched as her physical therapist shouted encouragement and clapped happily.

Hannah smiled in return, her bright eyes wide. "Look Mommy, look at how good I'm doing."

"I see, darling," she answered, biting back tears of pride.

"That's excellent Hannah! Keep coming, great. Good girl!"

Everyone clapped as Hannah completed her trek and sat down with a dramatic sigh. Diana went to her side and hugged her.

"You did great! You see? You've been so brave and worked so hard. You'll be all better soon."

"And then we'll go home, Mommy?"

"I hope so," she said with a smile.

A discreet throat clearing brought everyone's attention to the open doorway. Diana froze when she saw Devlan enter the large rehab room, arms loaded with several brightly wrapped gifts. Hannah's face lit up, and she laughed with happiness.

"Uncle Devvie! What do you have?"

Devlan chuckled and bent to kiss the top of Hannah's blond head. "Presents, of course. A new doll, perhaps. I don't know."

"Are you teasing me?"

"No, of course not, but you'll have to open them to see."

Hannah laughed. "You are teasing me."

His lips twisted into a sheepish smile. "Kathy picked them. You know I'm not good with girlie toys."

Hannah and her physical therapist laughed at his self-deprecation, but Diana remained unmoved. She watched silently as he handed the presents over to the two, keeping a hand on the roses that were tucked in the crook of his arm.

Since that evening, she had struggled to put Devlan in the back of her mind and deny her infatuation with his kindness, and it had worked - somewhat. At least until he began to show up at the facility to deepen the bond with Hannah. To her dismay, the pair hit it off and had become the best of friends. They communicated in their own little way, with secret looks and gestures that baffled Diana and remained private between the two of them. Though he consistently claimed to have no idea how to handle children, he sure did know how to charm them. Hannah was smitten, but Diana felt his visits were too frequent and difficult to pretend all was well between them.

"How are you, Diana?" Devlan asked, coming to stand beside her.

He stood close to her, too close, in her opinion. She shifted her weight to her other leg while her traitorous nostrils flared with the scent of his cologne. It brought back stirring memories of heavy breathing and urgent hands.

Shifting her gaze, she glanced at his remaining package. The roses, she noticed, were yellow. That was the rose of friendship.

"Better. Hannah's improving every day."

"I can see. She's progressed – just since Monday. I brought these for you," he said, handing her the flowers.

One eyebrow arched sarcastically. "Did Kathy buy those, too?"

"No, I did."

She accepted them reluctantly. There was no use in being peevish, although she longed to desperately. "Thank you. They're pretty."

"Is there somewhere we can talk? I have to go over a few things with you."

"There's an empty office down the hall."

Diana stooped to tell Hannah she would be right back then led Devlan to the small office. She was acutely aware of his presence close behind her, aware that his eyes were watching her every move while he closed the door behind them. For once, Devlan appeared unsure, and she felt some satisfaction for it – but not enough. The beautiful roses were tossed carelessly on the desk as she walked around it and took a seat on the small wooden chair.

Devlan watched with a raised eyebrow, the corners of his mouth turning down, but he remained calm when he spoke. "Hannah's due to be discharged the day before Thanksgiving."

Not as skilled at hiding her emotions, Diana felt her mouth drop open in surprise. "That's next week."

"Yes, but she will have continuing care, just not in the facility. It would be outpatient care."

"Oh, I see."

"Since I ended up postponing my vacation, I was planning to go to Hawaii for the holiday. I have a yacht there."

"Why am I not surprised?"

He remained unruffled and ignored her comment. "Will you and Hannah come with me to Hawaii?"

"I had no idea any of this was happening. I hadn't given any thought to what we were doing for the holiday."

"I'm giving you an option."

She thought for a moment. Though it pained her to say the words aloud, she knew what her best option was. "I guess the smartest thing to do is return home."

"No," he said firmly. "The smartest thing would be to go with me."

"Let's not get into this again," she retorted. "Hannah's only five. I don't want either of us to interfere with your private life, Mr. Doyle."

"Mr. Doyle?" She knew she finally struck home when he let out an angry curse and scowled at her. "So we're back to formalities again?"

"Well," she snapped. "Why don't you spell out exactly what our relationship is or should be? That way I know I can't misunderstand you again."

Devlan placed both hands on the desk and leaned forward until their noses were almost touching. He smelled of mint and cologne, a heady combination that sent her heart racing in her chest. Without warning, one warm hand came up to cup her cheek, his thumb gently stroking her skin, but she resisted the urge to recoil. There was no reason to be afraid of his anger.

"Our relationship isn't where I want it to be, Diana. We have something between us, and you know it."

"I'm not admitting to anything."

"I want you to go away with me. We're family, and it's the holidays. What's your other option? Spending them back in Denver in a small apartment alone?"

Diana opened her mouth to answer, knowing he was right, but he cut her off.

"This is just what Hannah needs. She can continue her care onboard."

Diana frowned, too afraid to respond. The idea of spending

Thanksgiving on a yacht in Hawaii was thrilling. It was her fairytale all over again. However, being there with Devlan when there was obviously a very possessive woman involved was not. She remembered all too well what happened the last time she believed in her dreams.

"What about Roxanne?"

"I tried to tell you it's not what you think," he said earnestly. "Roxanne was my friend. I've escorted her out on a few occasions. I've never given her any reason to believe we were serious, and I had no idea that she thought we were. That whole evening ended in disaster when I picked up that phone, and it was not how I had imagined it would end. I'm sorry about that."

She nodded slowly, so afraid to give in but growing weaker. He was making too much sense. "I don't know..."

Devlan hung his head and let out a heavy sigh. She resisted the urge to reach out and run her fingers through his thick, dark hair. When he raised his head again, the familiar look of determination had returned.

"I'll pick you both up Wednesday. We'll have fun."

Having said his piece, he straightened and gave her a tender half-smile. Then he turned sharply on his heel and strode back down the hall before she could protest any further. Once again, he had laid down the law as he saw fit, but this time she was not bristling or willing to fight any further. She just watched him go with a bemused smile.

~

Kathy Lei sported silky hair as black as obsidian that trailed down her back to the curve of her buttocks. Her face was a delicate, heart-shaped one, with wide, dancing dark brown eyes and soft pink lips that perpetually curved upwards in a smile. She carried herself with confidence and pride, her tall heels clicking rapidly alongside Devlan's long strides. The woman was smaller than Diana and barely came up to Devlan's chest, but she still managed to keep up with his determined pace. Diana watched them approach, feeling her spine stiffen and her hackles rise despite her best intentions.

"Are you ready?" Devlan asked in greeting.

It was rare that she saw his white teeth, but the smile he sported now showed most of them. As he dropped his haunches in front of Hannah, Diana's gaze returned to the well-dressed, petite Asian woman by his side.

"You must be Kathy," she said softly, holding out her hand. Kathy was a full two inches and at least ten-pounds lighter than she was, and Diana hated the sting of jealousy that would not ease.

"And you're the famous Mrs. Somerset. It's a real pleasure to finally meet the woman who has knocked Mr. Doyle off his feet."

She giggled behind her well-manicured hand when Diana's eyes widened in surprise. Nudging her in the side good-naturedly, Kathy gave her a wink before replacing her neutral smile.

Hannah was chatting to Devlan and had somehow convinced him to wheel her back to her room, so she could show him how carefully she had rolled up a poster to keep it safe. He pushed the wheelchair slowly, his head bent in intense concentration on Hannah's happy babble. They watched them go in silence before Diana turned her attention back to Kathy.

"I've heard so much about you, I was expecting someone else entirely. It seems Devlan can't live without you."

"That's true," Kathy said with a laugh. "Especially now that you and Hannah have entered the picture. It's a new experience for all of us."

"Why's that?"

Her eyes continued to glitter with amusement as she reached for Diana and linked her arm through hers. She led Diana down the hall and out into the bright California sunlight before speaking

126

again. There were two vehicles parked out front, the ever-present Wills with the Bentley and a large Tahoe. Diana offered him a smile in greeting, but she listened to Kathy carefully.

"Mr. Doyle's an all-out workaholic, Mrs. Somerset," she explained. "Of course, now all he wants to do is be with you and your little one. I've never seen him so distracted. Missing meetings, not returning calls, forgetting to approve things. He just has his head all up in the clouds. I don't think even he knew how much he liked kids, or at least your daughter." Grinning widely, she winked again. "I keep telling him to hang out around my house for a time, that'd do it pretty good."

"Where's Mr. Doyle?" Mike asked Kathy, climbing the stairs to greet them. He smiled at Diana.

"He's with that beautiful little girl inside."

"If you're in a rush, you might want to rescue him. Hannah will keep him in there all day given half a chance," Diana confessed with a smile.

Kathy's gaze followed Mike, who continued up the stairs. "Now he's a fine looking one, isn't he?"

Diana shrugged. "I suppose so, in a boxer-like way."

Kathy arched one of her perfect brows. "Good call. He was a boxer, a good one too, they say. Took one too many hits to the head and smartened up. Mr. Doyle picked him up as a bodyguard and has kept him on for years."

"He's loyal," Diana noted.

"Yes, very. Mike rescued him once from a stalker who pulled a gun. Took a bullet for him through the arm. They're more like brothers now."

"That's good," Diana admitted. That tidbit gave her a whole new outlook on Mike and Devlan's relationship. "Does he have many enemies?"

Kathy chuckled. "Only the ones I make for him."

"Seriously?"

"Well, he can be tough in business, but for the most part he's fair. I've seen worse in my day, believe me. Still, there are weirdos out there, and he can't make everyone happy. He's concerned for everyone's safety. We have security all over our buildings and parking lots. It's a sad world out there."

She glanced at Diana with apologetic eyes. "I'm sorry, hon. I've been going on and on. How are those clothes? I see you're not wearing them. Just as he expected."

Diana blushed as she looked down at her jeans. "It didn't feel right."

"That's exactly what he said," she said, laughing. "Listen, he's a generous man and loves to please people, especially you and that beautiful child in there. This is all new to him, and it's the only way he knows how to show you both how much he cares."

"It's new to me, too," she answered. "And that's why I don't like taking things from him."

"Don't worry about it, really."

"I don't know," she said, shaking her head.

Kathy placed her hands on her hips and frowned. "He's never been happier. Let him do his thing. He knows you're not after his money, and I hope he doesn't wreck everything before he realizes what a gem you are. Nothing would make him happier than you accepting his gifts."

"I don't need charity."

"It's not charity. It's honest to goodness caring." Kathy paused to shake her head thoughtfully. "I thought he was exaggerating when he went on and on about how stubborn and proud you were. I really figured that you'd break down and whip out the credit cards once you got here, but I was wrong."

"Thank you… I guess," Diana said stiffly.

Kathy laughed again. "There's a reason he hasn't settled down yet. Everyone he's even tried to get close to has done it. He sees that you're different and wants you all the more for it. Ah, here they come. Don't tell him I told you that."

Suddenly reminded of their conversation about the Irish walking stick, Diana considered Kathy's words carefully. Looking back at the doorway, she watched as Devlan cheerfully guided the wheelchair out, and Hannah waved happily. When they came to a stop, Hannah slowly stood and slid into the vehicle with Devlan's assistance. Diana smiled, pressing her hands to her chest.

"Wonderful job," she breathed happily.

Kathy quickly slipped into the Bentley next, sitting next to Hannah and leaving Diana next to Devlan. Not sure what to expect, Diana turned to Devlan with a wry smile. Still in his upbeat mood, his brows wiggled suggestively in answer, and he chuckled when she sent him a warning frown. However, he remained the true gentleman as she climbed in, and it was not until the limo was moving that he took advantage of their close proximity. Beginning with a heavy sigh, Devlan stretched out his arms, allowing one to casually drape around her shoulders. Diana stiffened and remained rigid, but he kept his arm there the entire ride to the airport. His thumb absently stroked her collarbone as he gave Kathy final instructions, and although she tried to follow their conversation, she was too distracted by his touch. It was a mixture of teasing lightness and insistent desire, and Diana could feel her skin prickle in answer. All the man had to do was touch her, and she melted, she realized miserably.

As soon as the vehicles pulled up to the airport terminal, Diana escaped his hand by leaning forward to look out the window. Strange that his touch could stir her so quickly, she thought with some concern. Though she had managed to keep her distance from him, apparently her body remembered his desire-provoking touch, and she was still willing to go out to sea with him? Not for the first time, she wondered if she was crazy.

"Where are we, Mommy?"

"We're at the airport."

"Why?"

Devlan beamed proudly. "Because I'm taking you two ladies away for a week. We're going on a plane and then on a big boat. How does that sound?"

"I want to go home, Mommy," Hannah said softly, her fingers reaching up to grasp a piece of her hair. She began twirling it, and Devlan sat forward and smoothed the soft strands away from her face.

Having never seen Hannah cranky before, he nervously tried to coax her. "We're going to have lots of fun. There'll be boats and buckets to play in the sand. We'll swim and build sandcastles together. You'll like it, I promise."

Diana nodded in agreement, but Hannah still looked unsure. Suddenly Diana was overcome with doubts of her own. Maybe she was making another mistake in taking her away. Maybe she would heal faster in their small apartment. Glancing at the pair, Kathy offered them a smile to ease Diana's doubts and Devlan's growing panic.

"It's nap time, isn't it?" Kathy asked. "My youngest – boy, if he doesn't nap, he's done for the day."

Giving her a stern look, Devlan growled his thanks. "Thank you for your opinion, Kathy."

Diana smiled at Kathy, who had sunk into the leather with her arms crossed. Seeing her reaction, Kathy's frown faded, and she rolled her eyes.

"Kathy's right. She's tired." She smiled at Devlan in an effort to reassure him, and when he saw it, he noticeably relaxed.

Hannah nodded slowly in agreement just as Wills opened the door with a wheelchair in hand. "Are you folks ready, sir?"

The strong youth assisted Hannah into the chair while Diana climbed out behind her. She stood by the door, but Devlan remained in the car to give more last minute instructions to Kathy. Diana stopped to listen when she heard his final words.

"I don't want her to know about any of that trash. Get on the phone and have them print a retraction. I'll handle Roxanne when I get home. Thanks, Kath, and have a nice Thanksgiving."

Diana glanced down at her beat up tennis shoes, knowing without a doubt they were talking about her. However, when Devlan exited the car, his excitement was unmistakable, as was the warm hand that wrapped around her possessively.

"I'm not cutting this vacation short," he said meaningfully. "Even if it means I have to take you out to the middle of the Pacific Ocean."

Feeling warm again, Diana quickened her step in order to catch up with Mike and Hannah, but Devlan's arm, still firmly around her waist, stopped her from going very far. His dark head bent down, and she felt his cheek press against her forehead as he spoke. "I'm glad you decided to come away with me, Diana."

Not ready to admit that she felt the same way, she regarded him cautiously. "I did it for Hannah. She's been working so hard. She really needs a break, and where can she play on a beach this time of year? Besides, Thanksgiving alone wouldn't be much fun."

"I don't care what your reasons were," he insisted. "All that matters is that you're here now. I have the whole crew decorating the ship, and our chef is baking the biggest turkey they could find down there."

She laughed. "Wow. Thank you."

"I plan on repairing that rotten evening and starting over again. It takes a rare woman to give a guy like me a second chance after our harsh words."

"I had nothing to lose," she whispered.

"We'll see about that," he countered.

As she pondered his last statement, Devlan ushered her along to the waiting jet. It was the same one they had flown in from Denver, and she glanced around with concern. The sleek white plane was large and luxurious inside, but smaller than the

131

commercial airliners she had previously flown in. Remembering her parents, she turned to Devlan with a worried frown.

"Is this safe to take over the ocean?"

Devlan threw back his head and laughed. "Of course. I wouldn't take you and Hannah on a plane that wasn't safe." Her dubious look prompted him to smile reassuringly. "This is a Falcon 900. It has three engines and can fly distances over four thousand miles, which makes it perfectly safe to take over water. Besides, I've had this jet for three-years now, Diana. I've flown everywhere in it. It's safe."

Diana gave him another worried glance before finally giving in and ducking through the open door. A beaming stewardess greeted her and sent a flirtatious smile towards Devlan.

"There's a bed in the back made up for the little one. Once we're at cruising altitude, she can rest there," she said to Diana. Then she looked past her and watched Devlan, who was making his way to his large leather chair behind the highly polished desk.

Diana smirked at him and found a seat next to Hannah on the long sofa in the back. The sleepy child pressed herself up against Diana's chest, and Diana wrapped her arms around her small shoulders. She pressed Hannah's head into the crook of her arm and smoothed her hair gently.

"Go to sleep," she whispered.

"I'm not tired," came the rebellious reply.

"Yes, you are," she said. She smiled soothingly once more. "We're going to have so much fun."

"I hope so, Mommy. I want to have fun."

Readjusting their positions, Diana urged Hannah to put her head down in her lap. The weary child did so, and Diana smoothed her hair away from her face with tender fingers. As the airplane slowly evened out, Hannah' eyes drifted closed, and she quickly fell asleep.

With Hannah settled, Diana took a moment to glance

around. Devlan was once again working. Two laptops were open in front of him, and he glanced between the two in rapid intervals. His long fingers typed while an occasional curse escaped his lips as he gazed at both screens before him. As Diana watched, she felt a flurry of emotions ranging from disappointment over his lack of attention to relief that he was giving her space.

She continued to glance around the pristine interior of the plane before her gaze landed upon Devlan's trusted bodyguard. Mike was now leaning back with his eyes closed in the plush seat across from his boss, his back facing her. With his seat in the reclined position, he appeared completely relaxed. His thick blond locks were windblown and free, unlike his usual impeccable appearance, and it appeared as if he too was looking forward to some time off.

The stewardess came along to offer her a glass of wine a short time later. She stopped for some time to chat with Devlan, but Diana noticed that he dismissed her quickly and went right back to work. Sporting a disappointed frown, the rejected woman returned with a warm blanket for Hannah before silently taking a seat in the front of the plane.

Diana was by herself, with no one to talk to. Already, they were over the clear blue expanse of water, and the monitor in her section of the plane was showing a Disney movie. She sighed. It was times like those that Diana wished she had a book, but, having none, she too closed her eyes.

It seemed as though she had just closed her eyes when she felt warm fingers gently stroking her cheek. Opening them reluctantly, Diana found Devlan standing before her with a wistful half-smile curving his lips. Her heart lurched in response, and she looked away quickly to turn her attention to the nearby window. As far as she could tell, they were still in the air, although the sun was fast setting in the western sky.

"Where are we?"

"Somewhere over the Pacific."

She frowned. "Are we almost there?"

"Yes."

Gently pushing her stretched out legs away, Devlan sat in the seat across from the sofa. Swiveling it around, he reached down and drew them onto his lap. She went still when his hands began a relaxing massage of her calves and ankles, but her tension did not last long. His strong fingers felt heavenly and were very persuasive. Just like the rest of him. Though her eyes drifted closed again, sleep was the farthest thing from her mind.

"What are you doing?" Diana murmured.

"Seducing you."

When her eyes flew open, Devlan released a throaty chuckle. His eyes twinkled in amusement when she sat up straight and jerked her legs away.

"Very funny," she snapped. "Why don't you try that with your stewardess? She seems more than willing."

"I would never get involved with an employee, Diana," he said, his eyes still dancing with delight. "As much as I appreciate your jealousy, I have to admit that woman doesn't interest me at all."

She scowled at him then turned back to look out the window, so he would not be able to see the tell-tale blush rising on her cheeks. Not to be ignored, he reached forward and caressed her knees, his thumbs stretching up to stroke the inside of her thighs. Though she wanted to pull away, she could not find the strength of will to do so. Instead, she reluctantly relented and watched the lazy patterns he traced on her legs.

"The last time we spoke ended badly," he commented.

"Yes it did," she agreed. "I'm sorry for being so stupid."

"Don't apologize. It was my fault. First Roxanne, and then… well, after I thought about it, I realized how easily it was to give you that impression. It hasn't exactly been a secret how much I desire you."

So there it was. She swallowed back her fear, knowing that to fight would be useless. "It was very arrogant of me to presume, but, for the record, I was willing."

"You know how crazy you make me, Diana," he said softly. "But I want you because you want me too, not because of a little bit of money."

Diana let out a short laugh. "That's not a small amount."

"You're worth every penny and more if you come to me of your own free will… It's just a matter of time."

The intensity in his voice gave rise to the familiar feeling of panic that stole through her belly. "I'm not sure I'm ready for that again."

"Don't worry, I'm looking forward to fixing that," he said with a chuckle.

She knew that she was not fooling either of them. He knew very well that their desire was mutual, and all he had to do was touch her, and she would melt in his arms. It may have been an oblivious move on her part, but her very presence on the airplane acknowledged her readiness to start over. When she was with him, her failed marriage was just a memory, a bad dream. Devlan's obvious admiration and yearning for her had the capability to wipe away those horrible years and give her back her confidence. So why did she hold back? Well, obviously she would lose her heart in a potentially temporary agreement. Was she strong enough to survive that?

Seeing her expressions change, Devlan sat back in his seat and spoke softly. "I really am sorry about what I said that night. I was shocked and angry…"

"I think we both made mistakes," she replied quickly. "I guess our assumptions were just a tad bit off."

"That's what we're going to fix."

When he spoke so confidently, Diana almost believed that he

could do anything. "I guess we'll see."

"We're going to make this work."

There was no hidden agenda behind his earnest blue gaze. All she saw was that familiar determination of a man who had no intentions of failing. He had made his goal very clear in his candid and honest way. At least she would be entering into an intimate relationship with no secrets. Her eyes were as open as his, so why could she not take advantage of this opportunity? Taking a deep breath, Diana studied him closely. Yes, she decided, she could go on. If it helped her get on with her life, she would take the chance. It was time she started enjoying life and enjoying Devlan.

Chapter 10

The flight took four hours, and with the time difference, it was evening in Hawaii when the airplane came to a smooth landing on Oahu. Under the lavender sky, the night air was balmy and filled with the scent of tropical flowers. The sea breeze was strong enough to stir Diana's hair, and she carelessly tucked some loose strands behind her ear. Across the air field, bright lights shined, and there they found a waiting helicopter with the pilot standing by.

Never one to enjoy flight, Diana was even more concerned about this contraption than she was of the small jet. While Mike strode ahead in his eagerness to get to the ship, Diana's footsteps slowed, and she ignored Devlan's sympathetic smile. She inspected the machinery with a cautious and hesitant eye.

"It won't bite you," he teased lightly.

"You never know," she replied.

Lifting Hannah into his arms, Devlan reached out with his free hand and captured her cool fingers. Before she could pull away, he lifted them to his lips and smiled encouragingly. They crossed the field to the chopper together and climbed within the small compartment.

"We'll be at the yacht in minutes," he promised. "It's just twenty miles off-shore. Then we'll get Hannah and you some dinner and tuck you into bed."

That was about all Diana heard above the roaring propellers.

She squeezed her eyes shut and clung to Hannah as the chopper lifted off the ground and sped out over the sea. All too soon, the lights on the ground changed to the deep blue of the ocean while Diana wondered how many helicopters went down on a weekly basis.

Fortunately, Devlan was right. It was a quick ride. Within minutes, she glanced below and saw the blinking lights of the waiting yacht beckoning to them. She sent Hannah a reassuring smile.

"How big is this boat of yours?" Diana yelled over the propellers.

Devlan squeezed her hand. "I'll give you a tour, personally."

She nodded and closed her eyes again as the chopper made a bumpy landing on the boat's upper deck. It took another few moments before the whine of the motor settled, and the doors were opened to allow them to exit.

Mike carried Hannah out, leaving Devlan to assist Diana to the safety of the deck. There were several people waiting in uniform dress beyond the helipad, and all of them wore matching smiles of welcome. Devlan made his way there, pulling Diana alongside him.

"Captain Adams, how are you?" Devlan asked with a broad grin. He reached forward and held out his hand, and the captain grasped it in a firm handshake.

"Glad to see you again, Mr. Doyle, sir. Welcome aboard."

"These are my guests," Devlan continued. "Diana Somerset... and this little beauty is Hannah. You already know Mike, of course."

The captain nodded curtly and gave them both polite smiles. "Welcome aboard *The Haven*, ladies. I hope your stay with us will be pleasant."

Diana smiled her thanks, but Hannah buried her face in Mike's shoulders. The cranky youngster was in no mood to socialize, and the captain noticed.

"Paolo, our first mate, will show you to the dining room, ladies. Our chef, Francois, has prepared a hot dog for Miss Hannah until he can consult with you on a menu for the week. I hope that is satisfactory?"

Diana glanced at Devlan, who nodded his approval. "I'll meet up with you on the main deck once you get Hannah to bed. Then I'll show you around the ship."

"Thank you, I'm sure that'll be fine," she answered the captain.

Paolo, an Italian born man with blond hair and blue eyes, bowed respectfully as he gestured for them to follow. His stilted English was somewhat hard to follow, but he spoke amiably about the ship as he led her through the main salon to the circular stairs. At the bottom of the first flight, he led them into the large, round dining room, once again holding out his hand for them to pass.

"Hannah's room is just down the stairs to the right," he finished, bowing out the room. "All the guest staterooms are down there."

Clinging to Hannah's hand, Diana took in the sight before her with awe. The room was surrounded by windows which overlooked the main deck. Though currently cast in shadow, she was fairly certain that the views afforded from this room could be breathtaking. It was deceptively large, and she took in the sight of the highly polished hardwood table with matching detailed chairs with dismay. More suited for a fancy banquet room, the table could easily seat fifteen, but only two places were set at the moment. A large platter of cheeses rested between the two settings, with a bottle of chilled wine and a single glass for her. Someone had gone to a lot of trouble for the two of them, and Diana felt a twinge of guilty pleasure.

While Diana and Hannah chose their seats, Paolo returned to ring a buzzer. Within moments, a stewardess arrived, carrying steaming plates with hot dogs and fries. "I poured milk for the lass, is that okay?"

Diana nodded and accepted the plate with a smile of thanks.

"My name's Betty. If you're needing anything, you just call on me," she said as she backed away.

"Thank you, Betty."

Hannah reached for her plate and drink like a fiend, and Diana realized that it had been hours since they had eaten last. Hannah had slept nearly the entire flight, and lunch had been hours before that.

"You poor baby," she murmured, cutting up the hot dog. "You must be starved."

She nodded enthusiastically. "I'm really hungry, Mommy."

"Well, eat all up, and we'll put you to bed."

"But we're supposed to have fun."

"Yes," she said nodding. "We'll have lots of fun in the morning. Tomorrow is Thanksgiving, and we'll have turkey for dinner."

"Will Uncle Devvie be there, too?"

"I would think so."

"Good," she said smiling happily. "I like Uncle Devvie a lot."

"I'm glad you like him, Hannah. He's a nice man who likes you a lot."

"He likes you too. I want him to be my new daddy."

Diana froze. "New daddy?"

"Yes, can he be my new daddy?"

"Jeez, Hannah, I don't know."

"But I like him. He's not mean."

"Mean? What do you mean by that?"

"Uncle Devvie makes you smile and doesn't yell at you like Daddy did."

Diana glanced out the window, too stunned to answer. Fortunately for her, Hannah did not press the issue. Instead, she dug into her meal and devoured it in record time.

"That was a yummy hot dog," she said as she smothered a burp.

Although she smiled down at Hannah, Diana was concerned with her growing attachment to Devlan. It would be okay for the child to enjoy Devlan, but for her to say she wanted him as her daddy, well that was worrisome. Fathers could not be replaced that quickly, and despite what had happened in the past, Peter was her father and always would be. Did Hannah want to replace him because of the way he had treated her mother? The concern would not leave her as she settled Hannah in the pink and white stateroom, for she realized that she had not considered the impact a new man would have on her daughter's life before now.

The room was small but perfect for a child Hannah's age. Devlan had obviously been hard at work to charm her yet again, for the second twin bed was loaded once more with toys and games to keep her busy during their time at sea. On the desk next to the TV/DVD player stood a small stack of movies, and there were coloring books and markers on the blotter.

Although Hannah was wild with excitement, Diana was able to calm her down long enough to prepare her for bed. While they were eating, the stewardess had unpacked Hannah's belongings and placed them neatly in the dresser across the room, and once Hannah had located her nightclothes, Diana tucked her in with a quick story. With promises of great fun in the morning, the door was shut soundly, and the light switched off.

Hannah's words still rang in her head as she returned to the main deck. There was no one around when she made her way to the back of the ship, and briefly she remembered hearing how discreet servants were. Appearing magically when they were needed, yet nowhere to be seen when they were not. A strange feeling of authority filled her. There were servants here to answer every one of her needs. She was with a very powerful man, a man who paid these people to cater to her. She could so easily take advantage of that. According to Kathy, most of Devlan's acquaintances did – everyone except for Devlan. As she had seen with her own eyes, he had retained a humility that seemed so out of character for his lifestyle, and he treated everyone with respect. It was merely another of the many wonderful qualities that made him so special, so unique.

Careful, the voice in her head warned her.

Devlan was waiting for her in the back of the ship. His dark hair was slicked back, still damp from a recent shower, and his jeans were slightly wrinkled from being crammed into a suitcase. Coupled with his short-sleeved casual shirt and sneakers, he had the appearance of being an ordinary man, even though they were on a huge yacht off the Hawaiian Islands.

"Would you like one?"

He held a beer in his hand, though there was a bottle of wine on the seat next to him. It rested on a tray in a bucket of ice, with two crystal glasses arranged with a red rose. Her heart fluttered in her chest when she saw the romantic arrangement. "No thank you, but I might try the wine."

Devlan gracefully poured her a glass and pressed the stem into her cool fingers. "So I see Hannah's all set. Are you ready for your tour?"

Diana took a long sip of the red liquid for courage and almost purred at the smooth, buttery taste. "Yes, sleeping like a baby. Ooh, this is good."

His eyes crinkled when he smiled and nodded his agreement. A lock of his damp hair fell forward when his head dipped, and she noticed that he seemed to have the thickest hair she had ever seen on a man. She had the urge to run her fingers through it again, but he beat her to it by pushing the wayward strands hastily back.

Dragging her eyes away, Diana took a deep breath. They

were almost completely alone now. Mike had long since retreated to his room, and the crew had all gone about their duties. That left just the two of them to enjoy the silence of the ocean. It was a strange feeling, one that left her feeling heady and reckless.

Off in the distance, she could see the lights on land. There were many different colored lights at varying elevations, giving it a kaleidoscope effect. Hotels and houses, restaurants and shopping plazas well lit within the tropical paradise.

"Which island is that?"

"Oahu," he said, coming up beside her. "Tonight, we'll sail up to Niihau and start our tour there. Niihau is privately owned, but we can see it from a distance. Then, this week, we'll keep heading south until we reach the big island."

Diana nodded and again stared out at the lights. Excitement filled her as she stared out at sea. She had always wanted to travel, but never in a million years had she dreamed of being in a situation like this. This was a dream. It had to be. However, with every passing day, she was growing more and more frightened of waking up.

Devlan's hands came to rest on her shoulders, and for the first time she took the initiative and leaned back against him. Yes, there were many worse places to be than being held by Devlan. A warm feeling filled her heart, and for the first time in many months, she felt happy.

"You want to take a look around, or are you too tired?"

"Tired? I slept on the plane, remember? I could dance all night," she joked.

"That could be arranged," he said, pointing to the full entertainment center.

"I was kidding," she said with a light laugh. "Maybe another time."

Taking her hand, he gave her a slight tug. "Come on, let's start top to bottom."

She smiled and followed him up the stairs to the helipad and then up one more flight to the bridge. A gasp of pleasure escaped her when she saw the large covered spa directly across from the wet bar. Plush seating and lounge chairs were also deftly placed for comfortable sunbathing.

"This is very private."

"Yes, to everything but airplanes." His eyes spoke volumes when he turned and gave her figure a sweeping gaze. "And Hannah."

She laughed. "Ah, you learn quickly."

Taking another sip of her wine, she noticed that Devlan had carried the bottle in his free hand as soon as he lifted it to top off her glass. He winked at her playfully.

The next deck sported the motor boat as well as two jet skis and other assorted water game equipment. There was also an outside dining table. Not accustomed to eating in such a formal setting as earlier, she delightedly planned on sharing her meals with Hannah there instead.

Beyond the table was a set of doors which Devlan led her through. On the other side was an enclosed lounge, with plush blue carpeting and mirrored ceilings. The long bar was fully stocked, yet Devlan made no move to stop and refill his drink. Instead, he placed down his empty and reached for another glass.

"Let's finish this off, okay?"

Once he poured himself some of the wine, he again refilled her glass. She watched him with a wry smile. If she did not know any better, she would swear he was trying to get her drunk. However, she did know him better and appreciated his attempt to put her at ease.

She smiled shyly. "Thank you."

Further down, the salon on the main deck sported a thick white carpet and attached wall-to-wall seating strewn with billowy pillows. There was a full entertainment center, and the mirrored bar had brass trimmings and full backed stools.

"There's a library of movies on board for Hannah," he commented as they passed.

"You didn't have to do that."

He smiled. "I didn't have to, but I wanted to. There will be times when she's bound to be bored."

In the corner behind one of the pillars she found a writing desk with an ocean view. A full computer was in sleep mode. It was so easy to imagine Devlan in this setting, entertaining high-powered officials of all nationalities here.

"This is just fabulous," she teased. "You can watch television while you work."

"There's more," he announced proudly.

Passing the galley and stairs to the crew's quarters, they went back to the round dining room, now in darkness, and again her breath caught at the night view. The ocean was a pool of ink, with gentle waves stirring against the bow of the ship. Off in the distance, she could see the land, still an oasis of glittering lights, and smaller craft tethered closer to shore. High rises and smaller homes dotted the landscape as far as she could see. It was so different from the peaceful solitude on the ship.

"This must be spectacular in the daylight," she murmured.

"It is," he said with a nod. He followed her gaze to look out at the lights. "I love it here."

"How long have you owned this yacht?"

"Four or so years. I really don't get to it all that often, maybe once or twice a year. It's an expensive toy, but I keep it because I still have hopes of using it more often."

She walked to the windows and leaned forward to get a good look. Devlan followed, wearing a smile of pure delight. Embracing her from behind, his chin came down on the top of her head. He inhaled deeply, and then let it all out in a deep sigh. Together they gazed at the island in the distance, their silence peaceful and serene for the first time.

The wine was working its magic. Despite her nervousness, she could not help but begin to relax. He noticed immediately and slowly turned her around to the circle of his arms.

"I'm glad you're here, Diana," he whispered. "I'm glad to have you and Hannah on my boat."

"Me too," she admitted reluctantly.

"Good."

Smiling impishly, she glanced up at him. "After all, it's a good experience for Hannah. She's never been here before."

Chuckling, he pulled her even closer. Her hips brushed against his thighs, and she could feel the hard strength there. Ever so slowly, his hands began to trace the outline of her back. She closed her eyes and leaned into him.

"Ever since our disastrous first date I've been planning this trip," he continued, his hands sliding lower then back up again.

"You have?"

His mouth was mere inches above hers, and she almost stepped on tiptoes to reach it. Yet his hands felt so good that she did not want to disturb their wandering. As if reading her mind, he lowered his head and brushed his lips against hers. Heat filled her belly, and her muscles tightened in answer to his teasing. She angled her chin higher, but Devlan did not deepen his kiss. Hovering over her mouth, his voice took on a deeper pitch.

"Yes, and I've imagined a million times throwing you on that very table and making you scream with pleasure."

Inhaling sharply, Diana opened her eyes and looked at the polished table. For a moment, erotic thoughts and scenes filled her mind. Images of them together with their limbs entwined caused her stomach to lurch violently. Then she glanced up and noticed the ceiling for the first time. Set inside a slight depression was a large, round mirror that ran the full length of the table. Biting her lip, she turned back to Devlan. His eyes were dancing, and he gave her his wide boyish grin. Unable to resist, she laughed.

"God, I love it when you laugh," he said earnestly.

Gathering her hand in his, he led her down the circular stairs to the stateroom deck. She began to feel nervous again, unsure what he planned to do with her but knowing without a doubt she did not want the night to end.

At the bottom of the carpeted landing, they came to the junction of the staterooms. Hannah's room was to their right. There was no noise coming forth, and all seemed settled for the night. Devlan looked at her questioningly. In the dim light in the narrow hallway he seemed taller and more sinister, and her breathing became shallow and quick. One of them would have to make the move to end their prolonged chess game of avoidance. She just did not know which one of them would.

"All that's left are the staterooms," he said softly.

"I've seen Hannah's, but I've no idea where mine is." Her voice trembled slightly, though from fear or excitement she did not know.

"Where do you want it to be, Diana?"

Her heart, previously beating fast, began to pound in earnest in her chest. He was leaving it all up to her this time. It was time to choose. Surprisingly, she wanted to scream at him to stop being so considerate and take control like he always did. That way, when all was said and done she would have someone to blame other than herself. However, despite the desire illuminated in his smoky gaze, there was absolutely no force coming from him.

"I don't know." She bit her lip. "I'm so confused. I just wish you'd help me."

"Stay with me," he said quickly. "The crew is discreet; no one has to know. Diana, stop this torture and stay with me."

The feeling in his voice betrayed the depth of his longing, and it filled her with a strange joy. Though he was leaving the decision in her hands, he had not been lying when he said he wanted her desperately. The realization was all she needed.

"Yes," she breathed.

With a triumphant smile, Devlan's head dipped swiftly in a move that took her breath away. Before she even caught her breath, she was kissing him back with the same urgency. Her arms wound around his neck tightly, and she pressed her full length against his. Without another word, he bent and gathered her into his arms. Feeling as light as a fairy, she was momentarily soaring through the air, and she gasped with delight.

His stateroom was right next to the stairs, and he deftly opened the door and switched on the lights before he allowed her feet to touch the ground. As her body slid against his, he groaned aloud. The familiar determined look appeared on his face as he gazed down at her.

"Do this because you want to, not because you think you've some stupid debt to pay."

Diana reached up to cup his face in her palms. "I'd be lying if I didn't say that I want this as bad as you, Devlan… It's just that I've made mistakes before. Big ones."

With a pained look on his face, he grasped one of her hands and placed it over his thundering heart. "Does this feel like a mistake to you?"

"No. Yes. I don't know," she whispered.

"How can something that feels so strong be a mistake, Diana?" he pressed urgently.

"I'm just so scared."

"Good lord woman, how can you be afraid of me? Don't you know the power you have over me?"

"Um, no," she whispered.

"It's time I show you then."

The door closed behind him with a kick from his foot, and suddenly they were alone. No interruptions this time. Out to sea, it was just the two of them, and Hannah sleeping peacefully across the hall. L.A. was a memory, thousands of miles away. Tonight, it was only two people, eager to explore each other's bodies, discover likes and dislikes, and ease the ache of unfulfilled longing.

Though casual encounters were new to Diana, it all seemed so natural with Devlan. His soft encouragement mingled with his awe when he touched her made her feel like a goddess instead of a failure. What she had done to capture his intense interest was beyond her reasoning, but he touched her with the gentleness and reverence of a man who treasured her completely. Diana could not help but melt into him. Tomorrow would be the day to regret her actions. Tonight, he was finally hers.

Much later, Devlan dimmed the lights and drew her close. His strength filled her with contentment while the light silk sheet felt cool against her burning skin. Unable to resist him, she snuggled against his chest, a move that brought a satisfied sigh from him. His arm tightened around her.

"Stay with me tonight," he whispered. "All night. Sleep beside me."

"I couldn't move even if I wanted to," she admitted.

"Good. Because I don't think I could either, and following you to another stateroom might be impossible."

She could not hide her giggle in the darkness. Not only had he just shown her how gentle a lover could be, but his tireless desire had nearly rocked her world off its axis. She felt as though she had died and gone to Heaven, and she was pleased that he felt as satisfied.

"You'd follow me if I left?"

"I finally got you where I've wanted you for forever. There's no way I'd let you leave again."

She heard his chuckle against her ear and placed a lingering kiss over the spot his heart beat most strongly. For the first time since her parents had died, Diana felt treasured. Everything about the way he had touched her that evening, even the way he was smoothing her hair down her back, was reverential. This was one special moment, and she knew in her heart she would treasure it always. Amazed with his gentle spirit, Diana drifted off to sleep feeling fortunate instead of scared that she had been able to experience it.

Chapter 11

Diana's eyes flickered before her long lashes fluttered open. The room was dark. It was the middle of the night. All was quiet except for the soft purr of the ship's engines. They were heading south back to Oahu on their second night of the vacation of her life, and the yacht was moving smoothly beneath her. All appeared to be well. So what had disturbed her?

Snuggling back under the covers, Diana closed her eyes and tried to relax back into sleep. Both she and Devlan had collapsed into bed that night, exhausted from their magnificent turkey dinner and quick sightseeing trip with Hannah to Kauai that day. Like a true family man, Devlan had escorted her and Hannah around enthusiastically, taking pleasure in Hannah's excitement and happy chatter until she had finally crashed into a deep sleep. Diana and Devlan were not long on her heels, and she now longed to find that deep, dreamless sleep that she enjoyed just moments ago.

Then she felt Devlan's hands on her. It was he who had disturbed her sleep, and he was pressing insistently against her back. She opened for him drowsily, and she sighed in pleasure as he began to move inside her. Even though she was still half-asleep, her body responded to the feel of him as if from pure instinct.

"Jesus, Diana."

Coming fully awake, Devlan suddenly went tense against her,

but it was too late. Unable to stop, his body stiffened then shuddered as he found his release. He buried his face in her neck with a ragged groan.

"Well, that was a completely reckless and foolish thing to do," he said softly into her hair.

Fully awake now too and feeling fairly stung, Diana rolled away from him with a scowl. "Reckless?"

"Yeah, I don't know what happened."

"It's okay," she snapped. "I'm clean."

"What?" he asked, his brow furrowing in confusion.

"Don't you think I immediately got tested after Peter?"

"What? Wait a minute." He reached for her but she resisted. "That's not what I meant... aw, hell!"

Devlan reached over to switch on the bedside lamp. Groaning, she squinted in the sudden bright light and brought a hand to shade her eyes. The relaxed feeling from a few moments ago had just about completely gone away. She grimaced.

Devlan was frowning at her, but his tousled hair and drowsy eyes softened the effect. His finger came up to trace a small scar under her eye. She turned away from the knowledge of what was coming.

"Why did you stay with him?"

She sighed deeply. "I don't want to discuss it."

"We're going to have to sooner or later," he said.

Diana shrugged and rolled back onto her side. "Then we'll discuss it another time. Just not tonight."

"He hurt you, I know. I would never treat you the way he did." Devlan tugged on her shoulder, once more rolling her onto her back.

"Then why do you care so much?" she asked. "You made a simple mistake, but it's fine."

Devlan shook his head. "It's not that, Diana. Other things could happen..." He fell silent, his blue gaze studying her intently.

When she did not respond, he spoke softly. "Like a baby. What if you got pregnant?"

"I see," she whispered, feeling tears fill her eyes. "I wasn't really concerned about that. I'm sorry."

In truth she could not blame him for his hesitation. A child could be confining for a man like him. Even though he truly seemed to love Hannah, the fact remained that he was single at present.

Oh, but he would make a fine father. The attention that he lavished upon Hannah was so wonderful for her, certainly better than the spare moments Peter had granted her. It was amazing how she realized after seeing Devlan with her daughter just how shallow Peter's parenting skills went. He had always been considered a doting father, but to him Hannah was only his little beauty. While he never reprimanded her, he never took the time to get down on the floor and interact with her either.

"It's not your fault, it was mine. But that sort of decision should be thoroughly discussed and agreed upon by both of us if the time came. Don't you agree?"

"I do agree, wholeheartedly," she said softly.

Bending his head, Devlan pressed a warm kiss on her shoulder. "At any rate, I'm so very sorry, Diana."

"For what?"

"Every day, I wish I had known what was going on with Peter." He took a deep breath. "Please believe me when I say that had I known, I would've put a stop to it a long time ago."

She snorted. "You would've been too busy to bother with him."

His face lowered to hers, and he studied her with deadly serious eyes. "No, I wouldn't. You've absolutely no idea how quickly I would've snatched you away from him."

"Oh." She could feel a softening in her face that belied her attempt to be emotionless and hard. The way he was staring at her, as though she was the most exquisite thing in the world to him, inundated her with joy. She was on the verge of letting him in for good; she was so close to trusting again. It was not difficult to imagine Devlan coming to her rescue. She could easily believe he would have intervened had he known the truth.

"I'm sorry for the way he treated you. I'm sorry that he scarred your beautiful face." Devlan bent to kiss her small scar. His lips were soft and moist, and his voice lightened as he continued. "And I'm sorry I was groping you in the middle of the night. It was a very ungentlemanly thing to do, but I just can't seem to get enough of you."

A small smile erased the concerned lines on Diana's face, and she reached up to hug Devlan tight. "Don't apologize. It was a nice way to wake up."

He chuckled. "It was an amazing way to wake up, actually."

Reaching over her head, he shut off the light again before returning her hug and pulling her onto his broad chest. He kissed her one more time.

"Go to sleep," he said softly. "I'll try not to do that again."

Diana closed her eyes, listening to the steady thumping of his heart and the rhythmic music of his breathing. Devlan was fast burrowing his way into her heart, and she knew that she was helpless to stop it. Perhaps it was that he had come into her life in such a lonely period. Or perhaps it was that he showered her with kindness when so few did. But whatever the reason, the one fact remained: she was fast losing her heart to the big, softhearted man.

Foolish, that voice reminded her.

Oh, she agreed with that voice, and she knew she needed to protect herself from hurt again. The question was just how she was going to do it. Devlan was making it so hard. How could she refuse the man who treated her as if she were a princess?

By making sure she remained clear that it was only

temporary. She and Hannah would be heading back to Colorado in a few short weeks, and what she needed to do was keep reminding them both of that fact.

~

The surf was high due to a storm further out at sea. Though it had passed south of the islands and continued east, Diana watched the waves cautiously as Devlan hefted Hannah up high over his shoulders and ran towards the pounding surf with a loud yell. Hannah was shrieking with delight, and her hands were balled into fists in his thick hair. With one last shout, Devlan rushed into the large crashing waves where he dunked himself and Hannah with him.

Both came to the surface sputtering. Hannah was clinging to Devlan like a monkey. Although coughing, her laughter was audible all the way back to the towels. Diana watched nervously from the shore. Shielding her eyes from the glaring sun, she worried what would happen to Hannah if Devlan did not calm himself down. Even though they were at one of the safest beaches in the island chain, Diana feared the waves were still large enough to sweep her away.

"Will you go get him?" She glanced at Mike. Having joined them on this day at the beach, he lounged on a towel nearby, totally at ease with Devlan's actions.

One fair brow raised in question as he lazily glanced over at her.

"Aren't you supposed to be a bodyguard? Can't you," she waved her hands, "guard his body?"

He raised his sunglasses and stared at the two in the water. "Leave them alone, Mrs. Somerset. They're both having a blast. No one needs rescuing here."

No one except me, Diana thought, shooting a peevish frown

at Mike as he lay back down to improve his tan. She stared out at the waves again, remembering how just that morning Devlan had again proven his infinite generosity and caring.

Early that morning, he had slipped away to pick up Hannah's new physical therapist in Honolulu. They were back by breakfast, much to Diana's surprise. To top it all off, he showed her the fantastic resume and introduced her to a most charming and cheerful young woman. Diana was surprised that she immediately liked the woman he had hired and had to admit that there was a reason Devlan was so successful in business. He was a good judge of character.

In addition to his thoughtfulness, he was wonderful with Hannah, attentive to her every need, and he truly seemed to draw pleasure in being with her. As she watched Devlan help Hannah move in the water, Diana was filled with so many more tender emotions for the man that she could not put into words. It was plain as day that she was falling hard for him.

Yes, she loved him.

Returning her attention to her book, Diana blinked back sudden tears. Falling in love with him should not have been a surprise, for she knew from the start that she would have a hard time resisting him. He was so charming and funny, and it had been so easy to let her guard slip. Diana could not remember a time when she had laughed so hard and long, and Devlan made her do it with utter ease. He had totally swept her off her feet in just a few days.

Now she needed to decide how to handle it.

Run away.

No, she could not run away. She was on a boat in the middle of the ocean, far away from cold and snowy Denver, but she would have to do something quick.

"Wow, Mommy, did you see what Uncle Devvie did?"

Hannah and her wet body were suddenly deposited on

Diana's lap, and she shot up with a startled yelp. Forgetting her somber thoughts, she watched as Devlan sat down on the towel next to her and shook out his hair. She was sprayed with the cool ocean water that caused goose bumps to rise on her flesh. She scowled, but Hannah giggled and imitated him, and together the two soaked Diana's warm skin.

"What are you two doing?" Diana shrieked.

She lifted Hannah off her lap and placed her next to Devlan. Grinning, the youngster whispered something in Devlan's ear. That was the last straw. Coming to her feet, Diana stood before them with her hands on her hips while Mike laughed from a safe distance away. With a fierce frown, she glared at them all, ignoring Devlan's appreciative stare. His gaze swept her from head to toe and took in the revealing bikini with approval.

Eyes twinkling, he nudged Hannah. "Tell your Mommy how pretty she looks today, and she's guaranteed to forgive you."

Hannah giggled again and stared up at her mother with wide, innocent eyes. "Mommy, you're very pretty."

Pointing her finger at Hannah's nose, Diana frowned as fiercely as she could. "Flattery will get you nowhere, young lady."

"But it is true," Devlan said with a wink.

She glared at him, but his wide smile left her feeling joyful inside instead of angry. Unable to resist, she relented and smiled back.

Still smiling happily, Devlan glanced at the three of them. "I hate to change the subject, but it's getting late. Are you ready to go?"

He came to his feet and began drying off his chest with the towel. Diana watched his smooth movements but hastily turned away when he turned back to her. "One second. I'll get our things," she said quickly.

Nudging Mike in the leg with one foot to force him up, Devlan wrapped the towel around his damp waist before briskly drying Hannah off as well. Mike carried everything the short walk down to the dock where they tied up the boat, while Devlan scooped up Hannah. Diana watched with her heart in her throat as her daughter wrapped her arms around his neck and held him tightly. It seemed all too soon that they were piling in to head back to the ship when she wanted to stay forever.

As they headed out to sea, Diana sent one last glance behind her. She watched the secluded area disappear with a sad eye. It was there she realized that she was in love with Devlan, and that would stay with her forever. No matter what happened to their relationship, Diana would always remember that short strand of beach, and the few moments of pure happiness that had touched her soul.

~

Francois Rat bowed politely and handed Diana the menu for the following day's meals. She smiled and thanked him again, all the while telling him to call her Diana. It was a futile gesture, and she watched the eccentric chef with the wild gray hair bow from the room with a bemused smile. Heading to the lounge to wait for Hannah to wake from her nap, Diana wondered yet again if she could ever get used to someone catering to her every need. At present, it was disconcerting.

She had just kicked off her sandals and reclined across the soft cushions of the sofa when the steward arrived carrying a glass of wine.

"Can I put on some music for you, Mrs. Somerset?"

"Thank you, Justin," she said, accepting the glass.

With a returning smile, he crossed the carpeted room on silent feet to the entertainment center and inserted a CD. Before she knew it, she was reclining to the music of "The Nutcracker". With a sigh of resignation, Diana accepted that he was doing his job and thanked him again before he stole from the room. The dark-headed college student left as quietly as he had entered, leaving Diana alone with her thoughts, and, of course, the menu beckoned.

Devlan was working hard in the library off their suite. She had been in there once, which had been enough. The room was fully equipped with computer, fax, satellite phone, and all sorts of devices she had no idea what they were or how to use them. While she completely agreed with Mike that Devlan needed to spend more time relaxing, he had made it clear that even while he was spending time with her and Hannah he still had to report in to work. There was a reason why the man had so much money – he worked for it. Kathy had not been kidding when she said that was all he did.

That he was enclosed in the electronics room served to remind Diana that they owed him so much. To let him get his work done was a small price to pay for such a wonderful vacation. Even if it meant she was left alone. Mike had retired to take a nap, the crew was busy preparing dinner and their next move, and Hannah's new physical therapist was unpacking her belongings in the stateroom next to Hannah's. That was the stateroom that was supposed to be hers, she thought with a flutter in her belly.

No matter what happened, she had to admit that this trip was truly an incredible experience. Though the attention from the crew was unnerving, she was smart enough to realize that she should enjoy it while she could. Devlan may be with her now, but that would not always be the case. For now, she could live her little fairytale dreams that she never realized she had, but instead of getting too comfortable and wishing for her happily ever after, she needed to use her quiet times to make a plan for when they went their separate ways.

She still could not trust him completely.

"Where's Mr. Doyle?" Mike asked. Fresh from his nap, he sauntered into the room and threw himself into a chair across from her, stretching his legs out before him.

Thrusting aside her thoughts, Diana sat upright and pasted a smile on her face. "He got a message. He's working."

She caught the flicker of exasperation in his eyes before he changed the subject. "Is the menu okay?"

Diana reached for it again and read it aloud. "Grilled salmon with Francois' special sauce, angel hair pasta with pineapples, papayas and mangoes, oven-roasted potatoes and white wine." She looked up at Mike with a playful smirk. "What more could you ask for?"

Mike grinned. "My thoughts exactly. It's a wonder I keep my trim figure."

Diana laughed and handed him the menu. "I can probably get Hannah to eat most of it, but there are a few mysterious things I doubt she'd even try. Francois tells me to make a list of things to buy her, but I don't want him to go out of his way like that."

"It's no trouble," Mike said with a shrug. "Besides, it gives the man a chance to get off the ship every now and then… I think everyone is so happy that Mr. Doyle is actually taking time to relax with you instead of working with a bunch of old men that they would walk the plank if you asked them to."

A small smile curved her lips as she envisioned the sight of the crew walking the plank. To think that it was her causing such a change in him was flattering and frightening at the same time. "I'm glad to help. It's just awkward to feel like you're taking and taking – all the time."

"I know what you mean, but I certainly have gotten used to it," Mike agreed cheerfully. "I see you're working on your tan."

She glanced down at her arms, which were fast becoming a light brown. Her legs too were starting to darken in color. "We've seen so much these past two days… Waimea Canyon and Na Pali Coast in Kauai, Waikiki and Pearl Harbor yesterday – well, you know. I've been outside, but not necessarily working on my tan."

"You look healthier."

"Thanks, Mike, you too." She laughed, her blue eyes twinkling. "Although you have more freckles than I."

As Mike looked down with a scowl, Hannah's new physical therapist entered the lounge. She was a small young woman, with large brown eyes and closely cropped brown hair. She sported a hesitant smile until Diana came to her feet and welcomed her in.

"I love 'The Nutcracker'," she said approvingly.

"Me too," Diana said. "It was always one of my favorites. My mother took me up to Boston once to see it when I was a kid. It was the most beautiful ballet I had ever seen, and it's stayed with me. One day, I'd like to take Hannah."

Mike cocked his head to the side, listening astutely to their conversation. It occurred to her that Mike may not have been introduced to her yet. She smiled in apology.

"Mike O'Hare, have you met Lani Matthews? She's here to help Hannah's leg get better."

Mike nodded politely and held out his hand, but he retreated to the back of the room while Diana and Lani shared small talk.

"He's so stiff," Lani remarked, nodding her head towards Mike.

"Not really. He just takes his job very seriously," Diana said.

"You can still do your job and have fun at it. That's my motto anyway. It also helps the patients when you make it fun. Today Hannah and I had such a good time, and she didn't even seem to notice the discomfort as much."

"Oh, Lani, I'm so glad to hear that," Diana said. "I mean, she's been so good and doesn't seem to be having nightmares like they warned me, but I still worry. She's been through so much."

"I know," Lani said with a sympathetic smile. "And it helps when they have someone who can relate to their confusion and loss."

"I hope you're right," Diana whispered.

"You have an exceptional daughter, and I'm happy to be

here. She's a hard worker."

"I'll make sure I tell her that you said so."

"She's going to do great."

Lani smiled encouragingly and continued to smile straight through dinner. Eager to chat, she was very attentive to Hannah, and Hannah was excited to have someone new to show all her presents to. The pair hit it off, and Lani good-naturedly went along with Hannah after dinner to play with her dolls.

Devlan watched it all and merely shook his head in wonder when the pair slipped away, but he was quick to capitalize on the missing distraction. No sooner had they left the dining room than he was reaching for Diana and leading her to the salon to watch a movie. Diana followed happily and tried not to see how easily their activity could become a nightly habit.

Justin and Betty had dimmed the overhead lights and lit candles to add a bit of romance to the room. Stretching lengthwise along the sofa, Devlan pulled her onto his lap.

"I missed you this afternoon," she said as she snuggled into his chest.

"I know what you mean. I can't believe I went three hours without seeing you," he teased.

Chuckling, Diana reached for the remote and leaned back against him. Though she knew he was teasing her, she could not stop the thrill his words gave her any more than she could stop the fantasies of this dream becoming a reality. However, reality was always close by, and they were just about to start the movie when Devlan's phone rang again. Straightening slightly, he pressed it against his ear but refused to let Diana pull away. She closed her eyes and listened to the deep timbre of his voice through his chest.

"Tomorrow?" He asked, sounding slightly irritated. "We're going to Molokai tomorrow. What? Maui? You couldn't...? All right, I'll meet him there. Thanks Kathy, I know you tried."

As he hung up the phone, he let out an exasperated sigh.

"What was that all about?" Diana asked.

His lips nuzzled the top of her head. "I have to go to Maui tomorrow. Business meeting on the green."

"Golf?"

"Yes."

"So? That sounds like fun."

"I haven't enjoyed a vacation in far too long. It's been great to get away and be with you and Hannah." Devlan sighed deeply. "It would be more fun to visit Molokai with you. It's one of the quietest islands here, and the most beautiful."

Feeling a twinge of guilt, Diana straightened. "Look, Devlan, we don't have to stop at every island. I know you're a very busy man. You've done so much for us; we're having a great time."

"I want you to go to Molokai with me. There are some beaches there that people rarely set foot on, which means privacy for us," he said pointedly.

"So we'll do it another day and skip an island further down."

The room fell silent as he toyed with her idea. Almost absently, his fingers went to her white cotton blouse and slowly the buttons fell open to reveal the pink bikini top. He glanced down and stared appreciatively. "Did I tell you just how beautiful you look in pink?" Devlan asked huskily.

Pushing his hand away, Diana ignored the flutter in her chest. "Have fun tomorrow, Devlan. Enjoy the day without your poor relatives."

His hand came up to cup her cheek, and his fingers stroked lightly before he drew her down once more. "I'd rather be with you and Hannah."

"We'll be here when you get back," she said with a teasing smile.

"You better be."

The sheer possessiveness she heard in his tone took her by surprise, for there was a depth of emotion that she was not accustomed to hearing from him. However, it also sent those familiar warning bells off in her mind. So he would go to the ends of the earth for her today, she thought, but what would happen tomorrow? More importantly, would there even be a tomorrow? That was still the greatest unknown.

~

It was a beautiful day of eighty degrees or so. The bright blue sky and warm sun shone down on their heads, warming them through their lightweight clothes. Glittering off in the distance, the aqua colored water contrasted sharply with the emerald green course. However, Devlan was not noticing the gently rolling green and well-placed palms. Instead, he stared out at the course impatiently. It was already nearing lunch, and they had only completed three holes. Not to mention that Hugh Davis, Hollywood director and successful leading man, had yet to reach the point of this critical meeting that could not be changed, no matter what.

Hugh was a handsome man in his mid-thirties, with golden brown hair and cheerful brown eyes. After making a start on Broadway, he had broken into film by starring in one of his own productions. When that project had succeeded beyond everyone's expectations, he had moved behind the camera as well. Since then, he had been nominated for an Oscar, received a Golden Globe and picked up an award at one of the European film festivals. A smart man, Hugh had made many friends in Hollywood, and his immense popularity had not come from rushing into things.

Kathy had told him that it was urgent that Devlan meet with Hugh today, and yet he was casual and laidback, purposely avoiding the issue. With other things on his mind, mainly Diana and Hannah, Devlan had enough of the small chat and decided to get down to business.

"So, what's up, Hugh? Why were you so urgent to see me?"

The other man straightened and shot Devlan a wide grin. "I have a favor to ask you."

"What kind of favor? Financial backing?"

"A friend of mine wrote a book back in college. Never published, just couldn't get his foot in the door, but boy is it a strong novel."

"Okay," he said carefully. This was not new to him. He was approached frequently from people who needed help. However, usually he would not interrupt his vacation for a sales pitch. His frustration deepened.

"Yeah, it is strong. Made even me cry."

Devlan chuckled. That was not so hard to believe. After all, the man was an actor. "What's it about?"

"Husband cheats, get AIDS, dies. Mother and small son left alone. No money, no friends, you know, all the tear-jerking stuff. She fights for her son, does whatever she can to get them out of poverty. Then mother finds out she has breast cancer. Dies. Leaves son all by himself. Like I said, a real tear-jerker."

"Sounds like TV to me, not big screen." Devlan frowned thoughtfully. The idea was appealing to him. It struck a chord within him since it was very close to what Hannah and Diana had gone through. Real life experience.

"That was my thought exactly." Hugh grinned from ear to ear. "Like a woman's network."

"I don't know anything about television."

"But you've worked with the networks before. You have connections." He grinned sheepishly. "I don't."

Devlan shook his head. "You'd have no trouble selling one of your projects."

"It's not a chance I'm willing to take."

He could understand his hesitation. If he were rejected once, it would be all over for him. Meanwhile, Devlan would have nothing to lose. At this point, he would do just about anything to get this game over with. "Do you have a script yet?"

"No, but I've spoken to a few good screenwriters about a screenplay."

"Send it to me when you get it. I'd like to give it a read before I agree to anything."

"You got it man," Hugh said. After a moment, he threw back his head and laughed. "I can't wait to start working with you. This is going to be great."

"I don't usually do this. I've got a company to run."

"I know. This will be a huge favor for me, and I won't let you down. I owe you one."

It was Devlan's turn to smile. "Yes you do… especially when you interrupt my vacation."

"You won't regret this. I promise."

He set his ball and tee down and squeezed his date's rump. His excitement was infectious and Devlan smiled too as Hugh swung nicely. They watched his ball land directly in front of the next hole while his companion, a young blonde who hung all over him, giggled and jumped enthusiastically. Frowning at her loud display, Devlan set his ball down. That was what he liked about Diana. There were no games. She gave him what she had with no drama or deceit. Everything about her was wholesome and real, including her body. Unfortunately, he reminded himself to concentrate too late, and his ball sliced to the right again.

"Wow, you're just not in the game today, are you?"

Devlan shook his head and sighed aloud. "I'm a thousand miles away."

"Wouldn't have to do with those new stories, would it?"

"Which ones? I haven't looked in the past few days."

Hugh laughed. "I don't blame you. Can be downright nasty can't they? These were pretty low. I dunno, something about that cute little widow using her daughter to get her hooks in you."

A sense of dread filled a pit in his stomach. "Oh, that's just lovely. What next?" Turning to Mike, he said, "Go find me a few copies. I want to know what's being said."

Mike nodded and began to turn away, but Devlan stopped him. "Call Kathy and have her get Teddy from public relations involved. Oh, and do whatever you can to keep it away from Diana. Got it?"

"You didn't know?" Hugh asked sympathetically.

"No. I thought I had the situation under control before we left the city. We've been at sea or sightseeing since. I haven't had time to watch the TV or read anything."

"Wow, sorry, man. I wish you didn't hear it from me first."

Devlan patted his back as they began walking to collect their balls. "Actually, it's better to hear it now than later when Diana finds out. At least I'll be prepared for her."

"A handful, eh?"

Knowing of her skittish attitude, Devlan knew that if she caught wind of what was being said, she would be ready to fly off again. The thought made him go cold. No, he could not allow that. He had to prevent it somehow. Suddenly, his good mood was shattered.

"More than you know," he said ominously.

Chapter 12

The sight that greeted Devlan when he returned to the ship was a scene of pure chaos. Betty and Justin were rushing back and forth, carrying their suitcases and bags of toys from below deck. They did not even stop to greet him as they passed. As he walked through the salon, he came face to face with Lani, who was sitting nervously on one of the barstools nursing a beer and chewing on her fingernails.

"What's going on?" Devlan asked, placing down his clubs.

"Oh, Mr. Doyle, it got so hot out that we decided to come in and watch TV until Hannah woke up from her nap. There were so many channels, and we were having fun flipping through. Then she saw herself on one of those programs. Of course, she stopped to listen. They said some horrible things. She was in tears."

"Wait here for Hannah."

Devlan's mouth thinned. He could figure out the rest from there, for it was just as he feared. Oh yes, she was ready to bolt. With the sight of toys and suitcases to meet him, he knew exactly what was going on in her head. A sudden possessiveness filled him as he imagined her leaving him. He did not want it to happen. Not yet.

All was quiet as he went further into the ship's body. The carpeted stairs muffled his rapid footfalls as he descended. It was too silent below, and the door to his suite was solidly closed. He turned the knob easily and entered the dark room, pausing only long enough to shut the door firmly behind him. Diana sat by the window, wearing her own clothing again, and her knees were drawn protectively up to her chin. Her forearms rested on her knees and her chin on her forearms as she gazed sadly out at the royal blue waters of the Pacific.

She did not move when he came to sit behind her, nor did she flinch when his hands went around her shoulders and pulled her against his chest. Wanting to enjoy the feel of her, he did not speak, and a comfortable silence filled the room with only the whoosh of the air conditioner breaking the silence.

"I was waiting for you," she finally whispered in the silence of the room.

"Why?"

He allowed his hands to slide up and down her upper arms. He noticed that she was tanning from her days in the sun. She looked good – healthy and happy. He was proud to know that he had a part in her current good health.

"I'm leaving."

"I noticed," he said dryly. He heard vulnerability in her voice and fear.

"I can't stay anymore. I can't have them saying those things about me. I mean, what if Hannah heard what they said?"

He heard the tears threatening in the back of her voice and stiffened in anger. His very public lifestyle had hurt her, and that was his fault. While he had worked hard to get to where he was today and was used to the scrutiny, Diana was not. She had jumped right in without any knowledge of how nasty rumors could be, and it was very possible that he could lose her and Hannah because of it. However, he wasn't ready yet. The truth was that he was not sure if he would be ready for quite some time.

"I heard about the rumors today too, Diana, and my publicist has been called. He's diffusing the situation now. He'll give them quite a statement, believe me."

"Now? But what about tomorrow? People will think; they'll remember the bad. I'll always have that stigma hanging over my head."

"I'm sorry that I'm in such a position that I have very little privacy. There was a time when I didn't mind, but now that I have others to think of, it's become a nuisance."

"You enjoy it though, and I don't."

"I tolerate it, not enjoy it."

"I don't want my daughter exposed to that kind of nastiness."

"Nobody thinks you used Hannah to get to me. Jesus, you'd have to be a real monster to have your child hit by a car to get me." She shuddered at the thought, and Devlan tightened his hands around her. "Besides, all the people that matter know the truth anyway, Diana. You don't have to leave."

Diana arched her neck to stare into his eyes. He could see a tear dangling just under her lid and reached up to wipe it away. Pain and anger pierced his heart as he realized just how upset she was and how serious about leaving. The idea scared him, more than he was ready to admit. He could not lose them now. Hannah and Diana had brought stability to his life. The two females had made him happy, and he had promised to do the same for them.

Slowly his hand cupped her cheek, and she leaned into his comfort. That small gesture of trust renewed his determination, but when she spoke, he was reminded that he still had a long way to go before he had it all.

"I can't stay. I don't belong in this lifestyle, and you know that as well as I. It's wrong to try and fit in here."

"No it's not. I want you here. You and Hannah will always have a place with me. I'll take care of you." He frowned fiercely in a small show of anger. "Let the tabloids have their day. You'll be tomorrow's news soon after. Somebody else will do something wrong and they'll be hounded."

She shook her head. "I have to think of Hannah."

"I'll always think of Hannah. She'll be sheltered from these stories. You know I'll do whatever it takes to ensure her happiness."

She sighed.

"Don't leave yet, Diana. I just got you here. You can't go. Not now." Though he knew he was beginning to sound desperate, all he cared about at that moment was convincing her that he was right.

There was a flicker of hesitation in Diana's wide eyes. He could see the fierce overprotective mother as well as the frightened woman struggle to make a decision. He pressed his slight advantage. "Please, Diana. I'm asking you to stay."

"I don't know, Devlan. I just don't have the strength to fight people's opinions."

"You won't need to. I'll take care of that. Anything you want; everything you need. I'll do it all."

"You make it hard to say no," she said softly.

"I'm trying to," he said fiercely. "I want you to stay. Getting away from it all and coming here with you and Hannah has reminded me of how much I'm missing in my life."

"I'll think about it a little," she said softly. She managed a tremulous smile that made his heart ache. Though still splotched with tears, her face took on a luminescence and beauty that stunned him. He hugged her closely and breathed deep her fresh scent.

"Good lord woman, you take my breath away."

Diana hugged him back, turning in his arms so that she could press her full length against him. He pulled her closer, loving the feel of her, the smell of her, and everything else about her. She was an enigma, a tease, and the very best thing that ever happened to him. He had never known what was missing in his life until he saw her again. Finally, after all the years of work, it all seemed to make sense, and now his heart pounded painfully as he thought how close he had come to losing her.

~

"A luau? Tonight?"

Devlan merely smiled with eyes shining with amusement. She glared at him furiously. After all, had nothing she had told him the day before meant anything to him?

"I can't go out tonight. What if people see me?"

"Diana, you can't hide." He wrapped his arms around her and pulled her close. "How can you not go to a luau while on vacation in Hawaii? Besides, I want to show you off. It's only a couple of friends. It'll be a big gathering with tourists who won't know who we are anyway."

"I don't know. Maui's busy. It'll have lots of people."

She reached up and toyed with the open buttons on Devlan's casual shirt. His skin had grown dark in the daily sunshine, and through the open neck of his shirt, she could see his golden tan and the dark curling hair peeking through.

"What's wrong?" he asked, tipping her chin up to meet his gaze. "There's something else bothering you, I can tell."

The fact that he had read her so easily caught her off guard. Her chin lifted stubbornly, even though she knew it was useless to try to hide it. "Do your friends know about those horrible stories?"

"Hugh's the one who told me," he said with a lopsided smile. "But he's used to it. He says all the time that the first rule in Hollywood is that you don't believe everything you hear or read."

Diana snorted in disbelief. Suddenly Devlan swept her into his arms and spun her around the room. His feet were smooth and skilled, and she laughed aloud when he continued to dance.

"You once told me that you could dance all night. Well,

tonight is the night to do it since our time here is almost over. It'll be just you and me, and we'll dance until dawn. I'll have Mike keep an eye open for photographers, and Lani can stay onboard with Hannah. Okay?"

He dipped her then and pressed a loud kiss to her neck. Diana held on to him with a yelp of surprise. Graceful, she was not, but he made her feel like a ballerina.

"Lessons?"

"Of course." He grinned and his eyes danced mischievously. "I dance so well now that I make anyone look good – even Mrs. McLean." At her look of surprise, he continued speaking. His lack of modesty made her want to laugh. "She was my date at our annual Christmas party a couple of years ago. I danced with her all night. She could barely move the next day."

Diana could feel her smile spread. The idea of him dancing with a stout housekeeper he described as a cream puff was comical.

"She particularly liked the tango."

Diana laughed and held out her hands in resignation. "All right, but promise me that if we see any unusual people we'll leave?"

"You have my word," he said solemnly.

Pulling her back up and releasing his hold on her, he stared at her until she reluctantly nodded. As she watched Devlan saunter away triumphantly, the feeling grew to dread. All her humor drained away as she considered being the center of attention again. Devlan could not shield her from everything. Things were bound to get worse. They always did.

~

They spent the rest of the afternoon sailing in the hot sun to Maui after a glorious day in Lanai's Manele harbor. Lanai had been a truly splendid place, one of the last untouched beauties in the world. Devlan had surprised her again with an off-road trip to the top of Lanaihale. They had been lucky. The day had been clear enough to see the other islands in the distance, and it was a sight that left her breathless.

Afterward, he satisfied Hannah by bringing them swimming at Hulopo'e. Like a true family, they had splashed in the water and played on the beach together. Hannah enjoyed every minute, and if Diana was not mistaken, Devlan had too. The three had held hands on the ride back, and Devlan was reluctant to let them go when they returned. He returned for several more kisses from them before heading back to work in his study. However, she had not seen him the rest of the day, even when Hannah and Lani went to eat their supper. Diana made sure they were all squared away before she went to prepare for the evening.

The stateroom was quiet when she entered. Tucked away in his office, she heard the deep timbre of Devlan's voice on the phone through the wall. There was tension in his voice that she was unaccustomed to hearing from him, so she tiptoed in and flipped on the lights as quietly as she could.

What met her eyes when the room was illuminated was a pleasant surprise. Strewn across the huge bed was a brightly colored mu'umu'u. She approached it slowly and fingered the cool material, taking in all the bright colors with an appreciative eye. Loving Devlan all the more, she held the dress to her chest. That he took the time to think of something so simple touched her heart, and that he had done it without Kathy's input warmed her to her toes.

Diana placed the cotton dress back on the bed and stripped out of her bikini. She glanced in the mirror as she passed and took in her newly tanned body. Even she had to admit that she was looking better than she had in ages. She was blooming almost as fast as Hannah was under Devlan's care.

Careful.

Ignoring the ever present voice of reason, she slipped into the bathroom and turned on the tap. The shower was tight and the water pressure not so great, but Diana still managed to enjoy a leisurely warm shower that relaxed her frazzled nerves enough to feel more excited about the luau. Of course, she and Lani had discussed the rumors, and Lani had displayed a true sense of confidence in her new boss. She was certain that Devlan would take care of everything.

As she was rinsing her hair, she felt Devlan's hand on her arm. Crying out in surprise, she opened her eyes and found his smiling countenance.

"I called you, but you weren't listening."

"Right," she muttered. She turned away from his grin and shut off the water, very conscious of her nakedness. He held a towel for her but was reluctant to hand it over.

Sounding more like a petulant child, Devlan winked at her. "I did, honest."

"Well, what's wrong?"

"I was wondering how I could fit in there with you."

Diana left the shower and squeezed by Devlan's tall form to the safety of the bedroom. "It's far too tight."

"I know," he said, raising his brows suggestively.

Though she rolled her eyes at his humor, she continued to smile. He was staring at her again as though she was the most beautiful woman in the world, and Diana wished with all her might that it could remain like that.

"I'm running a bit late. I need to shower, and then we'll take the launch over," he said as he stripped off his shirt.

It was now Diana's turn to stare, and she did so as unabashedly as he had. He was so beautiful, so virile - so male. His shorts fell into a pile, and she watched his taut buttocks as he ducked into his shower.

"Unfair that he's that old and looks that good," she muttered.

When Devlan again reappeared with only a pristine white towel around his waist, Diana stared and Devlan raised a brow in question. "Like what you see?"

Grinning at him over her shoulder, she nodded. "Very much so."

"Good answer." He smiled and released the towel. As it dropped to the floor, he reached for a long, thin box that rested next to their bed. He came to stand behind her and placed his hands on her shoulders.

"Have I ever told you how beautiful you are?"

"Yes, actually, you have."

Her abandoned lip gloss rolled towards her, and she reached for it quickly. She was not fast enough though, and it rolled to the floor. Devlan watched it go idly. His fingers began to massage the muscles of her shoulders, and she closed her eyes and allowed her head to fall against his abdomen.

"Well, I mean it, Diana. You are truly a most beautiful person." He glanced down at the new dress. "You like the dress?"

"Yes," she said softly. "I do, even with all the colors."

"I'm pleased you finally decided to wear something I've given you."

She smiled saucily, though her eyes remained closed. "You're slowly spoiling me rotten."

"I have another gift for you."

"I don't want it. You've given me and Hannah far too much already."

"If you were my wife, you'd be entitled to everything and then some," he said dryly.

"But I'm not your wife," she said carefully, aware that her heart had leapt to her throat.

"No," he said cheerfully. "You're right, but what we have here, how we've holidayed and spent all this time together, is the closest I've ever gotten to being married. Let me spoil you. I have all this money and no one to give it to except you and Hannah... Here."

He opened the box and handed it to her, and her eyes opened even wider. Displayed in front of her was the most beautiful gold locket she had ever seen. Such a simple gift, and yet she was totally enraptured.

"I picked it out all by myself," he said proudly.

The fine gold chain was a round snake design, sturdy and deceptively heavy when she picked it up. In the center, was a locket carved with Hawaiian flowers and hearts. She opened it to find a picture of him and Hannah already within.

He grinned. "Pretty arrogant of me, eh?"

Still too breathless to speak, she nodded wordlessly as her fingers smoothed the shining gold. He took it away and removed the necklace from the box.

"Wait," she said.

Reaching for the necklace as he raised it over her head, Diana caught his hand within hers. On the back of the locket were engraved words surrounding a tiny, intricately carved ring. "*A Vila Mon Coeur, Gardi Li Mo*? I only took Latin in school. What does that mean?"

Devlan secured the necklace around her neck and bent to place a soft kiss there. Then he straightened with a secretive half-smile. His face bore a strange expression as he moved away from her to dress. She watched him go, but her fingers still toyed with the heavy gold around her neck.

"I'll tell you later what that means," he said, nodding towards her necklace. "But for now you'll have to wait and stew."

When they boarded the launch, Devlan looked as handsome and debonair as usual. With his dark hair combed back and wearing white slacks with a Hawaiian shirt, he fit right in with the tourists. Surprisingly, the loud colors on his shirt actually complimented his dark good looks, and she proudly took his arm as he assisted her into the motor boat.

"I like that red dress on you," he murmured huskily, nuzzling at her cheek. "And I like your hair up, it leaves your neck wide open."

She was pleased that he noticed the extra care she had taken with her appearance. Because she wanted to make him proud in front of his friends, she had done her best to look good. However, she was at risk of losing it all with Devlan's nuzzling. Pulling away from him nervously, she glared at him.

"Do you mind? Don't mess my hair." She pushed playfully at his chest, and then placed a scarf around her head, trying desperately to protect her fragile inside-out French braid from the blowing trade winds.

"I can't help myself. You look and smell so good."

Though she rolled her eyes, she could not hide her laughter. He joined her as well, which earned them both a speculative look from Mike. Devlan winked in his direction and wrapped his arm around Diana's shoulders.

"You're something else," she said wryly.

Still smiling, he nodded in agreement. "That I am."

For the remainder of the ride, she relaxed against him and watched the shoreline grow closer. An SUV was waiting, and Hugh was standing alongside it when the launch pulled up to the dock. Devlan kept a proprietary hand around her waist as they all piled in and drove to the luau.

Just as Devlan had predicted, there were a few photographers hanging around, but they were tourists searching for autographs from Hugh Davis. While a small group of people descended on Hugh, it was Hugh's companion, a buxom blonde wearing a tight sequined dress more appropriate for a gala than a cookout, who urged them to continue to their table. Despite her nagging, she was quite lovely, and with a touch of jealousy Diana glanced in

Devlan's direction. Much to her surprise and pleasure, he appeared to not even notice her presence at all.

The luau was just getting under way when they found their seats. There were people mingling around in all directions, and the entertainers showered their group with beautiful leis. Diana accepted hers with a wide smile. Everyone was so happy and joyous that she could not suppress her growing enthusiasm. It would be near impossible that she not have a great time.

Not long after they had found their seats, they were called around the hollow to watch the pig come out of the imu pit. Diana could feel her mouth begin to water as the main dish was presented to all the guests.

"Looks good," Devlan commented, nodding in satisfaction.

"I'm starved," Diana said.

"Good thing. Looks like there's plenty to go around," Hugh said enthusiastically.

The buffet dinner consisted of the succulent pig, lomi lomi salmon, teriyaki beefsteak, chicken long rice, and a selection of Hawaiian dishes that made her mouth water. Devlan insisted that she try a taste of everything and laughingly filled her plate to overflowing. Diana went along with his idea and tasted everything, including the exotic Polynesian drinks from the bar, and pretty soon it took all of Devlan's power to keep her in her seat.

Hugh was more personable in the flesh than in the movies. He was childish and high-strung but funny and courteous at the same time. He sent her charming smiles and went out of his way to include her in their conversations even when he was promoting his new project to Devlan. Diana reached under the table to squeeze Devlan's leg in a show of support, and she smiled when he turned his attention to her.

"You must hear this kind of thing a lot," she said.

They had just cleared away dessert, a wonderful selection of banana cake with delicious frosting, macadamia nut bars and coconut cream cake. Diana had tried a little of everything on those plates as well, much to everyone's surprise. Hugh's companion stared at her with envy in her eyes, and Diana had smiled back. It was a slight consolation to see that she had to go without to keep her voluptuous figure.

Having finished his second pitch, Hugh and his date disappeared to try their lot at Hula dancing in the rear of the show. Devlan was staring straight ahead at the beautiful dancers, watching their hips sway in time to the music. When she spoke, he glanced down at her and shrugged one shoulder, but his exasperation was evident.

"It wouldn't be so bad if I wasn't on vacation."

"Vacation?" Diana blurted. "You've worked at least four hours every day."

"You're absolutely right, and I'm sorry if that bothers you."

"It doesn't bother me," she replied quickly. "I get angry that you never seem to be able to fully let go."

"Ah, but I've had fun letting you relax me after a long day's work," he teased.

She chuckled at his soft tone. Feeling the effects of the alcohol she had consumed, she reached up and laced her fingers in his thick hair. Slightly tugging on the silken strands, she pulled him closer to whisper in his ear. "And I *really* like helping you relax after a long day."

Her suggestive tone caused Devlan to raise a single eyebrow. He stared down at her for a moment, taking in her moist lips and heavy lidded eyes. His observant gaze also noted her growing intoxication.

"Perhaps I should've monitored what you drank instead of what you ate," he said thoughtfully.

"No, I'm fine," she said smiling.

"Because of you, I've been reconsidering all the work I've been doing, but unfortunately changes don't happen overnight."

"That's true… But you can relax now and enjoy the show."

Diana spun slightly to lean into Devlan when his arm came to rest on her shoulders. It felt good to have his arm around her. She felt warm and snug, but unfortunately their respite was brief. Taking in their cozy postures, Hugh frowned dramatically.

"Oh no, you don't. We can't have any of this. You're here with me tonight, so let's start the par-ty!" Clapping his hands together, he smiled widely at Devlan moments before he reached for Diana and pulled her to her feet. "Come on Diana, let's dance."

Before Devlan could object, Hugh sped her away to a clear spot on the dance floor and swept her gracefully into his arms. His movements were fluid and his steps light, and Diana noticed that in addition to being charming, Hugh was a skilled dancer. After several moments of feeling like a gawky schoolgirl, Hugh came to her aid by guiding her movements. She responded to his familiarity by dancing like never before, and she thanked the potent alcoholic beverages for helping her release her inhibitions. Fortunately, she was a quick learner, and soon Hugh was watching her move with new interest in his eyes.

From his seat, Devlan watched moodily.

"You dance well," Hugh remarked.

"Not at all, really. It's all you, Hugh."

"If it is, you make me look very good. Doyle's jealous as hell," he said with a broad grin.

"I don't know about that."

He shrugged. "At any rate. I've got you on my side. You'll plug this project for me, right? Any help you can give me would be great."

"I doubt he'd listen to me."

"He may not listen, but I can guarantee that he'll agree to anything you ask in order to get you away from me. Wow, I never knew he was so possessive."

"Possessive?" Diana asked breathlessly just before Hugh dipped her yet again. "Of me?"

He chuckled. "Yep, he's had enough and is on his way over now. Since he's looking very territorial right now, I think I should escape before he accuses me of stealing his date."

With one last spin, Hugh pressed a quick peck on her cheek. "A good word, right?"

Hugh abruptly thrust her away as soon as she nodded in agreement. She stumbled, but Devlan's hands were there to grip her waist from behind and prevent her fall. He scowled at Hugh, but the younger man laughed cheerfully and danced alone back to his pouting girlfriend with a happy wave. Diana leaned her head back into Devlan's chest and inhaled deeply.

"That was something," she murmured. "Did I tell you how good you smell tonight?"

"I thought you were supposed to be dancing with me tonight," came the sullen response.

"Are you jealous?" Diana teased.

"I think it's almost time to go," he growled. "They're beginning to clear everything away."

Stilling her hips with his hands, Devlan spun her around to face him, and she reached up to wrap her arms around his neck. "Dance with me now?"

"I can think of better places to dance."

Diana giggled, her eyes shining. "Later... But now I want you to dance with me. Hugh was right. You need to have a good time. Relax and enjoy yourself."

"You're drunk."

"And you're being a grouch. I never drink, Devlan, allow me one time."

Taking her words in slowly, his dark head nodded and then dipped as he pressed his lips against hers. She entwined her fingers in his hair and pulled his head closer to hers. After a moment of allowing her to deepen the kiss, Devlan pulled away and looked down at her. The corners of his mouth had turned up in a teasing smile. "If you're like this every time you get drunk, Diana, I may never let you get sober again."

Feeling slightly foolish, she giggled again. She noticed that her voice sounded high pitched and happy. "It's you, you know. You do this to me."

"Me?" His smile faded. "What do I do to you?"

"You make me all crazy. Fluttery." Waving her hands at her middle, she took a step away from him and pointed to her middle. "I've never felt like that with anyone but you. It's all you."

A slow and very satisfied smile appeared on his lips. "Must be love."

"Yep. Must be."

She leaned into him and placed her head on his chest. He was strong and felt so nice that she sighed happily. Raising his hand to press her head against him, Devlan tenderly smoothed the loose tendrils of hair from her face.

"I truly hope so."

Chapter 13

Darkness had overtaken the glorious night. The laughing voices and music were loud to her ears, but Diana was only aware that Devlan was finally dancing with her, and she again felt like her dream fairytale princess. The hypnotic music captured her, and they danced together in sync. It was as though they were one, for their feet moved effortlessly in the crowd under Devlan's expert guidance.

The warm night caused her dress to cling to her, and Devlan's hands seemed to be all over her, touching her in her sensitive spots that he had so studiously taken note of in the past few days. She was dizzy from alcohol and giddy from happiness. For better or for worse, she had been blessed with some sort of magic in meeting Devlan. It was because of Hannah that she was here. Though her accident was terrifying and painful, it had ended up bringing them both great joy. It was Hannah's magic, Hannah's blessing.

Too soon, the luau came to a close. Speaking on behalf of both of them, Devlan was quick to say goodnight to Hugh and his still pouting girlfriend. Her dramatics eased any remaining insecurities that Diana may have had. Of all the things that she had learned about Devlan in the weeks they had spent together, she knew there was no way he would accept that kind of behavior for very long.

As she watched them disappear in the evening, Mike

appeared from seemingly out of nowhere. His hair was slightly ruffled from the wind, and there was a ruddy glow on his cheeks, both signs that he had been having a good time as well. He was all smiles as he escorted them back to the dock, and he and Devlan fell into an animated conversation about the evening while Diana followed along reluctantly.

"I had a great evening," she whispered when he helped her into the launch. "Thank you for convincing me to go."

"I'm glad you had fun, Diana." Grinning with true pleasure, he followed her into the boat and pulled her against him for the ride back to the yacht.

She smiled at him teasingly. "How shall I ever repay you?"

His eyes danced with amusement. "Oh, I'm sure we can think of some way."

"I have a few ideas myself," she announced softly. "But it may involve a bedroom."

"Is that so?"

"Yes. I'd like to make sure you're a willing partner."

"I could probably be convinced," he said with a grin. "Are you up to the challenge?"

"Yep." Her hand went to his thigh, and she began to walk her fingers oh so slowly up until he captured her hand in his. Smiling impishly she pursed her lips. "But I guess you'll just have to wait and see to be sure."

Growling in answer, he held her hand tightly for the remainder of the ride. No sooner had they come to a stop alongside the yacht than Devlan was shuttling Diana from the launch and down to their stateroom. As they disappeared down the stairs, they heard Mike behind them laughing aloud in true amusement.

Diana paused long enough to read the note that Lani had left posted on Hannah's door. Her alcohol-fuzzed brain took a moment to decipher that the two had spent a leisurely evening watching movies on the big screen television before retiring early. It sounded great to Diana, but she still opened the door to check on her. Hannah was sleeping soundly, her small arms wrapped securely around her stuffed bear, and she did not flinch when Diana leaned over her and kissed her cheek. Nor did she move when Devlan pulled her covers up to her chin. Diana smiled up at Devlan and entwined her fingers with his.

Returning her smile, Devlan led her from the room. Hand in hand, they crossed the hall together and slipped into their room like newlyweds fresh from their wedding. No sooner had the door closed behind them than Devlan turned the lock. It was dark, with only the light to the bathroom casting shadows on their waiting bed.

"What does my locket say?" Diana whispered in the darkness.

Devlan glanced over as he pulled his shirt from his slacks. Gone was the tender man gazing down at the little girl as though she were his own. In his place was the male, the virile alpha who was remembering how seductively she had danced with him. His tousled hair gave him a rugged look, and his pupils were dilated with both hunger and promise. He strode to their bed and pulled back the covers before returning to her and pulling her into his arms. "Right now I have more important things on my mind."

"Like what?"

He smiled devilishly. "Like how you're going to repay me."

Remembering her earlier words, Diana tossed back her head and laughed. His eyes were dancing as he watched her display, but then his head lowered, and he became all business again. As if from a will of their own, their clothes seemed to suddenly disappear, and together they fell backwards onto the soft mattress.

When Devlan finally raised his head, Diana was breathless. She gazed up at him, holding him riveted as every emotion she felt and was feeling were exposed in her wide eyes. At the moment, she did not care if he saw how deeply she had grown to care. This night was their night; it was magical and the fulfillment of every one of her dreams.

"I want you, woman," he growled.

"Yes," she gasped in answer.

Their gazes remained locked as he filled her and suddenly they were flying, soaring high above with the blue sky and puffy white clouds of Hawaii. Right beside her was Devlan, his warmth and strength supporting her. For one night, they were completely in tune to each other, and after days of learning each other's needs and likes, they culminated their newfound knowledge with action. Her body answered his need, and she felt like a part of him as though they were truly one. Never taking his eyes from hers, he watched her lips part and her breath come in quick gasps as he moved inside her. Unable to stop, she finally broke their gaze when her eyes squeezed shut, and she cried out in a mixture of pure joy and pleasure. Though shaking from the effort, he allowed her to arch against him before he took his own release with a low growl of triumph.

After several moments, Devlan rolled to his side and wrapped his arms around her tightly. In the silence of the room, all Diana could hear was their mingled breathing while his fingers gently stroked the smooth skin of her back. Her eyes were just drifting closed when she heard him speak.

"I take it back," he whispered.

"Take what back?"

"I was wrong when I said that you rated yourself pretty high… I don't think you rated yourself high enough."

Though so tired that she could not open her eyes, Diana managed a short laugh. "I'm glad you can laugh about it."

She heard the rumble of his chuckle in his chest. "Who says I'm laughing? I think you damn near killed me tonight."

"Then you better get your rest and recover because I

definitely want to try that again tomorrow," she warned.

"Yes, ma'am."

Smiling against the velvety smooth skin of his chest, Diana pressed a warm kiss before snuggling deeper into his embrace. He continued to stroke her until long after she fell asleep, and when she awoke during the night, she noted that she was still locked within the safety of his embrace. It did not take her long to realize that it was exactly where she wanted to be.

~

A rustling sound awakened Diana, and when she reached for Devlan's warmth, she found only cool sheets. She sensed the early morning with a feeling of dismay and confusion. It was too early to be up while they were on vacation because it was still dark out. Dragging her sleep-heavy eyelids open, she saw him standing by his dressing room. He had just finished pulling the suit jacket over his vest when he caught her gaze, and he smiled as he hastily shut off the light.

"Sorry, did the light wake you?"

She stretched and sat up, wincing at the throbbing in her head. Oh my, she thought, what had she done? Certainly, she had consumed too much alcohol. Finding herself hesitant to meet Devlan's eyes, she shook her head. "What are you doing up this early? Are you leaving?"

She could see that he was freshly showered and clean-shaven. His hair was smoothed back, and as usual not one hair was out of place. Resting by the door was a suitcase, the seams bulging, and sadness enveloped her when she realized that she had just stated the obvious. Yes, he was leaving.

He came to sit by her side, smelling of his regular cologne and shampoo. One finger came to gently trace the outline of her lips as he stared down at her apologetically.

"I was going to tell you last night, but I didn't want to ruin the evening. I have to fly to New York. One of my subsidiary companies took a rather large dive in the stock market, and I have a meeting with the chief shareholders. It's not something I can miss."

Though she attempted to force a smile on her lips, it was so difficult that she was sure it appeared more like a grimace. Giving up the futile gesture, she reached up instead to cup his cheek in her hand. He seemed so sorry that she suddenly felt selfish. "I understand."

"I'm sorry, but it can't be helped. I've booked you and the others first class tickets back to California for the flight home. I'll have the jet, so you're going home on a commercial airliner. I hope that's acceptable."

"Of course it is," she said quickly. "When will you be back?"

"I don't know yet. The house in Malibu is ready for Hannah, and there will be a car at the airport to take you. I'll meet you there as soon as I can. I hope to be back at least by your birthday."

Diana gasped. With all the worry about Hannah and her progress and her new relationship with Devlan, she had completely forgotten that her birthday was a week away. She sighed and gave him her one of her exasperated looks, ignoring the stabbing pain in her head. "You had to bring that up, didn't you? How do you know when my birthday is?"

Though his eyes danced with amusement, his face grew serious. "I can't divulge my sources, but suffice it to say I know a lot about you, Diana."

She went still, knowing that it was probably a lot more than she even suspected he knew. Yet before she could question him further, he leaned over her and pressed a kiss to her forehead then her lips.

"Enjoy yourself and the rest of the trip. I'll see you back in California, okay?"

The words were tumbling out before she could stop them. "Shouldn't we just leave now too?"

"Of course not. I wouldn't expect you to cut your vacation short too."

"But – "

"No buts," he said, placing a finger against her lips. "Enjoy the ship; enjoy the islands. You're my guests, remember?"

Diana nodded, but she felt empty inside already. It would not be the same without him there. There would be no more laughter and fun sightseeing trips. The beach would be dreadfully boring without him tossing Hannah high over his head and splashing her with the spray from his hair. She and Hannah would be alone again.

Seeing her hesitation, he cocked a brow in question. "Tell me you're not feeling uncomfortable now."

No, she was uncomfortable for an entirely different reason. She just did not want him to leave. She shook her head in answer, too afraid to speak, and he removed his thumb to replace it with his warm lips in a long and lingering kiss. With a content sigh, she brought her hands from under the covers to his shoulders and hugged him tight, afraid to let him go.

"Stop now, Diana, or I'll never get out of here," he warned huskily. She pressed herself even harder against him.

She nipped his ear. "What's another fifteen minutes?"

"Mm," he responded reluctantly. "As much as I'd love to, I can't. I have to go now."

She released him with a sigh of regret. Lying back on the pillows, she primly pulled the covers back over her shoulders. "Okay then, fine. I'll see you next week. Have fun in New York."

"You're a vixen," he said with a chuckle. "Tell me you'll miss me."

It was her turn to laugh, and she did until her eyes watered. The dampness was suspiciously like tears though, and she swallowed a lump in her throat. "Sorry," she said saucily. "That's the last thing I'll do."

"I tried," he said with a shrug. Reaching down to give her thigh a gentle squeeze, he gave her one last smile that softened his eyes. "I'll miss you."

Coming to his feet, he walked away with confident and sure strides. With every step he took, she felt more alone. There was an emptiness growing deep within her breast, and he was just about to open the door when she called out softly. When he turned around questioningly, she smiled shyly. "I'll miss you, Devlan."

A slow smile of pure pleasure spread his lips, and he gave her an elegant bow before he continued out the door. It closed with a gentle click, and Diana sank back beneath the covers and curled into a tight ball. She tried to hold them in, but her tears trickled from between her closed eyes. Empty. The bed was empty, the boat was empty, and her heart felt empty. Without Devlan, she no longer felt whole.

A frightening thought, but she had to admit the truth. She was completely in love with him. Head over heels for sure. Clinging to the last thing that tied her to him, her fingers sought out her new necklace.

"*A Vila Mon Coeur, Gardi Li Mo,*" she whispered in the darkness. "I wonder what it means."

~

The answer was not forthcoming in the next week. Devlan called only once, and they were off the yacht when he rang. She was gripped with disappointment when she got the message and spent the entire evening hoping he would call again. Realizing that she was making a big mistake and that she had grown too dependent on him in just those few days they spent together did not help. Now the ship seemed quiet and empty, even with

Hannah's cheerful laughter. It was not enough to break her down mood, especially when her bed seemed so much larger and colder.

Beautiful Hawaii now seemed dull and boring. As she suspected, sightseeing was not nearly as entertaining without Devlan's extensive knowledge and playful antics. She missed his lust for life and adventure, and more than anything his willingness to try anything from parasailing and water-skiing to spending an entire afternoon with Hannah in the Children's Discovery Museum in Kaua'i. After spending one full day touring a sugar plantation and wishing Devlan was with them to enjoy it too, Diana and Hannah no longer tried to hide their loneliness. By evening, Hannah was voicing her disappointment that Devlan was gone. By morning of the second day, she was eager to go home, and by mid-morning, Diana had their bags packed and waiting by the helicopter to catch their pre-arranged flight.

After another white-knuckled ride to the airport, Diana, Lani and Hannah boarded the commercial airplane back to the mainland. Though she was eager to return, Los Angeles was noisy and dirty compared to the quiet serenity of Hawaiian shipboard life. The busy airport was crowded, and people rushed by them without any concern for Hannah. Nevertheless, she still felt somewhat closer to Devlan, and for that reason she was pleased to be back.

Diana stayed close to Hannah, pushing and shoving with the rest of them until they found their luggage on the carousel. The flight had been long and cramped, with Hannah sleeping across their laps the whole trip. Now it was the crowded airport that sent Diana's already frayed nerves over the edge. When she saw Wills saunter in through the glass doors and approach with a wide grin, she almost laughed aloud her relief. For a moment, Diana's heart leapt in her chest when she saw the dark-suited man behind their young chauffeur, but then she noticed that he was older and chubbier, and certainly not Devlan. She greeted the young man with a little less enthusiasm.

"Hi, Wills. Is Mr. Doyle here?"

Wills reached for their bags and effortlessly hauled them over his wiry shoulders. "Hey, Mrs. Somerset, Welcome home. No, he's still in New York. There's a message at the house for you. How was your trip?"

She sighed as she picked up the rest of the luggage while Lani helped Hannah into a borrowed wheelchair. "It was a great trip until the airport." She managed a laugh, but the sound was as frazzled as her nerves. "Isn't that always the way?"

Wills smiled sympathetically. "I know what you mean, but we'll get you home and settled. Mrs. Maclean has a meal all fixed up and waiting for you."

Diana remembered Devlan's warnings about Mrs. Maclean's cooking and shuddered. She wondered why he didn't bring home Francois to cook for them. After all, the wild Frenchman was a superb cook. Remembering some of the menu choices he had offered to her made Diana even more disappointed to leave.

"Mommy, is Uncle Devvie going to be there?" Hannah asked.

"No, he's still away."

"I want him to come back. Why won't he come home?"

Lani leaned over the wheelchair and made a hushing noise, but Diana sympathized with her cranky daughter. She was longing for his easygoing and cheerful presence as well.

"I'm hungry," Hannah whined.

"We're all hungry," Wills said over his shoulder. "Hurry up and we'll get home sooner."

Hannah giggled as the young man ran ahead of them and then turned around to wave at them to hurry. His antics drew a few curious looks, but his attempt to lighten the mood worked.

"Traffic was awful on the ride down," he said cheerfully as they loaded up the trunk.

"Lovely," Lani said.

"But I'm hoping northbound will be easier," he continued. "I'll try to get you back as quickly as possible."

With a weary nod, Diana slipped into the cool car and closed her eyes. Her head lolled against the back of the seat as she listened to Hannah's chatter. It would have been so easy to lose herself in the comfortable car, but she answered her daughter's questions as they came and endured the long drive to Malibu.

When they arrived, a stout woman was waiting on the steps. Without having to be told, Diana knew who it was. Biting back her laughter and the tears of loneliness that rose with it, Diana had to concede that Devlan had been completely right. Mrs. Maclean did look like a cream puff. She was short and stocky, with white hair and a round face, and her beaming countenance was the first thing Diana noticed when they pulled to the front of the house. With shuffling strides, she met them at the car with a wide smile.

"Why, hello, Mrs. Somerset. And Miss Hannah! How are you?"

Diana climbed from the Bentley and reached out her hand in a friendly handshake. "It's a pleasure to finally meet you."

"Oh, he tried to tell me how lovely you were, but I didn't believe him. I thought he was being a man and blind to all reason. I see now that I was wrong. Welcome home, ma'am."

Diana smiled shyly and ducked her head. All these compliments were welcome but definitely surprising. The close relationship that Devlan appeared to have with all his employees was remarkable. Their loyalty was beyond measure, and his trust and openness proved that the feeling was mutual. They entered the house together, stopping when Hannah gasped aloud at the gleaming luxury of the house.

"We're staying here, Mommy?"

"Yes, but don't break anything and don't dirty anything." She tapped her chin and sent a forlorn look in Hannah's direction.

"Actually, just don't touch anything."

Mrs. Maclean laughed. "Nonsense. She can go anywhere and do whatever she likes. It's her house."

Diana shook her head silently and narrowed her eyes in warning at Hannah. She nodded solemnly in return, her eyes wide with awe. She had never seen such luxury in her whole short life, let alone lived in it.

As they helped her up the carpeted stairs to her new room, Hannah glanced around with plenty of oohs and ahhs. Excitement radiated from every pore, and she was beaming with joy by the time they reached her new room.

"There's so much to do. Look at all these toys! Are they mine, Mommy?"

Diana listened to the chatter and answered when necessary, but all she wanted at that moment was to lie down and sleep. She half-heartedly played with Hannah, going through the paces on the floor with her toys like a robot. Although she knew that her downtrodden attitude was not good for her daughter to see, Hannah's excitement was so great that she did not seem to notice her distraction.

Once she was settled, Diana went to her room next door, opening the door and inhaling the clean salt air. It was here in this house that Devlan had begun his seduction – that is, until his girlfriend entered the picture. Suddenly reminded that Devlan had a whole other life that she was unfamiliar with, Diana grimaced. Now that they had become lovers, she wondered if Devlan would break it off with Roxanne. If he did not, she was not sure what she would do. The idea of packing up Hannah and going back to Colorado was becoming harder and harder to imagine, even though she knew that it was what she would have to do sometime soon.

Not yet, she reminded herself. She was not so blind that she could not see that he had been happy on the boat, too.

She walked across the room to open the French doors leading to the balcony. The swimming pool was just as she remembered, only without Devlan.

Hannah came slowly into the room, precariously holding a box full of new toys in her fingers. She was still smiling, and Diana noticed how quickly she was recovering from her accident.

"Look what Uncle Devvie left me."

"It was probably Kathy," Diana muttered.

"Who's Kathy?"

"No one, nothing," Diana stammered. "Let's have a look. Come to the bed."

Diana helped Hannah onto her mattress and together they opened all the new doll clothes. Hannah chattered excitedly the whole time.

"Mommy, is Uncle Devvie going to marry you and be my daddy when he gets back?"

Diana looked up in surprise. "I thought we already discussed this. Uncle Devlan is helping us out, but when you're well, we'll go home."

"I don't want to go home, Mommy. I like it here. I love Uncle Devvie."

Diana sighed, a frown turning the corners of her mouth down. "I know you do, but this is only a temporary thing. Uncle Devlan's trying to be nice while your leg gets better, but he's a very busy man. We can't intrude on him forever."

"I thought he loved me." Tears welled in Hannah's blue eyes, slowly overflowing and streaming down her face. Diana gathered her into her arms and stroked her hair, hair so like her own.

"You know what? I think we've had a long day and should get some rest. We'll talk more about this later, but remember that Uncle Devlan does love you. In fact, I think he loves you very much."

"I don't want to go to bed, Mommy, I want Uncle Devvie."

Diana came to her feet and carried Hannah to her room. Then she placed the sobbing child under the covers and lay down next to her, softly stroking her back. As Hannah settled, Diana realized that this was exactly what she had feared. Though she knew the two had bonded, it never fully occurred to her the extent to which Hannah would attach herself to Devlan. Mistake already made, the more important question became how to handle the situation. As she lulled her to sleep, Diana pondered her newest dilemma. She already knew that the longer they stayed, the harder it would be to leave, and it would be more difficult for Hannah to understand that they would have to do so sooner or later.

What was she to do?

Chapter 14

Back in Denver, there was a six-inch blanket of snow, and yet in Malibu, the sun still shone brightly. The day had dawned unseasonably warm, so Diana had donned her bathing suit and decided to lounge for a while out on the deck. She did not want to lose her Hawaiian tan too quickly, and Hannah and Lani were busy working in the indoor gym, giving her some quiet time. Since she was left with nothing to do, she decided to take advantage of the freedom. It had only been a few minutes before she was dozing under the soothing music of Devlan's iPod.

"Happy birthday," whispered a soft voice in her ear.

Diana's eyes opened suddenly, and she gasped her surprise. Devlan stood above her in the morning sunlight smiling broadly.

"You're looking great today, as usual," he continued. He hunkered down to rest on the balls of his feet, disregarding the creaking of his highly-polished Italian leather shoes.

With a squeal of pure pleasure, Diana reached forward and threw her arms around his neck, hugging him tightly and almost throwing him off balance.

"Whoa, hello to you, too," he said, laughing.

His hands encircled her waist, and he hugged her as he regained his balance. When they separated he placed a quick kiss on her cheek and handed her a brightly wrapped box.

"Mike's bringing this home even as we speak. If you throw on some shoes and something to cover your lovely little bottom,

I'll bring you out front to see."

Diana glanced at the box dubiously. "What's the box for?"

"Come with me, and you'll see."

Diana swung her legs over the deck chair and slipped her feet into her flip flops. As she came to her feet, she noticed Devlan was still staring at her. She flushed from head to toe with pleasure and excitement. He was finally home.

Home?

"I missed you," he said, wrapping his arms around her again.

"Where have you been? Hannah missed you dreadfully. She cried like the dickens when we got here, and you were nowhere to be found."

"What about you, Diana? Didn't you miss me?"

"I, uh, of course," she said with a shaky laugh.

"You did miss me. Admit it." He smiled lopsidedly. "I have never thought a king-sized bed too big until you came into my life, woman. I have to admit that I've never slept so poorly before."

Diana laughed, and her apprehension began to melt away. "I know how you feel," she admitted. "I haven't slept too well myself."

"I noticed. You were out cold underneath those headphones. All I could hear was Elton John's voice and piano. He's all you listen to, isn't he?"

"He's my favorite."

"Hmm, I'll have to keep that in mind." He released her and took a step back. "Come on before I molest you out here. I've got to go into the city for a while, but I wanted to give you your present first."

"It could've waited."

"I wanted to see you," he admitted softly.

Unable to hide her pleasure, she beamed. "I'm glad."

Reaching for a towel, Devlan wrapped it around her waist. "I'm not ready to share that luscious body with anyone."

She giggled and tied off the towel for him. "I have a sarong with me."

Devlan locked his arm around her waist and led her to the front of the house. As they passed the open door, he released her long enough to search out Hannah and emerged moments later with her in his arms. Hannah was clinging to him tightly and rambling on and on, and Devlan seemed to enjoy the sound of her voice. Diana's breath caught at the charming scene, for it still amazed her how well they got on. He understood her and had the patience of a saint. Not once had he lost his temper with her, and he really appeared to care for her. At the moment, he leaned over and planted a hearty kiss on her flushed cheek.

"Ready? Mommy's getting her birthday present."

Diana smiled at his reference to her. It seemed so natural for him to call her Mommy, and she liked the sound of it on his lips.

When they had all come to stand on the front steps, Devlan gave her the okay to open the box. With trembling hands, she untied the elaborate bow and then flipped it over to peel back the bright paper. The thick wrapping paper easily fell open, revealing a small box. It was too large to be a ring, but too small to be a bracelet or necklace. It was rectangular in shape and deep, so not earrings. With her heart pounding in her chest, she took a deep breath and opened the box. What lay inside caused her to frown in confusion. "What is this? Is this some kind of car key?"

Devlan smiled widely, his eyes dancing with excitement. "Yes, Diana, that gadget is a car key, and Mike will be here any – ahh, here he is now."

Diana spun around to see Mike pull into the driveway with a shiny, brand-new silver Mercedes sedan. Her mouth dropped open as the bodyguard halted in front of them, tooting the horn before he hopped out. "Happy birthday, Mrs. Somerset."

Diana glanced back at Devlan. "What's this all about?"

"Mike turned your rental in, and I thought it best to get you a car of your own."

"This is mine?"

"Yes," he said, nodding his dark head. His hands still had a grip on Hannah, but she could see that he wanted to embrace her. "It's all yours, to keep. Happy birthday."

She approached the car hesitantly and peeked in the window. She still held the triangular shaped device in her hand that was supposed to be her car key. On it were buttons to unlock the door as well as a panic button. She stared down at it and then glanced back at Devlan, her eyes wide. "How do I work this?"

The small group on the steps chuckled at her bewildered state, and Devlan put Hannah down before jogging down the steps to her side. His eyes were dancing with amusement. "This proves that your Corolla was ancient. Keyless entry has been around for a while now. Come here, and I'll show you."

She looked up at him hopefully. "Do you have time to go for a ride?"

"Of course," he answered with a slight frown.

"You said you had to go to the city for a while, but I'd really like you to drive first. I just want to look at it."

"Then let's take you for a ride."

Diana slipped into the soft leather of the new Mercedes and ran her hands over the seats. Despite her comfortable upbringing, she had never owned a new car. The only car that she and Peter had bought new was the Mustang, and that had been his car alone. This was her treat, her car. Closing her eyes, she inhaled deeply the scent. There was nothing like the smell of a new car. The cleanliness and newness permeated the very air. On top of that clean smell was the delicious scent of Devlan.

"This is amazing," she breathed.

"Ready?"

She opened her eyes and glanced at him. His eyes glittered with unconcealed excitement, and she could see that he was thrilled at having surprised her so much, but then her guilt returned. Fastening her seat belt, Diana smiled back, although her smile was slightly less confident and sure. "Devlan, I don't know about this. It's too much." She shook her head. "I can't believe you bought me a car…"

"Nonsense."

He deftly started the motor and put the car into gear, pulling out of the driveway with a slight squeal of the tires. They were silent as he put the car through the paces along the quiet back streets of Malibu before heading back to the Pacific Coast Highway.

"This car's magnificent," he said appreciatively. "Just wait till you drive it."

"It's beautiful… a work of art," Diana returned. Her long fingers reached out and gently stroked the walnut trim. "It's far too rich for me. Devlan, I really shouldn't accept such a costly gift."

With an uncustomary show of anger, Devlan pulled the car to the side of the road, and for several tense moments, the only sound was the low sound of the radio and the quiet purring of the engine. Mumbling under his breath, Devlan twisted in his seat and scowled at her. "Hasn't anyone told you that it's rude to refuse a gift?"

"Well, I –"

"Don't you think it's time to stop refusing me?"

"It's not that."

Lean fingers reached out and grasped her chin, lifting it to meet his penetrating stare. His touch was gentle, but she could see irritation and frustration in the tight lines of his jaw and grim line of his mouth. "Then what is it?"

She sighed heavily. "When you do things like this, I feel uncomfortable. I don't want people to think that I'm here for your money."

"Everybody who's anybody knows that you're my sister-in-law. They all know that you're here because of Hannah." His voice lowered an octave as he continued. "Only those who were present know about our fling in Hawaii. I've taken great pains to ensure that our private relationship remains thus."

Diana nodded, and he released her chin to sit back in his seat. *Fling?* Since when had what happened between them become a fling? She stiffened in her seat, her brain refusing to believe what she had just heard. It was painful to think that he only viewed their relationship as a fling, and her all of old insecurities came flooding back.

The car remained silent as they returned to the house. Devlan drove skillfully, though on the edge of reckless, and Diana knew that he was still irritated with her. She stared straight ahead until he pulled in the driveway and stopped the car.

"You're very quiet. Are you angry?"

She shook her head no, not trusting her voice to speak.

"I want to have dinner with you tonight. I'll be in the office this afternoon, but if you'll drive this into the city, I'll take you and Hannah out to celebrate."

Diana put on her best smile and nodded. He reached across the seat and planted a kiss on the top of her head. Even though she raised her chin to receive a kiss on her lips, Devlan released her and opened his door. He was at her side in an instant and gallantly opened her door for her.

"I've really got to run. I'll meet you at the office around seven o'clock, okay?"

"How should we dress?"

"As much as I'd love to eat dinner with you dressed that way, I can't think of a place that wouldn't frown. How about we have a family-style dinner? Something low key."

Before Diana could get a word in edgewise, Devlan had spun on his heel and climbed into the waiting car. She remained in the driveway, a frown marring her face. There would be much to discuss with him when she got the chance – and to Hannah as well.

~

Devlan sat back in his seat and breathed a sigh of relief. The day was beautiful and cool, but he felt downright hot underneath the collar of his suit. In addition, his palms were still moist even though she was gone. As they drove farther away from the house and Diana, he was able to breathe easier. That had been a close call. He had almost blurted out his plans when she bristled about the car. It was painfully clear that he still had not won her over completely yet. No, she made no qualms about resenting his desire to bestow frequent gifts on her. He would have to tread carefully and see how the night went.

Sighing in frustration, Devlan glanced down at his laptop without actually viewing the screen. He had not realized just how important it was to him to discuss his plans with Diana on this special day for her. He wanted to come clean, and he wanted more than anything to hear what she had to say about it. Yes, he wanted to see the look on her face when he told her that he wanted her in his life permanently.

What she did not know yet was that Thomas was right. He was ready to snatch her up before someone else did. Devlan Doyle, confirmed bachelor, had finally met the right woman and wanted to settle down.

Doyle Enterprises was bustling with activity when he entered the downtown skyscraper. Other than a cursory, "Hello, Mr. Doyle, glad you're back," no one seemed to notice his presence. He liked that. It reminded him how well his people worked under him, and why he had such a low turnover rate. Everybody knew their jobs, everybody did their jobs, and that meant everybody got paid.

Making his way up to the top floor where his office waited, he was finally surrounded by employees with questions and problems, all requiring immediate attention. Kathy appeared with flushed cheeks and her hair in mild disarray, and Devlan grimaced as she approached.

"You have to help me with this woman, Mr. Doyle. She's called at least ten times this morning, just in the last two hours. She wanted to make sure you remembered the charity dinner tonight. It's eight o'clock in Beverly Hills. She said you promised to pick her up at seven. Please call her back."

Devlan stopped in his tracks and signed the paper thrust before him by another desperate employee. Couldn't anyone live without his present for a couple of weeks?

"Who are you talking about?" he asked Kathy irritably. "Diana called?"

Kathy frowned and put her hands on her hips. Her foot was tapping rapidly on the carpeting below, muffling the furious sound. "No, Mrs. Somerset would never be so rude. I'm talking about Roxanne Lemieux."

"Roxanne?" Devlan frowned. "I have no plans with Roxanne tonight. I'm having dinner with Diana and Hannah. It's Diana's birthday."

"You bought tickets to a Hollywood charity dinner a couple of months ago. You're escorting Roxanne. Lots of press. It was supposed to be good for her career."

"Yeah, and bad for mine," Devlan muttered. "Damn it all, I forgot. Kath, do me a favor?"

"Oh, no," she said, backing away. "I'll not do your dirty work, Mr. Doyle. You call her, here's her number."

Kathy thrust the sticky note into his hand and stomped away, her stiff posture reminding Devlan how difficult Roxanne could be. With uncustomary briskness, he waved away the others pressing around him and stormed into his office, shutting the door behind him with a solid thump.

His briefcase was tossed on his desk before he threw himself into his plush leather chair. Oh yes, he was in for it now. Tonight would be one of the biggest battles he had yet to fight, and as he dialed her number, he could not shake the feeling that he would not be the victor this time either way.

"Roxanne? It's Devlan."

"It's about time, honey. Where have you been? I've been calling for ages."

"I've been in New York, Roxanne. I've been working."

"Yes, I heard about your vacation with your sister-in-law. The tabloids love it. She's prettier than I thought."

Devlan gritted his teeth. Her catty tone was not missed.

"Why didn't you visit when you were in the city? I was doing a show, and the tabloids noticed that I was there and you weren't."

"I told you, I've been very busy. It was a business trip in New York, not pleasure."

"Yes, you had that already, didn't you? A cozy little vacation on the yacht in Hawaii with your sexy new lover."

"That's enough."

She sighed and calmed her tone a little. "I'm sorry, hon, but I feel a little left out. Ever since she came into the picture, you've been neglecting me. I'm ready to move on. I want to go deeper."

Devlan drew his hand over his face and leaned forward in his chair. He truly did not wish to hear this now. "I can't think about that, Roxanne. The reason I'm calling is that something's come up and I can't – "

"You have to. Oh, Dev, you can't miss this. It's for children's cancer research. You're one of their greatest patrons. Every network is going to be there. It would hurt you and them if you didn't show up."

"What if you go for me?"

"Show up alone? No, I'm not doing that again."

Devlan scurried around his desk looking for the name of a few bachelors in his company. Roxanne heard him and started laughing. "There's no way you're sticking me with one of the suits in your company. You change your plans, Dev. You can't get out of this one."

Devlan cursed under his breath. "I'll see what I can do. Kathy or I will get back to you later."

"Fine, don't disappoint me on this one, Devlan. Don't you do it. It means too much to you and to me to blow this off."

He slammed the phone down and put his head in his hands. What a mess he had made. The question now was whether Diana would forgive him or not.

He pressed the button to the intercom and Kathy responded sharply. "Yes, Mr. Doyle."

"Call my house and let them know I have to cancel dinner. Tell them that I'll make it up to them."

"You're going out with *her* tonight?" Kathy asked angrily. "Are you serious?"

"I tried, Kathy." His scowl was fierce, and he was sure Kathy could sense it. "Just do it."

"But —"

"No buts," he snapped. "If this morning is any indication, it's going to be a helluva day. I don't need you on my case, too."

Ending the conversation, Devlan sighed heavily. There was much work to be done and many people to talk to throughout the day, so Devlan was busy. However, many of his people were rolling their eyes at him as he answered their questions distractedly or not at all. In the back of his mind for the entire day was his blown evening. All in all, he was very unproductive, and it was not until he was dressing in his tuxedo that he remembered he had not spoken to Kathy about Diana's reaction. Racing across his office, he reached for the door and yanked it open. Fortunately, she was still there and glanced up startled when he hurried out.

"Oh, good. You're still here," he said.

"I'm still angry at you." She gave him a once over, her eyes taking him in appreciatively. "Straighten your vest."

He glanced down and gave it a tug. Her mouth twisted and then broke into a smile, and she reached forward to do it for him.

"You need a good woman to take care of you," she said pointedly.

"I know. Will you marry me, Kathy?"

She laughed aloud. "Be careful, Mr. Doyle. People love to talk."

"Is Wills here with the Bentley?"

"He's downstairs."

"Did you call my house?"

"They're not pleased. I could hear Hannah in the background asking why."

He could not hide his disappointment. "It figures. I'll make it up to them. Any ideas?"

"An engagement ring?" she offered impishly.

Devlan stopped short and glanced down at his perky secretary. "What?"

Kathy shrugged. "She's the best thing that's ever happened to you, and you adore Hannah. I've never seen you so happy... or such a pest. Do you know how many people I had to calm down today? Just ask her and be done with it."

Devlan shook his head as he strode away. "You women are all out to get me today, aren't you? Is this some sort of conspiracy?"

Kathy just laughed.

Chapter 15

It was a mild evening, and Devlan felt stuffy in his well-fitted tux. The bright lights of the photographer's flashes were blinding, but Devlan knew he had to go through the paces with his customary smile in tow. In addition to the press, there were paparazzi, and he dodged the shouted questions as best as he could. If there was one good thing about his presence at the charity dinner with Roxanne, it would certainly take some of the heat off of Diana.

For her part, Roxanne looked stunning and happy, dressed in a slinky black evening gown and a wide smile. It clung to her long, thin curves, and not one touch of her professionally applied makeup was out of sorts or smudged. If he were any other man, he realized, he would be proud to escort her around. However, tonight his mind was fixated on the loving single mother, sitting home alone on her birthday. He was left feeling tense, resentful, and in no mood to be in the spotlight.

"Mr. Doyle! Where's that pretty relative of yours?"

Devlan gritted his teeth and ignored the question, but his grip inevitably tightened around Roxanne's arm. She stopped, turning to the photographer, and put on her best smiling pose.

"His *sister* is home watching us on TV," she quipped.

"Roxanne," Devlan muttered under his breath. "Move on now, or I'm leaving. Imagine what the press would do about that."

Roxanne hesitated for a moment, and Devlan imagined that

he could see her brain working, digesting his threat. Then she smiled brightly again and waved before wrapping her hand possessively around his arm and leading him away. No one noticed her mouth move beneath the smile, but Devlan heard her words quite clearly.

"You're hiding something there, aren't you?"

Those were the last civil words she exchanged with him until the end of the meal. Their actions were automatic with the appropriate laughs and applause, but Roxanne was obviously stirring something in her mind. He took the time to allow his thoughts free rein, and as soon as it was appropriate to do so, he politely insisted on being among the first to leave.

"Really, Dev, it's so early. Can't we stay for a little while longer?"

Devlan was struck at how phony she appeared. Her pout was perfectly staged, and he felt she could outdo some of the best actresses in the room. "Careful, someone might find you and put you in a movie."

She batted her eyes. "Would that be so terrible?"

Devlan sighed. "If it's that big of a deal, I'm sure I could find you a ride home."

Roxanne hastily put her napkin on the table and took one last sip of her wine. "No, no, I'll go with you. Maybe on the ride home I can talk you into stopping at a club for a while."

"I'm too old for clubs," he said wearily.

"That wasn't true six months ago."

Turning to the others at their table, Devlan bowed. "Ladies and gentlemen, I thank you for a pleasant evening."

They smiled and said their goodbyes. One boisterous Los Angeles trial lawyer grinned lewdly. "Can't wait to get her home, eh, Doyle?"

Devlan shot him a cold stare before turning to the others. "Would you believe I'm the one with the headache?"

Without another word, he turned and escorted Roxanne out of the hotel and into the car. All the while, he ignored her furious stare. Mike slipped in the front seat as usual, leaving Devlan alone with her. For once, Devlan really longed to have his friend's company with him, for no sooner had they pulled away from the curb than Roxanne was in his seat and pressing against him.

"Let's go to my apartment and make love, Devlan."

Her mouth pressed against his neck, her warm lips closing over his pulse there. Devlan's nostrils flared with the scent of her heavily perfumed body, the smell of which bothered him. He wanted a natural beauty, and the one he was envisioning did not need to apply strong perfumes and a lot of makeup to capture his interest.

He wanted Diana.

Once again, he was reminded of how much she had changed him. Gone were the days that he enjoyed being associated with the top beauties in the country. Right now, he wanted to curl up with Diana and watch a movie, just like all those pleasant evenings they shared on the yacht. He wished more than ever that he was back there at that moment.

"Roxanne, no. I can't do this."

He pulled away from her nibbling teeth. As she straightened, he turned to face her, knowing instinctively that she was tensing for a fight.

"What's with you?" Roxanne snapped.

"I have jet lag, and I haven't slept very well."

"Is this because of your house guests?"

"No Roxanne, I'm just not interested in you that way."

She smoothed down her dress, her long, painted fingernails nearly snagging the fine material. "I don't know why I waste my time with you, Devlan. Do you have any idea how many propositions I get a week? People are dying to date me."

He tried to hide his growing frustration, but his sarcasm did not escape her finely tuned ears. "Then maybe you should experiment with them."

She frowned at him, her beautiful face contorting with anger. "I don't want to, Devlan. I think that we have a future here. I think that you should go home thinking about that. It's time to make a decision as to where you think we're going. I'm tired of going out as friends. I want more."

With a weary sigh and an almost imperceptible shake of his head, Devlan answered her ultimatum. "I'm not prepared to go further with you, Roxanne. If you think that we can't be together as friends, then you should move on. You're a lovely, vibrant, beautiful and fun-loving young woman. I wouldn't blame you in the least."

"Go home and think about that before you come to a decision, Devlan. You're telling me now that you want to break it off, and I'm not sure you're ready to make that decision."

"I'm sorry."

She slid back into her seat and crossed her arms over her chest, but Devlan barely noticed. They were fast approaching her apartment, and his heart began to quicken. Soon, soon he would be home.

"I'm going back to New York Friday for ten days. I'll be back here until the holidays are over. Then, after Christmas, I fly to Italy to shoot a commercial. Try to work this out with me before then, okay?"

With a sympathetic smile, Devlan nodded his head. He was not a cruel man, and he was certain that once Roxanne came to terms with his lack of interest she would set her sights on someone else. The lights of the passing cars caught his attention, and he glanced out the window to help pass the time. The action effectively ended any further conversations for the remainder of the ride.

Ever the gentleman, Devlan escorted Roxanne up to her

apartment, but as soon as she was safely within her apartment walls he dashed back to the waiting Bentley. No sooner had he closed the door behind him than he was urging Wills to hurry home. Wills was apparently the only one at present feeling sympathetic and did as he was asked, managing to get them home in record time. However, the house was dark when they pulled into the drive. The fountain was brightly lit, and it was the only light as far as he could see. The dark interior and lack of outdoor lighting spoke volumes. He was in trouble here.

The three men stared at the house in silence.

"Uh oh," Wills said meaningfully.

"Just go to bed," he said.

With bated breath, he made his way through the front door and up the winding staircase to Diana's room. It too was dark, and she did not answer his knock. Unwilling to give up, Devlan opened the door and slipped into the room. The urge to see her and touch her was overwhelming. Too many days had passed since he had made love to her, and he needed to be with her again.

"Diana?"

Only silence answered his soft call, and to his dismay he saw that her bed was still neatly made and untouched. She had not retired yet. Where was she?

Stepping out onto her balcony, he looked down at the pool. The night had grown slightly chilly, but it was still comfortable enough to swim in. Although the whole house was dark, there were security lights illuminating the patio and the beach below indicating that someone had been out there. It took him a moment for his eyes to grow accustomed to the darkness.

Then he saw her.

A woman was running gracefully along the surf, her steps sure and methodical. The thick mass of blond hair was pushed away from her face by a black headband, yet the rest hung down her back in long blond waves. She was dressed in tight black shorts and an old gray zipper sweatshirt that was zipped halfway. Naturally, she did not wear anything he had purchased.

Devlan's breath caught at the sight, and suddenly he was reminded of the song that he had heard through Diana's headphones that morning. There were waves and soft sand all around her in the darkness, yet there she was enjoying herself and the night. It was a sight that burned itself into his memory, one that he would forever hold dear. He did not just want to continue their relationship, he wanted more. A lot more. All of her. Forever. The longed for discussion would not just be about a permanent relationship. It would encompass so much more, like a life together, children, family pets, and retirement.

Yes, he was in love with her. He loved the way she laughed and the way she smiled. He even loved it when she argued with him over his generosity. He loved her mothering skills, and he loved his niece. He needed her by him always. She was *the one*.

More determined than ever to tell her these things before the evening was over, Devlan hurried outside to greet her. She was still jogging when he reached the stairs to the beach, and he rushed to meet her halfway out. The sand did not slow him, even though it got into his shoes and scratched the fine leather.

"Diana," he called.

She stopped jogging and turned around, her eyes wide with surprise. "Wow, you're back early," she said, a little breathless.

"Why is the house so dark? Am I not welcome in my own home?"

His attempt at humor was lost on her ears. Her face remained still, although she began to jog in place as he continued to advance. "I saw you on TV tonight."

He nodded and stopped in front of her. Her chest was heaving slightly, and he saw the sweat glistening in her cleavage. Watching it drip lower and disappear into the cloth of her sports bra, Devlan licked his lips as he imagined tasting the saltiness on her skin, but he stopped from reaching out for her while he studied her closed countenance.

"I bought tickets to this charity a couple of months ago. I couldn't stand her up. It would've been humiliating for her and detrimental to me."

"Kathy told me."

"Oh," he said. He glanced down at his shoes. "Listen, Diana, I'm really sorry. I did everything I could to get out of it."

She held up her hand. "You don't have to apologize to me, Devlan. I understand."

It was plain that he did need to, more than anything. She was hurt, that much he could see in her otherwise guarded face. When Diana turned to jog away, Devlan reached for her and grasped her upper arm.

"What are you doing?"

He pulled her against him, his arms encircling her tightly. "I just got back from New York, and all afternoon I've been harassed by the women in my life. Right now I need you. I need your forgiveness."

"I don't know, Devlan. I'm all sweaty, please let me go –"

His lips came down on hers at the same time as he pulled her hips against his. Though he felt the breath rush out of her lungs, he did not release her. There was no way he could. Despite the damp sweatshirt that clung to her skin and her salty taste, Devlan thought she was freshest thing he had seen all day. His heart was pounding violently against his chest, and it was matched by her heart as well. No matter how long it took or how many kisses he had to give her, he was determined to ease her anger and make her smile for him again.

Luck finally seemed to come to his rescue when she began to relax slightly against him. Apparently, he was wearing her down, for her fingers slid through his hair and gave him a slight tug when he began to move away.

He raised his head a little, his tongue slipping out to taste her on his lips. "You truly are a sight for sore eyes," he whispered.

"Well, when you put it that way," she said with a brief smile. It was fleeting, too quick for his tastes.

He sighed in frustration. "I spent the entire day planning your birthday dinner. I had so much to discuss with you, and I was dying to see you and Hannah. Then I get called to this ridiculousness. I'm such a fool."

Nodding her head, she evidently agreed.

"Thanks for your support," he said wryly.

Her lips curved again, this time in a half smile. "Why can I not stay angry at you?"

"Because I don't want you to." When she shook her head and began to pull away, he grasped her tighter. "And I'm willing to work very hard to get what I want…"

She chuckled softly in the night.

"Let's go in before I ravish you on this beach where everyone can see us. I really do need to talk to you."

"All right," she murmured. "But let me at least shower."

"I'll join you," he said, raising his head and wiggling his brows at her.

She chuckled and pushed away from his loose grasp. "I don't know about that."

"Come inside," he said. "Now, before I do something stupid again like throw you to the ground and take you right here on the beach."

"All right, already."

Grasping her hand, he smiled when her fingers entwined with his. She laughed her magical laughter, and the sound warmed his heart. He really had missed her, and once more, he was overcome with the urge to discuss his plans with her, and he would have if her joyous laughter had not given away their precise location.

"Mr. Doyle, sir? Telephone."

Devlan stopped dead in his tracks, the blood rushing in his ears louder than the words he dreaded hearing. Mike stood on the steps, holding the house phone in his hands and peering out into the darkness. He looked uneasy, and his eyes remained averted when he spotted them.

"Take a message," Devlan said shortly.

"Uh… I'm sorry, but it's Roxanne. She said it was imperative that she speak with you now."

Devlan felt Diana go rigid beside him, and her fingers tightened around his. Devlan glanced down at her, very aware of her discomfort.

"Can't you see that I'm busy?"

His sharp tone surprised Mike, but he nodded and took a step back. "Yes, sir."

Devlan grasped Diana's hand and pulled her up the steps behind him, eager more than ever to lock them in his bedroom.

"Come on before something tragic happens," he muttered.

Diana smiled and picked up the pace, her long legs matching his strides easily. They were halfway up the stairs when Mike caught up to them. His face bore a pained expression, and he stared at a spot beyond Devlan mournfully.

"I'm sorry, sir, but she said it was an emergency. She said that she mistakenly overdosed on her sleeping pills tonight and is afraid she's going to die."

Diana gasped, but Devlan was unmoved. He spoke through clenched teeth. "Has she called an ambulance?"

"No sir, she's afraid of what the news would report. She's asking for you to come and drive her to her doctor."

"This is unbelievable."

"I'm sorry for interrupting. I wouldn't if it was unnecessary," he said again, his gaze flickering to Diana.

Before he could refuse again, Diana turned to face him and

placed her hand on his arm. "Go, Devlan," she said softly. "Go take care of her. Who knows what will happen next?"

Devlan glanced at Mike, who nodded in agreement. "She's right."

With a heavy sigh, Devlan turned to face Diana. He took her hands in his and pressed his lips to her forehead. "I'm so sorry to keep doing this to you."

"I do understand."

"I don't know how long this will take."

Though he did not hear it, he felt her heavy sigh. It matched his feeling of helplessness. Her disappointment was evident in the drooping of her shoulders and the strained look on her face. As he watched, she continued up the stairs slowly, her feet dragging and her head down. It made him feel a little better to see that at least he was not the only one affected.

"I'll call you tomorrow," he called after her. "We still need to talk, Diana."

She waved in answer and disappeared into the dark house. Devlan remained where he was, watching her balcony until the light went on. Then he gave Mike his attention.

"That woman is turning into a nightmare," he ground out angrily.

"This is pretty serious," he agreed. "Who knows what she's capable of?"

"I know, Mike." He took a deep breath and adjusted his clothes in an attempt to regain his composure. "Let's go and get this over with."

Mike fell in step beside Devlan. "You know, sir, you've stood Mrs. Somerset up twice tonight."

"You don't need to remind me," Devlan snapped.

Mike chuckled as he dropped the phone on the long dining room table. "I meant to say that it's her birthday and all, and you've left her twice for another woman. She's been pretty understanding about it."

"Scary, isn't it?"

"Well, yes. There's got to be a storm brewing."

Devlan's brows rose over his piercing blue eyes. "I can see what you're getting at, but I have a plan that will ensure my forgiveness. Tomorrow I plan to shop Rodeo Drive to find the perfect ring. I want to make this legit."

Mike's eyes widened in surprise, but his face broke into a wide smile. "Glad to hear it, sir. She's a fine woman."

"Yes. The finest I've ever met."

"Quite a catch when she doesn't give a hoot about your money."

"No," he said with a chuckle. "Actually, she would rather I didn't have any. That's one of the best things about her. She accepts me for the man I am, not the money I have. That's a rare feat."

"And she's a rare find. I'm very happy for you, and I hope you're both happy."

"Thanks, Mike. As soon as I can get Roxanne out of the way and work on my retirement, I plan to make her very happy indeed."

"Retirement? Does that mean…"

Devlan smiled at Mike. "It does. I'm cutting back on my work. I want to take care of my family. I want to spend more time with them."

Mike let out a low whistle.

"Let's take the Mercedes. I hate to get Wills out of bed for this."

"Very well, sir."

The two men strode to the garaged vehicle, and Devlan slid behind the driver's seat. As the engine purred to life, Devlan gave one more glance at Mike. "If you were me, Mike, what would you do?"

"I would grab her before somebody else does."

Devlan nodded, a smile brightening his angry countenance. "I thought so. Now I just need to explain all this to Roxanne. "

Chapter 16

Diana sat by the wall of windows in the white living room, the soft leather of the couch caressing her skin like a warm glove. The heavy rain pattered rhythmically against the ceiling high window. The droplets cascaded down the shining glass, and the small rivers caught her attention. With a finger, she traced the path of a single raindrop as it slid down the glass like a lone tear streaming down a smooth cheek. The day was as gloomy as she felt, for Christmas was approaching fast, and she had still not seen Devlan since the night on the beach.

Sighing deeply, Diana returned her gaze to the hardcover book on her lap. She was already halfway through, and she had only bought it yesterday. She, Hannah and Lani had gone to Beverly Hills the day before, shopping for Christmas gifts and just to have fun. Although the area was not quite what she had envisioned from the movies and television, it was the shopping trip of a lifetime. It was yet another moment in her life that she would remember always.

Not willing to forget her host, Diana and Hannah had chosen Devlan's Christmas gifts. Hannah had picked a sweatshirt that sported a child on a man's shoulders and read "World's Greatest Dad." Although Diana had objected, her stubborn child was adamant and stomped her feet so hard that tears had flooded her eyes.

Diana had also found the perfect gift for him. It took her a lot of soul searching, for what could she buy for the man who could have whatever he wanted? However, she knew the one thing he could not just take, one thing that he could only borrow. Hannah and Diana had treated themselves to a photo session dressed in fancy new clothes. To go with it, Diana purchased a costly frame with her own money and was having the items delivered on Christmas Eve.

The day had been perfect, although Diana had run out of steam a lot faster than the others did. It seemed to be the growing trend. Lately, she was tired all the time, with absolutely no true reason for it. She had no idea why.

Of course, now it was getting easier to go out with Hannah since she was continuing her recovery. She had put aside her cane, and Diana was sure that with Lani's help, she would regain the full use of her leg in a matter of weeks. As good as that sounded, it also meant that she would be free to leave Malibu – and Devlan.

With growing trepidation, Diana faced the reality of it all. Her fairytale existence was fast coming to a close. As hungry as he had been for her during their vacation, his desire for her did not overpower the demands of his friend and his work now that they were back on the mainland. He had always been so charming and open, but not once had he given her any indication of wanting her to stay when Hannah was better. In fact, his last reference to their relationship was that of a fling, and he appeared to have completely forgotten about them both now that their trip was over. That certainly did not bode well for any type of future.

Devlan had taken Roxanne to the hospital the night of the beach incident and stayed in the city for the next two days. He had called to tell her that Roxanne was going to be fine, but he was too busy at work to come home. Then he was again called to New York. It had been two weeks already, and he had yet to return.

Christmas was now only four days away. Devlan had called Mrs. Maclean the afternoon before and told her to hire a cook for a large Christmas dinner. With bated breath, the entire household assumed he would try to be home for that, but Diana felt that she would believe it when she saw it.

"Mrs. Somerset?"

Diana glanced up to see Mrs. Maclean standing in the doorway. Diana smiled in greeting and placed down her book. "Hello, Mrs. Maclean."

"Mrs. Somerset, you have a visitor," Mrs. Maclean said. The older woman appeared nervous, with her hands first twisting her apron and then smoothing it down.

Diana frowned in surprise and came to her feet. "I have a visitor?"

"Yes, ma'am," she said, her gray head bobbing. "It's Miss Lemieux."

Diana's breath caught. Suddenly the room began to feel warm. "Roxanne?"

"Yes, ma'am. She'd like to speak with you."

Before Diana could reply, the raven-haired beauty strode in. She appeared devastatingly beautiful in a white fur sweater and black leather pants. Her hair was flowing loosely down her back, and a wide red belt cinched in her narrow waist. Diana suddenly felt awkward and small next to this highly polished professional. She hated to admit that Roxanne Lemieux's startling beauty was perfect for Devlan's debonair good looks.

"Hello Miss Lemieux, it's nice to meet you," Diana said, holding out her hand.

Roxanne entered the room, leaving behind her the lingering smell of a costly perfume. She took in the magnificent living room with its fifteen-foot ceilings and smiled in approval. As she looked around, Diana stepped forward to greet her. She dismissed Diana's hand with a wave and entered further, crossing to the tall windows and glancing out at the pool below.

"You know, Devlan and I picked out this house together. It

was to be our home when we married. Malibu is private, and you know how much Devlan likes his privacy."

Diana watched Roxanne with a pained expression. She was no fool to realize that Roxanne was here for a reason, the question was - what?

"You would know better than I," she answered carefully.

Her hand fell to her side where it brushed against her tattered jeans. Next to Roxanne she felt plain, ugly, simple. It was like a glass of cold water in the face. Roxanne glanced at her with a sly look. It was the look of a cat that had swallowed the canary. Despite the outward show of friendliness, there was a palpable tension filling the air. Diana felt ill at ease.

"I do, don't I?" she said with a smile. "And I am just learning quite a bit about our handsome mutual friend."

Diana felt the urge to sit down, so strong was the dread settling in the pit of her stomach. She was too tired to fight, and she assumed that was why Roxanne was here. Taking in a shaky breath for courage, she attempted to smile. "You are?"

"Yes, well word leaked out today in the papers about his Christmas plans. Have you heard yet?"

Roxanne spun around to look at Diana, and her wide gray eyes watched for her reaction carefully. Seeing this, Diana schooled her features to remain impassive. After all those years with Peter and his ridicule, Diana was sure that she could maintain a poker face. With every ounce of strength she had within her, she held herself proud and emotionless.

"I don't usually watch TV," she admitted with an apologetic shrug.

Roxanne again smiled, knowing full well that Diana had watched the night of her birthday. It was the night that Roxanne had called; the night of the charity when Devlan had left her home alone. Diana remembered clearly what Roxanne had said.

"Ah, I see. Well, I had a minor accident a couple of weeks

ago and had to go to the hospital. Dev realized just how close he was to losing me and proposed right there on the spot. Now our little secret is out. He picked up the ring a couple of weeks ago. He had told me that he wanted to talk to you and his niece first, but I figured that since he was out of town, I'd stop in to say hello and pass on the good news."

Diana's heart came to a sudden stop before starting again in a rapid tempo. Her chest felt tight, as though a ton of bricks prevented her from breathing. Her head was spinning as she considered whether Roxanne was telling the truth.

Had there been any indication?

Yes, she thought wildly, Devlan had told her he needed to speak with her. It had been the very last thing he had said to her. Perhaps all this time he was afraid to tell her. Maybe that was why he had stayed away. Roxanne's chatter echoed in her ears, slowly drawing her attention back.

"I was so excited and just had to tell someone. I figured we should start to get to know each other. Especially since we'll be in close quarters until your daughter gets better."

Diana's world slid out from under her feet. She began to tremble in earnest. As badly as she longed to collapse into the soft sofa, she continued to hold her ground. Still, it was a tremendous effort to stay on her feet.

"Well, uh, congratulations are due you then," she stammered. Her voice sounded miles away, shaky and hoarse.

Roxanne's gaze never left hers, and she gave a small, almost imperceptible nod. "Thank you. I'm glad that we're going to be family. Even if it's only for a short time. I hear that your trip to Hawaii last month really did wonders for your daughter."

"Yes, she's healing quickly."

Not quickly enough!

"I think that's great news. She's a good influence on Devlan. He's suddenly more perceptive to children. I'm really so glad you're here."

"I'm sure," Diana muttered.

"Yes, because now he's eager to have his own children. You know, to pass on his name. I told him that he'd have to wait at least a year or two. I'm still in my prime, you know."

"I can see that."

A sleek eyebrow lifted before she smiled again. "Ah, well, as much as I'd love to stay and chat, I really have to get going. I'm planning on moving my things over after the holidays. I have to go to Italy, but when I get back, we're going to start making plans. It's so exciting."

A pained smile passed over Diana's lips, but she nodded in understanding. "I know. I've been there once myself."

"That's true. You have already been married. Well, me too. Second time is always the best they say. We'll see."

"I wish you the best," she murmured.

"Yeah, thanks." She raised her brows. "You know, Devlan told me how beautiful your daughter is. Maybe we can find a spot for her in the wedding party."

"Maybe," Diana echoed, although she knew she and Hannah would be gone by then.

"Again, we'll see after the holidays."

Diana could feel the tears welling in her eyes. It was getting increasingly difficult to hold them in. Children? Had he not panicked when they had unprotected sex? Did he not tell her that it would have to be something discussed and agreed upon?

Apparently, only when it involved her.

"I understand that Mrs. Maclean already hired a chef for Christmas dinner, so I guess I can leave you to handle the rest of the dinner plans for now. I'll be working right up to Christmas Eve."

All of Roxanne's chattering was driving her to distraction. Right then, all she desperately wanted to do was go and lie down.

She nodded distractedly. "Of course."

"Okay, then. I'll see you in a couple of days, Diana. May I call you Diana?"

"Naturally."

"Well good, Diana. Tell Hannah her Aunt Roxanne said hello and happy holidays."

"I will, thank you," she muttered.

Roxanne slipped out as easily as she had sailed in, leaving behind her the lingering smell of her strong perfume and the tattered remains of Diana's heart.

Pleading a migraine, Diana remained hidden for the rest of the day. At one point, she began to doze, her sleepiness overpowering her will to think. After a brief nap on the living room sofa, Diana sat silently with her chin resting on her knees. She stared blindly out into the rain, watching the wind tossed waves crash onto the beach. Tears blurred her vision and filled her eyes as sadness washed over her.

All along, you knew this would happen.

However, Devlan's callousness had taken her completely by surprise. He had always been so courteous and open. Why could he not tell her himself?

He tried that night on the beach.

He had gone away before he had a chance, but she could not believe it was out of cowardice. As she continued to think, she wondered over and over again if she had done something wrong. Maybe her cold reaction had frightened him off. In all their brief relationship, Devlan had always been honest and straightforward. It was so unlike him to do something so cruel, especially when he had said that Roxanne was nothing more than a friend. Had he lied because of his fear of her temper?

He had kissed her on the beach the night of her birthday until her head spun. He had told her then that he did not want her to be angry. So what had happened between him and Roxanne

227

that made him decide to marry her so quickly? Just a month ago, he had been making love to her on their private vacation, and now he was planning a wedding to another woman. She just could not believe it.

A confrontation was due here. He had to give her that one last courtesy before she left. If it was true, she and Hannah would leave immediately. She would figure out where to when the time came.

The rain eventually came to a stop, but the sky remained dark and dreary. Hannah popped in quickly, carrying one of her ever-present dolls. She was dressed in a short pink frilly dress that Lani had picked out, and it suited her fair coloring well. Diana smiled at her tremulously. It would soon be just the two of them again. Her wide blue eyes gleamed large in the darkness, and she fingered the doll nervously.

"Mommy, what's wrong?"

Diana had to smile at the beautiful young girl as she slowly made her way into the spacious room. "Nothing, I was just thinking."

"What were you thinking about?"

"It's a secret," Diana whispered, drawing her hand over her eyes.

"I like secrets," Hannah whispered back.

Diana pulled her onto her lap and hugged her tight. The little ragamuffin hugged her back, her actions bringing tears to Diana's eyes. How would she explain to Hannah her time of fun had ended? This poor child had been through so much already. Why did she have to suffer heartbreak again?

Lani poked her head in and smiled broadly. "Dinner's ready, Mrs. Somerset. Hannah, we made you some chicken nuggets, and Mrs. Maclean found some sauce. Are you coming?"

Hannah's face brightened. She pulled away from Diana with barely a glance. It was one of her favorite meals. Rushing for the door, she paused in the doorway and glanced over her shoulder at her mother with a bright smile. "Mommy, everyone here is so nice. I don't ever want to go home."

Diana tried to smile back, but her lips were frozen in place. She was exhausted, both physically and mentally. "We'll talk about that later. Go eat your dinner."

Hannah opened her mouth to argue, but Lani's insistent calling caught her attention. Spinning on her heel, she turned and fled the room, leaving Diana to watch her with a sad frown. According to Roxanne, soon this house would be full of laughing and running children. The sudden urge to run away from the house, from the visions of dark haired children giggling and playing on the steps, brought her to her feet. As soon as she stood, a wave of dizziness almost caused her to sit back down. Pressing her hands to her face, she was suddenly overcome with a thought. Their trip to Hawaii, as Roxanne had reminded her, had been a month ago. A whole month had passed since her week of pure bliss. That also made her menstrual cycle late.

She was late!

Desperation seized her, and she began to form another plan in her mind. With growing fear, she joined the others in the spacious kitchen and grabbed a bite to eat, ignoring Mrs. Maclean's curious stares and Lani's speculative one. Still pleading a headache, she picked at her food and ate silently while she formed her plan. As soon as they were done, she asked Lani to put Hannah down to bed. The child pouted briefly, but Lani was quick to make the idea sound fun. Diana concocted a story about doing some last minute shopping and slipped from the house as soon as she could. She had much to do and not a lot of time to do it.

She needed to be sure before Devlan returned.

~

"Mindy, I need help."

There was a brief silence before the woman on the other end of the line spoke. "Jesus Diana, where are you? On a payphone?"

"Yes," she said quickly. "I need help."

"Wow, I didn't even think they made those anymore. What happened? Is Hannah okay?"

"Yes, Hannah's fine. Actually she's doing fabulously. We're leaving Los Angeles, and I was hoping that we could stay with you for a short time. At least until I get myself settled in a new job."

"Of course, hon, when do you expect to be here?"

Diana took in a shaking breath. The conversation was proving to be a little harder than she had expected. The tears burned her eyes like fire, and no matter how many times she blinked them back they struggled for their freedom. "I would think in a couple of days."

"Oh, Diana, you can't come now. There's a big storm coming. They're expecting a foot of snow. The airport will probably shut down, and the roads will be closed."

A sob escaped Diana's lips as a wave of despair washed over her.

"Can you wait a couple of weeks, Di?"

"No," she moaned. "We have to leave now."

"Hold on a minute, hon, I'll go get Allan."

The tears began to careen down her face while Mindy called for Allan. Once again, they were coming to her aid. Diana glanced up at the foreboding sky, cursing the winter weather with a vengeance. She felt so trapped and alone.

"Hi, Di, how are you?"

Diana's attempt at laughter only came out as a moan. "I've got to get out of here now, Allan, and I don't know how."

"Were you going to fly or drive?"

"I wanted to drive out there in a borrowed car and pick up mine. Now I don't know what to do."

"You could head south, Diana. Phoenix is only six hours away from you. I have a friend in Scottsdale who can help us out. He has a big condo down there where you and Hannah can crash. I'll drive your car down and meet you there, okay?"

"Are you sure, Allan? I mean, it's so close to Christmas."

"Not a problem. You need help. Hold on, and I'll get Brad's address."

There was another pause during which Diana glanced at the bag in her hands. She had stopped at a drugstore on the highway and purchased a pregnancy kit. As she stared at the results in the McDonald's bathroom, the words of her high school guidance counselor rang in her ears.

"Ladies, it only takes one time. Remember that."

Now the bag with the incriminating evidence was clutched in her hands in the parking lot of that fast food restaurant, and she was once again in flight mode. She needed to get away. As far away as she could get from the crashing waves that seemed to scream the truth every time they broke on the beach.

"Okay, Diana, his name is Brad. Brad Vember. He lives in Scottsdale, off Scottsdale Road. I'll call him and let him know that you're coming. Do you have any money?"

"Yes, I have some. I'll pay him whatever he wants to let us stay until you get there."

"Don't worry about it. Brad's an old friend of mine. He's a real nice guy. He's an artist down there. You'll love him."

Diana laughed, but it sounded strained and shaky. "Please don't push any more men on me, Allan."

Allan laughed. "I won't push him on you. His tendencies go the other way. Brad is gay, Diana."

"Oh," Diana said, a true smile flitting across her lips. "That's even better."

"I'll be there as soon as I can, okay hon? Call me if you need anything."

"I already did."

He chuckled on the other end, although there was very little humor in it. "I'll see you soon."

Once they disconnected, Diana took a deep, steadying breath and reached into her bag. It was time to confront him. Diana pulled the business card from the bottom of her purse where she had stashed it among her lip gloss, discarded keys and Hannah's miscellaneous toys. She was relieved that she still had it, even though she had never had the need to use it. Until now. As she stared down at the handwritten number to his hotel suite in Denver, fresh tears flooded her eyes. So much had happened since then; so many things had changed. Her daughter was no longer near death. Devlan had made sure of that.

Flipping the card over, she ignored the office line and dialed his mobile. It was late in New York, but she knew very well how quick he was to take calls. On the fourth ring, it switched to his voicemail response, and the sound of his clipped voice was enough to throw her over the edge. A heartbroken sob escaped at the same time as the line beeped, and she hastily pulled the phone away from her ear.

Diana hung up the handset and leaned her forehead against the receiver. Unable to question him, her next step was to go back to the house and prepare for her departure. She still longed to confront Devlan, to find out why he had not just told her the truth, but that would be difficult when he was suddenly so hard to reach. So, should she stay long enough to speak to him first?

Returning to her car, she continued to allow her thoughts full rein. It seemed impossible to her that he would be so devious when all he had been was honest and up-front in the past. In fact, his candidness and determination were two of her favorite qualities about him. How could she have been so very wrong about him all this time? Because she was still overly trusting. Peter had done the same thing. Devlan's stepbrother had wooed her until she was hopelessly in love with him and then proceeded to stomp on her heart. He, apparently, was no different, and no matter what her heart told her, she had known this would happen before she had even entered the relationship. She had jumped in with both eyes wide open. It was no more than she deserved.

No, she would not remain any longer than it took to collect her belongings. There was no reason for her and Hannah to stay. Devlan had made his choice. She owed it to him to leave as peacefully as possible. She had learned her lesson once before. It was time to take matters into her hands and be strong. She would go to Phoenix and start fresh – away from Devlan.

The house was still well lit when she pulled to a stop outside the gates in the silent Mercedes. She sat in the soft leather of the front seat for a moment and stared at the beautiful mansion before her. The majestic front steps beckoned to her, reminding her that everything she held dear was within that house. Yet she also knew that she had to leave it, before it was too late.

She silently slipped through the side security gate and strode up the front steps. The door was unlocked when she entered, and the foyer was silent with no one appearing to greet her. There was a note on the crystal table, and Diana noticed it was addressed to her. She picked it up slowly and frowned.

"Two phone calls," she muttered into the silent room.

Devlan had called, the note said, leaving the phone number for his office in New York and a message to call as soon as possible. She grimaced. Roxanne probably told him of her visit.

The second phone call was from Esther Holmes. Diana glanced at the number again with a contemplative frown. Thomas was a lawyer. Perhaps he could help her. He would know exactly what to do about her newest dilemma and how to get Hannah out of Devlan's will.

Folding the paper and placing it in her purse, Diana shut off the light behind her and headed for her bedroom. She had much to do, and Esther could wait until Phoenix.

Once she finished packing, Diana slipped into Hannah's room and gathered up her belongings. Allan had said it was a six-hour drive to Phoenix. If she could do most of the driving that night, Hannah could sleep in the car. That would save her a lot of explaining during the long drive.

Glancing over at her sleeping child, Diana sighed sadly. How she hated tearing up her child's roots again. The lifestyle Devlan had given her had suited her well. She had blossomed in the care he offered. In fact, both of them had. It had been so easy to be spoiled by him.

Quickly throwing Hannah's belongings together, Diana returned outside to the car. Fortunately, the security guard was lax in the evening, expecting most of the mansion's inhabitants to still be coming and going. She encountered no one as she loaded up the trunk and returned to the house to gather Hannah. The sleeping child posed more of a problem for Diana. She was not pleased at being awakened and questioned Diana loudly. Diana hushed her as best she could while she supported her over the potty.

"We're going for a long ride tonight. You can stretch out in the back seat and sleep there. I've laid out nice soft blankets."

"But why, Mommy?"

"We have to," she replied as she pressed soft kisses all over her face.

"I don't want to."

Diana bit her lip as she sighed. She had to get Hannah outside without a scene. Smoothing her hair away from her face, she smiled more bravely than she felt. "We have to. It's very important."

"Why is it important? What's wrong?"

"Nothing's wrong, darling. We just have to."

"Are we going to see Uncle Devvie?"

234

"I don't know."

She helped Hannah slip on an oversized sweatshirt over her nightclothes, and then tied her sneakers. Hannah rubbed her eyes as she sat on the bed, watching her mother closely.

"Where are we going?"

Thinking quickly and taking a large gamble, Diana spoke quickly. "We're going to see Allan."

"Allan? Will AJ be there too?"

Diana sighed in relief. Hannah still remembered her old friends. Shrugging, Diana smiled at her daughter. "I don't know, we'll see."

"Okay."

Diana bent to pick up Hannah and rushed out the front door feeling like a thief in the night. Once again they were lucky, and no one spotted their speedy exit. Diana stood for a moment in the silence of the foyer, looking around as the memories invaded her heart. There was the bar she had seen Devlan stand at the night he took her to dinner. The outside lights were on, shining down on the pool where she had first seen his lithe length and thick muscles as he had angrily worked off the ruined evening. The beach lay beyond, where he would have seduced her if Mike had not found them and Roxanne had not called. So much had happened here, and it was all over now.

Soon they would be in a new area to start a new life.

Again.

Chapter 17

The blackness all around her was mesmerizing. There were no streetlights on this highway, and she had not seen another car in miles, only an occasional tractor-trailer. Beyond the windows was the vast emptiness of the desert and the secrets it held within. She had no idea how long she had been driving; she had lost all acceptable radio stations an hour before. Hannah still slept peacefully behind her, a good thing, for right then Diana needed all her concentration to stay on the road.

They were well within the desert now, miles from any civilization. This area of Arizona was rugged and beautiful in a dangerous and desolate way. The pale whitewashed sand of eastern California had been replaced with red, mineral-laden soil. The desert was desolate and dangerous, but full of life in the form of cacti and prickly brush. The occasional sight of a tall saguaro appearing out of the darkness frightened her even as it awed her, and the sky above was clearer and littered with more stars than she had ever seen in her life. They glittered so brightly above that she felt as though she could reach up and grasp one.

The next town would be another forty miles or so, and Diana watched the trip meter anxiously. The silence around her was eerie and hypnotic. She needed coffee or something. She was just so tired, with heavy eyelids that were growing harder to keep from slipping over her fatigued eyes. Yet, she pressed on. Her will was stronger than her exhaustion.

It was a long drive through Phoenix, and as she drove into the rising sun, a new feeling of hope dawned inside her. The sprawling city loomed ahead of her for miles when she entered its limits, an oasis of life in the middle of the desert. Surrounded by small mountain ranges and saguaro cacti, the vast, bustling city was magnificent, and as she drove she breathed a sigh of relief.

It was just past dawn when she made her way off the Route 202 onto Scottsdale Road. The wide road was already stirring with early morning traffic. She pressed on north through many traffic lights until she reached the heart of Scottsdale. From there, she made her way to Brad Vember's development.

The complex that Brad lived in was modern and spacious. She breathed a sigh of relief as she pulled into an open spot and glanced around. The multiple two-story buildings all looked very much alike. She could see a fenced pool and a community center across the well-manicured lawn. It was strange to see so much plant-life and grass in the middle of the desert, not to mention all the tall palm trees. It just was not normal.

But this was Phoenix.

Shutting down the car at last, she leaned her head back against the head rest. Her legs felt numb, and she really needed a bathroom. There was no sign anywhere of her small car, and she hoped that Allan was on his way. At that moment, she felt very uncomfortable about walking up to this stranger's door and announcing herself. Still, Hannah needed a place to sleep, a safe roof over her head, and food in her belly would be nice, too.

Hannah began to stir when Diana opened her car door. "Time to get up sleepyhead, we're here."

She moaned and opened her eyes, quickly squinting them against the early morning sun. "Where are we?"

"At a friend's house. We're going to stay here for a little while."

"Is Allan here? I want to see Allan."

Diana lifted Hannah into her arms and grunted under her daughter's weight. "Wow, you're getting heavy."

Hannah smiled at her and gave her a hug. "I love you, Mommy."

Diana hugged her back and grinned. "And I love you."

"Is Allan here?"

"I don't think so; we'll see when we get inside. Are you ready?"

Hannah nodded her blond head, her tangled hair falling into her face. Diana laughed and helped smooth it away. Her fingers were tender as she stroked the smooth cheek. It reminded her that although she had lost the two men in her life, at least she still had her child.

And another on the way, she reminded herself harshly, also with no father to care for it. She could almost feel her mother's disappointment from her grave.

"Come on, Mommy, let's go!"

Diana was jolted back to reality and nodded. "Right, let's go."

Her footsteps were slow and measured as she carried Hannah towards Unit 1112. The condo was on the first floor, and the door was firmly shut against her. Her first knock was timid, but when no one answered, her fist became more insistent.

Finally the door swung open, revealing a tall thin man around her age with long chestnut hair and partially closed brown eyes. He was bare-chested, wearing only baggy sweatpants that hung below his navel, and his toes were bare. She realized he had been sleeping.

"Come in. You must be Allan's friend."

Diana nodded and stepped in seconds before the door shut behind her with a dull thud. She was left standing in the open living room of his apartment while he strode away.

"Where'd he go, Mommy?"

"Back to bed, I suspect," she muttered.

Hannah giggled in response.

The living room had only a full-sized futon and a TV resting in the corner. The rest of the spacious room was filled with paints and easels, brushes and canvases. It was a total mess, but Diana suspected it was organized chaos.

"The second bedroom is safe to sleep in, but I don't have a crib for your little girl."

Diana's glance went back guiltily to the hallway where her host now stood. He still had not dressed, and Diana cleared her throat nervously.

"That's fine," she croaked. "Hannah can rest with me. Thank you for taking us in on such short notice…"

Brad nodded and waved his hand. "I'm sorry I'm so grouchy, but I sometimes work at night and just fell asleep a few hours ago. See me in the morning, and I'll be in a better mood."

"That's fine, I understand," she said nodding. Yet she was suddenly filled with apprehension. She was placing her trust in Allan completely and trusting that Brad was safe.

"I'm going back to bed," he announced, slipping back into his room and shutting the door with another solid thud.

Diana waited a moment before setting Hannah down on the futon. She placed the overnight bag beside her before throwing her a reassuring smile.

"Wait here, I just want to look around."

Hannah nodded, wide-eyed, and clutched the bag tightly while Diana advanced further into the apartment and looked around. There was a small dining table in the dining room, also littered with paintings, and the sink and counters in the kitchen were covered with dirty dishes. Diana sighed and shook her head. No matter what anyone said about him, he was still a man.

The bathroom was also unkempt. It was littered with his dirty clothes and the soap ring around the tub told the tale of many baths without a good scrub. She glanced into their bedroom and breathed a sigh of relief. The bed was neatly made with what appeared to be clean sheets, but she still stepped up close to check. Yes, she admitted with a sigh of relief, they were clean. There were several of his paintings hanging on the walls, but it was too dim to really look at them.

Their room was not as cluttered. There was a dresser and a small TV beside the bed, and a quartz alarm clock rested on the nightstand. She sighed and returned to the living room to find Hannah already near sleep again.

"Let's go. The bed's clean."

They tiptoed past Brad's room, and they could hear the sound of his light, even snores. Hannah glanced at Diana and giggled behind her hand.

"He's a silly man, isn't he, Mommy?"

Diana chuckled and shut the door behind them. As she steered Hannah into the bathroom she gave her a wry smile. "He's an artist, Hannah. Rumor has it that they're all a little odd."

"Why?"

She smiled. "How about you ask me in the morning after we sleep?"

Hannah nodded and slipped under the covers of the bed. She closed her eyes and sunk into the pillow just seconds before Diana did the same. They were out within moments, sleeping until well into the day.

The first thing Diana thought when she opened her eyes was that she was still dreaming. It was hard to believe that only yesterday Roxanne had uprooted her life. Then there was the still shocking fact that she was pregnant. So much had changed in the last twenty-four hours, she must have been dreaming. When she noticed that she was still dressed and sleeping under the covers of a complete stranger's bed, it all came back with a bang.

She sat upright and looked around frantically for Hannah. She was not within the spacious room, and not in the bathroom connected to their room. Diana tossed back the comforter and slipped from the bed to look for her daughter while a cold fear went straight to her bones.

"Hannah?" She reached out and opened the door.

"What?" Came the tenacious reply.

Diana heard laughter and sighed. At least Hannah was safe. She closed the door behind her and wandered down the hall to the living room. Hannah sat on the futon with a paper plate on her lap. There was a sandwich cut into fours on the plate, one of which was already eaten, and a glass of milk on the floor next to her. Their host sat cross-legged on the floor below her and was telling Hannah something that made her laugh outrageously.

"Hi," Diana said, her voice revealing her uncertainty. "What are you doing?"

"We're eating," Brad announced, smoothly coming to his feet.

Diana noticed first that Brad had dressed and apparently showered, for his long hair appeared damp, even though it was still tousled. His jeans were loose and paint-stained, and his oversized sweatshirt hung loosely to mid-thigh. He looked even thinner underneath the baggy clothes, and Diana winced at his lack of fashion sense.

"Nice to meet you, Diana. I'm Brad Vember," he said, smiling as he held out his hand. "I've made you and Hannah peanut-butter and jelly sandwiches. I'm afraid that's all I've got at the moment. I don't eat much when I'm working."

Diana grasped his hand and noticed immediately that, although his fingers were incredibly long and slim, there was a lot of strength in his grasp. She smiled shyly and shrugged politely.

"Please, don't worry about us. I'm just thankful that you were able to take us in. The last thing we want to do is put you out in any way."

"Nonsense," he announced, waving away her concerns with

his hand. "It's no trouble. When Allan called me last night and told me you needed help…well, it's the least I could do. You stay as long as you need to. You're safe here."

Diana smiled and nodded her thanks, too choked up to speak. "Well, the first thing I'm going to do is find a grocery store and fill up your kitchen. Then maybe we can clean it."

Brad chuckled at the sight of her wrinkled nose. "Again, when I work, everything is forgotten. The apartment could be burning down, and I wouldn't notice. One of the hazards of the job."

Diana rolled her eyes and glanced around again. Fortunately, he did not appear to smoke, and there were no candles in the apartment. Noticing her suspicious look, Brad chuckled and shook his head.

"I don't keep things like that around for that precise reason." He sat on the couch next to Hannah and resumed their conversation. Diana looked on as he and Hannah began chatting again, and then she went in search of her sandwich.

The clock on the microwave in the kitchen announced the time as one in the afternoon. She shook her head in self-reproach. She should never have slept that late. However, she had driven all night and felt so tired. Plus the warm bed and quiet apartment had lulled her into a dreamless sleep.

One o'clock in the afternoon. That meant that it was already noon in California and three in the afternoon in New York. Did Devlan know yet that she had gone? Did he care?

~

Devlan slammed down his fist on the table and came to his feet in a rush. Everyone in the large boardroom fell silent, and all eyes turned towards him in surprise. He had wanted their attention, and he sure had gotten it.

"You know, I pride myself on my patience, but you people are sorely trying it. For days now, we've sat here debating one simple problem, and no one has any answers. Instead, everyone is at each other's throats and placing blame."

"But, sir, this is a billion-dollar deal. If we mess up here, Doyle Enterprises will take a huge hit."

Devlan nodded in agreement. "That's true. But I have trust in you, where you don't trust yourselves. You people…" His hand swept through the crowd of forty people. "Are the smartest in the business. Lawyers, financial planners, stock brokers, all of you. You have the brains to pull this off." He stopped suddenly and glanced out the clear windows to the hallway outside. Kathy stood there, waving her arms frantically. Glancing back at the assembled group, Devlan smiled apologetically. "Will you excuse me for a moment? Continue discussing our options and get me answers."

A murmur went up as soon as the door shut behind him, and Devlan rolled his eyes at Kathy in frustration.

"That message you were waiting for from Malibu arrived early this morning. It took them all afternoon to find you here. I have a line if you want to return the call now, sir."

Devlan shook his head as he took the cup of coffee she handed to him. "It's just Diana returning my call. She never got back to me last night." He let out a heavy sigh. "I'll call her when we wrap up here. That is, if we ever wrap up here."

"Still no resolution, sir?" Kathy asked.

Devlan shook his head. "One more day of this, and I'm likely to go crazy. I'm getting too old to be up till all hours of the night brainstorming. I want to go home and celebrate the holidays."

"I know what you mean," she replied, her eyes taking on a faraway look.

Devlan cocked his head to one side as he contemplated her. She did look as lonely as he felt. Was she missing her husband and children?

"You know, Kath, I'm not likely to need you here. If you want, I'll have the jet fly you back to L.A. this afternoon and fly back later to collect me."

Kathy shook her head no. "This time of year, the airports are a mob scene. I don't want to add to that. I'll go back with you."

"Nonsense. We'll find you a commercial jet and get you a first class seat then."

Kathy's face brightened. "I'll get on it right away. Thank you Mr. Doyle."

Devlan smiled down at her, pleased that she was happy. He knew how she felt, for his whole being ached with longing for the woman and child awaiting him in Malibu. It seemed an eternity since he had held Diana in his arms and buried his face in her glorious hair. He missed the sweet sound of her voice and her light laughter, and he really missed the golden child whose speedy recovering made his heart fill with pride. He counted her swift recovery as his greatest triumph ever.

"I've got to get out of here soon too, Kath. The only way to do that is to finish up here. Just let me know if something else important comes up. I'll call Malibu later."

"Yes, sir," she said, grinning. She chuckled a little as she tossed back her hair. "Isn't love wonderful?"

Devlan shook his head in wonder. "I don't know how to answer that right now. So far, it's not so great when I'm stuck at work."

Kathy laughed harder. "It can only get better, sir. Just wait until you give her that beautiful ring."

Devlan winked and returned to the boardroom, leaving Kathy with the sound of his determined voice.

"Okay, ladies and gentlemen, I have to be in Malibu in two days. We have to settle this within that time, or I'm firing all of you."

There was a roar of laughter before the room settled down

once again. Kathy walked off down the hall, a wide smile on her face. She joined their laughter happily. "I love this job."

It was well after midnight when Devlan finally left for his apartment on the Upper East Side. He was exhausted but elated. They had finally reached an agreement and completed the merger, netting his organization a huge amount of money. The paperwork was in its final stages, and once everything was signed and sealed, he would be free to celebrate the holidays and hopefully his engagement. If that went well, his next project would be his retirement somewhere quiet with Hannah and Diana. It was no secret that Diana disliked being in the spotlight, and he too was growing tired of having his every move watched. With this new merger, he would be free to retire away from the spotlight, and he wanted to relocate somewhere quiet with the two ladies in his life.

Devlan glanced down at the pile of messages handed to him when he got into the car. There were three from Malibu, one saying it was urgent, as well as one from his lawyer out there, and one from Kathy saying she was on her way home. He grinned at the last one. It made him feel a lot better to see her happiness, and he hoped that his relationship with Diana would work out the way hers had.

The wide smile remained pasted to his face as he took the elevator up to his apartment and unlocked the door. He wandered into the library and settled down in his large leather chair with a large groan. As he reached for the phone, a new smile crossed his face. Just one more day and he would be home with the woman and child he had grown to love with all his being.

He quickly dialed the number to Diana's room and sat back in the chair, reaching into his suit pocket to pull out the box holding the ring he had purchased. As he waited for her to pick up, he flipped the lid off and stared down at the glittering ring. It was a beautiful ring, he admitted, taking pride in the fact that he had helped to design it. As Diana once said, he learned fast.

The diamonds were a rare blue tone, set in an antique platinum setting. The center large diamond was in the shape of a heart, with a crown of smaller diamonds around it. The band had engraved hearts along the sides and narrowed down into solid platinum underneath. It was not flashy or showy, just pure workmanship and detail. He really admired it, and he hoped Diana would, too.

The operator came on to the line and broke him from his reverie. "There's no one answering, would you like me to put you through to the main house, sir?"

Devlan glanced at the clock with a frown. It was after midnight in New York. Perhaps they were already sleeping. Diana was sure to have Hannah in her bed by seven thirty; it was quite possible that she retired, too. He felt the evening's elation drain from him to be replaced with disappointment and loneliness.

"No, I don't want to wake them up if they're sleeping. I'll call back in the morning. Thank you."

He hung up the phone and came to his feet. His hands tightened into fists clenched by his side. Another night was passing without hearing the sound of Diana's voice. It was torturing him.

He placed the ring in his safe and locked the heavy metal door. Tomorrow, first thing, he would call Malibu and talk to Diana and Hannah and give them the good news. He desperately needed to hear their voices.

~

"And nearly two feet of snow fell in Denver and Chicago yesterday and is due to hit us in the next day or so. Be prepared, the meteorologists are expecting over a foot of snow and plenty of disgruntled travelers. Merry Christmas, New York!"

Devlan opened his eyes wearily and reached for the alarm

clock. Snow? On Christmas? How often did that happen? The East Coast never had snowstorms like that this early in the season, let alone on Christmas. Why, he could count the amount of times he had heard of white Christmases in New York.

He slipped from between the sheets and let out a loud yawn. Another night of not sleeping well had passed, and he was growing more and more exhausted with his lifestyle. The lack of sleep and the stress of the last couple of weeks were beginning to wear on him. More than ever, he wanted to get home. The nights were lonely and cold without Diana in his arms. They spooned well together, and he missed sleeping with his face pressed into her hair. Not for the first time, he mentally shook himself for sounding like a lovesick fool. However, he could not help but wonder if Diana felt the same loneliness he was suffering from. He wanted to know.

Taking a long hot shower helped to soothe his tensed muscles and refresh his tired bones. Still, his mind was filled with thoughts of Diana and Hannah and how they were faring in his absence.

"Mike, get up," Devlan called to the closed door down the narrow hallway.

From the other side of the thick oak door, he heard a muffled curse and nodded in satisfaction. Mike too, for all his bluster, was just as anxious to get back to Los Angeles. It seemed they both were growing weary of three hours of sleep a night, and the chill of the east coast winter.

Marie, the French woman who maintained the apartment for him while he was in California, had already set coffee to brew and had fresh pastries laid out in the dining room for him. He finished buttoning his shirt and tucked it into his slacks, his movements quick and smooth. As he pulled out the chair, Marie appeared carrying his coffee and the daily newspaper.

"What's this about snow?" Devlan asked in greeting.

"Ooh, sir, a bad storm."

Devlan's dark brows raised over his blue eyes. "Bad? Any word on the airports?"

Marie tucked a piece of her graying hair back under the starched white cap she wore. "I don't know, Mr. Doyle. Do you want me to call someone?"

"No," he said, waving his hand dismissively. "I'll check on it myself. Thank you, Marie."

Marie bowed out of the room, leaving Devlan with a worried frown on his face. He reached for the remote on a table beside him and pressed the power button. Part of the wood paneling noiselessly turned in, revealing a full entertainment center. As Devlan flipped on the news, Mike appeared freshly showered and still scowling.

"I need coffee," he muttered.

"Get your coffee, and then call TJ, and find out if he can fly us out today, maybe before the snow starts to come down. I'll call the office and find out about completing our transactions now – this morning."

"What's going on?"

"Bad storm. Watch."

They sat back and watched the weather. The storm had buried the mountains and the Midwest, and now was making a wild dash east.

"Damn it all."

"Bad news," Mike stated. "Imagine how these holiday travelers are feeling."

"I know. I'm one of them," Devlan snapped.

"We'll work something out, sir."

Devlan reached for the receiver of his telephone and dialed a number, his fingers rough on the buttons. His voice was clipped when his lawyer picked up.

"Set up a meeting now, this morning. We need to finish this

by noon."

Devlan hung up the phone before his lawyer could answer and turned to Mike. "Get on the line and handle things from here. I'm going to head down now. Call me on my mobile as soon as you hear anything. I want to get out of here by noon."

"Right," Mike said, nodding his head.

Devlan pushed back the chair and came to his feet. With purposeful strides, he collected his heavy overcoat and briefcase. Nothing was going to stop him from completing this deal and returning to Malibu, not the weather, not the lawyers – no one. He had to get back to them. And he would. No matter what, he would.

Chapter 18

The phone in Devlan's pocket vibrated, alerting him to the incoming call. He reached for it, waving his finger at the secretary who offered him a pen.

"I'll be with you in a minute," he said to the crowd. Pushing back his chair, he came to his feet and raised the phone to his ear.

"What have you got?"

"Sir, I have some news."

Devlan frowned. Mike's voice was tense, and he sounded so far away. "What's wrong?"

"I just got off the phone with Mrs. Maclean. Wills has been out all night and just left this morning for the hospitals."

"Hospitals?" A cold feeling of dread landed on his shoulders with the weight of the world. All eyes in the room swiveled toward him, and a hush fell. "What's wrong?"

"They can't find Mrs. Somerset or Hannah, sir."

The words escaped in a rush, and then Mike fell silent. Devlan shook his head as if to clear it before pushing open the broad door. He needed privacy – quick.

"What?"

"Mrs. Somerset went out two evenings ago and was out late. When everyone woke up in the morning, she still was not there and neither was Hannah."

"Maybe they went shopping," he said hopefully, although he knew the truth. It hit him with such a sharp pain in his chest that he could barely breathe.

Mike's response was just as guarded. "She hasn't been home since, sir."

"Are her clothes gone?"

"They couldn't find anything missing but her suitcases. Everything else was left in their rooms."

There was a rushing sound in his head. Over that sound came the thundering of his heart. His voice caught as he spoke the dreaded words. "The car?"

"Gone." Mike said softly. "Miguel said he saw it last pull out around nine."

"No accidents reported?"

"Wills is still looking into it."

"Let me know as soon as you hear anything. Any luck in the airports?" Devlan asked hopefully.

"Not a chance. Too much traffic leaving before the storm. We're stuck here until it passes."

"At least it's a fast mover."

"Yes, sir." Mike's voice was solemn.

"No note?"

"They didn't say, sir."

Devlan shook his head again, stunned. He knew. In the back of his mind, he knew. He had been gone for too long, and she got scared. She had flown the coop again. There was nothing he could do about it now, not with a storm coming, and chances were that everything he had bought her was neatly where she had found it. Her pride would never have allowed her to take anything.

"Keep your ears open for word on the car. I'm sure we'll be getting it back," he said softly.

"Do you want me to hire someone to find her?" Mike's voice was hopeful.

Devlan sighed. "No."

Sudden anger filled him. If his love had not been strong

enough to hold her, there was no sense in keeping her against her will. If she did not want him, he sure as hell would not chase after her. He had tasted their sunshine, albeit briefly. Perhaps that would be enough for him. The stabbing pain in his heart told him that it never would be. The idea of growing old without them, without Diana's smile and Hannah's laughter, filled him with such loneliness that he thought his heart would tear in two.

"Let's watch for the car first," he conceded roughly.

"I'll pull whatever strings I can to get us back there, sir, and I'll keep an ear open for news."

"Good."

"Oh, and sir? They also told me her Christmas gift for you arrived. Mrs. Maclean says it's beautiful."

"That's great," he muttered.

He hung up the phone and wandered down the carpeted hall until he found an empty office. Shutting the door behind him, Devlan leaned against the wall and took in a harsh breath. He could not breathe, so heavy was the feeling in his chest. The room began to spin as he gasped for air. He lurched away from the door and staggered to the small desk. His hands fell heavy on the papers scattered about as he collapsed into the stiff chair. He felt lightheaded.

Glancing down at his hands, Devlan noticed he was sweating. Yet he felt so cold. Gooseflesh began to rise under his suit and shirt, the fine hairs sticking up straight to hold in the heat. It did not help. He was so cold. Was it possible to die of a broken heart?

Suddenly the door opened, and a young intern stuck his head in. "Mr. Doyle? What are you doing in here?" His head cocked to one side. "Are you all right, sir? You don't look too good."

Devlan opened his mouth to speak, but no words came forth. He still could not breathe well, and the heaviness in his chest grew more insistent. He shook his head. The intern approached cautiously and reached forward to touch the pulse on his neck. His keen gaze took in Devlan for another moment before he backed away.

"I'm going to go for help. Just wait right here."

Devlan wanted to shout for him to stay with him. Suddenly he felt scared. Something was most definitely wrong, but what he could not tell. Perhaps losing Diana and Hannah had done something to him, or maybe it was possible to die of a broken heart after all. The young man hurried from the office. As though from a distance, Devlan heard him shouting for help.

"Call 911. Man down. Quick, I need help!"

The next thing he knew there were people all around him, and his phone was vibrating again. Still in his hand, he glanced down. It was an unknown number with a strange area code. He ignored the call and closed his eyes briefly. Faces blended, but Devlan saw only one in his mind's eye. Just one woman with blond hair and bright blue eyes smiled down at him.

"Why?" Devlan whispered.

No one responded; no one had the answer. His shirt was loosened, and he was gently lowered from the chair to the floor. Someone came by with a blanket, which they threw over him. He noticed then that he was shivering violently. Voices were mingling around him. Then two dark figures arrived, and they were carrying equipment. A mask was placed over his face, and he was told to breathe in deep.

He was dying. He knew it, but he did not mind. Losing Diana and Hannah were too much for him to bear. So accustomed had he grown to their presence in his life, that one without them seemed too overwhelming to consider.

The huge deal he had made meant nothing. Nothing at all mattered anymore. Diana and Hannah were gone.

~

"Happy New Year!"

Diana lifted her glass of ginger ale and toasted the small party. Allan was there, as was Brad, his partner and some of their friends. Despite all these new faces, Hannah missed California desperately. Every day was a chore for Diana to explain again why Uncle Devlan was not there, and why he probably would not come back. It had been harder than she had imagined, for not only did she miss Devlan, but Hannah did as well. Allan's arrival just after Christmas had helped, but it was Brad's consistent tenderness and playfulness with her that smoothed the way.

"Smile Diana, have a good time."

Diana raised her glass at Allan and smiled. Once again, he had proven himself to be a true friend. Allan had arrived with her car, packed to the hilt with some of her treasured belongings.

She stood alone by the easel that rested next to the fireplace in the living room, watching the small party from a safe distance. Her heart was not in it. Luckily, Hannah slept peacefully in their borrowed room down the hall, the noise from the party not loud enough to wake up her exhausted child. The men and few women that mingled stood in cliques around her, and no one offered to speak to her. She did not mind; in fact, she preferred watching. Everyone appeared so happy and completely oblivious to the mess that she had made of her life.

"Hey, can you turn up that TV?" Someone shouted to her.

Diana glanced at the small TV before turning it louder. The scene in New York City was boisterous. There were people all over the place in Times Square. She noticed the huge crowds in addition to the big piles of snow and shivered. Had Devlan made it home before the storm last week? She had tried one last time to reach him using Brad's phone, but it had gone to voicemail, and again she could not speak long enough to leave a message. Hoping that with time she would be able to find her voice, she decided to take a wait and see approach.

Allan appeared by her side and took her arm. "Let's go outside. It's quieter out there."

She nodded and let him lead her out the front door just as the news came on. No one watched as they went over the headlines and the weather. Then came the news that caught some of the more right wing artist's attention.

On the screen was the view of a dark-coated man whose face was hidden under the raised collar. A biting wind pressed the coat against his long legs, the tails flapping wildly out behind him. He was climbing the stairs to a white jet, but his face remained downcast and his footsteps were slow. The newsman's voice suddenly interjected.

"And Doyle Enterprises', Devlan Doyle, left the city tonight for rest and relaxation in his Brentwood, California mansion. As you know, Doyle, on the day he made history with his huge company merger with SYTE Computers suffered a near-fatal heart attack. It's said that he will make a full recovery but needs to take some time off from his hectic schedule."

"Will his girlfriend, model Roxanne Lemieux, be accompanying him?" The co-announcer asked.

"Roxanne has left New York for Italy, and Doyle is due to start production of a new television movie in Hollywood. A spokesperson for the Doyle camp has released the news that Doyle and Lemieux are still friends, but probably will be seeing others. Sounds a little rocky to me."

The crowd jeered at the news, and Brad shouted at the others to turn it off. Through the closed door, Diana heard the sound of Brad's stereo and grimaced.

"I'll go tell him to turn it down," Allan said, coming to his feet.

"No, no," she said, putting her hand on his arm. "It's his house."

"That's why I asked you to come out here. Brad approached

me earlier tonight…"

Diana squeezed her eyes shut. "He wants us out?"

"No, no, just the opposite. He wants you to stay on as a roommate. It's cheap enough rent if you split it in half, and Hannah seems to like it here." Allan smiled and reached for Diana's hand over the glass table. "I noticed you were drinking ginger ale all evening."

Diana glanced down at her champagne flute and shrugged. "I don't like champagne."

Allan nodded, but the curve of his mouth told her he did not believe her. He leaned against the wall and crossed his legs at the ankle as if he had all the time in the world. "What happened in California?"

"I told you. Hannah's almost well. It was time for us to move on."

"In that much of a hurry? There's more."

Diana shook her head, but tears had begun to form in her eyes. She looked away from Allan's piercing stare and crossed her arms over her chest, wincing as she did so. The sensitivity of her breasts merely made matters worse, reminding her that she did in fact have a secret.

"I'd rather not pry Diana, but you sounded so desperate on the phone. I just want to make sure you're going to be safe here… Did he hurt you like Peter?"

Diana tried to laugh, but the sound was more like a sob. "Oh, no. Just the opposite, Allan. He was a true gentleman. He was so nice, so gentle and caring. Hannah loved him. He was just perfect."

"So why did you leave him?"

Diana returned her gaze to Allan's, her eyes bright with tears. "He's getting married."

"Married? To whom?"

She waved her hand. "It doesn't matter. Not to me."

"Did you tell him how you feel?"

"And how do I feel, Allan?"

"It's plain as day that you're in love with him. Maybe you should tell him."

"I can't."

"Why not? Maybe he'd change his plans."

"Roxanne is much more glamorous and beautiful than I. He's better off with someone more of his class."

"More his class? I don't know for sure, but when I saw him, he seemed pretty humble to me."

"Yes, but I didn't fit in."

"Tell him."

"I can't," she whispered.

"Tell him."

"I can't, Allan. Please, stop."

"Why the hell not?"

Diana glanced down at her hands. She was grasping her ginger ale flute tightly. "I'm pregnant. I confirmed it at a clinic Monday."

Allan's face paled for just an instant before all the color came rushing back. She watched as he swallowed hard. "What?"

"You heard me," she snapped.

"That's all the more reason to tell him. Don't be stupid, Diana."

She shook her head. "I can't right now. I've tried, but it's too difficult. I can't even leave him a message." Her voice broke, and she felt her eyes fill with all the unshed tears she had been bottling in. "Please, I need more time. It just hurts too much right now."

"He has a right to know."

"Please, Allan. When you return the car to him, don't say anything. Do you understand me, Allan? You can't tell him."

"How can you do that to him?" Allan frowned fiercely. "How can you be so cold?"

His words stung her. Cold? Is that what she had become? She needed to make her point clear. "It would kill me to know that he was with me when he loved another. Don't you see? He'd do that. He's such a kind man that he would drop everything and marry me. I couldn't live like that."

"I don't agree with this. Diana, I can't make any promises. If he gives me any inkling that he really wants to know where you are, I'm going to tell him."

"Please, don't do that to me."

Allan came to his feet. "I'd like to get some sleep before I hit the road later." Though he was furious with her, he held out his hand. "Come on, I'll tuck you in."

She gave him a watery smile. "Thanks for everything, Allan. I really do appreciate everything you've done."

"You may not say that if Doyle asks where you are."

"But I mean it now."

He smiled. "We know."

~

"Well, I've always wanted to be a daddy. I hope you don't mind me filling in for the guy?"

Diana laughed. It was a sound that was rarely made in the last month. "Really, Brad. Do you have to keep reminding me?"

With one hand on his hip, Brad waved his paintbrush around flagrantly. "So, will you marry me or what?"

Diana shook her head. "I've been married once, and trust me when I say that it's not fun."

"But this would be different. I'd be –"

"Saddled with a woman who has two children by two different men, neither of which is you." Diana glanced up and frowned. It really did sound bad, and even worse when she added that Devlan and Peter were stepbrothers. "You can be my coach.

Okay?"

Cocking his head to one side, Brad stuck out his lower lip and made a sad face. "Well, if you say so."

Diana gave her attention back to the papers in front of her. "You have over twenty thousand in your checking account, and you're getting reminder notices left and right." He shrugged. "And the mural you sold at your shop last week went for two grand less than it was worth. What are you doing?"

"I'm an artist, babe, not an accountant."

"You need help if you want to keep on doing your work. Maybe you should hire someone."

Brad leaned forward and dabbed furiously at the canvas before turning to her. He held his brush in his teeth. "Fine, you're hired," he said in a muffled voice.

She shook her head. "I'm not an accountant."

"No, but you're pretty, and you're smart. You're exactly what I need to keep the store running."

"You're doing okay, Brad, but you need a professional."

"Baloney. You need a job, and if I remember correctly you did major in business management and finance. You can help me out there and do my books. I'll pay your rent, health insurance, and a small salary, too."

"Finance was my major; business management my minor. That still doesn't make me an accountant," Diana murmured.

"I can offer you flexible hours, and you're going to need that soon."

Her hand fell to her still flat abdomen. She still had not told Hannah about the baby, even though she was now eight-weeks pregnant. It was too hard to explain. It had taken her a long time just to help Hannah get over the fact they were not going back to Malibu.

The new surroundings had aided Hannah in her recovery. She certainly did well in the dry desert air. She was now re-enrolled in school and an aquatics class, and Brad had helped her find a therapist to ensure that Diana was completing her therapy correctly.

However, Brad was right. She needed health insurance to ensure Hannah's continued care, as well as her own and that of her unborn child. It would not do to try and have a baby without prenatal care.

"Very well," she said, sighing. "But I can't guarantee the outcome."

Brad chuckled. "Baby, you're the best I've got. Besides, you managed the bookstore in Denver. You'll do fine, I know it."

"I hope I can fulfill that obligation."

"I have faith," he said with a gentle smile. "Besides, I can't wait to help you birth that baby. This is so exciting."

~

Devlan sat on the sofa in his library, reading a long overdue book. Though his retirement plans had been put on hold, he had taken time off at the insistence of his doctors. After a week of sitting at home, he was bored out of his mind. Mrs. Maclean knocked softly on the partially open door before popping her head around the corner.

"Tea, Mr. Doyle?"

"Thank you." Devlan placed down the book between his crossed legs and managed a small smile at his housekeeper.

"How are you today, sir?"

"Fine, thank you. And you?"

"I had a passable holiday." Her eyes seemed to fill with tears, and Devlan looked away quickly, knowing what she was going to say. "I had gotten used to a larger household in Malibu, so it was too quiet here for my tastes."

"I know what you mean," he said abruptly. He had spent

Christmas in New York, snowed in, hurting and recovering from a heart attack that made him feel twenty years older.

"I knew there would be trouble when Roxanne showed up that day, but I didn't do anything to stop it. I'm sorry, sir."

Devlan glanced up quickly, but the emotion and guilt on Mrs. Maclean's face made him regret doing so immediately. He was not yet ready to discuss what had happened. "It's not your fault."

"I'm glad to see you home again. We were all scared for a bit there."

Devlan nodded impatiently. Though the subject had changed, he was tired of hearing all the well wishes from people who had no idea what he was going through. "Has Mike called yet?"

"No, sir."

Just then, as if on cue, the phone rang. Devlan reached for it quickly, almost upsetting the book on his lap. Mrs. Maclean backed from the room as quietly as she entered, her eyes still brimming with tears.

"Yeah."

"We got a hit on the car. Kathy got a call from the guy in Denver, her friend."

Devlan pinched the bridge of his nose and forced his next words out. "Is she there?"

After a slight pause, Mike answered softly. "No. She collected her car and asked this guy, Allan, to call you."

Well, he thought miserably, that hurt. "I see... At least I know they're okay."

"I'll go out there and drive the car back, if you want."

"I'm going with you." Devlan put aside the blanket covering his legs and came to his feet. "Pick me up in an hour."

"But, sir."

"Just do it."

~

Denver was clear and cold when they arrived in the jet late that afternoon. Freshly fallen snow blanketed the city, and driving proved treacherous on the icy streets. Appearing completely oblivious to the cold, Allan Collins met them in the front yard of his home, his face grim. Devlan remembered the tall handsome man from the hospital. It seemed like a lifetime ago.

"Mr. Collins, thank you for calling me."

Devlan held out his hand, and the other man took it in a firm handshake. His voice was guarded as he answered. "No problem."

An awkward silence fell over the trio. As much as Devlan longed to ask where she was, he held himself in check. It would not do anyone any good to appear like the love-struck fool that he was.

As if sensing his discomfort, Mike stepped forward and reached for the keys. "Do you need to get anything out of the car before we go?"

Allan shook his head, but his eyes never left Devlan's. "No. I didn't have anything in it. I think Diana got all her things out."

Mike nodded his head and wandered back to the rented car to transfer over their baggage. Devlan stared down at his feet as he collected himself. The very sound of her name evoked memories that he did not care to think about at that moment. He had failed in his attempt to earn her trust and she had fled. For the first time in a long time, Devlan had made a serious tactical error, and he had lost what he had thought would be the deal of a lifetime. Happiness.

It was his inner strength that saved him from growing emotional at that point, the very power he possessed that had kept him so successful in business. A sense of cold detachment fell over him. It was the familiar feeling he experienced whenever he truly wanted something. It was wisest not to show that feeling to anyone, no matter the cost.

"They're okay?"

"Yes. I heard she tried to call you and tell you herself, but you didn't answer."

Devlan suddenly remembered the strange call the day of his heart attack. In fact, there had been two strange calls. He nodded shortly, wondering if he should pull out his bill and do a reverse lookup. No, his heart told him, still stinging from her rejection. Let her come to him.

"Do you know where she is?"

"I do," Allan replied. His voice was as cautious as Devlan's, yet Devlan's keen eye took in the look of hopefulness in his stance.

"Will you tell me?"

"Why do you want to know?"

That was a loaded question. Devlan's eyes narrowed as he stared at Allan intently. He was unsure which way to go. He decided it was best to remain careful, but he was certain the desperation he felt was mirrored in his eyes.

"I was... curious."

"She really doesn't want to be found right now," Allan said, his foot nervously kicking at the snow bank beside him. "But there's a hell of a lot more warmth where she is now than where she came from."

Devlan frowned at his evasive words, unsure how to take the riddle. He was about to question him when Mike appeared and shattered the moment. "I'm all set here."

Devlan nodded and reached out his hand again. "Thank you again, Collins. If you talk to them again, give them my best, and tell them to keep in touch."

Allan nodded his head again, though his shake was quick and weak. Devlan released his hand and turned away, hearing Allan's low voice behind him, filled with frustration and disgust. "This is all wrong."

As Devlan wandered away, he was suddenly overwhelmed with the feeling of failure. Allan had wanted to tell him something, and yet he had done something wrong.

But what?

Chapter 19

Phoenix Sky Harbor Airport was bustling with activity. Diana glanced at the terminal where the jet out of Denver was arriving. It was now August, and the searing desert heat was taking its toll on her. The monsoon season was in full swing, and while she enjoyed the nightly light show and pounding downpours, the additional humidity was making her suffer. She sat heavily in one of the seats just outside of security and took as deep a breath as her greatly rounded belly would allow. How she longed to kick off her shoes and soak her swollen feet, but now was not the time or the place.

"Watch for Mindy's plane, okay?"

Hannah made her way to the window and gazed out at the bright sunshine outside. "Is that her plane, Mommy?"

The big jet was slowly making its way to one of the gates, and the noise from the engines vibrated through the thick glass. Just beyond, across the tarmac, was parked a jet like Devlan's. It was the same white plane with a blue tail. Diana closed her eyes. Just thinking of him still made her heart ache. It had been almost eight long months, and she had never heard from him, not even when Allan had returned the car.

Allan had promised her that he had not divested her whereabouts, but Diana still had her doubts. If he had really wanted to find her, he would have had an artillery of hired hands track her down. Most likely, Devlan had not cared enough to ask, and that must have been why seeing the jet made her feel bitter and angry now.

"Mommy look, over there!"

Diana opened her eyes and followed Hannah's finger past the small jet to another landing plane. After murmuring her acknowledgment, Diana's gaze was drawn back to the small jet.

A group was descending the steps of the aircraft to slip into the waiting limos. Her breath caught as she took in the tall, dark man who descended last. He was dressed in a dark suit and carried a large briefcase. The people around him hovered, proving that he was the one in charge.

Was it?

Diana shook her head. It was too far away to tell for sure, but there was no tall blond head to indicate Mike's presence, nor was there a petite woman with black hair by his side. No, it could not be Devlan. It was merely wishful thinking on her part.

"Diana. Hannah!"

Diana's attention was brought back to the airport with the arrival of a very ecstatic Mindy. Slowly dragging herself to her feet, Diana waddled to Mindy's outstretched arms and embraced her friend. Hannah interrupted the two by placing herself between them and hugging them both.

"How are you, Di? My gosh, is that a big little boy you've got there?"

Diana took a step back and placed her hand over her abdomen. "You know what they say about those second children? Always more trouble and bigger than the first."

"Amen to that."

They laughed together before Hannah threw herself at Mindy once more. "Look Mindy, I can walk without a cane!"

"I see. You'll have to tell me all about your adventure."

As they chatted, Diana found herself drawn back to the jet. Everyone had piled into the limo, and it was just preparing to pull away from the jet. Her fingers went to the glass, and she closed her eyes tightly. It could not be him, but how could she know for sure?

"Diana? Are you okay?"

With a jump, Diana's eyes popped opened. Mindy was staring at her with concern written all over her happy face. She smiled. "Of course. It's the blasted heat. I'll tell you, Mindy; Phoenix is hot. There are no ifs, ands, or buts about it. It's hot."

"It's the desert."

Diana nodded. She did like Phoenix. It was better than Malibu and much better than Denver. She just wished that she had the man she loved to share it with.

"Let's go!" Hannah pulled Diana's hand, leading her away.

"Do you have luggage?"

"Just these two carry-ons," Mindy said with a grin.

"Oh, I love you!" Diana said gratefully.

"I'm ready and anxious to see this city everyone rants and raves about."

~

"Dammit!"

"What is it?"

Devlan stared down between his legs to see that he was truly missing his other laptop. After all these months, he still flaked out. Enough was enough! When would he get his senses back?

"I left my other computer on the plane."

"That's not a problem," Jones said. Jones was Devlan's new Phoenix lawyer, a bumbling idiot in Devlan's opinion.

"Fine, let's go back and get it."

Devlan sat back as the occupants in the limo scrambled to get the message to the driver, but their rapid-fire voices seemed to fade away and were replaced by the urge to look out his window. His gaze turned to the windows of the terminal above. The outline of a child was briefly visible through the mirrored glass, and the hair on the back of his neck prickled in awareness when he looked up. He was overcome with the urge to go up there and see what it was that held his attention. There was something there, but he had no idea what. All he knew was that it left him feeling lighter.

"Stay there, I'll get it."

"On the desk," Devlan remarked. His gaze returned to the airport, several stories up. He had never been to Phoenix before. What had captured his attention?

Before he could figure it out they were pulling away, leaving the airport and the fleeting feeling of happiness. It was something he had not experienced in a long time. They were trapped for a little while in the traffic around the terminals, and again Devlan turned his gaze outside the vehicle. He allowed the other occupants to discuss that afternoon's meeting since it gave him a chance to relax.

Through the concrete pillars to his right, walking in the shadow of the parking garage were two women. His gaze locked on the fair one, a heavily pregnant woman, with long blond hair so similar to Diana's that it took his breath away. It was tied back in a loose braid, with strands falling in her face, also like Diana's unruly locks. She was chatting excitedly with the other woman, who carried two carry-on bags, but he could not see her face as she was turned away from him.

As Devlan passed them in the limo, he saw the child appear from the other side of the darker woman. His breath caught at the sight of the small blond girl skipping alongside them.

"It can't be," he whispered against the hot glass of the window.

"Pardon me, sir?"

Devlan shook his head. "Nothing. Just remarking on the heat."

No, it could not be her. Hannah more than likely would not

be skipping alongside them yet. Besides, Diana could not have gotten pregnant that quickly.

With a heavy sigh, Devlan dragged his hand over his face and around to massage the back of his neck. He had heard of things like this happening in such extreme heat. He knew he had better slow down. Hallucinations were common, and here he was putting other people's faces on complete strangers. People that he just could not get out of his mind.

Yes, he would have to take it easy.

~

"Exciting!" Diana gasped. "Do you remember saying that? How exciting do you think it is now, Brad?"

"I feel sick." Brad's face was chalky, and it had taken on a slightly greenish hue.

The grip he held on Hannah's hand was so tight that the child frowned. "Lemme go, Brad."

Hannah jerked her hand away and hurried over to Brad's friend, Jimmy. The young man smiled and took Hannah's hand. "Come on kiddo, I'll take you to the gift shop."

Diana watched them go before turning her attention back to Brad. "This isn't exactly fun, is it?"

They were in the hospital now, in a birthing room awaiting the arrival of Diana and Devlan's son. She had been in labor for the better part of the day, and as the sun sank lower in the late summer sky Diana grew more impatient.

"I had no idea, Di. I wish you'd told me sooner."

"Told you what, Brad?" Mindy asked, smoothing Diana's hair away from her face. "This is natural. Transition is a part of a woman's labor. It means that the birth is imminent, usually within an hour or so she'll start to push."

"Will you shut up? You sound like a damn book," Diana

ground out through clenched teeth.

Mindy met Brad's eyes over her head. Brad swallowed hard. "So this is the part when the husbands get their ego shredded?"

Mindy grinned as she nodded.

"Cool," Brad said.

"What's so cool?" Diana snapped, a grunt escaping her moist lips. Suddenly another grunt escaped.

"Is it time?" Mindy asked, smoothing her brow with another cool rag.

"I think so. Will you call a nurse?"

Stumbling over his feet, Brad rushed to the door and began shouting for a nurse. Two came in quickly, frowns of irritation across their faces. Their strides were purposeful as they approached the bed, although they glared at Brad. "Please don't cause such a commotion. The other patients are frightened."

"I'm sorry," Mindy said smoothly. "We think she's ready."

Diana was aware of Brad pacing next to the bed, and she reached for his hand to grasp firmly. Her face glistened with sweat, and her blond hair was plastered to her face.

"How are you?" he asked in concern.

"I've been better," she muttered, squeezing his hand tight.

"Relax now, Mrs. Somerset," the nurse advised. She watched the monitor as the contraction came on, and then reached over to adjust the band around Diana's rounded belly.

"That's a big one," the other nurse remarked.

Diana groaned in answer, and her eyes remained glued to the monitor. The baby's heartbeat dropped slightly in response to the contraction, but the nurses did not seem concerned.

Diana tried to focus on her breathing technique, but it was so hard. The pain was so intense. She could do nothing to manipulate her body except to breathe through the contractions, but it was getting increasingly difficult. She wished it was all over. She also wished she had taken that epidural when it was offered.

"Please, can I push now?"

"We have to wait for your doctor, dear," said the older nurse.

Diana let out a loud sigh. "Where is he?"

"Coming. We paged him a few minutes ago."

Diana envisioned him downing a cup of coffee at his leisure while she suffered in the birthing room. She gritted her teeth in frustration. Suddenly cool hands were on her forehead again, and Diana smiled her thanks at Mindy. Her loyal friend smiled back and pressed some cool ice chips to her lips. Diana closed her eyes and lay back, sucking on the cold ice while she had a reprieve. It was almost over. Soon her baby would be born.

"Ah, and here's my lovely patient now."

Diana opened her eyes and saw her elderly obstetrician enter the room. He donned gloves and glanced at her record before sitting down at the foot of her bed.

"How are you, Diana?"

"I want this finished."

"I know."

She longed to scream out that he did not know, after all he was only a man. How could he know anything about birthing a baby? But she held her tongue and closed her eyes again as he did his exam.

"Ten centimeters, completely effaced." He straightened and smiled at her. "Are you ready to push, Diana?"

With a sigh of relief, Diana nodded her head. She felt weak already, and the hard part was not over yet. Then a vision of Devlan entered her mind. It was a sight she had struggled to bury far in the recesses of her brain, but there he was, and he was smiling with pride and joy, urging her to keep trying and not give up.

"Come on, Diana, give us a big push."

She raised herself and pushed with all her might. In the background, she heard one of her nurses counting to ten, and then she fell back against the pillows once more. More ice was pressed against her dry lips. And so it went for almost a half an hour she pushed before finally *he* was born. The room fell silent as the final push produced her son. The doctor and nurses worked quickly and wordlessly, doing automatically what they did on a daily basis. Diana lay back against the pillows and took a deep breath. It was done.

"Mrs. Somerset, it's a boy," the younger nurse said.

All around her they bustled with activity, drying and suctioning the baby. Then the room burst with the sound of the infant's angry cries. Diana nodded her head and glanced at Brad. Her roommate, boss, and now friend had tears streaming down his face. He approached the foot of the bed and glanced over the doctor's shoulder as he worked to suction the baby's airway clean. His digital camera dangled from his wrist, completely forgotten.

"He's just beautiful!"

Diana smiled at Brad and nodded again. She had known he would be. He was probably the very image of his father. Then she would be cursed with a daily reminder of him every day of her life.

"May I see?" Mindy asked.

The look on Mindy's face confirmed Diana's suspicions. "He is beautiful, Di," she whispered.

They brought the baby over to the heating lamps and continued drying him off. He howled angrily, his arms and legs waving wildly. Diana allowed a fleeting smile as she watched him. He was so round and red.

"What's his name?" The older nurse asked.

All eyes turned to her expectantly. She glanced at all the faces, waiting patiently for her answer. "Bryce," she said matter-of-factly. "Bryce Devlan Somerset."

The baby was weighed in and quickly swaddled. Diana held out her arms as the nurse approached and wrapped them around her new son possessively.

"Bryce," she whispered.

Tears filled her eyes as she stared down at the infant. He was beautiful already, with a head full of black hair and a strong chin like his father's. How proud Devlan would have been had he known.

Yes, she thought sadly, he would be proud and so very happy – if she were to tell him. But she selfishly had not, and that filled her with so much guilt that she was ashamed of herself. She still could, she thought. There was nothing to stop her. Unless one considered that he was probably already married to Roxanne and could sue her for custody.

She hugged little Bryce to her and stared down into his voluminous gray-blue eyes. No, she would not allow that. Bryce was hers and hers alone. She would never share him willingly with another woman, especially Roxanne Lemieux.

However, could she live with that selfish decision?

~

Diana picked up the receiver and pressed it to her ear. With one hand she held Bryce, howling loudly for his mid-afternoon meal, and with the other she quickly dialed the California number. Once done, she pressed her newborn infant against her breast and helped him get a grasp on her nipple. On the other line, she heard the steady sound of the ringer before a distinctly foreign voice answered.

"Hello?"

"Mrs. Holmes, please."

"May I ask who is calling?"

Diana sighed. "Diana Somerset."

"One moment."

After a decidedly long pause, she heard the click of another phone, and then suddenly there was the sound of Esther's excited

273

voice. "Diana, dear, how are you?"

Diana smiled. "I'm fine, Esther. How are you?"

"We've been waiting for ages to hear from you. I saw Devlan last week, and he told me that you weren't staying with him anymore. Goodness, it was as if you just dropped off the face of the planet. Are you okay? Where are you, honey?"

She paused for a moment, considering whether she could trust her parent's friend or not. However, if Devlan really cared she was sure he would have found her already. "I'm fine. We're fine. I'm in Phoenix, Esther, working with an artist. I run his shop in Scottsdale. It's been such fun."

"Oh, I'm glad to hear it. And your daughter? How's she now? Devlan said he hoped her leg was healing okay, but that he didn't know."

"Hannah's fine. It's been a long road, but she's running and playing again." Diana gripped the handle of the phone tightly. "Listen Esther, part of the reason I called was to see if Thomas still practiced."

"Law?"

"Yes, law."

"Of course, he's got an office downtown. Why? Are you in trouble?"

"No, no. I'm calling for my friend. You know, the one that I told you about? He may need some advice. That's all. Would you mind giving me Thomas' number at work?"

"Oh, sure, honey. Hold on, and I'll ask Marta to get it for you."

As Diana waited, she removed Bryce from her breast and began to burp him. He fussed a little after the first burp, nuzzling her shoulder to indicate that he was still hungry.

"Okay, Diana, do you have a pen?"

Diana scrambled for the pen, roughly jostling Bryce. The hungry infant began to cry harder, and Diana hurriedly put him to her other breast.

"Was that a baby?" Esther asked.

"It's okay," she muttered. "I have a pen now, Esther."

"Okay, dear."

Diana scribbled the number down and chatted some more with Esther while Bryce finished nursing. However, her main concern was Thomas and what he could do for her and Hannah, as well as Bryce. Though sleep deprived and completely hormonal, she knew she had to do the right thing and tell Devlan. Hiding his son from him was just not an option. He deserved to know after everything he had done for her and Hannah, but she needed a lawyer desperately, and a good one if she was to go against Devlan. She needed to be fully prepared in case he did try to take Bryce away. If Devlan wanted a battle when the time came, she would give it to him, and she would do everything she could to make sure her children came out the victors.

Chapter 20

Devlan watched the sun set over Los Angeles from his office window. His desk was piled high with urgent paperwork, and he knew it would be another long night before he could head home. With a wry smile, he glanced at the luxurious leather sofa in his adjacent sitting room. Perhaps he should just sell the Brentwood house and live right here in his office.

No, he corrected himself. The Malibu house should be the first to go. He had not set foot in that house since Diana and Hannah had left. The last time he had been there was to collect his Christmas present. It was a gift he immediately packed away since it hurt too much to gaze at the faces that still haunted his thoughts.

Devlan opened his center desk drawer and pulled the one hidden photo he kept of Diana and Hannah free. It rested just beneath the engagement ring he had never had a chance to offer her but never had the heart to return. A tender smile creased his lips as he stared at the well-worn picture. It was of Hannah and Diana on a Sea Doo in Hawaii. They were carefree and laughing, looking so much alike and having such a good time. It was a photo he treasured because he knew Diana had been happy with him then. There was no mistake or lie in that photo. She had been happy – both of them had.

The vibration of his mobile brought Devlan from his reverie. He put the picture away and shut the door with a satisfied sigh. It was slightly reassuring to note that it pained him less when he stared at the picture than it had a few short months ago. Perhaps he truly was healing.

"Yes?"

"Devlan, it's me… Roxanne."

Devlan's shoulders sagged at the sound of her voice. Following his heart attack, he had told Roxanne about his planned engagement to Diana. Shortly after that, Mrs. Maclean had told Devlan about Roxanne's visit the night Diana had left, but still Roxanne denied any involvement in her disappearance. Her continued refusal to divulge what had been discussed that afternoon was still a tender spot with Devlan, and he placed some responsibility for Diana's disappearance on Roxanne's shoulders. With the trust in their relationship so damaged, they had maintained a polite distance since.

"Hello, Roxanne. How are you?"

"I have tickets to a charity function tonight and wanted to take you out."

"I can't," he answered quickly. "I'm swamped here."

"Really, Devlan? Everyone is talking about you. They say that your heart attack at Christmas took all the fun out of you. Just come to this one thing. It's an auction for AIDS research, and it'll be lots of fun. Besides, you need to spend some of your money."

Devlan sighed. It was not his heart attack that had wounded him so deeply, and they both knew it. "Who's putting it on?"

"It's the Holmes'. Esther and Thomas. You know them."

"Yes, I know them," he said shortly. He rapidly blinked his eyes against the memory of Diana that first dinner they shared after seeing Thomas and Esther.

"Well, they found a place in Scottsdale that sells all kinds of artwork and artifacts. Treasures really. The artist donated a bunch of stuff for Thomas' AIDS cause a couple of weeks ago, and they threw this together. You'll love them."

Indecision tore at Devlan. The idea of staying in town at his desk held no appeal to him, especially when his thoughts were again consumed with Diana and Hannah, but a night out with Roxanne was undoubtedly just as emotionally exhausting.

"Dev, come on. You'll really like this stuff. The guy may be an unknown now, but he's sure to get your attention."

"Fine, what time?"

"Eight o'clock."

"I'll see you then."

~

A light drizzle began to fall as Devlan slipped from the Bentley into the posh hotel. They mingled with the crowd briefly before moving into the banquet hall, and that was where Devlan saw the unknown artist's first piece.

His breath stuck in his throat at the artist's rendition of the desert. The saguaro cacti were exquisitely painted, as were the organ pipe and prickly pear, all bearing the faces of children. However, there was a blond water sprite, soaring high within the clouds in a flowing blue dress that matched her eyes. The water that trickled from the jug she held gave life to the children below.

A chill passed through him as he stared at the sprite. She bore an eerie resemblance to Diana, so much so that his breath caught in his chest yet again. Forcing himself to look beyond the sprite, he realized that it was a moving piece. It depicted nicely the tenuous balance of water and life in the desert. Devlan loved it.

"You see," Roxanne whispered. "I told you. You do love his work, don't you? I can see it in your face, darling."

Devlan glanced at Roxanne, his eyes shuttered. "I admit that it's stirring. We'll have to see."

He guided Roxanne to their table and sat down heavily. So much for assuming he was on the road to recovery. He was envisioning Diana everywhere. First he conjured her and Hannah in an airport, and now in some stranger's oil painting. It had to stop, he mused as he gave himself a mental shake. He needed to get on with his life.

"Here's your program," Roxanne said, handing him a catalog of the artwork up for auction.

Devlan flipped through it, hurriedly finding the page. "Brad Vember?"

"Yes, that's the one from Scottsdale."

"Never heard of him."

"He's still pretty local, but his pieces are huge and sell for a lot of money in Arizona. Everyone's hoping this will help get him worldwide. They say he's the next great realist."

Devlan stared down at the shots of the paintings. Once again there was the blond sprite in the desert. It was the only one the female model appeared in. There were some of children as well, a dark boy and light girl, but nothing moved him like the first desert scene... the one he dubbed "Diana" in his head.

For most of the evening, Devlan sat motionless, watching the proceedings through bored eyes. Roxanne bought some nice pieces, but Devlan waited for the large painting. Whatever the cost, he would have that painting.

"Are you going to buy anything?" Roxanne whispered as another piece was sold. "There are only a few more."

"Yes, as a matter of fact, right now." Devlan straightened in his seat and watched attentively as they produced the painting.

"That one?" Roxanne snapped. "You like it only because the woman is a blonde."

Devlan gave her a withering glance. "No. It's a beautiful piece."

"Ladies and gentleman, may we start the bidding at two thousand please?"

Devlan signaled, as did a dozen others. "Great," he muttered. "I'm obviously not the only one who appreciated that painting."

"Lots of men prefer blondes."

Roxanne rolled up her catalog and tapped it angrily on her knee, but Devlan ignored her. His concentration remained on the bidding war that went on in front of him. It finally boiled down to two, himself and their host, Thomas Holmes. Devlan shot him a quick glance, and the older man raised his program in response. Devlan smiled and raised his bid, finally causing the man to back down amid awed gasps and cheers.

"I can't believe you spent that much on that painting," Roxanne snapped, huddling down within her seat.

Devlan came to his feet and bowed to the cheering crowd before sitting back down and grinning at Roxanne. "You said yourself that it was for charity. Eighty isn't really all that much."

She grunted in answer and continued to scowl as Devlan pulled his checkbook from his inside suit pocket. "I'll catch up with you in a few minutes," he said.

She nodded and came to her feet, preparing to give her information to the woman on the side. Devlan watched her go with a feeling of immense relief. While he was glad the evening was almost over, he was also pleased to have found this new treasure. He couldn't wait to get it home and take a good look at it, and he was just signing his name when he felt a hand on his shoulder.

"Congratulations, Devlan."

Devlan turned around and came face to face with Thomas Holmes. "Why Thomas, it's good to see you."

"Ah, baloney. You're just happy to outbid me on that painting. Priceless, isn't it?"

"Yes, it's very nice."

"I saw the lust on your face the minute it went up for bids. I knew you'd get it."

"Then why'd you let me spend so much?" Devlan asked, chuckling.

Thomas threw back his head and laughed. "It's for charity,

isn't it? Besides, that's hardly a penny in your bucket."

Devlan nodded solemnly, though his grin was wide. "True."

"There's one thing that I know that you don't," Thomas continued.

"What's that?"

"I know the artist, and he has another piece just like that one in his shop in Scottsdale. His model was sad to see this one go. She really had an attachment to it, probably because of the children in it. Brad went right to work to get her another one."

Devlan's curiosity was peaked. "Who's his model? His wife?"

"No, a good friend, shall we say?" Thomas' eyes glittered with mischief, and Devlan frowned at his evasiveness.

"You'll have to get me his address. I've been doing some work in Phoenix lately. Maybe next time I'm in Scottsdale, I'll check out his shop."

Thomas looked satisfied and began to slip back into the crowd. "You do that, Devlan, ol' boy. His address is stamped on the back of the painting. It should also be on your receipt."

Devlan glanced down and nodded. "I've got it."

"Good. Oh, and I've called you a couple of times but haven't heard back from you yet."

"You have?" Devlan asked with a frown. Had Kathy given him messages from Thomas? He really could not remember.

"Yes. I heard from Diana recently. She contacted me. We have a few things to go over with you."

Devlan's head snapped up. "Wait a minute," he said, reaching for Thomas' arm. "Diana called you?"

"No," Thomas said, grinning. "Actually, I saw her just a few weeks ago."

"In Los Angeles?"

Devlan's heart began to pound furiously in his chest. Excitement flooded through him. Could it be? Had she come back?

"No. She's got a new job now and is doing fine. Hannah looks great; she's in the first grade now… Devlan, Diana hired me to represent her against you."

Suddenly the evening's jubilation seemed to drain out of him. Although not overly surprised, Devlan was still hurt by her newest action. What had he done to wrong her so terribly?

"Against me? Did she say why?" Devlan asked, his voice hoarse.

Thomas' face softened. "Let's discuss this in my office, not here with all these people around. We'll need a bit of privacy when we go over things. I have a lot to share."

Though it took every ounce of strength in him, Devlan straightened and stood tall. Putting forth one of his best business-emotionless faces, he gave a nonchalant shrug. "I understand completely," he said evenly. "I'll have my lawyer contact you in the morning."

Thomas cocked his head to the side and contemplated Devlan. "That's a real special painting you just bought, Devlan. Go home and enjoy it."

Devlan nodded, but his excitement was gone. When he again turned his attention to the waiting young woman, his words were curt. "Have that delivered to my office."

"Yes sir, Mr. Doyle," she replied with a smile.

"Thank you," Devlan said, walking away. He wanted to find Roxanne and go back to his office. He had a lot of work to do, and work was the only way to erase Diana from his mind.

~

The painting arrived the following evening. Kathy had stayed late that night, and she opened the door to his office with a curious look on her face. "You have a delivery, sir."

Devlan glanced up as the men entered with the painting

safely wrapped and balanced between them on a dolly.

"Come in," he said, rising from his chair. "Put it in the other room, next to the couch."

"What's going on?" Kathy asked, following the men.

Devlan watched them remove the painting from the dolly and carefully stand it up. In addition to the blanket that covered it, the piece was wrapped with tan paper to protect it from the elements.

"I bought a painting last night," he replied. "Thank you."

The men nodded and slipped back the way they had come, leaving Kathy to watch Devlan with a frown. Together they slowly unwrapped the painting, and Kathy gasped as she took in the scene. "My God, it looks like..."

Devlan glanced at her. Kathy had stopped suddenly and bit her lip to keep the words in. "It's okay," Devlan said with a smile. "I liked the comparison of water and desert, life and death. That's why I bought it."

She snorted and came to her feet. Her lip curled as she stared down at the painting. "Sorry sir, but I don't buy that for a minute." As Devlan opened his mouth to speak, she put her hands on her hips and glared at him. "Why don't you stop being so damn stubborn and just go find her? Stop torturing yourself and admit that you're still in love with her."

At his angry glare, she softened her tone.

"How can you go on with your life if you don't have the answers you're looking for? That's the hardest part, sir. You should find her long enough to ask why. Then move on."

Devlan chuckled. "Really, Kathy. You need to get your nose out of those romantic novels. You make it sound so easy."

"It is that easy, especially when I know Roxanne and how she works. It wouldn't surprise me in the least if she chased that special woman away."

"If that is true, she should have talked to me first. But she didn't; she just left."

"You didn't ask either. What if Roxanne said something terrible about you? Did you ever think of that?"

Devlan glared at her in response.

"What about the rest of us? Shouldn't you talk to her to give the rest of us some closure at least?"

Devlan had to admit that she had a point there. It was true that Kathy, Mrs. MacLean, Mike and even Wills had all felt defeated following their disappearance. Each one of them felt as though they bore the guilt for Diana's actions.

However, in truth, only he did. He shook his head. "You don't understand."

She groaned and held her hands up to the sky. "I give up. Goodnight sir, I'll see you in the morning."

"Goodnight. Oh, and send Mike and Wills home too. I'm going to be late tonight."

As Devlan watched her go, the loneliness began to fill him again. Maybe she was right. Maybe he needed to stop being so stubborn and confront her to find out why.

Sitting heavily on the sofa, Devlan turned on the light next to him to get a better look at his newest acquisition. It illuminated the dim room even more, shining its light on the new painting. Yes, he had to admit that the sprite did look an awful lot like Diana. Same blue eyes, same small nose. Even the rounded chin was hers. But then again, it was an artist. Who knew what the real woman looked like? Brad Vember could have been generous with the model and just made her look exquisitely beautiful.

Devlan nodded as his eyes slowly closed. A brief nap, he promised himself. Then he would get up again, order a take-out dinner, and start working. It was Wednesday already, and if he finished up this week he would have the whole weekend to relax. Then he would start Monday with a new slate.

It was more than a brief nap. When Devlan again opened his

eyes it was pitch black outside, with only the few lights from the other skyscrapers and the moon casting any glow in the night sky.

"Great." He glanced at his watch and his scowl deepened. It was near midnight.

Shaking his head, Devlan swung his legs over the side of the couch and put his head in his hands. He stared down at the painting, taking note of the two children. The blond child was female, and most definitely Hannah.

The words rang in his head.

"There's a hell of a lot more warmth where she is now than where she came from."

Devlan sat up straight. It could not be. Had Allan Collins really told him the truth back in January? The 480 area code on the day of his heart attack? Could it be? Thomas said he had seen Diana right around the time he found this new artist. In Scottsdale, Arizona.

A bitter laugh echoed in the quiet room. Devlan fell to his knees in front of the painting and studied it closely. Roxanne had told him that this new artist was the next great realist. Of course it was Diana. There was the same wary look in her eyes, and the same shy smile. Hannah, too. There was no way he was wrong about her. The beautiful golden child had grown up a little, but he would recognize that playful grin and those happy blue eyes anywhere.

"I'll be damned," Devlan muttered.

Coming to his feet, Devlan went to his office and picked up the phone. He dialed TJ first, and the exhausted pilot grumbled his agreement before hanging up on him. His next step was to dial Mike. A true bear when awakened from his beauty sleep, it took several tries and several times of hanging up on the phone service before he could entice his bodyguard to pick up.

"We're going to Phoenix. Throw together some clothes for me and meet me at LAX."

"Right."

Mike hung up on him. Devlan sighed and dialed the number impatiently yet another time. Any other time, Devlan would be irritated at his bodyguard's lax manner, but Devlan was too excited to be angry.

"Meet me at LAX. We're going to Scottsdale to find Diana."

"Whoa, what?"

"Are you awake?"

"I'm out of bed."

"Good. See you there in an hour."

He was about to disconnect when he heard Mike's jubilant voice. "Finally!"

Devlan returned to the sitting room and glanced again at the painting. Was it just him, or was there loneliness in Diana's eyes that mirrored his own? He stared for a long while, remembering Kathy's words. She was right. It was beyond past the time when stubbornness was the right response. They needed a confrontation to sort things out once and for all. He did need to know why. With growing hopes, Devlan prepared to go to Phoenix.

Chapter 21

Devlan gazed down at the sea of orange lights in the darkness with growing trepidation. Just below him, in one of those cookie-cutter housing developments and apartment complexes, Hannah and Diana could be soundly sleeping. The trepidation grew to a nervousness he had not felt since he was an inexperienced teen. Even after all this time, it was still a complete mystery to him how Diana made him lose all control. Usually the one to handle everything, Devlan found himself acting like a schoolboy. Right now he felt more vulnerable than ever.

The night was hot and dry, reminding him again that he was now in the desert. The hotel limo Mike had called for was waiting for them as they stepped off the plane, and its sleek black lines and soft, plush interior relaxed Devlan slightly. This was familiar territory, something he was accustomed to. As soon as they were safely seated, it pulled away from the curb and headed to the most luxurious hotel in Phoenix. From there, it was a short ride to the art community of downtown Scottsdale. His plan was to visit Brad Vember's shop first thing in the morning and find out where exactly Diana was. Then he would take it a little more slowly. He did not want her to flee again.

He gazed out the darkly tinted window at the luxurious hotel as they pulled onto the red stone drive. Despite the late hour, the hotel manager was standing outside to greet them with a wide smile. Behind him stood two young bellboys, eager to gather his bags and escort them to their suite.

"Good morning, Mr. Doyle. My name is Williams, sir, Neal Williams."

"Hello Williams," he replied.

"Welcome back again. I've put you in our best suite. It's on the main floor, but very quiet. I hope you'll find it acceptable."

Devlan nodded absently. "I hope so, too."

Mike followed the two bellboys while Devlan reached for his computerized key. The manager bowed as he passed, and Devlan shook his head. As much as he hated to admit it, he was not royalty and, thanks to Diana, he had grown to despise being treated like that.

"By the way Williams," he remarked, turning back. "What can you tell me about the art galleries in Scottsdale?"

"Oh," the man said, beaming. "They're world famous."

"I know that," he answered dryly. "I'm looking for one artist in particular."

"Every Thursday night this time of year, they have what's called the Art Walk. Sometimes the artists are there to meet with people, and some of the galleries serve refreshments. It's actually quite fun."

"You mean tonight?"

"Why, yes, sir, tonight would be Thursday."

Devlan nodded his head and strode away, tossing a cursory thank-you over his shoulder. This would be perfect. As a tourist, maybe he could find Diana and Brad Vember at the same time.

Devlan and Mike followed the staff to his suite on the main floor. As the door opened, Devlan stepped in and took a glance around. It was spacious, with two bedrooms, a large living room, and a large wet bar with a refrigerator. He took everything in with appreciation and then turned to Mike with a curt nod. Without a word, Mike reached into his pocket and pulled free some cash to tip. The two young men thanked them profusely before backing out of the room and shutting the door behind them.

"Now what?" Mike asked.

Devlan strode to the patio and pulled back the heavy curtain. He could see the pool outside and took a deep breath. How Hannah would love this place.

"I'm going to bed for a while. Then we'll have a late breakfast and find this shop."

Mike took the paper with the address written on it and stared at it for a moment. "Okay," he said, tucking it in his pocket.

"Tonight there's some sort of gathering. Some of the artists will be around downtown. I was hoping to get a look at this Brad Vember. Maybe I can find out where they are through him."

"Phoenix is a big city."

"Yeah," Devlan said with a nod. "But I have you. See what you can find out about where she lives while I check out the shop."

Mike grinned. He took the four steps to the sunken living room in one lunge and sat heavily on one of the velvet sofa chairs. Letting out a loud yawn and kicking off his shoes, Mike placed his white-socked feet upon the nearest chair.

Seeing his friend relax was tempting to Devlan, but instead he found his laptop and plugged it in and immediately began typing an email to Kathy to explain his disappearance. He still had plenty of work to do, even if he was almost four-hundred miles away from the office. He paused in his typing and thought for a moment. Perhaps that was why Diana left. Though she had given him a new outlook for the future, he never had the chance to tell her so. He had planned to tell her after he proposed that he wanted to retire and focus on his new family.

How quickly that had changed.

Closing his laptop with a determined snap, he went down the

hall to the bedroom. Work could wait. When he began his search for Diana, he wanted to be fully rested and completely focused on the task at hand. For far too long, he had put his business first, and everyone was right. This time around, he needed to put old ghosts to rest before moving on with his life.

Later that morning, Devlan emerged from the hotel freshly showered and determined. He greeted the hired driver with a smile and climbed into the car, thankful for the blasting air conditioning. Traffic was steady, and the limo pulled out slowly. All at once, they were caught up in the other cars, heading into Scottsdale – and to Diana.

Devlan took a breath and held it. This was a moment he had truly longed for since she had left. He just had never admitted it to himself. Oh yes, he desired to find out answers, to see where he had gone wrong, for one thing remained, and that was that Devlan Doyle rarely made mistakes.

Yet, as the time grew closer, he felt more and more uneasy. There was anger brewing within him. He was angry with her for running off without a word to anyone. While he could forgive her for not completely trusting him, he was not so forgiving that she hurt others. Obviously, she did not care that there were many people who had feared for her safety.

"We're getting into Scottsdale now, sir."

Devlan nodded at the eyes staring at him through the rearview mirror. "I need Vember's gallery. It's off Scottsdale Road somewhere."

The driver nodded. "I'm sure it's in the Old Town area. I'll head that way."

"Good."

The day was bright and warm, and the sun rose high in the sky. It was turning into a beautiful day, with warm, dry air and a mild breeze. It would be the perfect day to track Diana.

He saw her car first. It pulled out into traffic just two cars ahead in the right lane. He saw the back of a blond head and sat up straight. "Wait a minute," he snapped. "Follow that Toyota."

He could not be positive since the car now had Arizona plates on it, but Devlan was pretty sure it was Diana he was following by the small dent in the rear bumper. He had studied that dent when she splattered him with dust the day of Peter's funeral. The driver remained a discreet distance away from her as they followed the traffic, too far back to make a positive identification. Then the car pulled into a strip-mall parking lot, sliding into a space in front of a grocery store.

"Stop. Pull in there and park, please."

He need not have asked, for they were already following. The driver eased into the fire lane but left the car in drive. Devlan watched the blue car intently, not even aware that he was holding his breath until he let it all out when she emerged. Her hair was in a loose braid and trailed down to mid-back. He had loved her skill with braids; they had been her specialty. With the unrelenting desert heat, he was surprised to see that she had let it grow in the past year but not surprised to see it so skillfully done up.

From behind, he could see she had put on a few pounds and smiled. They were needed. Her long legs were tanned under the short skirt she wore, and her baggy, pale pink top came down below her waist. Even so, she was still beautiful, and Devlan's breath caught as a flurry of long-buried emotions rose within him.

"Don't leave yet. Give me another minute."

The driver did as he was told, and Devlan watched Diana hurry into the store. He was tempted to go in after her but eventually thought better of it. They needed privacy for their long-overdue confrontation. With bated breath, he awaited her, his hands clenched into tight fists on his knees, and noticed that his palms were sweating.

"Follow her when she comes out," he said.

Again the driver nodded, and he held his tongue despite the obvious questions in his eyes. Devlan decided he liked the young man. Obviously, he knew how to do his job well.

Diana emerged a few minutes later carrying two large packages, one appearing to be diapers. Devlan frowned. Hannah was potty trained and had been since long before he met them.

The packages were hastily tossed into the back seat of the car, before she again slipped into the front and started up the motor. Devlan had seen her face long enough to see that she appeared frazzled or rushed. He remembered that look; it was one he had seen on her face many times.

Devlan sat back as the limo pulled back into traffic and willed his racing heart to slow down. They followed several car lengths behind her small car, finally stopping in front of an apartment complex.

"Drive by and turn around," Devlan said. "Maybe we'll catch her on the way in."

"Yes, sir."

From the opposite side of the road, they watched Diana as she unloaded her car and rushed to a first floor apartment. She soon disappeared inside.

"Okay, let's go," he said, his tone thoughtful.

He could not believe his luck. In a city of over four million people, he had managed to stumble into Diana within minutes of beginning his search. Perhaps it was meant to be after all?

Diana was here, within reaching distance. Now what was he going to do? Devlan idly rubbed his chin. It would be so easy to confront her, right in her apartment. Then again, he could not know for sure that it was her apartment. She could be running errands for a friend, or picking up Hannah from a play date.

"Where to now, sir? Should I pull in?"

"Keep heading for the shop. I'm not sure this place is hers."

"Yes, sir."

It was apparent that the shop had closed with Diana's departure when they pulled up. It was not an unusual thing, since most of the shops lining this part of the strip were small and artsy. There was a sign on her door, and Devlan got out of the limo to read it. She was taking an hour for lunch but would be back later. Devlan returned to the car.

"Do you have to be anywhere?" He asked the driver.

"No sir, I'm at your disposal."

"Good. Let's get some lunch. My treat."

The driver's eyes widened. "Thank you, sir."

Devlan sat back and gave the young man a smile. He needed to plan his next step, and tell Mike he had found her. He was curious now to see what Diana had been doing since he had seen her last. At least she was well. In fact, she looked pretty good. The added weight looked great on her.

After a quick lunch and some small talk, Devlan and his young driver friend were back in the vehicle and heading straight for the art gallery. After negotiating light traffic, they once more hunted for a parking space in the busy area. After a few circles, they pulled into a small lot and parked.

Devlan eased his length out into the bright sunshine and strode purposefully up to the door. It had taken them longer than an hour to find a place and then eat their lunch, so Diana had already re-opened the gallery some time before. He was pleased, for at least then he would not catch her at a busy time.

Little bells overhead jingled as he opened the door, and he stood there for a moment, his heart pounding as his eyes grew accustomed to the darker interior. The moment had come. Diana was there, only feet away. He could feel her presence.

Glancing around casually, Devlan took in the interior of the shop. There were small statues and Native American pieces on the tables scattered throughout the shop, but the most eye-catching parts of the nice little shop were the magnificent and colorful paintings lining the walls. They were also stacked haphazardly near the entrance to the back room, a surprise to see since they were worth so much money now.

As Devlan stared around him, a man appeared from behind the partially closed curtain leading to the back and approached him quickly. He wore a bone-colored, finely tailored suit, and his blond hair was slicked back to a tight ponytail in the back of his head. Devlan sensed immediately that he was not the artist.

"Can I help you?" He stopped in front of Devlan and stood resting on one leg. His gaze on Devlan was almost predatory, and Devlan was immediately seized with discomfort.

"Diana Somerset?" Devlan asked.

"Yes," the man said, waving his free arm with a sigh. "She's around here somewhere, even though she's not supposed to be. Hold on a sec, and I'll go find her."

Just then, Diana appeared from behind the same curtain, holding a bronze statue, which she stared transfixed at. She did not give them the slightest glance as she wandered over to a shelf where some slightly similar pieces were on display.

Devlan watched her move, his gaze devouring her. She was still so damn beautiful. In that, nothing had changed. Several loose strands of hair had escaped her braid and hung loosely around her face as usual. The fine pieces beckoned to his fingers, and he curled them into a fist as he tried to fight the rising tide of emotion that flooded through him.

"Jimmy, do you know where 'Walking Man' has gone? This isn't the right piece. Mrs. Oberman asked specifically for 'Walking Man.'"

The sound of her voice had not changed either, but he could

see the panic in her face. It must have been an expensive piece.

Jimmy waved his hands again. He wandered back the way he had come, throwing one final inviting look over his shoulder at Devlan. "Diana, go home already, will you? I'll find it... By the way, there's a guy here to see you."

Devlan raised an eyebrow at his description, unaccustomed to such a casual reference. Shaking his head, he approached Diana silently and came to stand behind her just as she turned around.

"Hello Diana," he murmured.

Had he not been there to catch the bronze piece she was holding, Diana would have lost two items up for sale. Her whole body jerked, and the exquisite artwork slipped from her stiff fingers. As he watched, all color drained from her face. She frantically took him in, and her bright blue eyes widened with what appeared to be panic. Devlan frowned in concern, and he awkwardly handed her the statue he had caught.

"I'm sorry," he said softly. "I didn't mean to startle you."

Diana's lips were opened in a silent gasp as she continued to stare at him mutely. She took the piece he held out to her with visibly shaking hands. He had no idea what he had done to frighten her so, but it bothered him to see her so shaken.

"Are you okay?"

She let out a deep breath before nodding slowly.

"Is there somewhere we can talk?"

Diana shook her head, tearing her gaze from his long enough to gather her bearings. She stared down at her feet then over at his just a few feet away. Devlan watched the top of her head, sighing in relief as the color slowly returned to her ashen face. As his concern eased, the anger began to come back. The fierce emotion fought for supremacy over his continued desire.

"Who told you where to find me?" Diana asked in a voice barely above a whisper.

Devlan shrugged. "No one told me where you were."

She looked up at him with wide eyes. He felt the urge to reach out and stroke her smooth cheek and caress the worry lines away, but anger stayed his hand.

"No," he said a little louder. "No one told me where you were, although I must admit I wished someone had."

He spun around and closed his eyes. It was proving to be a lot harder than he thought. There was just something about her…

Opening his eyes, Devlan glanced at some of the objects on display. Behind him, he could hear Diana take another deep breath.

Her voice was soft. "You did?"

"Yes," he said, picking up a small crystal vase. "How much is this?"

Diana shook her head again, as if trying to keep track. She hesitated a moment before clearing her throat. "Ninety-nine, ninety-nine."

"Yes," he continued. "I did. But no one told me anything. You were just gone, without a word to anyone. Instead of buying a car for you, I spent months wishing I had just gotten you a damn mobile phone."

The blond head lowered again to stare at her shoes. Devlan almost felt sorry for her, for he knew that she must have had her reasons. However, he still hurt too; he even had the pieces of his broken heart to show her.

"So when I went to an auction a couple of nights ago and bought a painting, imagine my surprise when I saw who the model was."

Diana's head snapped up, and her mouth fell open. "You bought the desert scene?"

The corner of Devlan's mouth rose. "I gather you heard about it already."

"Yes. Thomas called me this morning and told me how much it sold for…" She trailed off, as if just realizing that she had spoken.

Devlan nodded and wandered to the other side of the shop, silently thanking Providence for giving them an empty store to play this game.

"I was surprised that it was you. It took me a few hours to really convince myself that you were still with us in the land of the living." He shot her another look, but she stood silently, her teeth gnawing on her full lower lip in that oh so familiar way that she had whenever she felt torn. His heart stirred slightly, but he reined in his emotion. "And Hannah, too. She looks great. How's her leg? You left without finishing therapy."

"She had a therapist here," Diana said, her voice stronger. "She's in school now and just started first grade. She's doing well."

"I'd like to see her," Devlan said quickly. "I've really missed her."

Diana nodded and looked away quickly. Devlan thought he may have seen tears glistening in her eyes, and her voice quivered slightly when she answered. "She's missed you, too."

Seizing upon the moment, Devlan crossed the small shop and again came to stand in front of her. She continued to avert her eyes, but Devlan saw one tear escape her lashes to slip down her cheek. Before he could stop himself, he reached out and wiped it away, but Diana jerked as though his touch burned her and gave him her stiff back. Disappointed, he allowed his hand to fall back to his side while the wetness of her tear quickly evaporated in the dry air of the shop. He wished he could pull her into his arms and hold her while she cried.

But he did not. She had hurt him, too.

"Why couldn't you stay long enough to tell me you were leaving?"

297

"I tried to call you a couple of times," she whispered. "But I couldn't leave a message."

"Why did you leave?" He asked, his voice remaining neutral.

"I couldn't stay," she stammered. "I didn't want to get in the way."

"Get in the way? Of what?"

"Roxanne told me about your engagement, and I thought it would be easier for us both if we were out of the way."

Devlan forced himself to chuckle, although the very thought of laughter revolted him. She turned around and raised a curious brow. Shrugging, Devlan gave her a wry smile. "My marriage plans were canceled."

"Oh." Diana's eyes flickered. "I'm sorry."

"Yeah," he said abruptly. "Another notch on my stick, actually. I was stood up by the woman involved."

"Roxanne stood you up?" Diana asked, her open mouth and wide eyes giving away her astonishment.

"Roxanne was never my intended, Diana," he said forcefully. "You were."

A heavy silence fell around them, with only the sound of their breathing and the soft classical music playing throughout the shop audible. Devlan saw the glint of her gold chain and reached into her pink top far enough to pull the charm free.

"You actually kept something I gave you," he said softly. His long fingers flipped it over, and he read the inscription. "*A Vila Mon Coeur, Gardi Li Mo.* God, woman you still have it."

The charm fell back against her heaving chest, and Devlan turned to go. Diana watched him, her tear-filled eyes glued to his person. Her face was a mask of fear and confusion, and Devlan did not doubt for a moment that she felt as mixed up and torn inside as he did.

"I just wanted to see you once more. To make sure you were

okay," he said. "I'd still like to see Hannah. Would it be okay to stop by tomorrow?"

She nodded.

"Fine. By the way," he said over his shoulder. "You look great. You needed a few extra pounds."

The door jingled again, and Devlan stepped aside so a young man with long, brown hair could enter. Dressed in a threadbare T-shirt and cargo shorts that hung from his tall, thin frame, the man looked as out of place in this fine gallery as Devlan felt. He stopped long enough to stare at Devlan unabashedly, his eyes squinted as though with recognition. Then his gaze settled on Diana, and he smiled.

"Excuse me," he said, advancing in the shop.

Devlan glanced back, but Diana had turned away and was wiping her eyes. The intruder stood in the middle, staring from one to the other while Devlan quickly made his escape. He needed time to think, time to reorganize, and time to heal the wounds that had reopened when he saw the only woman he had ever loved.

Chapter 22

"I would never have known it if I didn't see it with my own eyes," Brad mused, placing his hands on Diana's shoulders.

Diana sniffled and again wiped at her face. "What are you talking about?"

"Bryce's father."

Immediately Diana stiffened, and she pulled away to glare at Brad. "Bryce is *my* son."

"Ah, but he wasn't conceived via the Immaculate Conception," Brad said lightly, pulling Diana against his chest.

She immediately resumed her crying. Through her sobs she managed to pinch Brad's arm. "Don't be so crude."

Brad chuckled and held her gently. "I'm not being crude… I'm being honest."

"Where's Hannah?"

"She's in the car with the air conditioning on, I promise. I just dropped by to bum some cash off you. I told Hannah I'd take her to the zoo before the Art Walk gets started tonight. Is that okay with you?"

"Yes," she said quickly. "That would be good. I don't want her to see me like this."

"Is he giving you trouble?"

"Of course not. He would never…"

"Where's Bryce?"

"Asleep in the back."

Brad released his grip on her and watched as she patted the tears away. "Did he see him already?"

"No, he didn't seem to know. I guess Thomas hasn't told him yet."

"So he searched you out on his own?"

"I guess."

"He looked as upset as you, Di. Maybe there's a chance."

"God, I was so stupid!" Diana smiled bitterly. "He wanted to marry *me. Me*, Brad! Not that lying bimbo, but I ran away before he could even ask me… and I don't think the offer still stands."

"Wow, Di. You really lost a good catch."

"Stop teasing," she said, a small laugh escaping her. "Jimmy already gave him the once over."

"That slut."

Diana giggled through her misery. The relationship that Jimmy and Brad shared was playful and teasing. They bickered all day long, and Diana's head spun as she watched their arguments. Yet as volatile as their relationship was, she sensed they shared a bond that went way beyond her comprehension.

Face serious again, Brad met Diana's gaze and held it. "Are you going to be okay here?"

"Yes," she said with a sigh. "I've got to get myself together. He just took me by complete surprise. I never saw him coming."

"How did he find you?"

"The painting."

"You mean?"

"Yes. He's the one who bought it."

"You see? I said you were my good luck charm. And see, I was right."

"I'm a mere woman whose heart is so confused right now that I can't think straight." She lifted her hands to her head and massaged her temples. "Go away, Brad. Leave me in peace. I need to think."

"Fine. I'll meet you and Bryce here at five o'clock sharp."

Diana nodded her head and waved him on. She knew Brad was just trying to help, but she needed to be alone. Her mind was spinning. Never had she considered that Devlan had planned to marry her. What a fool she had been for running off like she had. She should have found the strength to stay and confront him like she had planned. Instead, she had done what she always did – run away.

Sighing deeply, Diana stopped the inner accusations by placing her hand over her eyes. It was plain that she had allowed her fear to override her common sense, and what she had done was done. She and Devlan could not turn back the clock and go back to those few days of panic. The best she could do was move on with her life and continue trying to heal her heart. It sounded so easy, but the truth of the matter was that she would never forgive herself for being so irrational.

~

"Jimmy, we'll be back in a little while."

"Okay!"

Diana watched as Brad pushed Bryce's stroller ahead down the crowded sidewalk. She walked a little more slowly, her grip on Hannah's small hand tight.

"Stay with me," she advised.

"I want to go with Brad, Mommy. He walks faster."

Sighing heavily, Diana nodded. "Fine. Go catch up with him."

She watched as Hannah skipped off, once again sending a prayer of thanks that her daughter was completely healed. However, no sooner had they slipped out of sight than she felt a presence very close to her. She placed the Kachina doll she was examining down and turned around to see Devlan once more standing close behind her. Her sharp inhale was cut short as a large crowd of people bore down on them. Diana was pressed against the table where the dolls were housed by Devlan's large body, and her eyes widened even further. Fortunately, Devlan looked as taken aback as she, and as uncomfortable.

"Good lord, man. Must you keep sneaking up on me?" She snapped, relieved that the others had long gone on ahead.

"I'm sorry."

"Are you following me?"

He had the good grace to look uncomfortable, though he shook his head adamantly. "No, I was told about the Art Walk before I saw you. In fact, I was planning to find you here tonight, but as luck would have it..."

"As luck would have it?" she repeated. Her heart was thrumming at a bird's rate, yet she struggled to remain calm. He did not appear to have any inkling about Bryce, and she still had no idea how to approach the topic.

"Well, you know what I mean."

"When are you leaving?"

Devlan chuckled, though his face appeared strained. "Not soon enough for you?"

"No, no," she said hastily. "It's just that I'm trying to arrange a time for Hannah to see you."

"Why not now? She's here, isn't she?"

"Actually, she's with some friends."

"I see. How about tomorrow? When does she finish school?"

Out of the corner of her eye, she saw Brad returning with Hannah and Bryce. Her baby was howling at the top of his lungs, but when Brad saw her with Devlan, he quickly turned them around.

In her desperation, she grasped Devlan's lightweight suit jacket. "Tomorrow's fine. Come around three or so?"

"Three. Fine."

Diana smiled evasively. "I've got to run. I'll see you later."

Though he appeared confused at her sudden change of heart, Devlan nodded again. He opened his mouth to say something else, but Diana quickly slipped into the crowds. She headed straight for the cries of the baby, leaving Devlan to remain where she left him, a frown marring his handsome face.

Little Bryce had worked himself into a full frenzy when she at last met the frazzled trio. She managed a small laugh at Brad, who was gently bouncing the baby over his shoulder.

"He's hungry," she explained.

Brad rolled his eyes. "I can't help him there."

"Give him to me." She took the hungry baby and immediately he stopped fussing. He sucked furiously on his fist and continued whimpering in discomfort. "Can you drive us home? I'll take care of him there."

Brad nodded, but he had a worried look in his eye. "He followed you here?"

"No. He said he wanted to see the sights. I'm pretty sure I lost him in the crowd."

"Diana, when is this guy leaving? Things could turn very ugly if he finds out by accident. He's going to think you're keeping his son from him."

"I know," she moaned. "I made plans for him to meet with Hannah tomorrow. I'll figure this out by then."

She grimaced as she spoke, and Brad eyed her speculatively. "You don't want him to go, do you?"

She shook her head, but Brad pressed on.

"You don't. Somewhere in the back of your mind, you want to tell him how much you love him, don't you?"

304

She shook her blond head. "You don't understand... you don't know."

"Know what?"

"He's so powerful and can have anything he wants. It's a whole different lifestyle. I'm happy here, with you and Jimmy."

"Because you think I'm safe. Hell, you think it makes you safe, but you can't hide forever. Sooner or later, you have to take a chance."

"That's not fair."

He was unapologetic. "But it's the truth."

"Just bring me home," she said. "My head hurts from all of this."

She really did not want to think about things so far in the future. Besides, from the way he had sounded that afternoon, he had no intentions of seeking her out after they said their farewells. She heard from his own lips that he had just come to see that she was all right.

Oh, how it hurt to admit how badly she had botched such a good thing. She had set her guard so high that she had run at the first sign of trouble. Despite her vows of protecting her heart, she had broken it herself – and his. It had been hard enough to move on with her life, let alone now seeing him again after all this time. Knowing she had hurt him too just seemed to make things so much harder.

No matter how much she wished for it, she knew their time together was over. They had shared some beautiful moments, and he had truly given her the most precious gift of life and love, but she had been foolish and trampled on that gift.

"We're home!" Hannah hollered.

Diana returned to the present and smiled at her daughter. She would need to explain to her about Devlan's return to the scene. The very idea saddened her. Once more, she was teasing her firstborn with Devlan's companionship when she knew it would only be fleeting, but how could she say no?

"I'm going to go work out. I'll bring Hannah with me, so you'll have time to think and relax with Bryce."

Diana smiled her thanks to Brad and concentrated on getting Bryce in the house and fed. She retired to the rocking chair in her and Hannah's room and tried her best to soothe the fussing baby. Outside her room, she heard Hannah's chatter and smiled. How she loved her two children. She had truly been blessed.

Bryce's avid sucking had quieted down to an occasional one as he fell asleep. She gently shifted him to her shoulder and began to pat his back. The overtired infant continued sleeping, even when three burps erupted from deep within his small belly.

She carefully placed him in his small cradle and smoothed back the dark hair. What a joy her son was becoming. Just a few days before he had bestowed upon her a gas-induced toothless smile which was so like his father's that her heart truly melted. She had to tell Devlan. He had to see his son. Hopefully, they could be strong and provide him with the best upbringing possible.

She covered the sleeping baby and exited the room, closing the door softly behind her. Then she strolled down the hall to the kitchen, only to find Hannah and Brad munching on tortilla chips.

"Aren't you going to work out?" She picked up their empty glasses and washed them, then began working on the rest of the dirty dishes in the sink.

Flashing her a wry grin, Brad pushed aside the bag of chips. "You're right. We're going. Come on kid, I'll take you to the workout room and you can help me lift weights."

"Promise?" Hannah asked, her eyes gleaming with excitement.

Brad shrugged and tossed a towel around his neck. "Only if you're nice. Come on, I'll race you."

He allowed Hannah to beat him to the door, and her nimble little fingers hurriedly unbolted it and pulled it open. Much to their surprise, she revealed Devlan standing there with his hand poised to knock.

"Uncle Devvie!" Hannah screamed.

Brad's eyes widened in surprise, and he glanced over his shoulder at Diana. "You've got company."

Too stunned to move, Diana watched as Hannah threw herself at Devlan with a squeal of joy. "Oh Uncle Devvie, we've missed you so much!"

Devlan laughed and swung her into his arms. He spun her around and around until she laughingly begged him to stop. With a squeeze and a chuckle, he set her down on her feet and squatted to her height.

"Let me get a look at you," he said, holding her at arm's length.

"I've grown," she stated.

"I see." He nodded his head. "Yes, you have, and you've gotten even prettier."

"I have a loose tooth," she announced. He watched proudly as she opened her mouth and began to wiggle her tooth.

"It's going to come out soon," he said.

Diana approached, drying her hands on a dishtowel. Devlan's gaze met hers, and he regained his full height. He astutely took in Brad's change of dress and impending departure.

"Good evening, Diana. Are you on your way out?"

Diana opened her mouth to answer, but Brad beat her to the chase. "No, Hannah and I are."

Brad stepped aside so Devlan could enter, and Diana watched as her former lover took in Brad's painting supplies and canvases scattered in the living room. Sensing the direction of his thoughts, she stepped forward and came to stand between the two men.

"Devlan, may I introduce Brad Vember. Brad, this is Devlan Doyle."

The two men eyed each other with newfound interest. She saw how Brad's eyes widened in recognition. Not surprisingly, he had heard of Devlan before, and Devlan was meeting the artist who had painted her as a water sprite.

To her surprise, Devlan continued to remain impassive. He held out his hand with a polite smile. "Nice to meet you, Mr. Vember. I admire your work."

"And I yours."

Devlan cocked his head, and his eyes narrowed suspiciously when Diana's sharp intake of breath reached his ears. Fortunately, Hannah came to the rescue by throwing herself once more at Devlan.

"Look, Uncle Devvie! I can dance now."

She did a clumsy pirouette for him, and then waited expectantly for his applause. Instead, he reached forward to hug her tightly again. His eyes appeared suspiciously moist. "Goodness, I missed you, little one," he breathed into her golden hair.

"Well, we should get going," Brad announced, scowling meaningfully at Diana.

She watched with growing panic. If Hannah and Brad left, she would be alone with Devlan. There was no way of knowing how that would turn out. "Why don't you stay and let Hannah visit with Devlan for a while? That way he can go home in the morning."

Devlan released Hannah and smiled at Diana. "No. That won't be necessary. I've already got a time slot to leave tomorrow afternoon. I can still visit with Hannah after school." He glanced down at the child. "Would you like that? Do you want me to visit with you tomorrow?"

"Oh, yes!"

"Then it's settled," he said triumphantly.

Diana clenched her teeth. She could not understand why Brad was not helping her. Instead, her traitorous friend took a hold of Hannah's small hand and led her to the door.

"We'll be back in a little while," he called over his shoulder.

As the door shut behind the pair, Devlan advanced even further into the apartment. His keen eyes took in everything, from the scattered dolls to the numerous paints. The cluttered scene left no doubt that they all shared an apartment. Devlan's mouth thinned as he glanced around.

"I'm sorry for all the clutter," Diana said as she came forward to clear off the small futon. "I haven't been home long enough to pick up."

"Home," he repeated, as if not wanting to believe it. "You all live here then?"

"Yes," she answered. "Brad took us in when we left California."

Devlan's head inclined slightly at her words. She saw his fists clench by his sides, but he showed no emotion in his angular face. The silence that followed hung heavily in the air, and Diana busied herself by returning to the small kitchen and drying the freshly washed dishes. Remembering her manners, Diana grudgingly spoke up. "Can I get you anything? Water, soda, tea?"

He shook his head in the negative, and silence once again fell.

Thankfully, there was nothing about that would indicate an infant in the house, and Diana felt relief at the reprieve. How she would approach the subject was still up in the air, and she wished she could have had the chance to call Thomas first.

Devlan followed her in and took a seat at the small dining room table. He watched her work intently, and Diana felt his gaze burning her where it landed.

"You do look good," he commented.

She gave him a sarcastic look. "I look chubby. Admit it, Devlan. I know I've put on weight, but it's okay, I don't mind."

He smiled, though it did not quite reach his eyes. "So where did you meet Brad Vember?"

"I see," she said. "Is this about Brad?"

His brows lifted over falsely innocent eyes. "No. I was merely curious to know who it was that stole you away from me."

She threw back her head and laughed, but it was a nervous laugh, and she felt none of the humor she displayed. She could not understand how he could not see how much she still ached for him. "Brad's a friend of Allan's. He sent me to him when I called for help."

"Called for help?" He frowned, his despair plain in his intense eyes. "Why is it you'll ask anyone for help but me? A complete stranger? You would even go to a man you had never met, but you wouldn't come to me?"

Diana finished putting away the last dish before she answered him. "Look, Devlan, Brad is gay. He has absolutely no interest in me whatsoever. He's been involved with Jimmy for as long as I've known him."

Devlan had the grace to look surprised before he chuckled. "Jimmy? The one at the gallery?"

"Yes," she said, unable to hide her own smile. "We're all one, big happy family."

Devlan came to his feet and approached Diana. She backed away until she rested against the counter. Suddenly, she was transported back in time to the day he had first kissed her. Unconsciously, her mouth opened for his kiss, but Devlan stopped too far away to touch her.

"Why are you here?" Diana asked, her tone revealing her

irritation.

Devlan sighed. "I don't know, Diana." He nodded in the direction of the coffeepot. "Maybe we could share a cup of coffee."

"You came here for a cup of coffee?"

His face broke into one of his heart-stopping smiles. The sight brightened up the room in addition to his face. Diana longed to reach out and touch his shadowed cheek. She wanted so desperately to huddle within the strength of his arms. However, she did neither, and her hands remained by her side. As he watched her, Devlan's smile slowly faded, and his eyes began to gleam. Diana saw the look, one she had seen before, and quickly turned away before she exposed too much.

"No, I didn't come for a cup of coffee." His voice was warm, and he continued talking as she hastily filled up the coffeepot. "I don't know for sure why I came. All I know is that all this time I've suffered, wracking my brain to figure out why you left without saying a word to anyone. I couldn't figure out what I'd done to scare you away… Now you're here, right in front of me, with such a simple excuse that I feel like I'm missing something."

She refused to look at him for fear he would be able to see the lie on her face. "Missing something?"

"Yes, like there's more to the story that I don't know about. I mean, why run away so quickly, without even questioning me? What drove you to sneak off in the middle of the night without a word to anyone?"

Finally, she turned around to face him, her eyes again filled with tears. She wished so desperately that she could tell him the truth. Tell it all to him. About the baby, about Roxanne's visit, but it would do no good. He made it plain earlier that his offer was no longer valid. She had already hurt him so much.

"I'm sorry," she whispered. "I never meant to hurt you. I was so scared."

"Scared? Of what?"

She shook her head. "It doesn't matter now, does it?"

Devlan reached forward and took a hold of her arms. His eyes burned with urgency. "It does matter. I think it does."

"Devlan, please."

"I need to know, Diana. It does matter to me."

"There are other things to talk about now. We shouldn't be looking at the past. We need to discuss the future," she said quickly.

"I'm still stuck in the past."

Diana struggled to catch her breath. Things were moving so fast. Devlan's warm grasp was burning her arms, and he was so close she could smell the familiar scent of his cologne. It was the same scent that she had fallen in love with so long ago, and it hurt her so much to be so close to him again.

"It shouldn't matter anymore, Devlan. Please. I've tried to put you out of my life, to move on. Don't make it any harder than it has to be."

Devlan inched closer in the small kitchen, and his breath fell heavy on her upturned face. It smelled like mint, like the freshness after the rain. "You're so wrong. I'll always be in your life, no matter what. We shared something that was very special. You can't deny that." His voice grew husky as his face lowered to mere inches from hers. "Or this…"

He continued his descent, and Diana's eyes drifted closed. She could not stop him, even if she wanted to. She felt the softness of his lips brush against hers just as the first cry went up. He froze where he was, his full lower lip just barely touching hers.

The cry came again, and Diana squeezed her eyelids together. Well, she had tried. Devlan released his grip on her and took a step back. "That was a baby."

Diana bit her lip as she nodded. Devlan continued to frown. "But I thought you said you and Brad…" His voice trailed off as he inspected her again. "You're not chubby. You've…"

Diana stood so still she felt she could have been molded from clay. Devlan continued to fight against the odds, obviously afraid to admit the truth. Throughout his inner debate, Bryce's cries grew stronger as he became more fully awake. Suddenly, Devlan turned and stumbled down the hall, one hand reaching out to guide him along. The door to her room was opened, and he approached the small cradle by the light of the nightlight while Diana scooped the baby up. A small burp broke the silence as the child moved, explaining his sudden wakefulness, and Devlan's mouth hung open as he stared at his very likeness. His face appeared pinched, and it was void of any color. It was plain to Diana that he did not know where to go from here.

"This is my child." His voice was soft, almost a caress.

Diana nodded. "Yes, that's what I was trying to tell you."

"And this child is the reason Thomas told me to contact him?"

Again she nodded. How dubious she had been. How selfish. The pain mirrored on his face was second only to hers. She was the cause of his pain. It was her actions that had hurt him so terribly. "I never meant," she stammered. However, she stopped speaking for she knew she would only lie.

Handing him the small bundle, she watched as he took Bryce in his arms and held him close. Through her own tears, Diana thought she saw some glistening in Devlan's eyes. He held their child so close that Diana's heart ached for them. They did belong together; she could not hide it.

Devlan raised his face from Bryce's silky black hair and glared at Diana. "How could you have kept this from me all this time? You were pregnant with my child and ran away?"

She shook her head wordlessly. If only he knew how badly she had longed for him through it all.

"You realize that I will change my will to include this infant."

"Bryce," Diana offered.

"Bryce." He again kissed Bryce's warm head and rubbed his cheek against the soft skin, but his voice was like ice. "And you realize that I will take custody of this child."

Diana reeled back as though he had struck her, and all the blood drained from her face. Was Devlan playing a cruel joke on her? Try as she might to deny it, the cold, hard look in his eye told her he was deadly serious. He handed the baby back to her, but one hand lingered momentarily on his small head. His voice was every bit as cold and clipped as his eyes when he backed from the room.

"My lawyer will be in touch with yours, Diana." His voice was severe, as sharp as the edge of a knife. She had never heard him speak thus, and it frightened her to see him so angry. He took a step backwards, but his eyes still glared at her. Hating her. "I can see myself out."

Devlan slowly backed from the room and out of Diana's sight. She heard the door slam shut seconds later and collapsed to the floor. Sobs of heartbreak came forth as she lamented the loss of the man she loved – and the son she was bound to lose as well.

Chapter 23

The door opened with a flash of light from the hallway. Diana was still on the floor, although she had moved until her back rested against the mattress of her bed. She squinted as Hannah reached up to flick up the light switch. Suddenly their room was illuminated fully with bright white light. It hurt her head, and her tear-swollen eyes burned in protest.

"Hi Mommy!"

Brad shushed Hannah and sent her back to the living room with the promise of a video. After reaching down and hugging her mother, she happily skipped out and left them alone.

"Jesus," Brad said, coming to kneel in front of her. He took her cold hands into his own and gave her a light squeeze. "What happened to you?"

"He said he's going to take him away."

Diana cradled the sleeping child against her breast. There was no way she would ever give up Bryce willingly. No matter what, she would fight for her child.

"I won't give him up," she said fiercely. "There's no way he'll take him away from me."

"Do you really think he meant it?"

"Of course he did. He doesn't bluff, Brad."

"If he's that successful in business, he must bluff," Brad said dryly. "Think about it, he's the king of cool."

Unknowingly, Diana's fingers went to the necklace Devlan

had given her so long ago. She began to finger the heart-shaped locket nervously, tugging it along the chain.

"I don't know," she whispered. "He was so angry. I've never seen him like that before."

"Can you blame him?" Brad frowned at her. "It's plain that he loves Hannah a lot, and she's not even his kid. I don't blame him at all for wanting to hurt you. I would, too."

"Thanks a lot," she muttered. "Whose side are you on anyway?"

He reached forward and stilled her hands. "I'm on your side, Diana... I see that you love this man. Call me a romantic fool, but it bothers me to see you hurt so much. You want to trust him, but you can't, and that's your problem. Maybe you should trust him more." He glanced at the intricate locket. "What's this anyway?"

He opened it and glanced at the two pictures inside. The look he gave her was deliberately wry, and she blushed. "You kept his picture next to your heart all this time, and then you expect me to believe that you're happy without him?" He flipped the locket closed and glanced at the inscription on the other side. "*A Vila Mon Coeur, Gardi Li Mo?*"

"Do you know what it means?" she asked, sniffling.

"Of course, I took years of French in school."

"What does it say? Devlan never told me."

"It says, 'here is my heart, guard it well.'"

As the words sunk in slowly, Diana threw back her head and laughed. Bryce startled at the sound, and she absently pulled him closer. "I don't believe it."

"Hey," Brad grunted. "My French isn't that bad."

"What a fool," she gasped. Brad was right. There was still hope.

Brad frowned at her in confusion. "I'm not a fool."

"I have to go," Diana said. "Bryce has been fed and has a

clean diaper. Put Hannah down no later than eight. She has school tomorrow."

Diana came to her feet and handed Brad the sleeping baby. "Wait a minute," he protested. "Where are you going?"

"I'm going to try to fix things. I'm going to say I'm sorry."

"But how? Do you know where he is?"

"I can guess."

Finally understanding, Brad smiled. "Good luck Di. I'll miss you."

She glanced at him over her shoulder. "I'm not there yet."

~

Diana drove straight to the finest hotel in Phoenix. Although there were dozens of fine resorts and spas in the Valley of the Sun, there was one hotel that stood apart from the others. The hotel that harbored presidents among the rich and famous, and Diana knew without a doubt that Devlan would be there.

The red-paved drive led to the fine stucco front. She slid into a parking space without any aid and rushed into the front lobby, and the concierge glanced up in surprise at her hurried entrance. She had tried to straighten her loose hair and fix her face, but the tears had washed away all traces of the makeup she had applied earlier that day. Her clothes were casual and not nearly as finely tailored as the patrons of this exquisite hotel.

"Mr. Doyle's room, please," she said breathlessly.

There was a collective murmur behind the desk as the employees glanced at one another in uncertainty. Diana watched them with growing exasperation, her face growing stiffer with tension.

"Please, I need to know where he is."

When they continued to hesitate, Diana glanced around the

lobby frantically. Out of the corner of her eye, she saw Mike
O'Hare appear from the lounge and breathed a sigh of relief.
Shoving herself away from the desk, she pursued the tall
bodyguard, calling out his name from across the lobby.

"Mike!"

He spun around, and his eyes widened when he saw her
there. "Mrs. Somerset?"

"Please, Mike. I need to see Devlan."

He shook his head slowly. "I don't know... He's locked up in
his suite. Told me to go away for a while and ordered a bottle."

Diana grimaced. "Will he see me?"

"I don't think so."

She felt the tears begin to fill her eyes as despair filled her.
Her shoulders slumped as she sighed in resignation. Mike watched
her closely, his eyes narrowed. Finally, with a groan, he reached in
his pocket and pulled free his room pass. "Take this. The
number's on the jacket. I'll find somewhere else to go."

"Thank you, Mike. Thank you so much."

He waved his hand and turned away, but not before Diana
saw the red stain on his cheeks. She would have hugged him had
he not slipped out of sight.

Diana was left clutching the treasured pass. She remained
rooted to the spot for another moment before gathering up all her
courage and striding purposefully to Devlan's room. She could do
this, she told herself. It was time to admit that she had changed
quite a bit since her terrible marriage to Peter. She had learned
how to stand up for herself and her daughter, and it was mostly
due to Devlan. Now she needed to repay him that favor. It was
time they were completely honest with each other, and she had to
tell him the truth straight out.

The door was closed, and she could not hear any noise
coming from inside. She remained outside for a few minutes,

insecurity staying her hand. She had to thrust her pride aside now. It was all up to her. But deep down the fear was there. Haunting her. She was still afraid to open her heart to never-ending pain. Just like before.

The door swung open silently to reveal the darkened suite. The only light came from the bedroom, where the door stood partially open. No sound came from the sunken living room, and Diana squinted into the blackness ahead. Fear made her mouth dry, and it took all of her strength to advance into the room and shut the door behind her when all she wanted to do was run away.

"I thought I told you to go away."

Diana startled in a mixture of surprise and alarm. Devlan's deep voice was as harsh as it had been at her condo. He was seated in the living room in one of the plush white chairs. As her eyes grew accustomed to the darkness, she noted that he was facing away from her, and a bottle of whiskey was on the floor by his side. His dark head was resting against the back of the chair, and she could see that his eyes were closed. In his hand was an eight ounce glass, partially empty, and the bottle already had a pretty good-sized dent in it. She inhaled sharply. Peter had never been a nice drunk. She had no idea if Devlan would be any better.

"Go away," he insisted.

The words were cold and clipped. Diana squeezed her eyes shut and took the carpeted stairs slowly. She felt as though she were walking to her doom. However, she knew she could be strong. She could survive this. She would simply tell Devlan the truth and see what he had to say. It would be so easy.

Although she advanced slowly, she saw Devlan's nostrils flare seconds before he raised his head and opened his eyes. She froze when he pinned her with his angry blue gaze, unable to move a muscle. "What are you doing here? I told you my lawyer would be in touch with yours."

COLLETTE SCOTT

Diana steeled her resolve and dropped to her knees in front of him. He did not move, although he watched her intensely. When her hands came down on his knees, he jerked away, but it was the only move he made.

In an effort to appease him, she held her hands up for a moment before letting them fall to her side, but he continued to glare at her. "I'm here to say I'm sorry."

Devlan shook his head and emptied his glass. When it was gone, he inhaled harshly and scowled at her. "Go away, Diana. I'd rather not look at you right now."

Diana shook her head. "No. You asked me earlier to tell you why I left. I'm here to tell you now."

"I can't listen to your excuses right now."

She hesitated long enough to gather her courage and put her pride aside. "I was so scared Devlan."

"So you say."

"I was. I was so terrified that I panicked."

"I really don't want to hear this now, Diana. I'm in no mood." He waved his hand and reached for the bottle. Diana was tempted to pull it from his hand, but she did not want to inflame him any more than he already was.

"Devlan, please. Listen to me. That's all I ask."

"I can't anymore. I've tried to be patient, but never in my wildest dreams did I ever suspect you of hiding your pregnancy from me. *My child*, Diana."

She bit her lip. He was totally and absolutely correct. However, she had reasons, and she wanted him to hear them before she left. "Devlan, please, just listen. Just give me these last few minutes, okay?"

When he did not answer, she jumped at the chance to speak. "Roxanne came over and told me that you realized how in love you were with her after her trip to the hospital. She said you were announcing your engagement to her on Christmas Eve. Who was I to doubt her?"

"I told you we were nothing more than friends."

"But you have to admit that she came first with us several times. After all, you left my bed to be with her on two occasions."

"Then why didn't you rage at me, and get it out in the open? Why did you bottle it all inside you?"

"I was afraid. She was there a long time before I was."

"But I told you."

"Yes, but you showed me something different."

"I had commitments to complete. You should've trusted me."

"I'd been wrong to trust before. I still couldn't know for sure."

"Because you didn't have any confidence. I told you I'd take care of you while you found your self-esteem again."

"You also told me that you would follow me if I ran away again." Diana laughed bitterly. "You never searched me out until now, and I know that you could have easily found me. Besides, who am I to compete against a woman as beautiful as she is?"

Devlan shook his head. With a feeling of some triumph she noticed that he almost reached for her. "You are every much as beautiful as she is, if not more so. I used to think that you had more caring and depth than she did."

She could feel a blush rising on her cheeks and ducked her head. "I didn't know. I was going to stay and question you, but then I realized that I might be pregnant. I went to a drug store and bought a kit. When it came up positive, I went wild. I assumed that you would take the baby away and want to raise it with Roxanne. The very idea of Roxanne holding my child made me crazy. I was so scared that I ran away."

"If you had stayed long enough to ask me, you would've

realized Roxanne would never touch my son."

"But it wasn't just her. I was afraid to tell you, too. I admit that. You had referred to our vacation as a fling and had already expressed your reluctance to have children with me that night on the boat."

"A fling?" he frowned as he struggled to remember. "I never…"

"You did. On my birthday, you said no one knew about our fling in Hawaii."

"I was trying to reassure you that what we had would remain between us," he said angrily. "Why are you twisting everything?"

"I'm not twisting," she insisted. "I'm trying to explain my point of view. You said things and then did others. I came to my own conclusions."

"Yeah, the wrong ones. You once accused me of refusing to commit, Diana, but you should take a look at yourself. I offered you everything I had. I committed fully to you."

He was right; she knew that now. How she had despised the very thought of him because she believed he was a commitment-phobe, but she had proven herself to be just as guilty. "There was never talk about a future. Everything we had in that time was under the understanding that I would leave once Hannah had recovered."

"You never gave me the chance. I was going to talk to you the evening of your birthday. I was going to ask you to stay with me. You were the one who took off."

"I was wrong. I know that. And it was wrong for me to wait to contact Thomas, but the idea of you and her sharing my baby, or you marrying me out of duty was just too much to bear. I thought I was helping you from facing an awkward conversation. Never, Devlan… never did I think I was hurting you."

"But you did," he said softly.

322

"And I am so very sorry." She reached for him again, and this time he did not pull away. She threw herself at him, wrapping her arms around his abdomen and burying her face in his chest. "Roxanne said that you were planning a family together," she said brokenly. "I figured that Hannah and I would be like a bad memory, the black sheep of the family, and I wanted to save you from having to tell us to leave. I had to protect my daughter. She loves you so much."

He did not push her away, but neither did he participate in her tight hug. His arms remained over the chair as he sat, unmoving, beneath her. Having said her piece, she finally released him. She came to her feet slowly and stared down at him. Her face was completely unguarded as she managed a small smile for him.

"I came here tonight to tell you. You deserved to hear the whole truth. You're such a wonderful person, Devlan, and you truly deserve the best. I know that I reacted too quickly, but I have no intentions of keeping you from Bryce. He's your son, and you're an amazing father. My children are the world to me, and I only want what is best for both of them."

Waiting for a response that never came, Diana slowly nodded her head in understanding. She had come to say what she wanted to say and had survived it. It was now time to bow out. She turned and headed for the stairs with heavy feet and an even heavier heart. Disappointment at his continued coldness filled her, but she had hurt him deeply. He needed time to digest it all, and she had to be willing enough to give him all that he needed. Patience. Devlan had always been so patient with her. It was her turn to do the same for him.

Dropping the room pass on the glass table beside his chair, she glanced once more at Devlan as he sat unmoving. With her head held high, Diana placed one foot on the bottom stair. "Goodbye, Devlan."

Tears blinded her in the darkness, and she stumbled on the last step. She quickly regained her balance and hurried to the door, hoping to escape before he heard her sob again.

She was just pulling the door open when his hand snaked past her and held it closed. His fingers splayed across the door, his arm perilously close to her nose. The tears that threatened to spill over her lashes obscured his features, but she could see that he was staring right at her when she turned to face him.

"Don't open that door," he whispered.

"But…"

His finger covered her lips. "Sssh."

She could smell the whiskey hot on his breath and grimaced. Was he drunk? She could not tell. "I don't understand."

"I'm furious with you," he said.

"I know."

"Hush," he hissed. "Just give me a damn minute."

He continued to stare at her, his eyes burning into her as though he was trying to see into her soul. Unsure what to do or how to respond, she met his gaze wordlessly, patiently waiting for him to speak. Finally, with a muffled curse he slammed his hand against the door. The loud smacking sound caused her to jump, but she remained rooted to the spot.

"How could you be so goddamned blind, Diana?"

"I said I was sorry."

"God, I don't think I can stand to look at you right now."

"Then why are you blocking the door?"

He took another deep breath and let it out slowly, shaking his head as he did so. His hand slid from the door to her shoulder in a firm grip. "I'm afraid that if I let you walk out that door, you'll disappear in the night, and I'll never see you again."

She shook her head adamantly. "No. I swear to you that I'm done running away, Devlan. I won't do that to you or to Bryce."

The name of their son cooled the air between them. Devlan loosened his grip upon her but did not yet let go. Her vision had cleared enough to see the emotion on his face. It was reassuring to see that he was as confused as she was.

"I won't let you," he whispered.

"So what do you plan to do?"

"I don't know what to do."

He released his grip on her and thrust her away. Stumbling back a step, she bumped into the door. When she again raised her frightened gaze to his, he raised his hands to the ceiling in frustration and groaned aloud.

"Damn woman, what am I to do with you?"

"I won't keep Bryce from you, Devlan, I promise you that. Thomas and your lawyer will help us work something out. I don't want to complicate things any more than I already have."

"Is that what you want? Don't you want anything from me? Child support?"

She shook her head. Then she lowered her face to stare at her hands. Honesty, she reminded herself, she had made a promise to clear the air between them, and that required honesty. "I've never wanted anything from you, Devlan, except…"

"Except what?"

She shook her head and chuckled wryly. "Nothing. It's not important now."

"It is important." Devlan's approach was rapid, and he had a hold on her before she could move away. His eyes burned with an urgency that took her breath away. "Tell me, Diana. For once, tell me how you really feel instead of forcing us both to assume."

His husky words tickled her ears. How she had missed that deep and gentle voice. She would always remember the feel of him, the taste, and the smell of his clean skin. That was all she wanted.

She wanted him.

With shaking hands she reached up and cupped his cheeks. The sharp stubble there scratched her palms, but she did not care. He felt so male and alive, so familiar and so desired. She loved him with all of her heart and soul. She wanted him so much that her heart ached.

"I love you, Devlan. I don't love your money or your power. I love the man that you are – the gentle and kind man who would do whatever it took to protect me. That's all I wanted from you. Just your love."

"Is that all?" His sudden laughter caught her off guard, and her hands fell away from his face in a mixture of surprise and shame. "Christ, woman, I've loved you for as long as I can remember. How could you have doubted that for an instant?"

She shook her head in confusion.

"I was attracted to you the first time I ever laid eyes on you."

"But how? You didn't even know me."

"No, but you were so beautiful and pure. The memory of you on your wedding day, that day that I met you for the first time, was enough to make me fly to Denver when he died."

"I thought you came for Hannah?"

He nodded slowly. "I did. If you proved to be a bad mother, I was prepared to take her away, but when I saw you again, I saw the real you behind your tough words. You were scared and lonely."

"That's true."

"Everything I did from there, I did to make you see that I'd take care of you. I wanted you to know that you would never have to worry about anything anymore. The yacht, the house – it was all for you, Diana."

"But I didn't want any of that. All I've ever wanted is you."

"I know that now. You had said many times that you were

intimidated by my life, but you have to realize that I felt the same. Sure, I have money and everything I could buy, but you had the most precious thing of all – a family. Money can't buy family. When I realized that, I started to fall in love with you."

"You never said anything," Diana sputtered.

"Neither did you."

"But I assumed that you knew."

"As did I."

They stopped talking and stared at each other. Suddenly, Diana laughed nervously. "Such a silly mess. What should we do about it?"

"I don't know," he said softly, his jaw hard. "This lack of communication has caused a lot of pain."

Diana stared up at him. Her face was hopeful but guarded. "I'm so sorry, Devlan. I never meant to hurt you."

His lips compressed to a thin line. "I want to believe you."

"Please do," she said quickly. "I was hurt and frightened. That's all."

"But how do I convince you that I love you? How can I prevent another misunderstanding like this one from happening again? What's to stop you from running away?"

"Tell me," she breathed. "Tell me you love me. If you really do, say it out loud."

"I love you, Diana."

She smiled brightly, her white teeth flashing him. "I love you too, Devlan. Not a day has passed that I didn't think of you, miss you, or stop loving you. Seeing you today just brought it all back."

His hand rose up to cup the back of her head, and he drew her to him. His soft lips brushed hers, once, twice, three times before he deepened his kiss. She accepted him eagerly, her heart pounding in her chest. When he broke away, his voice was rough with emotion.

"There hasn't been and never will be a woman that could ever mean as much to me as you do. You and Hannah brought me so much joy in the time we spent together, and I still can't understand how you would ever think otherwise."

"I love you, Devlan. Please believe me. These past few months have been pure hell."

"Then you never should've left. What you did was stupid, Diana. Next time you believe these rumors, I want your word that you'll talk to me before jumping to conclusions. Remember the first rule of being in the spotlight?"

She grimaced. "Never believe everything you hear."

"That's right," he agreed. "Roxanne had her own selfish motives, but I swear to you that I was telling the truth from the start. You're a smart woman, and I'm sure you can see that."

"Next time someone shows up at the door and tells me about your wedding plans when I think you've been avoiding me for a couple of weeks, I promise I'll ask you first," she conceded.

"There won't be any other women showing up at the door, Diana. There has never been another woman in my life – ever. You're the only woman I've ever loved."

She smiled. "I hope you can find it in your heart to give me another chance because I love you so much."

"There's not a chance of that happening until you're ready to commit to me, and I mean all the way. Marry me, Diana. Tell the whole world you love me by becoming my wife."

"Yes," she breathed without hesitation. "Yes, yes, yes!"

"I have your word?" He asked sternly.

"Oh yes, Devlan."

"Then we're not leaving Arizona until it's done."

She nodded in complete agreement.

"And first thing tomorrow I'm getting you a cell phone. No more assumptions and miscommunications."

"Okay," she said.

"Even better, I'll just take you with me when I go out of town, at least until my retirement is squared away."

"But Hannah has school," she paused. "Wait a minute. Retirement?"

"I can't leave you and Hannah again. It damn near killed me being apart from you both. I'm doing this all the way, Diana. I want to spend the rest of my life with my family."

Family, that beautiful word that meant so much to them both. Diana's heart melted as she glimpsed that powerful emotion called joy. "Oh Devlan," she breathed.

"I'm serious," he responded roughly. "This is it. Be prepared for everything or nothing at all. You're agreeing to me full-time."

"I wouldn't have it any other way," she said adamantly.

Finally giving in, Devlan gave her a blinding smile and swung her up into his arms. She wrapped her hands around his neck and clung to him as tightly as she could, hoping to never have to let go. Devlan strode purposefully to his bedroom, and Diana smiled against his neck.

"Remember one thing," she warned. "I do have a midnight curfew."

He frowned. "Midnight?"

"I have to get home to Bryce."

"But you're all mine until then? We still have a lot to talk about, Diana," he said sternly. "After we make up."

She nodded again. He deposited her on his bed and turned around to kick the door shut behind him.

"I have a son, *I have a son*!" One last cry of surprise escaped through the closed door, along with the muffled sound of laughter as they came together. In love.

The End

About the Author

•¶•

A lifelong writer and storyteller, Collette began her first novel at the age of eight. Since then, she has obtained her bachelor's degree in literature and master's degree in education while squeezing in her writing whenever she can. The New England native now resides in Arizona with her three children and multiple family pets.

Hannah's Blessing is Collette's second novel. It is the follow up to *Forever Sunshine*, a novel of hope, survival, and the prequel to the Evan Family series. To view more information about Collette, including her current and upcoming titles, please visit www.collettescott.com.

Facebook page: AuthorColletteScott

Twitter: @collettescott

8357084R00198

Printed in Great Britain
by Amazon.co.uk, Ltd.,
Marston Gate.